Hot Magic

"Harder," she commanded. "Kiss me harder."

"Julie." Harry's arms tightened.

Her name, a rough murmur that was both a plea and a prayer, reached inside her like a fist and pulled out a hunger that she hadn't known was there. She pushed closer, lost in the sensation, lost in him. Violins sounded in the air around them and fireworks filled the sky. Julie broke away and took a step back, breathing hard. Harrison's chest rose and fell as furiously as hers. He tracked her movements, his eyes glowing like amber coals. Why had she ended the kiss? She took a step back toward him.

"Mom!" Tasha burst out onto the deck. "Did you see those fireworks? I haven't seen anything that amazing since we went to Detroit for the Freedom Festival. It's not even dark and you could see them light up the sky."

Julie turned toward her daughter and shook her head to clear it. "You saw actual fireworks?"

"And heard violins." Tash looked across the yard. "Is Dorie learning to play the violin again?"

Julie dropped down, directly on the deck, and buried her head in her lap.

"Yoga? Now?" Tash asked uncertainly.

Hiding her head in her lap did not block out her thoughts. With a sigh, Julie looked up at Harrison. The heat had banked and his eyes now held a hint of amusement. "Did you do that? The fireworks, the violins?" She braced herself for the answer.

He shook his head. "No."

Her shoulders sagged in relief. Her world still made sense.

His lips twisted slightly. "You did."

HOT Magic

Magic Destiny Book 1

HOLLI BERTRAM

This is for you, Cols.
I met you when I first set foot on this crazy, winding road.
I'm thankful for that every day. You're the best, kiddo!

One

"HARRISON CHEVALIER is sitting in a tree," Doreen announced as soon as Julie Dancer answered her phone.

"The new neighbor? I didn't know he'd moved in already. Why is he in a tree?" Julie leaned over the kitchen sink to look out the window. She gently pushed several small pots of fading herbs off to the side of the windowsill with a silent promise to water them later. "I can't see him from the kitchen. His garage is in the way. I'm going upstairs to look out my bedroom window."

"He's in that old oak next to my property line." Doreen Lessing lived in the split-level behind the small cedar shake bungalow that Harrison Chevalier had just rented. She had a much better view of his backyard than Julie. "Do you think he has some kind of mental illness that involves a compulsion to climb trees?"

"You mean OTCD, obsessive tree climbing disorder?" Julie took the steps two at a time. "That's usually accompanied by an excessive ingestion of bananas. Unless there's a mound of peels on the ground, I'm thinking he's an entomologist, studying a rare species of oak mites."

"We have a rare species of oak mites in Ann Arbor?"

"I don't know. Ask Harrison."

"Ha-ha."

Julie hopped over the dirty jeans scattered on her bedroom floor and pulled aside her bright, yellow bedroom curtains. From this angle she could see most of Harrison's tidy backyard. Sure enough, one shiny wingtip moved back and forth amid the leafy branches of the oak tree near Dorie's yard.

"This is so weird," Julie murmured.

"I say he's a spy for the CIA, and Cindy is really an international terrorist. He's keeping her under surveillance." Cindy Lui, also referred to as Sexy Cindy, Sin Cindy or Luscious Lui, depending on Dorie's mood, lived in the beige, vinyl-sided ranch on the other side of Harrison's house. "Why else could he possibly be in that tree?"

"She rented him the house. She'd have to be a pretty inept terrorist to do that. You've been reading suspense novels again, haven't you?" Julie pushed aside a couple of books that had fallen onto her bed from her nightstand. She sat and thumped her bare feet into her running shoes, which she never used for running. "I'll go welcome him to the neighborhood and find out what he's doing in the tree."

"What?" Dorie's low screech made her wince. "Grown men in shiny shoes don't sit in trees. Seriously, what if he has some kind of problem?"

"I'm a trained social worker. I can handle it." Okay, she worked in research and hadn't actually counseled anyone since her practicum training. Still, it was like riding a bike, right? It would come back to her. "I'll call you as soon as I get back in the house."

"I'll keep watch. I'm not comfortable with this, Julie. If things get rough, tuck your hair behind your ear as a signal, and I'll send the twins into the yard. They'll be the perfect distraction."

"If things get rough? This is not a military campaign." Though Dorie's six-year-old twin boys probably qualified as weapons of mass destruction. "I'm going to introduce myself to our new neighbor."

"Who happens to be sitting in a tree," Dorie pointed out.

"He's probably trying to rescue his cat."

"Julie, he just suddenly appeared in his yard in a tree. No car, no moving truck, nothing. Seriously, don't you think that's strange?"

"I think it's strange that you know that."

"I'm a stay-at-home mom. It's important to keep abreast of changes in my work environment."

Julie paused, impressed. "That's a really clever rationalization for being nosy."

"Thank you."

"His car's probably parked in the garage, and the moving truck is coming later. I'll talk to you soon." Julie pressed the off button and shoved the phone in her pocket.

She jogged down the stairs, lifting her knees high so she could consider it her exercise for the day, and stopped in the kitchen to look for a new-neighbor food offering.

When Tasha left for college, Julie pretty much quit making dinners. The planning, buying, and cooking of healthy meals took time and energy that could be better used for…okay, she currently used it for watching movies and catching up on old television series she'd missed over the years. But hey, *Firefly* with oatmeal or Chicken Marsala with lots of dirty dishes—not a hard decision.

Unfortunately, that meant her cupboards were fairly empty. She hit the jackpot with an unopened package of Krispy Kremes in the freezer. They'd been an impulse buy, frozen once sanity returned so they wouldn't become dinner. While they defrosted in the microwave, she grabbed a serving plate out of a bottom cupboard. The dish was fine china with little stars decorating the scalloped edges. She piled the slightly warm but now soft donuts onto it and headed out the back door.

Harrison had a detached single-car garage that sat behind his house. She followed his driveway and veered off around the garage into the backyard. A tangle of rose bushes bloomed in the September sun, adding a sweet note to the perfume of freshly cut grass. The foot still hung from the tree, a well-shod pendulum.

"Hello! Mr. Chevalier?"

The shoe abruptly stilled and the branches of the oak tree began an ominous rustling. Two legs, clad in perfectly creased black slacks, appeared beneath the lowest branch. In a rush, a large, lean male body dropped to the ground. The man crouched for a second, then straightened.

Julie brought the plate of donuts closer to her chest. "Mr. Chevalier?"

He was not the quirky, little Frenchman that his name and actions might suggest. He was not at all the type of man you'd expect to find sitting in a tree. High, haughty cheekbones graced a too-serious face. Thick blond hair brushed the collar of his black shirt and seemed more suited to a surfer than the elegant man in front of her. Eyes the color of old gold watched her with unnerving intensity.

"I saw you in the tree." The words were breathless and not at all the welcome she'd intended. She shoved the plate into his hands.

The man glanced down at the donuts. "You saw me in the tree?" He had a British accent. She was a sucker for a British accent.

"Your foot, actually. I saw your foot hanging from the tree when I just happened to glance out my bedroom window."

She shifted uncomfortably under his steady stare. Walking into his backyard and calling him out of a tree to welcome him to the neighborhood suddenly seemed more intrusive than friendly. "Uh, I thought you might be stuck and need some help," she improvised.

"You thought I might be stuck and you brought donuts?" He nodded as if this made perfect sense. "Were you going to arrange them into a soft landing spot in case I fell?"

Julie sucked in her breath and kept a pleasant expression on her face. Did he mean to be rude, or was this an example of the wry sense of humor the Brits were rumored to have? She managed a laugh, just in case he'd said something funny.

He didn't smile. "I'm quite capable of getting myself out of a tree."

"Obviously." She had the ridiculous urge to apologize for

doubting him. She stifled it. "Welcome to the neighborhood," she said belatedly.

"Thank you."

They stared at each until Harrison shifted the plate of donuts and glanced pointedly at his watch.

"I know it's none of my business, but why were you up in the tree? Do you own a cat?" Julie was usually better at polite small talk, but her brain felt unaccountably scrambled.

"No, I don't own a cat. And you're right. It's none of your business."

She laughed again, turning it into a cough when he looked at her as if she were a lunatic. Okay, so he meant to be rude, not funny. She could handle that.

She gave him her most charming smile. "Being the new guy on the block means everybody is curious about you." She leaned in slightly. "Rumor has it you're a spy. If you give me the real scoop, I can let everyone know that you're actually a bird lover or an arborist or…whatever."

She caught a flash of alarm in his eyes.

"There's talk about me already? I only arrived fifteen minutes ago."

Julie waved a hand in the air. "Small-town America. Gossip, gossip, gossip. You can't avoid it."

"You consider Ann Arbor, a city of over a hundred thousand people, small?"

Julie shrugged. "It's all relative. We have some really big cities in America."

His lips curved in something that was almost a smile. "I've heard that. What's your name?"

"Julie Dancer." She pointed to her right without looking away from his face. "I live in the Cape Cod next door."

"Julie." His gaze intensified, and she felt sudden empathy for every amoeba ever examined under a microscope. He studied her from the top of her head down to her toes, absorbing the boring details of her brown hair, brown eyes and short nose. She became conscious of her worn University of Michigan T-shirt and khaki shorts. Had she shaved her legs recently?

"Julie Dancer." The way he repeated her name—slowly, like he held it in his mouth and savored it—sent a dart of unexpected heat through her. "At last."

"At last?"

He took a step closer to her. "I've been waiting to meet you."

She took a step back. Maybe Cindy had told him a lonely divorcée lived next door. Maybe he had plans to hit on her. Her pulse beat faster until reality intruded. If he wanted to hit on anybody, it would be Cindy, who far outclassed her as potential hit material. Which was fine by her because she didn't *want* to be hit on.

Wait a minute.

"You moved in fifteen minutes ago and have been waiting to meet me while sitting in a tree?"

"Of course not." He frowned up into the branches of the tree. "Don't be ridiculous."

She pulled herself to her full five feet, seven inches. He didn't look impressed. Maybe because he still towered a good six inches above her. "I'm not ridiculous."

He lifted an eyebrow.

Americans cock a brow and look amused or perplexed. Only the British could convey such arrogance with a simple facial movement. They probably employ specially trained nannies to teach the skill— "A little higher, Master Harrison, or there will be no bangers and mash for you."

Fascinated, she watched until the brow dropped. "Why don't you explain what you meant by the 'I've been waiting to meet you' remark?"

"Certainly, though I prefer to do so in private."

Could Dorie be right? Was he a spy? Or maybe he was a serial killer, trying to get her indoors where he kept his electric saw. She took another step back. "This yard is private. No one can hear us here."

His jaw firmed, and she had the distinct impression that people didn't argue with him very often. "I'm Harrison Chevalier." The words reverberated like a note rung on a gong. He paused, obviously waiting for a response.

Julie nodded. "I know. Cindy Lui, your landlord, told my friend Dorie you were moving in. Cindy was pleased to get another renter so quickly. Eugene, who used to live in your house, had to leave suddenly when he got an unexpected transfer. He's an engineer at Ford. He's in Germany now."

Harrison crossed his arms, a furrow of impatience between his eyes. Obviously, he couldn't care less about Eugene.

"I should recognize your name, right?"

"Yes, you should."

She gave him a half-smile of apology.

His frown deepened. "I'm one of the Penumbrae," he said, as if that would make everything clear. "It's time for you to assume your rightful place in the Triad and help block a curse that is being placed on me."

Several heartbeats passed in silence. A slight rustling in the branches above broke the unnatural quiet. Harrison grimaced as a twig fell on his head and he brushed it aside.

Julie assumed the accepting, non-judgmental expression that she'd perfected during her last research project on psychosis. "What is the curse?" Her brain hummed as she searched her mental files for a diagnosis fitting a man who believed he was cursed. Schizophrenia? Psychotic disorder? Smart ass?

"It's a binding curse. The Walker who attempts it wishes to become my consort."

"Your consort." Add a delusion of royalty to the mix. Fascinated, she decided to keep him talking. The more she knew about how his mind worked, the easier the decision about buying a privacy fence would be. "Does this curse make you impotent?"

"Excuse me?"

"Consort's an old-fashioned word for a royal husband or wife, right? It's just that if I wanted to be your consort and I was able to curse people, I'd curse you to impotence until you agreed to…consort with me."

He cocked his head and considered her with more interest. "You are truly evil."

"Well, what's the point of a curse if it's not evil?"

"I'm not impotent." He stated the words flatly.

"I'm glad for your sake." Her biggest problem during that study had been a tendency to become too immersed in her subject's fantasy lives. She forced herself to rein in her curiosity about the imaginary curse and stick to the basics. "How can I help you?"

"Have sex with me."

This was her fault. She'd introduced the topic of impotence and had gotten the man thinking about sex. She really needed to be more careful about what she said. She pulled out her phone. "Look at the time! I've got to run. It was nice meeting you, Mr. Chevalier."

"You're scared." He sounded surprised.

"Don't be ridiculous." She backed up a few more steps. "It's very hard to be frightened of a man holding a plate of donuts." That, of course, was untrue.

He smiled. His eyes warmed with a hint of amusement that had the oddest effect on her. Did a little delusional thinking really matter in the big picture? They had meds for these sorts of things. Harrison looked down as if he'd forgotten the donuts, and she began to breathe again.

"We've gotten off on the wrong foot. I can explain. Come inside and share a pastry with me." He looked up, his expression wry. "I promise to keep holding the plate of donuts if it will make you more comfortable."

How could she even think of stepping into a house with this man? He tugged at her in a way she didn't understand. She nervously flicked a strand of hair behind her ear and heard a door bang shut.

Dorie must have had the twins revved at the starting block,

ready to explode into the yard if needed. When the first plastic arrow tipped with a suction cup bounced at Harrison's feet, Julie muttered a weak, "Maybe later," and beat a hasty retreat into the safety of her own home.

Harrison carefully set down the plate of donuts, ignored the steady stream of sucker-tipped arrows flying over the chain link fence along the back of the yard and hoisted himself back into the tree.

"This is uncomfortable, Bascule." He straddled an upper branch, brushing a leaf from his pants. "There is no reason we need to meet in a tree."

The great horned owl, perched on an adjacent limb, blinked. "Fun, Harrison. Sitting in a tree is fun."

"Only if you're ten years old." Though he'd never sat in a tree when he was ten, so he couldn't be sure of that. "Are we just about done convincing the neighbors that I'm an oddball?"

"Not quite. I have two more things to discuss with you. Word has reached me that small groups of Triad members have begun to organize and are fighting back against the demons."

"Finally." A surge of hope lightened Harrison's mood. "Our work is paying off. We have to build on this."

"You can't do anything until you get rid of the binding." Bas ruffled his feathers. "I also came to offer advice on how to handle the Dancer. Obviously, you don't need it. Your charm and persuasive abilities have rendered me speechless."

"One could only hope." Harrison lifted his foot, reached down and unstuck an arrow that had attached to the bottom of his shoe. "You sent me here." He narrowed his eyes at the owl. "Marguerite's curse is already distracting me or I would have questioned you first. Is there another way to break the binding?" The Dancer was not ideal. Her flip attitude irritated him.

"The old-fashioned way is the quickest, most efficient way. Marguerite wove the first tie of the binding with earth energy," Bas responded. "There is tremendous power involved in creating and sustaining such a tie. Theoretically, a Dancer who can channel enough light energy could undo it. The problem is finding someone with that capability. I sense the potential in Julie Dancer. If you two join together, the power should be enough to sever the tie."

"Join." Harry repeated the word. Bas didn't usually use euphemisms.

"Shag, boff, bonk," he promptly clarified. "Sex has power. Even humans use it as a tool in their magic rituals. But be careful. There's something about this Dancer that I don't understand, something that feels different."

"The difference is she doesn't bloody know who I am." Harrison said as he rubbed at his temple.

Bas blinked slowly. "Marguerite bothers you more than I thought."

The fact that Marguerite had successfully completed the first part of the binding curse didn't bother Harrison. It enraged him. She sat in his mind like a weed that couldn't be plucked. He wanted her out. Yesterday. "Julie Dancer may have been raised human, but she is one of us." A connection that gave him a dark sense of satisfaction. "Once she understands the consequences of this curse, she'll agree to help."

The owl made a strange, gravelly sound.

Harrison looked at him suspiciously, but Bas merely spread his wings. With a powerful thrust, the owl lifted off, a soaring shadow against the sun-bright sky.

Julie almost ignored her phone, not wanting to rehash the whole strange Harrison encounter with Dorie until her head stopped pounding. At the last minute, years of conditioning triumphed. She picked up her phone, tucking it to her ear as she reached for the ibuprofin in her kitchen cupboard.

"Hi, Mom." The voice of her nineteen-year-old daughter made her pause.

"Hey, Tash. Is everything going okay at school?"

"School is fine. Grandma just called me."

Julie put four extra-strength tablets into her mouth and swallowed, without water. Her mother had promised not to tell Tasha her news until they were all together over the Christmas holidays, about three months from now. Darn the woman. She couldn't be trusted.

"Could this be a symptom of menopause?" Tasha's normally soft voice held an edge of anxiety.

Julie closed her eyes and slumped into one of the maple chairs that matched the small kitchen table. "As far as I know, homosexuality isn't a recognized symptom of menopause. Besides, I think Grandma went through menopause a good decade ago."

"Then what's wrong with her? It's ludicrous for a sixty-eight-year-old woman to suddenly decide she's a lesbian."

"She's sixty-five," Julie offered weakly.

"I know she hasn't been in the closet all these years. You used to cover my ears when we'd be watching those old Paul Newman movies together because of the comments she'd make."

True. Her mother was quite the Paul Newman fan. And not because of his acting skill.

"Is she supposed to even be thinking about sex? I thought the whole libido thing wound down as you got older and that people had to use drugs or lubricants to even do it."

"Well, no. That's not exactly...." Julie stopped, and tried again. "Homosexuality isn't just about sex."

Tash wasn't listening. "I bet she's going through the early stages of senile dementia. We need to get her help. I think we should fly to Chicago together and do one of those intervention things."

"Calm down." How like her mother to drop this bomb and leave her to deal with the aftermath. They'd both known Tasha would not easily accept her grandmother's change in sexual preference. Tash didn't have a problem with homosexuality; she had a problem with change. Her daughter craved stability. "You don't do interventions for senile dementia or homosexuality. You do interventions for substance abuse." Thankfully her child was studying English, not social work. "And many older people have active, satisfying sex lives." So she'd heard.

"Does this mean she never loved Grandpa? Oh, Mom! Thank God he's dead. He'd be so devastated!"

"Honey, why don't you let this news sink in for a while before we talk about it. Can you come over for dinner tomorrow?"

"Tomorrow's busy. I have a paper due Monday for Great Books." Tasha attended the University of Michigan, and lived in a dorm about fifteen minutes from their house. "How about next Sunday?"

"Call me if you want a ride."

"Okay." Tasha sounded calmer. "Maybe this is one of Grandma's passing fads."

Not likely. Last time she'd spoken with her, her mother had begun organizing a Chicago chapter of the Gay Grays. "Just get your studying done and we'll talk about this next week."

"Mom." Tasha sounded surprisingly serious. "You're happy, right? You don't have any big changes planned that I should know about?"

The fact that she even asked the question was progress. Tasha had learned that she handled transition better when she could prepare for it in advance. Tash's father, Jack, was the exact opposite. He didn't know the meaning of the word "stable." An adventure junkie with a degree in archeology, he flitted from dig to dig like he was Indiana Jones with attention deficit hyperactivity disorder. When Tash started middle school, Julie had decided the family should settle in one place. Jack had decided they should get a divorce.

Julie sighed and glanced out the window. She did a double take. Was that an owl swooping across her new neighbor's back lawn? An owl? In the middle of the day?

"Mom!"

Tasha's voice brought her back to their conversation. She turned away from the window and what was probably just a very fat sparrow. She'd have to quit putting leftover buttered popcorn in the bird feeders. "Don't worry, honey. I'm very happy with my life. I'm always going to be your predictable, dear old mom."

"Which is just the way I love you." Tasha hung up, sounding comforted.

Predictable, comfortable, safe—that's just the way Julie wanted to live the rest of her life. She'd had enough adventure with Jack, and then with single parenting. These were going to be her quiet, peaceful years. She glanced out the window again trying to see Harrison's oak tree. So why was she suddenly feeling restless?

TWO

TWO HOURS later, a knock sounded on her front door. Julie set down her coffee cup and muted the baseball game before she answered. Harrison Chevalier stood on her doorstep, dressed in his elegant tree-climbing attire.

"Thank you for the donuts."

She took the clean plate he handed her. "You're welcome."

"The plate is beautiful."

Julie looked down at the perfect circle in her hands. The tiny silver stars along the rim winked at her. She'd counted them once when she was little. Exactly forty-two perfectly formed stars. Her age now, she realized.

"It belonged to my grandmother. I never met her." Julie had no idea why she told him that.

"May I come in?" He sounded very proper, very polite.

Julie became immediately aware of the old but comfortable sweatpants and sweatshirt she'd put on after her shower. When had she become such a slob? Oh, yeah. She'd always been a slob. "Um…well, I'm watching the Tigers."

"Watch your nature show later. We need to talk." Polite morphed into autocratic with startling ease.

She'd never taken orders well. Her smile firmed. "I'm sorry, but now is not a good time."

"I need your help, Julie."

His clear eyes looked remarkably sane for someone with a

thought disorder. "I have the names of a few good therapists in town," she offered.

"I don't need therapy." He sounded exasperated. "How about if we have dinner at a public restaurant? I just want a chance to talk with you."

"I have a policy not to date neighbors."

"This has come up before?"

He didn't need to look so surprised. "Well, no. It's a new policy. Specifically geared toward neighbors who believe they're cursed."

"I know I haven't made a good impression," Harrison said, which wasn't quite true. He'd made a very strong impression and it wasn't all bad. It wasn't even mostly bad.

He paused, as if considering what to say, and ran his hand through his hair. The golden strands fell perfectly back into place. Like magic. Julie's shoulder length brown hair tended to wave into soft curls at the least provocation. Just once, she wanted a straight swing of shiny hair like the women in shampoo commercials.

A startled expression crossed Harrison's face. He reached out and touched a curl with one finger. "Your hair is very nice. You don't need to change it."

Julie took a quick step back, out of Harrison's reach. "How did you know what I was thinking?"

Harrison frowned. "That shouldn't have happened. I apologize."

There must be a logical explanation for this. But, first things first.

"Do you know what I'm thinking now?" She tried to visualize something innocuous, just in case—children laughing, dogs cavorting in a flowery field, a blue sky shimmering with sunshine. Unfortunately, her slutty brain kept inserting totally inappropriate pictures of Harrison without a shirt. Beneath that proper clothing, light hair dusted his wide chest and well-defined stomach muscles begged to be touched.

What was going on here? Men didn't interest her these days

unless they were safely on a movie screen or in a book.

Harrison shook his head. "No. I have no idea what you're thinking."

Thank you, God.

His hand reached out and she took another step backward. It dropped to his side.

"Mind touch is a private form of communication used by blood-bonded mates," he explained. "I assure you this was highly irregular and purely unintentional."

She nodded, not really listening to his gibberish as she came up with a reasonable explanation for his apparent mind reading. Non-verbal cues. He noticed her staring at his hair and correctly interpreted that to mean that she was dissatisfied with her own hair. Mystery solved. On to other things.

He'd called her hair very nice.

Granted, that wasn't a particularly extravagant compliment, but she savored it for a moment before she remembered the man also believed in curses and mental telepathy. Not to mention he sounded like a science fiction geek or a dog breeder, with all his talk of mates. Aliens and animals have mates. People have partners.

"Julie." His voice commanded her attention. "Will you have dinner with me tonight?"

Spend a whole two hours with this man? Something—okay, his accent and his incredible face and body—almost compelled her to say yes. "No. I can't."

He looked at her as if she were a particularly frustrating puzzle he needed to solve and then he smiled a slow smile that made her quickly review what she'd been thinking. Nope. Nothing to cause a smile like that.

He took a step back and gave her a brief nod. "Perhaps another time. I'll be seeing you again soon."

Julie quickly shut the door before she could ask when. Harrison's delusional system might fascinate her on an intellectual level, but somehow she doubted intellectual interest alone was bumping up her heart rate.

Which meant trouble. Because on a personal level, Harrison Chevalier was definitely not the type of man a comfortable, predictable woman should be interested in.

Marguerite Deschamps moaned and kicked aside the bedcovers as she twisted her body, trying to wake. Grand-mère Belle was sobbing again, begging Marguerite to save her. With a quick, sharp move, Marguerite threw her body into an upright position and broke free of the dream.

She pulled in deep breaths, trembling in the aftermath of the tormenting vision. "I promise, Grand-mère." She repeated the words she'd spoken since the first dream when she'd been a mere eleven years old. "I promise I'll save you."

Now, after years of helplessly listening to her grandmother's pleas, she'd finally found the key to free her. Marguerite automatically felt for the tie with Harrison.

Blank nothingness.

Her muscles tensed and panic iced her body as she desperately searched for the presence that had been with her since she'd cast the first words to bind him. There, he was there. Her heart slowed. For a moment she had lost the powerful, angry hum that should have scared her but instead had become oddly comforting.

Marguerite put a hand against her head, as if doing so would keep him there. She shuddered as she mentally touched the edges of a bitter essence she couldn't identify, a sour presence that had laced her psyche ever since she'd cast the curse. No matter. She knew freeing Grand-mère would not be without price.

She glanced out the window at the sun still high in the sky. She never woke until dark. Only her dreams had roused her now. Unlike the flower she'd been named for, the ox-eye daisy, which grew like a weed across the grassy hills and was called moonflower because it bloomed both day and night, Marguerite preferred to stay in the shadows.

She dressed quickly in beige linen trousers and a loose silk shirt of the same shade. She slipped on a pair of low-heeled sandals and walked down the long marble halls of the family wing to the library. No windows marred the rose-colored walls, built centuries ago from the very stone that formed the rolling French countryside. The shadows soothed her and she slowed her frantic pace as she traveled the long, cool corridor. She reached out and let her fingers slide against the walls, feeling the strength and support of her ancestors in the very foundations of the castle.

The library doors stood ajar. As expected, her brother, Luc, sat in one of the burgundy leather chairs, reading by the light of the large mullioned windows. He looked up, surprised, when she entered the room.

"Marguerite. What's wrong? Why are you awake?" He set his book on a small wooden table, concern marking his expression.

She glanced at the windows and the outside shutters banged shut, cutting out the natural light along with a view of the wooded slopes of Montagne Noire. Two lamps flicked on, emitting a soft glow. She wouldn't tell him of the dream. She never did. "We have a problem. The link wavered."

Luc tapped the cover of his book. "I'm not surprised."

"You're not surprised? What does that mean? I performed the first tie to perfection." Marguerite paced the room. Her pale hair whipped against her face with the force of her movement. "Harrison is always in the corner of my mind, but suddenly, for the space of several heartbeats, he was gone. That's impossible, Luc!"

"Magic is nothing more than the manipulation of energy. As such it can be transformed or re-routed by anyone who has knowledge and skill."

"Not a bonding curse." Marguerite argued with certainty.

"A curse is just the name given when power manipulation is used for evil. The mechanics stay the same. You've only placed the first tie on Chevalier. Two ties are required, each bound during a new moon when you're able to access the most earth energy. You have almost three weeks to wait until the next new moon." He paused. "This may not proceed as smoothly as you plan,

Marguerite. It's wrong, not to mention dangerous. Chevalier is powerful."

She shivered, uneasy. "Trust me, Luc. I won't tell you why I'm doing this, but it must be done."

Luc watched her with eyes that invited her to confide in him. They shared almost everything. She wouldn't have survived their parents' death without him. Yet, she'd never told him of the dreams. And she couldn't explain the path she now walked to free their grand-mère. She wouldn't taint him with the evil, also.

The lights in the room flickered and power flowed in her veins, washing out her need to confide in her brother, washing out her doubts. "I am the most powerful Walker of this generation. Harrison will be my consort, tied to me."

Luc folded his arms across his chest. "So you'll have a fierce lion by the tail." When Marguerite didn't respond, he shook his head. "You've changed. Power was never so important to you. Why, Marguerite?"

"Power frees you."

"What do you need to be freed from?" His eyes narrowed.

"Power creates opportunity." Marguerite quickly tried to deflect his line of questioning.

"This power you wield creates the opportunity for much sorrow." When Marguerite didn't respond, Luc frowned, but continued. "While you slept, I've been studying. I found an obscure reference that I think we need to pay attention to."

Marguerite picked up the book he'd been reading, relieved he'd changed the subject. "*Mots de Sagesse?*" She read the title aloud. "*Words of Wisdom?* This book is read by school children." She dismissed it, tossing it back on the table beside Luc.

"The book is read by children because it forms the foundation of Triad teachings. It tells the story of Patre and Yesmi, father and mother of energy wielders. It outlines the prophecies. You would do well to remember these, Marguerite. To remember the balance that must be maintained."

Marguerite laughed. She couldn't help it. He sounded so sure of himself, so passionate, so full of book learning instead of life learning. She leaned over and placed her hands on both sides of his beloved face. "Sanctimonious drivel, mon frère. Close your book and look around you." She patted his cheek and stepped away. "Balance is an illusion. The ones with the most power will always control the scale." Soon she would have the strength to free Grand-mère Belle—and in doing so, be free of her.

Luc didn't take offense. He never did. "The reference I found is in the prophecies. The verse talks of one who will rise to great power in the aftermath of a divisive war. 'A daughter shall be born in light and shadow, a guardian who rises out of evil. Wild power circles her and chaos follows in her footsteps.'"

Cold settled across Marguerite's shoulders. "Fifty years ago the Great Rift tore the Triad apart."

Luc nodded, silent.

"We were born during a lunar eclipse, as the earth's shadow darkened the moon—in the light of the moon, and then in shadow." Marguerite swallowed, tasting fear. The dreams and the surges of power she experienced might all be signs. "Perhaps it speaks of me. Perhaps I'm the one prophesied."

Luc watched her, a serious expression on his face. "Prophecy does not equal destiny, Marguerite. You are free to make your own choices."

She'd not been free since the dreams first came, but soon, soon she would be.

"Today while you slept I felt something." Luc said. "A wisp of Dancer power."

"There are no Dancers in the area." None had lived in the Montagne Noire area since the Great Rift. Luc, however, was a powerful Sensitive. He would not be mistaken. "Where is this Dancer?"

"Very far away." He looked thoughtful. "And the energy was Dancer energy, but different. Perhaps I felt it though your tie. It may be the reason your connection with Harrison faltered."

Marguerite clenched her fist, muscles tensing all over again.

Only a very powerful Dancer could help Harrison break the bonding curse. She knew of none with that much power.

"I contacted London," Luc continued. "Harrison left the city over a week ago."

Damn the limitations of the first tie, which told her none of Harrison's actions. "Where is he?"

"He's gone to the States. To a town in Michigan."

She made her decision quickly. "We leave for Michigan as soon as can be arranged."

Julie stopped by the grocery store after church the following Sunday to stock up on as many of Tasha's favorite foods as she could find. If she kept her daughter's mouth full, maybe Tash wouldn't spend the entire dinner discussing her grandmother. This was, admittedly, a coward's strategy. A true social worker would encourage Tash to talk out her feelings. Tash, however, being a true social worker's daughter, didn't need the encouragement. Julie added a gallon of cookie-dough ice cream to the cart, Tash's absolute favorite.

She parked in her driveway and walked around to the trunk. How to get the bulging plastic bags into the house in the fewest trips?

The handles of the four lightest bags went around her left wrist and she hooked the handle of a gallon of milk with her fingers. Two bigger bags fit around her right wrist and she cradled the twelve-pack of diet root beer in her right arm. The case of water would have to stay in the trunk for now. She staggered back from the car and realized she didn't have a way to close the trunk. She'd have to put something down.

A large hand reached from behind her and lowered her trunk lid. "Can I help?"

"Harrison!" Harrison had become the hit of the neighborhood. In the last week, several neighbors had had him over for tea. If he planned to stay for any length of time, the local Starbucks might be in serious trouble. "You move very quietly."

"So I've been told. Your hands are turning purple."

She looked down. Her hands *were* purple and quickly turning numb. "You're right. Better get these groceries in the house. Thanks for closing the trunk." She hurried up the front walk, only to stop before the front door, stymied as to how to open it.

"Do you have a key?" He stood behind her.

"It's not locked." She couldn't see his face but she felt his disapproval.

"Crime is on the rise everywhere. It's dangerous not to secure your home."

Julie glanced over her shoulder and met his steady gaze. "You're right. I'll start locking the door from now on." Especially since he now knew she kept it open. Her hands had passed the tingly stage and were going numb. "Would you open my door, please?"

He reached past her, his knuckles brushing her bare arm, and turned the brass knob. She rushed inside, almost ran through the small living room, and dropped the bags on the kitchen counter. Instant relief. She flexed her wrists a few times to get the blood flowing.

Harrison stood in the arched doorway that led from the living room to the kitchen. Today he wore khakis and a brown shirt, making them look more formal than they were. Even though he leaned a shoulder against the door frame, he had a presence that made her stand up straighter.

She smoothed her dark blue capris and tugged at the sleeveless white shirt she'd changed into after church. The early October weather was unseasonably warm. She'd tamed her hair and even put on makeup. She wasn't always a slob. She could hold her own with this man. Maybe.

"Making two trips would have been more sensible," he commented, nodding toward her hands.

"Next time I'll do that." Of course she wouldn't.

"You're lying." His eyes watched her steadily. "Don't."

His words didn't sound like a threat. There was no invisible "or else" tagged on to the end. That would almost have been easier. She could have gotten angry at his arrogance and presumption.

Instead, his simple request for honesty struck her as intensely personal and scared her more than any threat. Which was stupid. If you asked most people if they wanted you to lie to them or tell them the truth, they'd pick the truth. So why did his asking for it outright shake her to her core?

"Okay, here's the truth." She spoke louder than normal, trying to dispel the growing intimacy building in the room. "I hate making two trips and next time I'll load up with as many bags as I possibly can to avoid it."

He smiled slightly and then nodded once. "Excellent."

She was breathing too quickly. Who was this man?

His expression serious, he straightened, the spell he'd woven between them gone. "All week you've avoided speaking with me privately. We have to talk. Marguerite will undoubtedly show up soon."

Julie sighed and began to move efficiently around the kitchen, putting away the groceries. She'd forgotten for a moment that this man was crazy. "I don't know who Marguerite is, Harry," she said gently.

"I'm aware of that. Stop patronizing me and give me your full attention. I'll explain."

Julie paused, a box of lasagna noodles in her hand. "Does this have something to do with you wanting to have sex with me?"

"Yes." His face was expressionless.

"It's not going to happen."

He studied her a moment. "Would it make a difference if I told you that you'd enjoy yourself?"

"Please." Julie shook her head. He might be crazy, but his ego was doing just fine.

"You'd no doubt get offended if I offered you reimbursement for your services."

"You think? Don't even go there."

He ran a hand through his hair in a motion she was beginning to recognize as frustration. "I thought Americans weren't as hung up about sex as they used to be."

"Where did you get that idea? Of course we are." She put the cheese in the refrigerator, stuffed all of the now empty plastic bags into one bag and shoved them under the sink, then straightened. "You've been watching American television, haven't you?"

"Everyone watches American television."

"Television is fantasy," she said. Just like the delusions buzzing around inside your head, handsome man.

Harry took a step toward her. "Define fantasy, Julie."

"I know you have that word in England. You're from the land of Tolkien and Rowling."

When he continued to watch her, waiting, she elaborated. "Fantasy is make-believe. Pretend. Dragons and magic." She waved her hands in the air. "Happily ever after."

"What if I told you dragons once existed?" He took a step closer.

"I'd ask for fossil evidence."

"What if I told you magic exists now?"

"I'd say prove it." He stood so near she could smell him, an elusive scent of earth and sun that made her want to breathe deeply.

His voice lowered. "What if I said happily ever after is a possibility?"

"I'd say you've never been married." The words came out as a whisper. He stood too close. She should back away, but she didn't want to. A frisson of heat built from the soles of her feet to her shoulders. The warmth spread out and filled her.

Harrison's eyes darkened to rich amber and his breathing deepened. He didn't touch her, but it felt like he did. It felt like he moved his hands over her, learning her skin, the space inside her elbow, the curve of cheek.

"Have you ever been married, Harry?" She forced herself to talk, to back away from him and the odd, intimate sensation.

He frowned, but answered. "No."

"Take my advice. Stay single. Life is so much simpler that way."

"I haven't noticed that my life is simple." He stood still, his gaze following her movements as she picked up a washcloth and began to wipe the tile counter, just for something to do.

She relaxed when he maintained a safe distance. "Only because you don't have the married state to compare it to."

"You're cynical for one so young."

Julie laughed, truly amused. She tossed the cloth in the sink and folded her arms. "I'm forty-two. I have a child in college. The gray in my hair is gathering momentum for a scalp takeover. I have to eat one less meal a day just to maintain a weight that is ten pounds heavier than it should be. I'm losing so many brain cells that my head may be hollow by tomorrow morning. Thank you, but I am not young."

"I don't see any gray in your hair."

"Hmmmm." She tilted her head and pretended to consider him. "Maybe I will sleep with you after all."

"Yes. You will." The calm assurance in his voice caused a tremor of anticipation in the pit of her stomach.

"Harry, I'm joking. Listen, you're an incredibly attractive man, if a little tightly wound. Find yourself someone younger, more adventurous." Before I get hurt again.

"No."

She tried again. "I'm not going to do something stupid like sleep with a man who believes he's cursed."

"Would you sleep with me if I didn't believe I was cursed?"

Hoo boy. She didn't want to think too closely about that one. "Of course not."

"Why not?"

"AIDS. Sexually transmitted diseases. Sagging breasts."

"You're not planning on getting married again?"

"Been there, done that, have the scars. No."

"You're not planning on having casual affairs?"

"Of course not." She had a strong moral code, a daughter to

set an example for. Though her daughter really wasn't around all that much to appreciate the good example she was setting.

"So you're never going to have sex again in your life?"

Julie pulled out a chair from the kitchen table and sat down hard. "I hadn't thought about it like that. That's sad, isn't it?"

"It's not sad. It's bloody ridiculous."

Julie rested her chin in her hand. "Let's not talk about this. I'm getting depressed."

The front door banged and quick footsteps sounded across the living room. Tash appeared in the kitchen doorway, her thick, red hair pulled back from her face in a ponytail. She wore black running shorts and a white sport T-shirt that molded to her torso. She bent over, hands on thighs, and took a deep breath. "I knew you'd make lasagna, Mom, so I decided to run over and pre-burn the calories."

Julie glanced at Harrison. He stared at Tash with surprise. Tash straightened and stretched before she noticed Harrison. She gave her mother a startled look, then stepped forward, her hand outstretched. "Sorry, I didn't see you. I'm Natasha Morgen."

Harry took her hand with a smile. "Harrison Chevalier. I just moved in next door."

Julie saw her daughter's eyes widen under the full impact of the Chevalier charm. "Welcome." Tash's voice sounded breathy. Julie suspected it wasn't from her recent run.

"Thank you." Neither had released the other's hand. Julie fought an urge to rip them apart. She felt an equally strong urge to stamp her foot. She settled for clearing her throat. Loudly.

Harrison took a step back from Tasha, dropping her hand. "I didn't realize your daughter was fully grown."

"I told you she was in college."

"Yes, but...." He paused, looking at the young woman still smiling at him. A calculating glint glimmered in his eyes when he turned back to Julie. "Perhaps Natasha might be willing to help me break the curse."

Three

"EXCUSE US, Tash." Julie marched over to Harrison, grabbed his arm and pulled him across the black and white linoleum, out the kitchen door and onto the back deck. He came a bit too easily. She shut the kitchen door and turned, angrier than she'd been in a long time.

"Touch my daughter again and I'll have your butt in jail, you pervert."

"She's of legal age. She can make her own decisions."

"She's not making this one. Stay away from my daughter, Harrison." She punctuated her words by poking her finger at his chest.

He grabbed both of her upper arms, holding her still. "Why are you so upset?"

"Because you're old enough to be her father and you're probably insane."

He smiled slightly. "At least you said 'probably.' I'm making progress."

She wanted to kick him. Hard. Where were these violent thoughts coming from?

His hard eyes gentled. "I don't want to have sex with Natasha."

"You don't?"

"I don't."

She blew out a breath of air. "You meant me to think that."

"Yes."

"So that I would sacrifice myself to save my daughter from you."

"I hadn't viewed it in quite that light, but yes."

"This honesty thing works both ways. Don't play games and don't lie to me."

He tilted his head slightly, studying her. "You are an interesting woman, Julie Dancer."

"Not really." Ask her ex-husband Jack. "I'm actually kind of boring."

He laughed, an almost rusty sound that flowed through her like water over sugar, dissolving the residue of her anger. Then he grasped her arms, and with a smooth motion pulled her against his chest and kissed her.

Harry's lips weren't awkward or hesitant. He kissed her like he knew her. Like he had kissed her a thousand times before and her mouth was a welcome home. Julie kissed him back, seduced by the sense of belonging. Her tongue whispered across the inside of his lower lip and then went back for a slower, longer taste. Something suspiciously like a purr vibrated from her throat. He was addictive. She was in trouble.

The purr, or maybe it was her tongue, had the same effect as a blowtorch on dry firewood. The kiss went up in flames.

She was suddenly arched over Harrison's arm, her breasts pressed into his chest. His hand cradled the back of her head and his lips covered hers, hard and hot. Julie's circulatory system went haywire. Blood rushed so quickly through her heart that it pounded like a jackhammer and yet that same blood pooled and settled with a slow heated pulse between her legs. She had no chance to respond to the kiss before he eased his mouth away and took an unsteady breath. He gently nipped at her lip and then soothed the small sting his tongue. When he did it again, she circled his neck with her arms and tugged. "Harder," she commanded. "Kiss me harder."

"Julie." Harry's arms tightened.

Her name, a rough murmur that was both a plea and a prayer,

reached inside her like a fist and pulled out a hunger that she hadn't known was there. She pushed closer, lost in the sensation, lost in him. Violins sounded in the air around them and fireworks filled the sky. Julie broke away and took a step back, breathing hard. Harrison's chest rose and fell as furiously as hers. He tracked her movements, his eyes glowing like amber coals. Why had she ended the kiss? She took a step back toward him.

"Mom!" Tasha burst out onto the deck. "Did you see those fireworks? I haven't seen anything that amazing since we went to Detroit for the Freedom Festival. It's not even dark and you could see them light up the sky."

Julie turned toward her daughter and shook her head to clear it. "You saw actual fireworks?"

"And heard violins." Tash looked across the yard. "Is Dorie learning to play the violin again?"

Julie dropped down, directly on the deck, and buried her head in her lap.

"Yoga? Now?" Tash asked uncertainly.

Hiding her head in her lap did not block out her thoughts. With a sigh, Julie looked up at Harrison. The heat had banked and his eyes now held a hint of amusement. "Did you do that? The fireworks, the violins?" She braced herself for the answer.

He shook his head. "No."

Her shoulders sagged in relief. Her world still made sense.

His lips twisted slightly. "You did."

"You're a witch and you didn't tell me." Tasha paced around the kitchen, upset. "First Grandma tells us she's gay, now you turn into a witch. You promised not to get weird on me, Mom."

"I am not a witch." Julie put the lasagna noodles in boiling water, wishing she had some wine to dull the energy fritzing through her.

"Harrison said you have powers."

"Harrison is crazy," Julie retorted.

"Harrison is hot. And he didn't look crazy to me." Tasha

crossed her arms and her face turned stubborn. "Mom, I saw the fireworks and heard the violins. *I'm* not crazy."

"I can't explain that right now. I don't understand it myself. I do know that if I were a Sun Dancer, or whatever Harry called me, I'd know it." She slammed the cheese down and leaned back against the counter. Her skin felt tight, like it couldn't contain all the energy whizzing through her veins. This was embarrassing. She really needed to get out more. Kissing a man shouldn't mess with her this way. "I'm over forty. You don't start discovering totally new things about yourself when you're my age."

"Grandma discovered she's gay, and she's a lot older than you." Tasha pointed out with irritating logic.

Julie turned to get a cold glass of water from the sink. She was burning up. "Grandma doesn't count. She's in an orbit all by herself." Julie put a hand against her forehead. "I think I'm catching the flu." That was it. She was running a high temperature and this was all a fever hallucination.

"Mom?" Tasha had a funny note in her voice.

"Yes?" Maybe she should lay down with a cold compress or something.

"Uh, Mom. You're glowing."

"That's nice of you to say, but I know I look as yucky as I feel."

"No, Mom. You're *glowing*. You have a halo all around you."

Julie ran into the small bathroom off the kitchen and stared into the mirror. A pulsing light surrounded her body. Her daughter crowded in behind her. Tash reached out a hand and passed it through the light.

She yanked her fingers back quickly. "It's got an electrical charge."

Julie closed her eyes. "I am sleeping. This is all a dream."

"Mom, I know you sent Harrison home, but I think you better go talk to him."

"No need." Julie opened her eyes, surprised to see the glow building in intensity, just at the thought of him. "I'm sure I'll wake up in a few minutes."

Tasha backed away. "Okay. Listen. You go watch the noodles and I'll just step outside for a breath of fresh air. I'll be right back." Tasha turned and raced through the kitchen. Julie stepped out of the bathroom and watched her practically leap over the deck as she headed toward Harrison's house.

Tasha looked so athletic and beautiful. Her little girl was all grown up. Smiling, Julie stepped back into the bathroom. The white pedestal sink and bright yellow walls made her feel safe and happy. She'd bought white hand towels for the room when Tasha had left for college. Ha! And Jack thought she wasn't a risk taker. She fussed with the towels and noticed her fingers left small, brown singe marks. Good thing this wasn't real.

Getting into the spirit of things, she pointed her finger at the toilet. "Be clean!" She squinted at the porcelain. The toilet hadn't been all that dirty to begin with and she couldn't tell if was any cleaner. The bathroom mirror began fogging over and she walked into the kitchen to turn down the fire under the noodles. Her brain felt fried by the heat consuming her. Too much. Everything was too much. She wanted a normal, boring dream. The tears starting down her cheeks hissed and evaporated into puffs of steam.

"Mom. I need you." She whispered into the empty air of the kitchen, hugging herself. She wasn't at all surprised when her mother popped into the room.

Her mother, on the other hand, screamed.

Harrison had just ended a phone call to his secretary when the banging on his door started. He stalked through the empty house to the door, not in the best of moods, and threw it open. Young Natasha's fist landed square on his chest.

"Ow!" she yelped and sucked on her knuckles. "Are you wearing a cement vest or something?"

He would have felt flattered, but the minute he opened the door, he sensed the tsunami of power. He grabbed Natasha and pulled her close. Fear trickled into him for the first time since this whole fiasco began. In a heartbeat, they stood in Julie's kitchen.

Natasha crumbled to the floor the moment his arms loosened. An older woman stood in the middle of the room, a startled screech echoing from her lungs. Julie smiled at him, glowing like a bloody angel. Only the immortals could contain that much power without bursting a blood vessel. Julie certainly couldn't.

He scooped her up like a baby, the glow dampening slightly. What the hell was happening to her?

"Harry, this is my dream, and I want you to kiss me again." Julie's arms, hot as pokers, circled his neck. Her power pulled his head down. He met her lips, jolted again by the taste of her— sweet, salty, addicting. For a brief second, he lost himself in the absolute rightness of the hot press of her mouth. The fiery burn of her body against his. He lifted his head and met her dreamy eyes. He thought one word.

Bascule.

Tasha struggled to her feet, sucked air into her lungs, and watched her mother disappear from the kitchen with Harrison. She didn't faint and she didn't scream. She didn't even have a panic attack. Instead, she stumbled to the closest chair and sat down. "I'm hallucinating, aren't I?"

"I saw it." Jean Dancer wore a particularly grim expression on her face.

Tasha rubbed her head. "Unfortunately, you're in Chicago, so I'm hallucinating you, too."

Jean reached over and pinched her arm, hard. "Hallucinations don't pinch."

"Ow!" Tasha had no idea if that was true, but she decided to go with it. "Is Mom all right?"

"No. But if anyone can help her, the Balance can." Her grandmother lowered herself into a chair slowly, as if every muscle pained her. She wore a flowery, flowing skirt and a peasant style blouse. Grandma changed styles on a daily basis. Sometimes she went for sleek and sophisticated, sometimes hip and fashionable. Today she'd been caught in a sixties time warp—a decade she'd no doubt owned.

"Who or what is the Balance? What's wrong with Mom? How can people teleport through space?" The words tumbled over each other. Her mouth and tongue couldn't move quickly enough to frame the questions in her head.

"Slowly." Jean drew out the word.

Tash took a deep breath and put a brake on her racing thoughts. One question at a time. "How can Harrison zap in and out of places like a *Star Trek* character?"

"In *Star Trek*, you need a transporter device. Totally different thing," Jean said absently.

"Grandma. Look at me. Tell me what you know about this." The soft demand sat between them like a grenade.

Jean looked up. Lines creased her usually smooth skin. "I know I've been incredibly foolish. Something triggered a release of Julie's power."

"I don't understand."

Jean put her head on the table, the soft blonde curls she currently clutched in her hands a tribute to her hairdresser. "I don't, either. This is impossible. Besides, she's Sun Dancer and he's Penumbrae."

Harrison had called Mom a Sun Dancer, too. When Jean kept her head on the table, Tasha pulled out her phone and googled Sun Dancer. Mom was not a member of a Native American or First Nation tribe. She was also not a nudist or a boat. No help there.

"This is not the time to be chatting with friends." Jean sat up. "Put your phone away, and tell me exactly what happened before your mother went nuclear."

Tasha stuck her phone in her pocket and then repeated the story of the kiss, the violins and fireworks and her mom's odd electrical glow.

Jean's frown deepened. "Using power is a balancing act. There are three parts to it—absorbing energy from the environment, transforming that energy and releasing the power back into the environment. Your mother hasn't been trained. If she begins absorbing energy without knowing how to release it...."

"Are you saying Mom might die?" Tasha put one hand against her chest, to physically hold in the hysteria she could feel pushing for release.

"No. No! The Balance has her. He'll take care of her. He'll help her."

Her grandmother's words didn't sound as certain as Tasha needed them to sound. She stood up but there was nowhere to go. Nothing she could do. No way to help her mother.

Steam from the simmering lasagna noodles fogged the windows. She carried the heavy pot to the colander her mother had set in the sink, her heart twisting as she thought of her mom bustling around the kitchen. Her strong, dependable mom. Her steady rock.

She tipped the noodles and hot water into the colander and stood, taking the full force of hot steam that bathed her face. Hair that had escaped from her tight ponytail twisted into corkscrew curls. Hair color from her dad, hair curls from her mom. What else had her genes gifted her with?

She turned and braced both hands behind her on the counter. "Grandma, who are we?"

The man lounged in a camel-colored vinyl armchair, watching reruns of The Simpsons. One long, leather clad leg draped over the side of the chair, his foot ticked a lazy rhythm. Not a muscle in his lean body jerked when Julie and Harrison appeared in the hotel room with him.

Julie gasped at the lightning-quick change in venue and tightened her grip on Harry's neck. He sucked in his breath, and she smelled burning hair. Now that was definitely bizarre. She'd never been able to smell in a dream before. She moved her arm and saw singed neck hairs on Harry. She turned her head and spit on her skin. The water danced like moisture on a hot griddle. Oh man. How would Freud interpret this?

She loosened her death grip on Harry and looked around, storing details for later therapy sessions. She appeared to be in a small, bland hotel room decorated in shades of pale beige. Okay, Freud would think she was boring. No surprise there. She turned her attention again to the room's single occupant and stared in growing wonder at the man sitting in the armchair. Thank you, deep unconscious. "I've dreamed up a young Johnny Depp!"

The man lifted a dark brow. "Johnny Depp?"

"She's about to ignite, Bas." Harry's deep voice broke in. "Her abilities have triggered, and she's absorbing power."

The man stood quickly. "How did it happen?"

"I'll explain later." Harrison's accent sounded more clipped than usual. "Can you siphon off any of the power?"

The man held out both hands toward her. Julie felt a moment of intense relief, a chill breeze that quickly got sucked up in the heat. She smiled at him. "I loved your pirate movies."

He looked at Harry. "We need an angel. There's too much energy."

"The angels aren't allowed to interfere," Harry bit out. A muscle in his jaw twitched once. Julie resisted the urge to put her hand against his cheek. He probably wouldn't appreciate having his facial hair burned off.

"Rules are like rubber bands. They can stretch more than you'd expect before they break. Something you, Harrison, have yet to learn." The man called Bas held up both hands in a simple, fluid gesture. He murmured a word that Julie didn't catch. A flash of light, gaining in intensity like an expanding star, filled the room.

Julie realized she'd finally exploded. Her soul floated free into blessed cool. So this was death.

Wait! She frowned and tried to put the brakes on her drifting consciousness. No fair. She refused to enter into the Great Beyond before her life passed before her eyes. She didn't mind missing a replay of the Married Years, and strangely, she felt no tinge of sorrow at leaving Tash and her mother behind. She did, however, want one last memory of that kiss with Harrison. Death had obviously released her inner floozy.

Try as she might, she couldn't hold her thoughts together. They slipped out of her head like wisps of morning fog meeting the sunrise. The last thing she remembered was a remarkable feeling of peace.

Grandma's head jerked and she stood. Her whole body trembled. "Something's happened."

"Of course something's happened. People are teleporting all over the place and Mom has disappeared." It only took Tasha a moment to realize her grandmother meant something else. Dread filled her and a band tightened around her chest. "What? Is Mom okay?"

Grandma sat down again, a shaky hand running through her short curls. "I don't know. I'm a bit of a Sensitive. I just felt a huge jolt of power. I don't know what it means." Her brown eyes, usually bright and laughing, were full of despair. "I don't know what it means."

Tasha sat down beside her and took both her hands. "I need you to tell me what is going on." She still managed to speak slowly, even though her heart felt like a ping-pong ball bouncing against her ribs. "Tell me about Sun Dancers, the Penum-whatever and Sensitives. Tell me where Mom has gone and what is wrong with her."

Grandma nodded, taking a deep breath. "I thought I could escape all this. Keep you and your mother free of it."

"Escape what? Keep us free of what?"

"Your heritage. Your birthright and your birth curse." Her grandmother spoke in a voice of doom.

"Stop with the mumbo-jumbo horror movie stuff, Gram. Talk in clear English."

"All is not what it seems."

"Grandma!"

The older woman shuddered and gave Tasha a defensive look. "Well, it's not. There's more to this world than meets the eye. Humans are only part of God's grand equation. There are immortals, spirits and mortals with special powers. You, my dear, are a mortal with special powers."

Tash didn't say anything for a moment. Obviously her special power was her ability not to scream in frustration at the craziness coming out of her grandmother's mouth. Instead she said, very slowly, "Tell me more."

"Several types of these special mortals exist. The ones you need to be concerned with now are the Sun Dancers, the Shadow Walkers and the Penumbrae. These three together form the Triad and serve as a buffer against evil. 'Wherever three or more are gathered, evil cannot prevail.'" Her grandmother spoke the last sentence as if it was a known truth.

"Is that a Bible verse?" Tash's head felt like it was whirling. She had so many questions.

"No. I really have no idea where that came from or even when it was said, but it's something all Triad learn in the cradle."

Except, apparently, for Tasha and her mother. "I don't have any powers."

"Your mother didn't either. Your grandpa was human, and I thought you'd both somehow missed out on the magic gene."

Tasha closed her eyes. If she hadn't beamed from Harrison's front porch to this kitchen, if she hadn't seen her mother blink out of the kitchen in Harrison's arms, she'd think her grandmother had truly taken a dive over the edge. "Do you have powers?" She opened her eyes to see Grandma shrug.

"I'm a Sensitive, which means I can sense others with power. I'm very rusty at the whole energy wielding business."

"Grandpa was a normal human?"

"As normal as they come. Not a whiff of power about him."

Soft, cuddly Grandpa Abe had loved nothing better than to

sit on the couch and tell Tasha endless stories. He always smelled like he smoked a pipe, and she often thought of him on cold winter nights when Mom had the fireplace going. "Did he know about you? About the power?"

"Yes. And he loved me anyway." Grandma smiled sadly. "He made me feel safe."

"Why did you need to feel safe?" Didn't power give you... power?

"Many years ago, there was a huge civil war in the Triad. We call it the Great Rift." Grandma stopped abruptly. Her eyes widened and she looked around the kitchen like a cornered rabbit. Before Tasha could reach her, she slid off her chair to the floor. Grandma placed a trembling hand over her heart.

Tasha knelt beside her, grabbing hands suddenly gone cold. Was she having a heart attack? "Grandma!" Tasha stared at the stricken, pale face, desperately wishing for help, for sanity, for Red Cross first aid training.

"Shadow Walkers." Grandma said the words so softly Tasha had to lean forward to hear. "There are Shadow Walkers near."

A husky laugh broke the silence that followed her statement. "How astute of you."

Tasha's head swung around at the softly accented voice, and she jumped to her feet. A crowd of people filled the kitchen. She blinked rapidly, but they didn't disappear. Slightly in front of the rest, two people stood side by side—man and a woman, both beautiful beyond anything Tasha had seen outside of touched-up magazine photographs. Both were tall, the man topping the woman by four inches. Even standing still, they radiated an innate grace. Their faces were long and fine-boned, their hair a slide of silver moonlight that reached the shoulders of the woman and touched the collar of the man. Both had deep blue eyes and dark lashes, striking against their otherwise pale coloring.

The group wore modern clothes—cotton slacks, khakis, jeans, and a variety of shirts and tops all in subdued colors— but something about them felt ancient. Tasha stiffened her spine.

"What are you doing here? Who are you?"

The woman took a step forward. "We are the shadows that frighten you at night. We have come for the Dancer."

Four

"'SHADOWS DON'T scare me.'" Tasha tried to squash the quaver in her voice as she stepped in front of her grandmother. "'There are dark shadows on the earth, but its lights are stronger in the contrast.'"

The quote came tumbling out without thought. She threw back her shoulders, going with the theory that if she looked brave she might feel brave. Her heart rate slowed when the lips of the silver man quirked in amusement and his eyes lit with interest. A man with a sense of humor wouldn't hurt her, right?

"Dickens," he murmured. "*The Pickwick Papers.*"

Shadow Walkers read Dickens. And had French accents. They couldn't be all bad.

Drama Queen—as Tash had mentally tagged the woman—crossed her arms and sighed heavily. "Let's gather the chairs in a circle and form a book group, why don't we?"

Silver Man's grin widened, but the men behind him looked alarmed. One of them cleared his throat. "Uh, I haven't read that one, Marguerite."

She gave the man a blistering look. "I'm astounded, Adrian." She turned back to Silver Man, her voice clipped. "Are these Dancers? Is this the one I'm looking for?"

Silver Man shrugged. "There's Dancer energy here. Difficult to tell if the power is coming from these women or if it is a residue from the one who was here. The one who exploded."

Tasha's legs gave out, just like that. She sank to the floor beside her grandmother. Harrison and her mother were the only other people who'd been here. Harrison hadn't looked anywhere close to exploding.

Marguerite frowned. "No matter. The bond has not wavered again. We'll go to the Balance's house and wait for him." With a graceful swipe of her arm, the bizarre entourage disappeared.

Tasha barely noticed. She turned and buried her head against her grandmother's shoulder, refusing to believe what she'd just heard. Her mother couldn't be dead.

"Is she dead?" Harrison asked. The pace of the blood thundering through his veins had nothing to do with the angel who had just left the room. It had everything to do with fear. The unfamiliar emotion made him want to roar in protest.

The angel had absorbed the excess energy, allowing Julie's own system to begin processing the energy, but had left her slumped and unconscious. Angels were never chatty, and this one, after a long look at Bas, left without saying a word.

Bas contemplated the still body sprawled on the floor. "No, she's alive. It's night though. Since she's triggered, she'll be more attuned to the power rhythms of light. She may not wake until morning."

Harrison knelt beside Julie and gently picked her up. She felt cool to the touch, her skin faintly pink. He pulled her close for a moment and caught the faint scent of cinnamon. Each angel had an individual scent. He'd heard it said that while humans usually have no conscious memory of their contact with the Seraphim, that scent could invoke feelings of comfort and safety afterward.

He moved to the bed and pulled off the covers with one hand. He laid her down, removed her black loafers and then pulled the sheet and blanket up to her shoulders.

"I never knew you were so nurturing." Bas stood near the wood laminate cupboard that held the television and watched him.

"I'm not," Harrison said shortly. He moved to sit where he could see the bed.

"How many times did you get tucked in at night?" Bas asked softly.

"You know the answer to that." He glanced at Bas. "I couldn't leave her on the cold floor."

"Two minutes ago I'd have predicted that's exactly what you'd do."

Bas was right. Harrison didn't spend much time worrying about how comfortable anyone was. His worries were confined to restoring the Triad and to seeing justice served.

He stared at Julie's face. Her eyelashes fluttered as if she fought to regain consciousness. Most people who had their conception of reality torn apart would welcome the quiet respite of sleep. This one's mind refused to close down. He could almost feel her neurons firing and her brain sifting information.

He admired her spirit. He admired the way she protected her daughter like a fierce lioness. Perhaps that's why he didn't want her scared or cold. He glanced at Bas. "She's over forty, and her powers just triggered."

"I told you she'd been raised human."

"But she still should have come into her powers, whether she developed them or not. Why did you send me to her? How could a powerless Dancer help me?"

"She was never powerless."

Harrison had no patience for Bascule's riddles. "I'd like to keep her here until she regains consciousness. Her family will hover, and I need to talk with her. Is that all right with you?"

"Of course." Bas looked at the woman on the bed. "I was planning on leaving this evening anyway. The room is paid for until tomorrow morning."

"Thanks." Harrison looked toward the balcony. "Where are we?" Judging from the angle of the sun, they were in the same time zone as Michigan.

"Just outside of Tampa."

"Is there trouble here?" Prior to the Rift, the Farnsworth family had been one of leading Triad families in Florida. Jerry Farnsworth had recently agreed to assume the position of Lion of Florida and was beginning to rebuild trust here, along with a governing structure.

"No. Jerry was a good choice. The Farnsworth family has branches throughout the state and are well liked." Bas picked up a piece paper from the small desk and crumpled it into a ball before throwing it in the empty metal wastebasket.

Harrison didn't miss the fact that the paper hit the can with more force than necessary. "You're here searching for your mystery person." About five years ago, Harrison had deduced that Bas was looking for something or someone. Bas had never confirmed nor denied it. He simply ignored Harrison whenever he had asked about it.

Harrison was therefore not surprised when Bas nodded toward Julie. "Tell me what happened." The paper ball burst into flames, quickly burning to ashes.

"We kissed. Our powers resonated. Julie began pulling power and couldn't release it."

Bas pulled out the chair next to the desk and sat down. "This changes everything,"

"No, it doesn't." Harrison wouldn't let it. Marguerite had to be pushed out of his head.

"You can't use Julie to break the tie. It's too dangerous. The fact that your kiss triggered her latent abilities could mean that you two are what people used to call 'in harmony.'"

"Harmony? Not bloody likely." Julie defied him constantly. She thought he was insane.

"It really has nothing to do with your personalities or how you get along." Bas smirked. "Obviously. We now think couples like you and Julie manipulate energy in such a way that your power attracts like opposite poles of a magnet. This is rare among our people. Diksen was doing some research on the phenomenon in Sweden before the Rift. I recall hearing that intimate contact,"

Bas looked at Harrison and clarified, "*shagging*, could force a blood bond in a small percentage of cases."

Harrison looked at Julie. "How small a percentage?"

"Around ten percent in his small sample."

"If there were ten percent chance of rain, you wouldn't bring an umbrella. Stop worrying."

"Worry is useless, caution is not."

"If she can break this sodding curse, I will have sex with her." He'd consider sex with a monkey if it would get Marguerite out his head. Julie was a no-brainer. The idea of a forced bond occurring because of sex was ludicrous. "The Balance doesn't bond with one person. If anything, his bond is with the whole Triad." Harrison believed his words, but looking at Julie, he felt a whisper of rebellion. "Does *Mots de Sagesse* say anything about this?"

"Why do you ask?"

"You wrote the bloody thing."

Bas curled his lip. "Yes, I remember that. I'm merely surprised at your sudden interest in the prophecies."

"I have interest in anything that might give me a clue as to how to solve this problem. I read the book while at school. The writing is pretty dense and archaic. Unfortunately, I don't remember much beyond the basic stories."

Bas sighed. "Why did I even bother to have a scribe in my room for the five years I was in and out of that vision trance? Read it again."

"Do you keep a copy with you?" He'd probably have a few hours to kill while he waited for Julie to wake up. He could skim.

"It would be a bit puffed up to keep a copy of my book on me at all times."

"Which is why I assumed you'd have one."

Bas grinned. "I'll hunt one down for you. Do you still feel Marguerite's presence in your head?"

"Yes." Like a dull ache that never left him, a constant distraction.

"She'll try to place the final tie during the next new moon."

"Unless I've broken her hold by then."

"Do not continue with your plan to use the Dancer."

"My plan?" Harrison looked away from Julie to glance at Bas. "I believe it was your plan."

"Whatever." Bas studied Harrison. A fleeting shadow of regret and sorrow darkened his eyes. "Regardless of what you think, shagging the Dancer is too risky. Don't do it. We'll have to move to Plan B."

"You didn't mention a Plan B in our previous discussions." Harrison spoke calmly, but he didn't feel calm. Stopping this curse was too important for Bas to just dole out information as he saw fit.

"I gave you what was supposed to be the simplest, quickest way." Bas shrugged. "Plan B means waiting. If the Council weaves a protective circle around you during the night of the next new moon, it should block Marguerite's attempt at placing the second tie and break the curse."

Waiting until the next new moon to rid himself of Marguerite was almost unthinkable. Harrison paced the small room. The constant wrongness of her presence already affected him, played with his mood, his thinking. "Do you really think sex with Julie is a risk? I don't form attachments. You know how I was raised."

Bas walked over to Julie and touched a soft curl resting on her cheek. Harrison's stomach muscles clenched, but he didn't say anything.

Bas didn't look at him, but as if he sensed the volatile emotions that Harrison couldn't define, he stepped away from the bed. "She's lovely and strong-willed. A fitting mate for anyone."

Harrison moved between Bas and the bed. He picked up the lock of hair Bas had touched and rubbed it between his fingers. "Not for a man like me."

"I'm sorry you believe that." Bas's spoke seriously, his stare steady and unblinking.

For a moment, Harrison wanted to comfort Bas, which was an odd feeling. Bas walked to the sliding glass door that led to a small balcony and slid it open. He turned, his gaze encompassing both Harrison and Julie. "Call me if you need me." In the blink of an eye, a great horned owl sat on the iron rail beyond the door. With a single, silent flap of its wings, it soared into the night.

Julie opened her eyes to darkness. She reached out for her bedside lamp, confused when she touched only air. Last night's dream rushed back in a jumble of bits and pieces.

She sat up and peered into the unrelieved black. This was not her bed. This was not her bedroom. "Hello?" She whispered the word, not sure she should let whatever lurked in the shadows know she was awake.

"You're awake."

Her heart jumped at the immediate response. Not because of the fact that the voice belonged to Harry. "Where am I? Is Tasha okay?"

"She's fine. She's at your house."

Her shoulders relaxed and she let out a breath she hadn't realized she'd been holding. "What happened? Where am I?"

"What do you remember?"

A collage of images flashed through her head. She focused on one of the clearest. "I remember being angry with you. We kissed and then…." And then everything got hot and fuzzy. "Have you been sick recently, Harry? I think when we kissed I must have picked up a virus from you that caused me to spike a fever and start hallucinating." She put a hand against her now-cool brow. "That could be why you've been having delusions about a curse."

A light clicked on, and she squinted at the bright flare. She pushed herself to a seated position and looked around. She appeared to be in a hotel room. Harry sat in a tan vinyl chair, facing the bed. He had his hands in his pockets, and he watched her with brooding intensity.

"I'm sick with some super bug that made you instantly ill. That's your explanation for all of this?"

"It's one possibility." Okay, so not a very good one.

Harry gave her a look that said he doubted her sanity. Which was another possibility. Maybe she was really in a psych ward, and this hallucination was just a residual fantasy not controlled by her antipsychotic medications. That was the reason for the twist of heat curling through her and the almost uncontrollable desire she had to crook her finger at him and lie back on the bed. No sane person would be thinking about sex when there were so many unknowns on the table.

With a sigh, Julie put her feet over the side of the bed, relieved to see that except for her shoes, she still wore her clothes. So she wasn't a total slut, even during a psychotic break. Was she happy or sad about that?

Harry's eyes narrowed. "What are you thinking?"

"Nothing." She immediately tried to blank her mind in case he was trying to read it. "There's absolutely nothing in my head. I'm very boring." So boring and uninteresting her ex-husband had packed up and left. Okay. Where had that come from? Apparently, in addition to not being slutty, her psychotic brain was a whiner that wanted to have a pity party.

Harry stood in a single, supple move and walked toward her. "You are many things, Julie, but boring is not one of them. Your mind is an intricate puzzle. Ten minutes spent with you is more adventure than most men can handle."

Was that a compliment? Whether it was or not, his words soothed parts of her she hadn't realized were raw. Of course, he had an ulterior motive for flattering her. He thought he needed her to break the curse. "You're just saying that because you want to get me into bed."

"You're already in bed," he pointed out with a small smile.

"You know what I mean. If we slept together, got married and had a daughter, you'd stop thinking life with me was an adventure. I'd be the woman who was holding you back from your dreams." Oh, great. Just spill all your hurt and insecurities out on the guy, Julie.

"How do you know having a family isn't my dream?"

"You want to get married?" she asked, incredulous.

"Of course not." He spoke quickly, as if afraid she might drop to one knee and propose. "That will never happen."

"You getting in bed with me is something that will never happen, either."

"We resonate, Julie." He snapped the words out, obviously irritated.

"What on earth are you talking about?" Tuning forks resonate, not people. Her intricate puzzle of a brain felt like it was missing a few pieces.

He took a step and suddenly he was towering over her, his knees almost touching hers. Her heart fluttered at his nearness.

She scooted backward across the bed and stood on the other side. The gleam in his eyes gave her the sinking feeling that she'd pushed his predator button.

She held up a hand. "Enough."

"I merely want to remind you how it feels to resonate, since you've apparently forgotten." He put a knee on the bed.

The focused look on his face held her still. Had anyone ever looked at her as if the rest of the world didn't exist? She lost time in that look, felt a strange yearning burst to life.

Then he shifted, and she blinked, suddenly aware of her surroundings again. "Resonate! Of course! Silly me. Now I remember. Violins, rainbows. No need for a refresher."

She thought she heard a snort, though Harrison wasn't the type to snort. He took his knee off the bed and looked at her with an expression that she couldn't quite interpret. "I like you, Julie Dancer. And they were fireworks, not rainbows."

The sweetness of his sudden smile caused an ache in her chest. "Right." She took a deep breath. "Enough of this…nonsense." She waved a hand between them. "Let's order a bracing cup of tea from room service, and you can tell me what is going on and how I can get home."

The smile disappeared from his face. "If your parents hadn't been so irresponsible, you would already know what's going on.

Jean Dancer has a lot to answer for."

"Tell me about it." She was going to have a serious discussion with her mother the next time she saw her. Her mother. Who had popped into her kitchen out of thin air. "I'm a witch. That's what you told me after we kissed." Oh. My. God. Flashes of light danced in front of her eyes.

"Breathe, Julie. You're a Sun Dancer. You wield the energy of light."

"So…sort of like a witch?" She took a deep gulp of air but couldn't get rid of the funny buzzing feeling that seemed to zip through her body. "Or would that make me more like a Jedi knight," she asked, "tapping into the Force?"

He crossed his arms and thought for a moment. "The Jedi knight analogy is closer, but our people have been called witches for ages."

The funny feeling grew stronger. Our people? Witches? "I'm not in Kansas anymore, am I?"

He looked puzzled and then recognized the reference. "You watch a lot of movies."

"My laptop is my Friday night date. Okay, Saturday too. We're very close." She rubbed her hands up and down her thighs. "You're not crazy like I thought, are you?"

"Not yet." He didn't smile. "Prolonged exposure to you might change that."

She couldn't argue the point. She was driving herself crazy as well. Her head began to ache. She needed time, maybe a lifetime, to digest everything that had happened. "I want to go home."

"You've always had that power, Dorothy." Harry paraphrased Glinda without a pause.

She let out a startled laugh that edged into a sob.

He considered her for a moment. His hard face softened. "You're handling this quite well, but you need time." He spoke slowly and calmly. "Think of your mother. Think of Natasha. Gather the energy around you."

Where was a pair of ruby slippers when you needed them?

She had no idea what he meant by gathering energy, but she pictured Tasha standing in their kitchen. A stab of heat rushed through her. "Ouch!" Her mental image dissolved in panic. Not again.

"That won't happen," Harry reassured her. "Before, you tapped into the energy around you and didn't have an avenue to release it. Your body has opened channels and reached equilibrium. You haven't yet learned to transform the energy but it's ebbing and flowing through you. It's an unconscious process, like breathing, unless you reach for large amounts of power."

She narrowed her eyes at him. "Get out of my head, Harry.

He jumped on the bed and walked over it, making the awkward move look graceful. He stepped down beside her, and with a smooth move pulled her into his arms.

"We'll use my power this time." Without another word, he fastened his mouth against hers.

This heat didn't hurt. It seduced and warmed. For just a moment, she let go of the desperate struggle to make sense of everything that was happening to her. Her fingers spread against the back of his neck and compulsively curled as he deepened the kiss, his tongue boldly stroking into her mouth. A moan caught in her throat, the slight sound bringing back a rush of reality.

She pushed, and he lifted his head. "Do you have to kiss me for this to work?"

His lips curved into a wicked half-grin and sent another wave of sensation through her. "No."

Then his eyes darkened, and his arms tightened their hold. She closed her eyes and let his hand push her head against his chest. He felt right. A solid anchor in this sudden whirling void.

She didn't open her eyes until she heard her name called.

"Mom!" Tasha jumped up from the kitchen table, almost knocking over the cup of tea her grandmother had just placed in front of her. She elbowed Harrison out of the way and buried her head in her mother's shoulder. Her mom's arms came around her and the world began rotating again. The air finally held enough oxygen for her to breathe.

Her mother squeezed her tight. "I'm okay, sweetheart."

"It's morning," Tash accused, not lifting her head. "You've been gone all night. We didn't know where you were and weird silver people popped into the kitchen and—"

"Weird silver people?" Harrison interjected.

"The Balance." Grandma sounded awestruck. Tash swung her head around to stare, startled by her grandmother's pale face and wide eyes. Grandma stood from the table, her whole body trembling, her head lowered. "The Shadow Walkers are here. They're at your house."

Harrison looked cold and frightening. "You've caused problems, Jean Dancer."

Grandma—outspoken, bold Grandma—said nothing, but kept her head bowed. Tasha shivered and moved closer to her mother.

Harrison turned, his gaze skimming over Tasha to rest on her mother. His expression didn't change, but his face softened somehow. "I have to go. I'll return before nightfall."

Mom sucked in her breath. "Harry...?" His name was a question.

"Later." Harrison blinked out of the kitchen, which was both scary and seriously cool.

An odd, heavy silence filled the room. As usual when the three of them were together, silence didn't last long. Jean spoke first. "Tell me you didn't sleep with him."

"Mom!" Her mother didn't sound as outraged as Tasha would have expected. "Forget about sex, and tell me what the hell is going on."

"Do you know who that man is?" Jean persisted.

"Sort of." Mom shrugged. "He says he's one of the Penumbrae and that we're Sun Dancers." Her mother shot Grandma a look. "I'm expecting you to explain."

"He's not just any Penumbra, Julie. He's *the* Penumbra,

the Balance. He's above the very law that he enforces. He holds power over all in the Triad—Shadow Walkers, Sun Dancers and Penumbrae alike. I don't want you involved in any of this. You can't sleep with him."

"Will you please stop talking about sex?"

"Julie, I saw the way he looked at you."

A knock sounded on the front door.

"I'll get it." Tasha grabbed the excuse to escape from the kitchen. She didn't want to hear about her mother and sex. Way more information than a daughter should have to deal with. She trotted through the living room and opened the front door, belatedly wondering who would visit at seven in the morning.

Silver Man stood on the porch.

Tasha froze, unable to slam the door shut. He could probably walk through it anyway.

"Little Dancer." The frown on his face smoothed. "We must speak." He glanced over her shoulder toward the voices in the kitchen. "Privately."

"I don't think so." He was a Shadow Walker. Whatever that was.

He pointed toward the morning sky. The moon glowed feebly in the growing light, a thin crescent. "Sun rise is in about five minutes," he said, as if that should reassure her.

"'The nearer the dawn, the darker the night.'" The words popped out of nowhere. Great. First Dickens and now this. Way to show what a major nerd she was. The words she read lived inside her, her lens through which to understand the world when her own experience wasn't enough. She'd never actually quoted those words out loud, though. Social suicide was not her thing.

"Henry Wadsworth Longfellow." Silver Man stepped inside the house, looking delighted. He started to say something, then shook his head and blinked his incredibly long lashes. "Marguerite is with Le Bilan, then she will rest. We can talk without interruption."

When Tasha frowned, he smiled an apology. "The Balance,

your neighbor, Harrison Chevalier."

Tash was too tired to ask who Marguerite was, why she needed to rest, or why she would want to interrupt them. "What do you want to talk to me about?"

"An ancient prophecy that I believe impacts us both." His voice lowered and deepened.

Tasha sighed, unmoved. Maybe it was lack of sleep or too many traumas in a twenty-four hour period. "You must be related to the Drama Queen."

"Pardon?"

"Nothing." Tasha held out her hand, determined to act as normal as possible. "Hello, I'm Natasha Morgen."

His hand felt cool and firm as it grasped hers. "Die Morgenrote," he murmured in German, releasing her hand to touch her her fiery hair. "The flush of dawn."

She pulled back, aware that dawn was probably flushing her cheeks as well. "How pretty. Much nicer than being called Red. You're a poet?"

"I'm French," he said, as if that was the same thing. "My name is Luc Deschamps." His eyes met hers, his expression both serious and determined. "The Drama Queen, Marguerite, is my sister. We must speak."

Five

"WHO ARE you and why do you need to talk to my daughter?" Julie hurried into the living room, hearing a voice at the door that she didn't recognize.

Standing way too close to Tash was a ringer for one of Tolkien's elves, movie version. Slender and long limbed, he stood over six feet tall, with white, almost silver, hair just touching his collar. He had high cheekbones, a high forehead and wide-set eyes, all arranged above a strong chin that saved his features from being delicate. Bright blue eyes watched her with curiosity and a trace of wariness.

Julie grabbed Tash's arm and dragged her toward the middle of the room. Legolas made her nervous.

"You are she."

He had a French accent. For Tash, a French accent beat a British accent, hands down. Of course, accent aside, what he had just said made no sense, something Julie was getting all too used to, so she merely waited.

The man studied her, taking his time before he spoke again. "You are the one the Balance hopes will break Marguerite's spell."

"Did Harry take out an ad in the paper or something? Does everyone know he wants to have sex with me?"

"Mom!" Tash's voice was faint.

Julie sent her an apologetic smile and focused on the man. "Who are you?"

"He's Lucien Deschamps, a Shadow Walker," Jean, suddenly a font of information, announced from behind her. "A very powerful Shadow Walker."

The man slowly dipped his head in acknowledgement. "And you are Jean Dancer. Many searched for you after the Rift."

"Many must not have looked in the Chicago phone book," her mother retorted.

The man frowned, as if such a mundane search tool hadn't occurred to him. Many hadn't tried Google either, or they'd have found PrewashedJean.com. The full title of her mom's webpage was *Pre-washed Jean: Tips from a well-worn and comfortable woman.* The site got an amazing number of hits. Apparently a crystal ball, or whatever the voodoo of choice was for Triad members, bypassed modern technology.

"You left the Triad."

His phrase wasn't accusatory, but her mom reacted as if it were. "And my responsibilities? Is that what you're implying? Are you telling me Shadow Walker assassins weren't gunning for me?"

"The war is long over. We need to restructure. We need all of our powerful families working together." The Walker said the words gently, but they had the effect of a match on gunpowder.

"How dare you!" Jean wasn't very big, but she could be scary when she lost her temper. She marched up to the Walker and poked a finger in his chest. He took a step backward. "Go. Get out of this house."

"Grandma!" Tasha looked apologetically at the man. "It's been a confusing twenty-four hours."

He nodded. "These are confusing times for us all." He hesitated. "Now is not a good time to talk."

Bright boy. Julie frowned at the look that passed between Tasha and Lucien. The Walker turned and walked out the door.

"Good riddance!" Jean slammed the front door shut after him.

"What did he want, Tasha?" Julie asked.

Tasha shook her head. "I'm not sure."

"I don't trust him," Julie said. "Until we can figure out this new world we've been thrust into, you need to be very careful."

"I don't think he wants to hurt us." Sensible, careful Tasha had a small smile on her face. Uh oh.

"Get that look off your face, Natasha." Jean folded her arms across her chest. "He's the bad guy."

"Is he?" Tasha lifted her chin. "You and I often see things differently, Grandma."

"Your view is fogged by hormones, young lady," Jean snapped.

"Well, that wouldn't be a problem for you, would it?"

A nasty temper went along with Tasha's red hair. Julie stepped between the two. "Tasha, you're being disrespectful to your grandmother. Apologize now."

Her temper might be nasty, but it burned out quickly. Tasha ran to Jean and enfolded her in her arms. "I'm sorry, Gram. My mouth got away from me again."

"You didn't say anything that's not true." Jean's hand came up and touched Tash's hair. "That Walker family is bad business, baby. Stay away from him. His people killed your great-grandmother."

"What?" Tasha and Julie gasped the word out together.

"Your mother was murdered?" Julie had never heard this before.

"Kidnapped by a Shadow Walker and killed in cold blood. That's what started the civil war that blew the Triad apart."

"What happened?" Tasha perched on the arm of the couch, leaning forward with interest.

"They stole her right out of her bed, in the middle of the night, while we all slept. My father went after her and found her dead the next morning. Something in him broke and he went a little mad. He gathered Dancers from around the world and waged war on the Walkers. Hundreds of Walkers and Dancers died in one terrible week, including my father. Only the fact that the rest of the world was involved in a war as well saved us from discovery. After it was over, I moved away from New York. I cut all my ties with old friends and family. I wanted nothing to do with the Triad or what was left of it."

"Wow," Tasha breathed.

"Why haven't you told me this before?" Julie spoke through gritted teeth. How could her mother have kept this very important part of their history hidden?

"I don't want you involved in the Triad. Either of you."

"I don't know if we have a choice, Mom. It looks like the Triad has become involved with us."

"Ignore them. They'll go away."

Julie and Tasha exchanged a skeptical look. "Harry isn't easily ignored," Julie finally said.

"Drama Queen and Luc aren't either," Tasha added.

"And what about these powers I suddenly have? Shouldn't I use them for good, or something?" With great power comes great responsibility—or whatever it was Spiderman had said.

"No, no, no. Just forget about them."

Easier said than done, especially when she had no idea what her powers were. A terrible thought occurred to her. "What about Tasha? Is she going to have to worry that every time she kisses a guy, she may blow up?"

"A kiss doesn't usually trigger a release of powers. Your case is not normal, Julie." Her mother gave her a look that made her feel guilty.

"What is normal?" Tasha asked.

"Triad children come into their full powers at puberty. Before that, they have a very limited ability to transform energy. Most kids can light a candle or give another child a small shock, that sort of thing. During puberty, however, that changes and Triad children are sent to boarding school where they are taught how to control and use the energy they gradually become able to absorb."

Tasha looked thoughtful. "And that's where they learn how to fight demons in groups of three?"

Fight demons? Groups of three? What was Tasha talking about?

"Those are advanced skills, not taught until what would be

late high school here." Her mother nodded.

Julie didn't even know where to start asking questions. "Tasha and I didn't come into power at puberty. Why not?"

"You're of mixed heritage. When it didn't happen, I just assumed you didn't have the ability."

"So now that we know I do and we know that I'm not normal," Julie slanted her mother a look, "we don't know what to expect for Tasha."

"Right. My advice is that she stay away from men." Jean turned to Tasha. "There are really some very lovely lesbians, dear. I don't suppose you'd consider coming out of the closet?"

Tasha turned to Julie. "Grandma's driving me crazy."

"Tasha." Julie gave her daughter a severe look and turned to her mother. "Mom. You're driving me crazy. Gay people aren't gay just because it's convenient for them. You know that."

"Not all gay people are alike. Sexuality exists on a continuum. Some people are born gay, and some choose the gay lifestyle. It's not fair to say you can't be gay just because you don't have the right genetic make-up. That kind of closed-mindedness isn't like you, dear."

"I'm very closed-minded at the moment." Julie sat down. "In fact, my brain is in lockdown. I officially have information overload. And I haven't even asked you about demon fighting." When her mother started to speak, she held up a hand. "Hold that explanation until later. I have to go to work, and I don't think I can process anything more at the moment anyway."

"Good." Jean patted her shoulder. "Go to work, and forget all about this."

Julie straightened. "Mom, life has changed." She sighed. What an understatement. "I can't ignore Harrison."

"Of course you can ignore Harrison. You ignored me through most of your teens. You ignored the fact that your husband would rather sleep next to a dusty hole in the ground than in your bed for most of your marriage. You're very good at ignoring things."

Julie tried to stir up self-righteous anger, but her mother

was right. She didn't precisely ignore things, but she focused on what she wanted to think about and didn't focus on the rest. Julie rubbed her head. "Can you stay for a few days?" Her mother nodded. "We'll talk at dinner then."

"I'll cook," Jean offered.

"Will you drop me off at my dorm, Mom?" Tasha looked lost, like she didn't know what she should do next.

"Of course, honey." Julie put an arm around her shoulders. "Do you want to have dinner with us tonight? We have a lot to discuss."

Tash nodded. "I'll meet you at your office at six." She looked over at Jean. "Grandma, promise you won't make anything with tofu, okay?"

Jean nodded, not even arguing like she usually would. "You know I love you both with my whole heart. I won't lose you. I won't let anything happen to you."

Her indomitable mother looked suddenly vulnerable. A strong wave of love pushed aside Julie's irritation and anger at the dangerous secrets her mother had kept. This woman had lost both her parents in violence and was doing the best she could to keep her child and grandchild safe.

Julie reached her at the same time Tasha did. The three of them hugged, forming a triangle of strength and support.

"There's something different about you." Joe Kradeno, one of her coworkers, stood in her office doorway holding a file folder. "Are you all right?"

Julie sighed and rested both elbows on her desk, hands cupping her cheeks. She was tempted to tell him that she'd found a man she resonated with, come into some super powers and discovered that weird beings existed in the world. But she didn't have time to be evaluated by every psychiatrist in the building. "I'm just tired. Rough night."

"I can smooth things out for you." His voice lowered to what he probably thought was a sexy drawl.

"The results from the new study look that good?" Julie sat up straight and smiled, despite herself.

Joe stepped into the office and frowned at her apparent obliviousness to his flirting. He tossed the folder on the desk in front of her. "We don't have enough data to run the stats yet. The interviewers are still in the field."

"What's this, then?" Julie picked up the folder and opened it. Two tickets fluttered to her desk along with a piece of paper. She picked up the paper. It was an advertisement for a marathon of Jane Austen movies at the local theater. Joe knew how to tempt her.

He'd been trying to get her to go out on a date since he'd joined the lab a year ago. He wouldn't succeed. Short and wiry, with a full head of gray hair, he had the slim build of a distance runner. Aside from the big-mistake-to date-a-colleague thing and the fact that she didn't want to get involved with anyone at this point in her life, she could never date a man who weighed less than she did.

Which might severely limit her options if she ever did decide to date. Then again, she could stretch out on the couch, munching buttered popcorn for a long time before she outweighed Harry.

"Come to the movies with me, Julie."

Julie brought her focus back to the man watching her. "I don't date people I work with. I've told you that," she said gently.

"I'll quit."

She grinned and picked up the tickets and advertisement, putting them back in the folder. "Have fun at the show. And thank you for inviting me." She held out the folder until he took it.

"I won't give up, Julie."

"Which makes me worry about you, Joe. Go find somebody exciting. I'm a middle-aged woman enjoying a quiet life."

"Hey, I like the quiet life, too. After a glass of warm milk, I'm in bed by nine o'clock most nights. Maybe you could join me sometime."

She laughed. "I'm serious. I've raised a good kid and crafted a decent career. All I want is to relax during my off time. I'm not looking to start anything new."

"Want to go for a double mocha latte and see if a spurt of caffeine won't oil your aging engines?"

You had to give the guy points for persistence. She really was tired, coffee really would help, and going to the cafeteria with a colleague wasn't even close to a date. But most important of all, Joe was so blessedly normal. No fireworks or violins to distract her. No talk of curses and strange powers.

"Coffee sounds great." She stood and walked around her desk. The office was small, and Joe just had to reach out a hand to touch the smudges beneath her eyes.

"Is everything okay, Julie?"

"No. Everything is pretty much shot to hell, Joe."

When she didn't elaborate, he draped a supportive arm around her shoulders and guided her out the door. She paused, surprised by the sudden rumble of thunder that reverberated against the windows lining one wall of the hallway. "Wasn't it sunny out two minutes ago?"

Black clouds covered the sky in an ominous blanket. Lightning lashed out at the ground.

"This blew up quickly," Joe commented, dropping his arm when she stepped away from him. "It'll probably blow over just as fast."

The drum of thunder pushed against the glass with an insistent fist. Julie paused, unsettled. "'You can't stop a storm, but you can shut a window so it doesn't get in the house.'"

Joe gave her a strange look. "Is there a window open somewhere?"

Julie shook her head. "No, that's just something my Mom always used to say whenever it stormed." She shook her head as if to clear it. "You know Michigan weather. Storms can pop out of nowhere."

Joe grinned and pushed the button for the elevator that

would take them up three flights to the sixth-floor cafeteria. "That reminds me of a study I just read on the effect of weather on mental health. This study didn't just look at amount of sunlight, but took temperature…."

Julie nodded a couple of times, not really listening. She stared at the rolling clouds outside the windows until the elevator doors closed, blocking her view.

Harrison stood in her office when she returned. Julie almost dropped her half-empty cup of coffee.

"Hi." She sounded more breathy than she wanted to. He wore black pants and a white shirt open at the neck. A casual look for him. He stared at her, cold and silent.

"Um, should I kneel or something? Mom says you're a pretty important guy."

"I only want to see you kneeling in front of me for one reason." He didn't even smile when he said it.

"Funny man." She stepped into the room and shut the door. No need to fuel office gossip. "You look angry. I take it your chat with Marguerite was not productive?"

His facial muscles became more rigid. "Do not mention that woman's name."

"That bad, huh?"

"I need to return to London and meet with the Council."

"Right now?" She leaned back against her door. She was more tired than she'd thought.

He nodded. "Julie, did your mother explain bonding?"

"No. That didn't come up. She had a lot of other explaining to do."

"This is important. The Dancers and Walkers who commit to each other usually get married, just like most humans. A very few, however, choose to enter a relationship that can't be broken, called a blood bond. It's a powerful ceremony, twining the couple's power together through the mixing of their blood."

"How romantic. Young Triad girls must dream about it."

Yuck.

"I believe some of the sillier girls do." He looked like he found the whole concept as distasteful as Julie did. "Bascule has determined that our power is aligned in such a way that there is a pull, an attraction, for the energy to bond."

Julie let out a disbelieving laugh. "Between you and me? Good one."

"Bascule is rarely wrong."

Julie shook her head. "You're the great and powerful Balance. I'm a half-breed with no abilities. I don't think so."

He gave her one of his brooding looks. "We don't know what your abilities are yet. You are highly unusual."

Julie's hands flew up in the air. "I'm a little tired of everyone inferring that I'm not normal and all this weirdness is my fault. Go away. Go to London. Have a good life. I have work to do."

Harrison ignored her outburst. "The Council must be informed of this."

"Are you also going to inform them that you want to have sex with me to break the curse or have you already consulted with them about that?"

Harry had no expression on his face. "That plan has changed. Bascule has researched this phenomenon and has confirmed that if we have sex, we could bond without the blood ritual. I can't take that chance."

"So the bottom line is you don't want me anymore. I'm off the hook." She didn't know why she was acting all pissy. Bonding with him, with anyone, was nowhere on her list of things to do.

"Balances don't bond. They belong to the Triad."

"So, you're sort of like the Triad's version of a priest? Married to the entire Triad, not just one person?"

"No, not at all."

Argh. A thought occurred to her. "If we don't have sex, you remain under Marguerite's curse."

"There is an alternate option." A muscle in his cheek twitched. "The curse can be broken with the aid of the Council during the next new moon." His hand went through his hair in the now-familiar gesture. "In the meantime, if this invasion by Marguerite becomes too difficult to bear, I will sleep with Dancer women of lesser power in the hopes of finding one who can break the curse."

"No!"

"Excuse me?" His gaze focused on her.

"I said 'Oh!'" She stared down at her feet and willed herself not to stomp over to Harry. She had a strong urge to grab him and divert his attention away from other Dancers. What on earth was wrong with her?

She looked out her window, not trusting herself to look at Harry's face. "Did you come to say good-bye?"

"No, I didn't come to say good-bye."

The cool note in his voice didn't bother her. She felt too relieved by his words.

"I've put you in danger. Marguerite knows I intended to use you to break the spell." Harry's tone was brisk. "To protect you, I told her that you don't have enough power to stop the curse." Harry gave her a stern look. "If she discovers how powerful you are or the potential for our bond, she'll seek to neutralize you. It's important that you don't use your power until after the new moon on October sixteenth, when the curse is broken."

His grim face convinced her that Marguerite's idea of neutralizing her wouldn't be pleasant.

"I have to go to London, but I'll be back soon. I'm leaving Linda as your guard. She'll contact me if you need me."

Linda? Julie looked around, half-expecting someone to pop into the office and join them. "I don't like this, Harry." Julie sank into the office chair she kept pushed against one of the walls.

"I know. You'll handle it, though." He surprised her by crouching down in front of her. "Before I go, I want to make one thing clear. You said that I don't want you." This close she could feel the tension in him, the tight control. "Make no mistake. I want you."

The quiet intensity of the words caused a hot shiver to spread through her, but his expression remained cool and remote. He stood, backing away. He wanted her, but he made it clear that wouldn't guide his actions.

"Until the danger to you is over, I will be in your life." He paused. "My control is not what it should be in this situation." He drew in a deep breath, and she heard the faint echo of thunder. His face was calm, but his amber gaze held a heat she could feel on her skin. "Don't let that man touch you again."

Julie mentally went through the extremely short list of men who had touched her recently. Did he mean Joe? "What man?"

Harry paused, as if considering the question. "Any man."

Without even a wave of his hand, he disappeared from the room. Before she could blink, a woman appeared in his place. The tall, muscular blonde, dressed in leather pants and a purple shirt, regarded her with interest.

"So you're the Dancer who has the Balance's knickers in a twist."

Six

LINDA WASN'T so bad once you got past the purple outfit. Okay. Yes, she was. The woman paced Julie's small office nonstop, making small grunts of disgust. Her leather squeaked and she smelled like dead cow. Her vocabulary contained more names for animal excrement than Julie would have believed existed.

When Linda stopped in front of her desk and began leafing through some of the papers, Julie gave up on trying to work. "Linda, I appreciate your help, but I'm sure I'll be okay. You can go home."

"Brilliant idea. I'll just pop off." She planted both hands on the black laminated desktop and leaned forward, a disgusted look on her face. "Not. The gaffer would be cheesed off if I did a bloody stupid thing like that. He told me to protect you."

"Harry's got a lot of things on his mind right now. I'm sure he'd understand that I told you to leave."

Linda's mouth dropped open, but no noise came out of it. That blessed state lasted for all of ten seconds. "Have you got fewmets for brains? The Balance doesn't get upset. He's the Balance—get it? And he doesn't 'understand' when people don't do what he says. He just makes them do it."

Julie sat straighter, irritated that this woman would presume to know Harry better than she did. Then it struck her. This woman did know Harry better than she did.

Linda was not just a voluptuous, atrociously attired Amazon.

She was also a golden opportunity to find out about Harry and the Triad. Her mother might eventually cough up information, but she'd take two hours to impart two minutes of highly screened knowledge. With Linda, she could learn the real scoop. She'd need expert help to extract the information, though.

Dorie had the boys in daycare while she went to the health club on Mondays. She might just be free for lunch.

"From now on," Dorie stated, as she and everyone else in Zingerman's crowded dining area watched Linda plow her way through the tables toward the bathroom, "you're not allowed to make new friends without first passing them by me."

"She's more a friend of Harry's."

"Who is some cool-headed leader of the Council—a group of people who act as judge and jury for the rest of the Triad. And you're a powerful Sun Dancer who can wield light energy with her bare hands."

"Theoretically," Julie interrupted modestly.

"The bad guy, a Shadow Walker, is out to get you because your woo-woo can break a curse she has on Harrison."

"My woo-woo? Hello. Talk grown-up."

"Woo-woo's a legitimate word for magical power in the paranormal circles. A fact you would know if you ever picked up a decent horror novel."

"Stephen King uses the term woo-woo?"

"I don't remember." Dorie narrowed her eyes. "You should have told me about this sooner, but I guess you've been busy."

"What do you make of all this?" Julie asked. Dorie had a clear-sighted, practical perspective that Julie relied on. "Have I stepped down a rabbit hole?"

"Nope. I believe it's all true. There's more to this world than we know." Dorie broke a corner off the massive brownie beside Linda's plate and popped it in her mouth. "Can you believe she ordered this brownie? There's not a spare inch of fat on that woman. I wonder what her exercise routine is."

"Dorie."

"Sorry. I think we need to begin experimenting with your powers."

"How? I don't even know where to begin."

"Sure you do. Didn't Harrison tell you how in that hotel room? Something about imagining the place you want to go and then gathering power around you. That sounds simple enough."

"I don't want to go anywhere."

Dorie lowered her brows and gave Julie a look that made her squirm. "We'll start simple." She lifted the saltshaker and set it back down on the table. "Move this."

When Dorie said to do something, people generally did it. Julie closed her eyes and tried to shut out the chattering voices that filled the dining area, the colorful posters that lined the bright walls and the smells of fresh bread and rich, brewed coffee. She tried to clear her mind of everything but the small, glass saltshaker, half full of salt. Instead, she saw Harrison, standing at the head of a long, polished wooden table, blond hair touched by sun from some unseen window.

"Why are you smiling?" Dorie asked suspiciously. "Concentrate. The purple warrior will be back soon."

Julie shook her head to clear the image of Harrison and replace it with a saltshaker, but he wouldn't leave. Dorie's voice became a background hum as Julie settled back in her chair, lost in her fantasy.

The room Harry stood in blurred around the edges, like her mind had decided to add low-budget dream sequence special effects. Only Harry was clear. He wore a white button-down shirt with a brown tie. His cuffs were held together by amber cufflinks that glinted in the light. He appeared to be talking to people in the room, his brow furrowed, his face serious. Suddenly, his head jerked slightly and turned. He looked directly at her, surprised. A woman, young, blonde and too pretty, came up behind him and put a hand on his arm. Her hand moved in a caress down his forearm, settling at his wrist.

Annoyance shot through Julie. Just for fun, she aimed an imaginary bolt of energy at Touchy-Feely Girl. The woman opened her mouth and jumped back, dropping the papers she'd been holding in her other arm. Flustered, she bent to pick them up, going out of Julie's sphere of vision.

Harrison stiffened, an alert expression on his face. Julie had the urge to duck, like he could see her. Someone at the table commanded his attention and Harrison began talking, one long-fingered hand automatically reaching down to straighten the cuff the woman had pulled crooked. The man really needed to loosen up. Nobody should look that perfect. It made the rest of the world feel inferior.

With a wicked grin, she set about to muss him up. She mentally pulled off his boring brown tie, slowly unfurling the knot and dropping it on the table. Next, the top button of his collar flew off, landing with a ping on the table in front of him.

Cool. She was getting sound effects in her fantasy now. In fact, there was an irritating noise building in her head that sounded like rushing wind. She ignored it. She was having too much fun.

She popped his next button and then the next. Hmmm. Why not just do away with the shirt entirely? Poof. The shirt disappeared.

He was beautiful. Hard, muscled and just…beautiful. Julie took a deep breath and could swear she smelled him. Warm, clean, Harry. She wanted to kiss the blond hair on his chest, to look up and watch his expression while she did it. She leaned forward, felt his hair tickle her nose, heard the angry rumble in his chest. The angry rumble?

She opened her eyes when water splashed over her face, drenching her.

"Julie, what is wrong with you?" The panic in Dorie's voice snapped her into awareness.

"I must have fallen asleep."

"In the middle of lunch?" Dorie grabbed her arm and shook

it. "Jules, we have company."

Julie brushed her wet hair off her face. She focused on the man and woman across the table from her—Luc Deschamps and a person who had to be his sister, Marguerite. So this was the woman who had put the curse on Harrison and disrupted Julie's life. Julie stood, feeling the hair on the nape of her neck begin to sizzle.

"They just appeared out of nothing!" Dorie whispered the words frantically, but judging from the excited buzz circling the restaurant, the way these two had arrived wasn't a secret.

Tall, graceful and confident, Marguerite made her feel damp and dumpy, though the damp part was technically Dorie's fault. Marguerite's long, straight, hair looked exactly like she had just stepped out of a shampoo commercial. She wore a cream-colored silk jacket and pants that molded the slim curves of her body. Her feet were encased in three-inch heels that exactly matched her outfit. Blue, blue eyes held contempt, as they looked Julie up and down, pausing on the comfortable black loafers that she wore with almost everything.

"You are the woman who thinks to block my curse?" The disbelief in her musical, lightly accented voice was insulting.

"I look more competent when I'm not dripping lemon water." Julie shot a reproachful look at Dorie. "Have we met? I think you may have mistaken me for someone else. I don't have plans to block any curses." She glanced at Luc, not able to decipher the expression on his face.

"There is no mistake." Marguerite almost spat out the words. "Even I felt your power, and I'm not a Sensitive."

Power? What power? "Honestly, I don't know what you're talking about. I didn't get much sleep last night, and I fell asleep and…." She was babbling.

"Stop. You spilled enough power to light Paris in a blackout." The woman took a step toward her. "It may be daylight, but I'm still stronger than you, old one." She raised a slender hand. The air in the room began to push against Julie.

Sensing danger, Julie picked up the dessert menu, holding it like a shield. Luc put a hand on his sister's arm. Dorie launched another glass of water, this time toward Marguerite. The water formed a graceful arc through the air, exploding into droplets as it hit Marguerite's chest. She gasped, her hand dropping to the front of her silk jacket.

And then Linda appeared, standing between Marguerite and Julie. She twisted her head and glared at Julie. "I can't leave you alone for a minute, can I?"

"Hey, it's not my fault. I just took a little nap, and then she showed up. We old people need our naps."

"Nap. Right. Next time you decide to nap just put a frassing neon sign over your head with the words 'Attack Me.'" She turned toward Marguerite and positioned her sturdy back against Julie's nose, a living shield. "The sun is high, Marguerite. You can't win. Leave."

Julie peeked around Linda's arm. Marguerite met her gaze. "I want the Dancer." She said the words quietly and with such purpose that Julie huddled closer to Linda's back.

"For what?" Linda snorted. "You want to kill her and start another war?" A small rose-colored stone appeared in the air before Linda. "You're already wanted by the Council for gross infractions of Triad law. Don't make it worse."

Linda's tension alerted Julie to that fact that this must be really, really serious. Dorie crowded behind her, taking advantage of the human shield. Her warmth comforted Julie.

"You know what I said about there being more to this world than we know?" Dorie whispered.

Julie nodded, not looking away from Marguerite and the strangely mesmerizing floating stone.

"I think I'd like to go back to not knowing."

"Ditto," Julie agreed, even while something unfurled inside her, something she recognized but hadn't felt for years and years—a sense of excitement and wonder, of being truly alive.

"Rose topaz?" Marguerite's tight laugh brought Dorie closer

against Julie's back. "That puny stone can't absorb my power. You underestimate me, Guardian."

No light flashed from Marguerite's raised hand, no thunder rolled, but Julie felt the shock of something ripple through Linda's body. Only the fact that she and Dorie acted as buttresses kept the woman on her feet. The rose topaz dropped to the floor and rolled under the table.

Julie and Dorie came around to Linda's side, and they supported the sagging woman between them. Linda turned her head and gave Julie a look full of meaning. "Use your power. Now."

What? How? Anxiety surged through Julie. Think, think, think. She tried to concentrate, tried to visualize power gathering around her, tried to imagine Marguerite and her brother poofing into the Grand Canyon. Nothing happened.

Another wave shuddered through Linda. She groaned. Julie met Dorie's expectant gaze. Dorie wanted her to do something, too. A feeling of helplessness gripped her.

Marguerite moved quickly. Her hand reached out and grabbed Julie's arm, hurting her.

"Don't touch me." She yanked her arm out of Marguerite's grip and backed away, pulling Dorie and Linda with her.

"The Guardian will die if you don't come with me."

Julie looked desperately at Luc, who still stood silently at his sister's side. "Are you going to let her do that?"

He smiled slightly. "Are you?"

She hated people who answered a question with a question.

Linda struggled to stand straight. "You can't kill me, Marguerite. And you can't have the Dancer. She is under the protection of the Balance."

"Yes, she is."

Julie almost fainted with relief at the sound of Harry's voice. He stepped into the loose circle formed by the nervous but fascinated restaurant patrons. His shoes were polished, his black slacks wrinkle-free and perfectly creased, yet his shirt hung open, exposing his chest. Several buttons appeared to be missing. He met her eyes, his expression inscrutable.

"I thought you were in London." Marguerite's voice was brittle.

"Marguerite, I tire of your games. You have managed to place a tie on me, but don't overestimate your powers." He flicked a casual hand. Marguerite slumped in a dead faint. Luc caught her in his arms.

"Take your sister away," Harry instructed.

Luc nodded once and they both disappeared.

The hushed crowd suddenly began talking, everyone at once. Phones were held up and pictures were snapped. Harry looked around, his brow furrowed. Before he could say anything, Bas appeared at his side. A collective gasp went up from the crowd.

"They're making a movie!" A man's voice, filled with some relief. "That's the actor from *What's Eating Gilbert Grape*."

"Oh my God." This was a woman's voice. "Thank you, Michigan film tax credit!"

Harrison turned to Bas. "You turn up in surprising places."

Bas shrugged. "I have an interest in what is happening here." He looked at the crowd. His expressive face stilled, silence surrounding him like a cloud. All movement in the room, outside their little group, stopped. Then, as if a switch had been flicked, people began moving again. Like good little robots, phones went in pockets and everyone went back to their tables or work as if nothing had happened.

"The pictures?" Harrison asked.

"What pictures?" Bas responded, as he reached over and plucked a piece of Linda's brownie. "This is really good."

"Wow." Dorie breathed the word. "Did he just do a mind swipe on those people?"

"Looks like it." Julie knew her own eyes were wide.

Bas gave Julie a wink and a wave and disappeared as quickly as he had appeared. She looked around, but no one seemed to be paying attention anymore.

Linda moved, shaking off their hands. "That bitch of a Shadow Walker has more juice in her than we imagined. The rose quartz did nothing." She sounded more like her old self.

Harry looked at Julie and his lips tightened. "Go home, Julie. Marguerite won't bother you anymore today."

"I can't go home." She'd go absolutely crazy if she didn't keep busy. "I have to work and Tash is meeting me at the office at six."

He took a deep breath. "Will I ever hear you say 'Yes, Harrison?'"

"Try asking 'Would you like everything to be the way it was forty-eight hours ago?'"

He took a step closer to her and she forgot all about Dorie and Linda and the hundred other people in the restaurant. Her eyes rested on his chest. He smelled like wind and rain, earth and sun. Like a force of nature.

"Would you like everything to be the way it was forty-eight hours ago?" He spoke softly, so only she heard.

"Yes." The word almost stuck in her throat.

His hand wrapped gently around the back of her neck and he urged her closer. Her cheek rubbed against the skin of his chest. The soft, springy hairs sent spikes of pure pleasure through her body. He leaned down, holding her against him, his cheek against the top of her head.

"I asked you not to lie to me, Julie Dancer."

What could she say? He was right. She was a liar and a total idiot. Not knowing that he existed, that the world was full of magic, seemed too great a loss to bear.

"The next time you take off my shirt, make sure we're alone."

Julie jerked back and looked at him, embarrassed. "I'm so sorry. I don't know how that happened. I thought I was dreaming."

"The Council thought they were dreaming, too." His thumb played along her cheekbone. He didn't seem aware of the action. "You shouldn't be able to manipulate energy at such a distance."

"Maybe I did it through you because we're in sync." She could barely breathe. Her entire focus was on the movement of his thumb. She wanted to grab it with her mouth and suck.

"First we're in harmony and now we're a Nineties boy band?" Amusement and heat warred in his expression for a brief moment before he reverted back to cool, business-like Harrison. "I have to go. The Council is still in session. I'll be back tonight."

"Marguerite?"

"Her power is drained. Her brother has likely taken her somewhere to rest. She'll sleep through this night." His eyes searched her face. "Don't be afraid. I won't let her harm you."

Julie didn't like having to depend on him or on anyone for her own protection. Should she get a gun? She'd never considered that before. She'd ask Linda if she needed silver bullets or anything special. Maybe she couldn't kill someone, but she could aim for an arm or leg if she had to. Her stomach twisted.

Harry backed away and took Linda aside, saying something to her. Dorie hooked an arm through hers, watching the two Penumbrae talk.

"He looks different, not like our crazy neighbor who climbs trees anymore. He looks," she paused, considering, "dangerous."

"People are afraid of him." Even her mother, who feared nothing.

"He's got the hots for you, kiddo."

"He's got big commitment issues." He had wanted one thing from her—sex. And now that was off the table, big time. "He feels responsible for me, that's all."

"Nope. That look was not mere responsibility."

Julie took a good look at Harry. With his legs slightly apart, one hand in his pocket, his posture straight and confident, he appeared regal, even in his button-less shirt. He looked golden and true, like the fictional knights of old who came charging to the rescue on white horses.

Whoa. Stop the runaway imagination. Next she'd believe in happily ever after. She needed to get her hands on one or two of Tasha's literature books and read them for a reality check. Or better yet, she should just take a trip down memory lane and review the Married Years.

Dorie might have good instincts, but she didn't know Harry. He was a master game player. And while she had no idea what the rules were, she knew she was definitely just a piece on his board.

Harry lifted his head and looked directly at her, almost as if he could read her thoughts. Oh, damn. She'd forgotten about that! And then he was gone. No one in the restaurant seemed to notice. Cutlery clanked and conversations continued as if nothing unusual had happened.

Scary stuff, this magic.

Seven

HARRISON STOOD in the reception area outside the solid twin oak doors that guarded the Council meeting. His secretary, Heidi, cast furtive looks at him as she pretended to watch her computer screen. Etiquette demanded that he enter the Council room through the door. Popping into a meeting with no warning would be considered rude. Materializing into the reception area, on the other hand, was perfectly acceptable, even expected.

But now, instead of immediately reaching for the bright brass doorknobs that led to the meeting he'd so precipitously left, he strolled over to the large bank of windows that gave him a view of the London business district. He watched the muted rush of traffic below, insulated from the noise and smells of the city by thick windows and ten stories.

He tried to absorb the silence, to slow his still-pounding heart. Absently, he rubbed a hand over his bare chest, and then grimaced when he realized he was rubbing a hand over his bare chest. With a negligent flick of his wrist, three new buttons appeared and his shirt closed.

Earlier, at the meeting, Marguerite had been the usual, irritating background buzz in his head. But Julie's fear had jolted him, even here in London. Emotion had rushed through him, paralyzing him, until adrenalin pushed him into action. He'd left the Council without a word. Protecting Julie had been all that mattered.

Why? He couldn't use her to rid himself of Marguerite's tie. He was, however, responsible for the danger she was in now from Marguerite. She'd become a duty.

A duty that made him crazy.

She tugged at his senses making him think of nothing but sex. She ignored his dictates and she spoke to him in a way no one, except Bas, ever dared. She amused him and frustrated him. This was the woman who, based on her energy frequency, was perfectly suited to him? Impossible to comprehend.

"Skipping out on the Council meeting after your late lunch?"

Harrison looked over his shoulder at Bas, standing behind him in human form. He shot a quick glance at his secretary. Heidi loved Bas. As expected, she'd given up all pretense of work and was gazing in adoration at the man.

"Can't you put on a cloaking spell when you come to the office? Heidi's drooling on the computer keyboard again."

Bas smiled at Heidi. Her ample chest heaved with a sigh. "I can't stay long. What happened with Marguerite before I arrived at the restaurant?"

Harrison studied the man he'd known most of his life. "You showed up at precisely the right moment. Thank you." There was much about Bas that he didn't understand. He definitely wasn't human, Penumbrae, Walker or Dancer. All Harrison knew for sure was that Bas had been alive for a very long time, and had written a book of prophecy—*Mots de Sagesse*—that was regarded as sacred by members of the Triad.

Bas probably could have been regarded as sacred, too. But he didn't allow it. Bas considered himself a Lutheran.

Harrison had been eight the first time he'd seen Bas. He'd been sitting in the nearly empty library at the boarding school, staring at Hammurabi's Code, while he listened to the distant laughter of the other children playing football. He'd already been chosen as the next Balance, and had been given special tutors to begin his instruction in the laws of ancient societies. On that day, Bas had appeared in front of him and slammed shut his book.

Ignoring Harrison's gawking tutors, Bas had whisked him outside into the sunshine. The tutors had never said anything about it.

After that, Bas began appearing on a regular basis. They'd have long discussions about everything—the Triad, humans, beings of power, God, how everything fit together into a whole.

But even better than the conversations were the games. They played chess, backgammon and Diplomacy. On rare occasions, Bas would pop them into the woods behind the school, and they'd walk, Bas pointing out the antics of the wild life. Once, a squirrel had dropped several nuts right on Bas's head. Harrison had laughed so hard his stomach hurt. Bas had filled the dark hole of loneliness he'd almost smothered in.

"Harrison." Bas's voice interrupted his memories. "Tell me what happened at the restaurant." Bas leaned against the glass window, one ankle crossed over the other.

"Julie used her power and Marguerite zeroed in on her like a guided missile."

"Didn't you warn Julie about that?"

"Of course I warned her. And I left Linda with her as protection. Julie claims using her power was an accident. She thought she was dreaming."

"Did Linda have to hurt Marguerite?"

"Not quite. Marguerite almost disabled Linda."

Bas narrowed his gaze. "Marguerite doesn't have that kind of power."

"I had to drain her to control her."

"You drained Marguerite?" Surprise lifted his eyebrows.

"That's what I said." Harrison stifled the urge to shift his weight from foot to foot. Bas could make him feel like a little boy again.

"No wonder you don't want to go back into the Council meeting."

"I am the Balance." The Council didn't intimidate him.

"You are judge, not police. Your ability to drain power can only be used in times of war, when Council has pre-approved the action."

Harrison looked out the window. A pigeon perched on a ledge, two stories below. What must it be like to be a bird, to follow only your instincts? No wonder Bas spent so much time as an owl. "I know Triad law better than you, Bas."

"Have you ever broken the law before?"

"The Balance can't break the law. The Balance is the law."

Bas's solemn face lit with a sudden grin, causing Heidi to drop something heavy on the desk. Probably her chest. He clapped Harrison on the shoulder. "I'd say it's about time you took advantage of that little perk of the position."

"Superseding the written law is not to be done lightly. Rules provide order and structure to our society."

"I'm all for rules. How could you have the fun of breaking them if they didn't exist?"

Harrison shook his head, wondering how a man could be so old and not grow up. "You're supposed to teach me, not tempt me."

"Sometimes they're the same thing."

"Bascule, the Obscure," Harrison said, naming one of the many appellations assigned to the man in front of him.

"Don't be a concrete thinker. Look beyond the surface, Harrison. A good judge is interested in justice, not strict adherence to rules."

"Rules ensure justice."

Bascule shrugged. "Rules are just a tool. They can be used for good or evil."

Harrison nodded. "So you've said. Many times. I have to go back into the meeting. Will you be here when I'm finished?"

"Maybe. Maybe not. I'm thinking of taking Heidi out to dinner." Bas looked over at the dreamy-eyed woman.

"If you do, I'll expect you here in the morning, ready to work, because Heidi will be useless. For approximately a week."

Bas laughed. A thick, leather-bound book appeared in his hands. "I dug up an old copy of the *Mots de Sagesse*," he said, his voice suddenly serious. "You asked for it in the hotel. Read it."

Harrison took the book. "Is there a prophecy germane to the situation I find myself in?"

"Read the book," Bas responded.

"No offense, Bas, but this is dryer than dirt in the desert."

"Nothing worth knowing comes without great effort."

"Bollocks."

"Read it." The easygoing voice contained a thread of command.

Harrison looked at the book, then at Bas. He nodded slowly, an uneasy feeling settling at the base of his spine.

"And remember," Bas said, as he took a step toward Heidi. "Destiny doesn't play by the rules."

"Julie." A deep voice barked her name from her office doorway. Why hadn't she shut her door and locked it? Because Linda wouldn't let her. She'd given the woman a magazine and made her sit in the hallway so she could get some work done, but she'd had to agree to leave the door open. Of course, 'work' was a term she was using loosely after her lunch experience. Her brain couldn't handle anything more stimulating than deleting the cascade of messages that kept clogging her email program.

Julie looked over from her screen to see Dr. Phoebe Waters, primary investigator on the Bad Luck study—officially known as *Mediating Factors in Negative Life Events*—standing in her doorway. Joe stood slightly behind her.

"Hello, Phoebe. Joe." Julie straightened her shoulders and swiveled her chair to face the duo.

"We have a problem." Dr. Waters walked briskly into the room. The woman was often referred to as the grandmother of social psychology. Julie figured people who called her that had never seen her. She didn't look like any grandmother Julie had ever met.

At seventy years old, Phoebe Waters stood close to five feet, ten inches tall. Her face almost glowed in pale contrast to the dead black hair that hung in a braid down her back. She had piercing green eyes and skin so tight it wouldn't dare sag into a wrinkle. Her lips, soft and full, contrasted with the angles of her cheekbones and drew the eye. Julie watched them pull into a frown.

"What's up, Phoebe?"

"We've got the results back on the first field interviews."

Julie sat forward. The new study fascinated her. Their research team hoped to identify the factors that caused some individuals to always get dumped on by life. The hypothesis was that people with a proportionally higher amount of negative life events were poor decision makers. Eventually, Julie planned to develop a decision making training module that would halt or slow the bad luck cycle for these individuals.

Julie had screened each subject in the study, both the control group and the bad luck group. She could vouch for the fact that every person in the bad luck group more than met the study criteria for negative life events. Interviewers were now in the field—in this case, the subjects' homes—administering a questionnaire that Dr. Waters and Julie had developed to assess the past month of their life.

"How are the results?" Julie prompted when Phoebe didn't immediately continue.

"An odd thing happened between your baseline screening and the field interviews." Phoebe didn't look happy.

Julie's gaze darted to Joe, wondering what could possibly have gone wrong. She'd trained the field interviewers and they were a bright and eager bunch.

"Everyone's luck changed," Phoebe stated simply.

"What?"

"People who have had years of karmic crap piled on them are suddenly winning the lottery. One of the respondents got a promotion out of the entry-level position he's worked in for fifteen years. A woman who'd been homeless for five years had a miserly uncle die and leave her over a million dollars. A third found the title to some New York City property that had been missing for generations. The list goes on and on."

Julie blinked. "How amazing."

Phoebe nodded. "More than amazing. What is the probability of something like this happening by chance?"

Julie glanced at Joe, their statistics expert. He shrugged, a small smile on his face. "I could run the numbers, but so far the interviewers have completed questionnaires on twenty subjects who are in our bad luck group. All twenty have had an unprecedented run of good luck this past month."

"Which is bad luck for our study," Phoebe said. "The odd thing is, this isn't as unusual as you might think. I spoke with Dr. Bartel and Dr. Jacobs at lunch today. A similar thing happened to Bartel during his study on divorced parents delinquent with their child-support payments. Before he could begin any of his planned interventions, the checks started rolling in. Jacobs said that on his study of sex offenders, erectile dysfunction became rampant among the offenders, skewing data on the effectiveness of his group therapy. He ended up having to treat everyone in his subject pool for depression."

"I remember that. I—"

Phoebe interrupted her. "I don't want all the time and money we've put into this study to go to waste, but how am I supposed to study adverse life events when everyone in my sample is acting like they have a four-leaf clover tattooed on their forehead?"

Excellent question. Another glance at Joe showed no help coming from that quarter. In fact, he seemed highly amused.

"Well, perhaps our focus is too narrow," Julie said slowly. "Perhaps we should be looking at the mediating variables that impact both positive and negative life events to help guide our intervention." Julie took a deep breath. "We can modify the questionnaire and send back the interviewers."

Phoebe stared at her for an endless second, and then nodded. "That might work. I'll research what standard instruments are available to assess this. Call the interviewers. You can train them on the new instrument next Monday. You'll need to call the Institutional Review Board and get an okay to revise our protocol to include the second interview."

Julie nodded, relieved a crisis appeared to have been averted.

Phoebe paused on the way out the door. "Good thinking, Dancer."

Julie smiled weakly and watched her stride through the door. Joe chuckled.

"What's so funny?"

"Didn't you work with both Bartel and Jacobs on those studies that Phoebe mentioned?

"Yes, I did."

"Interesting coincidence. If I believed in coincidence." Joe crossed his arms over his chest. She caught the familiar scent of the citrus cologne he always wore. He watched her as if he knew something she didn't, and waited for her to make a connection.

The puzzle pieces clicked together. "You think that I had something to do with this?" Julie stared back, aghast. "How? Aside from the ethical issue of messing with subjects in a study, it would be impossible to do something like change everyone's luck."

Joe's expression didn't change.

Julie gave him an exasperated look. "So, what's your theory? I have pixie dust that I throw on the subjects or something?"

He cocked his head and studied her. "I don't know. Do you?"

She glared. "Joe, you're not making sense. It's not as if I have some kind of woo-woo...." Julie's voice trailed off as she used the word Dorie had just used at lunch. She did have woo-woo. At least according to Harry. Could she have screwed up the Bad Luck study without even realizing it? And the other studies she'd worked on? No. The alimony checks and limp penises had nothing to do with her. They couldn't. Her ability to absorb power hadn't started until she kissed Harry. But hadn't her mother said that even before Triad members came into their full power some of them were able to use small amounts of energy? Could she have been somehow using energy without even realizing it?

Joe stood and pulled Julie to her feet. "Don't look so frazzled. The study will still yield interesting data." He squeezed her hands, which he still held. "There's no need to feel guilty."

She met his eyes, almost on a level with hers. His were full of laughter. Why was he taking this so calmly?

Before she could question him, Tasha breezed into the office. "Mom, who is that sitting outside your office? Are you doing a study on women wrestlers or something?" Tasha stopped when she saw her mother wasn't alone. "Oh, hi, Dr. Kradeno."

"Tasha." Joe dropped Julie's hands and took a step back.

"Are you still working, Mom? Do you want me to," Tash hesitated and looked over her shoulder toward the door with obvious reluctance, "wait out in the hall?"

Julie shook her head and reached for her briefcase. "No, it's late. Dr. Kradeno and I will finish talking tomorrow. Let's go home."

Jean's meatless chili had everyone reaching for water glasses. Only Linda seemed unaffected.

"Thanks for dinner, Mom," Julie gasped, surprised when flames didn't erupt from her mouth.

"You're welcome, dear. I called Phyllis this afternoon and got the recipe."

"Phyllis?"

"One of the Gigis." At everyone's blank look, Jean elaborated. "You know, one of the Gay Grays—the G.G.s."

"Ah." Julie nodded. "Of course."

"Every Monday night," Jean continued, "the girls have a themed dinner get-together and Phyllis cooks. She's a bit territorial about the whole thing." Jean frowned. "She hasn't let me have a turn yet."

Smart woman, that Phyllis.

"What's tonight's theme? Fire-breathing dragons?" Tasha asked dryly.

Jean beamed with approval. "Actually, it's Sean Connery

movies. I chose *Dragonheart*, so you're close."

"Weird theme for a group of lesbians, isn't it?" Tasha muttered, pushing beans around her plate.

"We've already covered male-bashing and vibrators, so…."

"Grandma!"

"Mom!"

Linda doubled over, sputtering with laughter.

Jean folded her arms and looked at Tasha. "I'm still your grandma, Tasha. I still love you. The Gigis aren't defined only by our sexuality, baby. We're particularly into community service these days."

"I think that's great, Mom." And Julie did. She could see that Tasha was about to comment, so she quickly continued. "Now that dinner is over, we need to talk about this Sun Dancer business."

Tasha nodded. "Speaking of that, you'll never believe who I saw today in the library."

"Who?" Julie asked, wondering at the soft smile on her daughter's face.

"Luc, that Shadow Walker who dropped by this morning."

"He gets around," Julie said, sudden fear for her daughter spiking through her. Why hadn't she thought they might go after Tasha? Only the fact that her daughter sat at the table, safe and sound, kept her hands from shaking. "I saw Luc today, too. He was with his sister, and they tried to…." She paused. What had they tried to do? Kidnap her? Out of a public restaurant? That sounded too bizarre to say out loud.

"They tried to kidnap her out of a public restaurant," Linda inserted.

Tasha shot Linda a disbelieving look—which was actually the type of look Tasha had been giving Linda ever since they met. Then she turned to Julie.

"Mom?" She wanted Julie to deny it.

"I don't think they like me, Tash. Luc's sister thinks I'm out to thwart her evil plans or something. Did Luc say anything to you at the library?" Julie tried to keep her fear for Tasha's safety out of her voice.

"We went out for coffee. I don't know where you get the idea he doesn't like you, Mom. You must have misinterpreted something he said." She sounded desperate. "Are you sure they tried to kidnap you?"

Jean jumped up, knocking over her chair, startling everyone. "You are not to go out with him again. Stay away from him, Natasha."

Julie stared at her mother, but nodded. "I have to agree, Tash. Something is going on here that we don't understand. I think it might be a good idea if you move back home for a while."

Tasha frowned. "I can't do that. I have classes, a roommate, a pre-paid dining plan." Her voice grew softer. "A life."

"Just until we know there's no danger." Julie paused. "Marguerite, Luc's sister, attacked Linda. She's playing for real."

Tasha looked at Linda, her face pale. "Are you okay?"

Linda nodded her head briskly. "The b—witch caught me by surprise, otherwise I would have taken her." She flexed her arms and they all watched her muscles bulge.

"Mom," Tasha turned back to Julie, who was rubbing her own less-than-ripped biceps. "I didn't know he threatened you. I never would have gone with him."

Julie pushed away from the table and walked over to Tasha. She put an arm around her shoulders, and Tash leaned into her. "He didn't threaten, but he was definitely playing wingman to his sister. I think his sister is the one we have to worry about."

"And you think I'm in danger?"

"She might hurt you to get to me, Tash." Julie ran a hand down her daughter's soft hair. Fire hair, she'd always called it.

Tash pulled away and looked at Julie. Her lips set in a straight line that Julie knew meant she was thinking things through. "Can't you renounce your powers so this will all go away?"

Julie looked at Jean to see if that was an option. Jean gave a negative shake of her head.

"Apparently not."

Tash nodded and straightened her shoulders. "Okay. I'd worry about you all the time if I were at the dorm, anyway. But I still need to go to classes and the library."

"Linda will go with you." Thank goodness Tash wasn't going to fight her on this.

Linda shook her head. "No way. I'm stuck to you like glue, Dancer."

Jean spoke up. "I'll go with her. I can call a couple of Gigis if we decide we need more protection. They can be here in a flash."

"The Gay Grays are going to be my protection?" Tash rubbed her head as if she suddenly had a headache.

Julie knew exactly how her daughter felt. She headed for the cabinet next to the sink. "Ibuprofin, anyone?"

They'd made a quick trip to Tash's dorm so she could pick up clothes and books and tell her roommate she'd be gone for a few days. Tash was now upstairs in her room, studying. Julie sat, legs curled, on the soft, brown couch. Her mother sat in the matching chair, a laptop on her knees, probably online with the Gigis. Linda perched across from her on a wooden chair she'd pulled in from the kitchen. It felt strange to have so many people in the house. She'd been alone since Tash went to school. Which, okay, had only been a month, but it felt like longer.

Linda stared at her, unmoving.

She'd never hosted a Penumbrae Guardian before and wasn't sure whether she was supposed to ignore her or entertain her. But, since ignoring her was impossible, her decision was made. "Would you like a magazine, or should I turn on the television?"

"American TV is crap."

Brief and to the point. "Um, I could go through my movie collection. We could watch *Pride and Prejudice* or *Sense and Sensibility*."

Linda perked up. "Do you have any *Monty Python*?"

"No."

She slouched back.

They stared at each other in silence until Julie started to feel prickly. She reached for the remote. There must be a repeat of *Fawlty Towers* on one of her two hundred odd channels.

The house phone rang at the same time that a knock sounded on the door. Julie jumped up, glad for something to do. She hurried to the kitchen, grabbed the phone and clicked it on as she walked back toward the front door, still feeling the weight of Linda's gaze.

"Hello."

"Don't answer your front door!" Dorie's breathless voice squeaked over the line.

Julie froze, hand on the brass doorknob. "Dorie? What are you talking about?" Another knock sounded—a soft tap, as if the person on the other side sensed she was near and just needed to nudge her to open the door.

"Dorie, who's at the door?" Julie whispered. Linda sat up straighter, eyes narrowing on Julie. "Marguerite, Harrison, Vampires, Werewolves? Talk!" Julie hissed into the suddenly silent phone.

"Oops. Sorry, Dylan just put gum in Danny's hair. Why don't they just make peanut butter shampoo for kids? I don't know how many times—"

"Doreen! The door?"

"Oh. It's Super-Slut Cindy. And unless you want to go to her Halloween party and watch her prance around in a skin-tight Catwoman costume, don't answer the door."

"Are you going?" Cindy was ringing the bell now.

"Duh. Jim answered the door. We're going, but you still have time to be saved."

Dorie was diabolically clever. The adult party would be held after the kids finished trick-or-treating. If Julie didn't answer the door, she'd be available to babysit that night for the devilish duo. And they would be a devilish duo—even without the cute little pointy-tail costumes Dorie was already sewing. Dylan and Daniel on a candy high were not a pretty sight.

Julie would take a bullet for Dorie. But she would not babysit for her on Halloween night. She opened the door.

All five feet eight inches, one hundred and twenty curvaceous pounds of Cindy Lui almost fell into the living room. Cindy had an African-American mother, a Chinese father, and she was the most stunning woman Julie had ever seen. To top it off, she taught Biology at the University of Michigan and would probably win a Nobel Prize someday. She wasn't a slut—Dorie just called her that because Jim couldn't say a straight sentence whenever Cindy looked at him. If it wouldn't mean giving up her daughter, Julie would want to be Cindy Lui.

"Julie! I thought you were home." Cindy handed her a sealed envelope with little ghost and witch stickers on it. "An invitation to my annual Halloween Party. It's the night of a blue moon this year, so the goblins and ghosts will be out in full force." She smiled and glanced around the room, her eyes widening as she got a look at Linda. She took a step backward. "I'm getting the invitations out early so my party gets on your calendar first."

"Thanks, Cindy. I'll be there."

Cindy dragged her gaze away from Linda. "You wouldn't happen to know if Harrison is out of town? I've knocked on his door a couple of times, but haven't gotten an answer." A long-fingered hand tucked a strand of her short, wavy hair behind her ear. "I'd hate for him to miss the party."

"I don't know where he is."

"Isn't he the most amazing man? I had him to dinner the night after he moved in." She lowered a conspiratorial eyelid at Julie. "As his landlord, to welcome him to the neighborhood."

"I'm sure he appreciated it." The air seemed blocked in Julie's lungs. She concentrated on taking deep, even breaths.

"Oh, he did. Yes, I'd say he definitely appreciated it." Cindy looked closer at Julie. "I'm not stepping on any toes, am I?"

"No. No. My toes are just fine," Julie wheezed. It was her breathing she was having trouble with. Suddenly, Linda stood behind her.

"You're sucking in air like you just choked on a pile of buffalo chips. What's the matter with you?" Linda plucked the extra invitation out of Cindy's hand. "Shoo. We'll give this to Harrison."

Cindy tilted her head to look up at Linda, something she probably rarely had to do with another woman. "I can—"

Linda pushed her out the door. "Get going while you still can." She didn't give Cindy a chance to reply before she slammed the door shut.

Immediately, Julie could breathe easier. She put her hands on her knees and pulled in a deep whiff of Cindy's tantalizing perfume. "That woman is such a slut."

Her mother clicked shut her computer and looked up. "You wouldn't think that someone who came into her power at well past her prime would have such problems controlling it."

"I am not well past my prime! Was that my power? You told me to ignore my power. How can I ignore suffocation?" Julie wanted to yell at someone and Cindy wasn't handy.

Jean sighed. "I was wrong. You need training. You shouldn't have had difficulty breathing. I think that was a panic attack. Probably triggered by the fact you wanted to blast Harrison's girlfriend but wouldn't let yourself."

"She's not Harrison's girlfriend! I do not have panic attacks!"

"You're not in denial either." Jean shook her head.

Harry and Cindy were not a couple. One dinner did not make a relationship. Then again, what did make a relationship? She hadn't seen all that much of Harry herself, but there was certainly something between them. And that something made her want to be as tall and pretty as Cindy Lui.

Maybe all this emotion was hormonal. Maybe she was starting menopause. Maybe she'd been around her mother for too long. "I'm going to sit on the back deck." When Linda made as if to come along, Julie shook her head. "Alone."

Surprisingly, Linda just shrugged and went back to her chair.

Julie took a sweater off the hook by the back door and walked out onto the deck. The early October evening held just a hint of the cooler weather soon to come. She shrugged into her sweater, more for comfort than for warmth, and sat down on a white plastic chair.

She wasn't surprised when a figure stepped through the bushes that separated her yard from Harry's. His white shirt glowed in the light from her kitchen window.

"You're back."

"London is five hours ahead of Michigan time. The Council meeting lasted until midnight."

Julie did the math while he walked up the deck steps. He leaned against the rail, an arm length from her. "That was an hour ago. I take it you didn't take a commercial flight here."

"Right."

"How did your meeting go?"

"The Council wants Marguerite. They're angry I didn't bring her in."

"Why didn't you? You said she placed a curse on you. Can she control you?"

"No. Not with one tie. Tying her consciousness to mine takes an enormous amount of power and can only be done in two steps. Once the second tie is placed, however, she may be able to influence my actions."

"Why didn't you bring her in?"

"I'm judge, not police. That isn't my duty."

"Couldn't you perform a citizen's arrest?" The guy was way too rule-rigid.

"The Dancers and Walkers must police their own. Without that check in place, the Penumbrae would become nothing more than dictators."

Julie stretched out her legs, propping them on the rail of the deck. "So this Triad you keep talking about, this society of Dancers, Walkers and Penumbrae, they have to answer to both Triad law and human law?"

"Yes. Before the Rift, Triad neighborhoods existed in most large cities or towns. Regional heads, called Lions, settled disputes and kept order. After the Rift, the Triad mission was shattered, along with our sense of community. I've been trying to build trust and reinstate some of the old structure since I became Balance. You're aware of the growing violence both here and abroad?"

"Yes. I worry about Tasha and her friends."

Harry nodded. "Demons are becoming bolder. The strength of the Triad, our Threes, used to keep them in Gehenna. I need to convince our people to work together again, and I need to do it quickly. If demons grab a foothold on earth, life as we know it will be altered forever."

"Demons?" The thought scared the hell—ha-ha—out of her. "Why is saving the world your responsibility, Harry?"

"I could say that someone has to do it."

"Don't."

He lips curved in a small smile. "I trained my whole life for this responsibility. But more than that, the Triad is my family. I want our people united, strong and healthy. I want us to do the work we were born to do."

"No wonder you're so upset about Marguerite placing this curse on you. If you don't have your wits about you, the repercussions could be major."

"She will not place the second tie. The Council will block it."

"When is the next new moon?"

"October sixteenth. A week and a half from now."

"What if the Council thing doesn't work? What happens if she succeeds?"

"She won't."

"But if she did? What happens?"

Harry shifted and looked out into the cedar trees edging one side of her yard. "She will walk through my thoughts. Know where I am, hear what I hear. Talk with me at will."

Julie's feet thumped back on the deck, and she reached out and put a hand on his arm. "That's the ultimate in lack of privacy."

He looked down at her hand. He gently removed it. "This thing would be a rape of my mind. I think it would drive me insane."

Julie suddenly wished she could just sleep with him, break the spell and make it all go away. But he'd made it clear that wasn't an option anymore.

"Harrison, why are you here?" Perhaps the better question was why she wanted him to stay.

"Linda is not adequate protection against Marguerite, and she is one of our strongest Guardians."

"You're saying there isn't a way to keep me safe from Marguerite?"

"There is a way. You're a woman of great power. You must be trained to protect yourself."

"Right. I've been meaning to talk to you about my powers. When I try to use them they don't work. Then they kick in without me even realizing it."

"I'm arranging the best teacher I know for you."

"Not you?"

"Definitely not me."

She ignored her disappointment. "How long does this training take? I have a full-time job." If she didn't screw up the study so they couldn't run it.

His expression darkened. "Why are you concerned about your job? You don't want to be away from the colleague who took you for coffee?"

"No. I don't want to be away from the paycheck that gives me money." She suppressed a small smile.

"Take a vacation," he ordered.

"Can't I learn at night, after work?"

"You're a Sun Dancer. You work best in daylight."

Actually, time of day really didn't seem to matter, but she did need to learn about her power. "I'll see if I can get some time off. Will the teacher pop in and out for lessons or will I go someplace like Hogwarts and have classes like Harry Potter?"

He ignored the last part of her question. "The teacher will live with me, as will you."

"You mean, next door?"

"I mean London."

"No way. I'm not taking off to London and leaving my daughter here when Shadow Walkers are flitting around, asking her out."

"She can come." He gritted the words out between his teeth.

"She won't. She'll lose a semester at school. We can't afford that."

"I'll pay for it."

"No. We stay here." She folded her arms and stared him down. Her stubborn determination not to go to London had more to do with needing the familiarity of her home base than money.

His face stilled. "You have said "no" one time too many, Dancer."

The air pressure seemed to change and Julie swallowed. This was the Balance. The man who made her indomitable mother tremble. Nervousness trickled down Julie's spine. She looked into the flat, amber eyes and tried to find the Harry she knew. "Please, Harry? Tash is already dealing with a lot of changes. *I'm* dealing with a lot of changes. I'd really appreciate it if the teacher could come here."

For a moment his face didn't change. Julie cleared her throat and tried a small smile. It wobbled at the edges.

His face softened. Just a fraction. "Perhaps it will work. The danger to you will be over when Marguerite fails to place the second tie. I'll commute to London until then."

Relief brightened her smile. "Thank you."

"Linda and Bas will protect you while I'm away." He seemed to be trying to convince himself.

"Bas? The pirate guy from the hotel room?"

"I'm surprised you remember."

"Even when one is about to explode, he's pretty hard to

forget."

Harry's jaw clenched. The man was going to have dental problems if he didn't loosen up. Still, his reaction sent a thrill through her. She was only human. Maybe.

"Go to work tomorrow," he instructed. "I'll be here by the time Marguerite rises. She won't be in a very good mood, and she may come for you."

"Marguerite's in a very bad mood." Marguerite's soft voice drifted out of the darkness. "You really didn't think I'd have to wait until tomorrow evening to get my power back, did you?"

Eight

MARGUERITE FELT like a piece of overcooked pasta as she stepped out of the cedar trees bordering the Dancer's yard. True dark hadn't fallen, and the deepening shades of gray soothed her.

She needed soothing.

Her system hadn't recovered yet from the lunchtime fiasco when Harrison pulled the plug on her power. She'd fainted, but even that hadn't brought peace. The visions of Grand-mère Belle had followed her even into the dark void of her unconscious. She'd awakened, weak and nauseated, filled with renewed resolve to complete the melding spell and end this madness by freeing her grandmother.

One insignificant Dancer wouldn't get in her way.

She considered the couple on the deck, reassured by the golden presence of Harrison still tucked in her brain. Either the Dancer wasn't powerful enough to break the tie, or Harrison hadn't had sex with her yet.

"Marguerite." Harrison's deep voice flowed over her. He stepped closer to the Dancer. "How have you regained your power so quickly?"

Marguerite ignored the question. "I could bring you up on charges for what you did, Balance."

"The Council will be happy to see you," he said, not at all concerned.

"You think to use this Dancer to break my hold." She

confronted him directly. She didn't have the strength for small talk.

"No." He spoke softly.

"She hasn't the power?" Marguerite took a good look at the Dancer. The woman didn't look powerful. Brown, curly hair framed a slender face filled with large, brown eyes, a small nose and a mouth that was just a shade too wide. Attractive, not beautiful, definitely past her youth. Not someone she would normally give more than a passing glance. And yet, tension arced between this woman and Harrison. Too much tension. Perhaps they hadn't mated yet.

"She won't break the curse." Harrison said.

"Won't or can't?" If he hadn't yet slept with the Dancer, then Marguerite would ensure he didn't. She needed to know for sure. "I've been hearing rumors lately, Le Bilan. You're thirty-five. You have no children. That's unusual for a Penumbra. I wonder—is there a problem? Some physical difficulty?" She smiled, her gaze running down the length of his body.

The Dancer spoke before Harrison could. She slid an arm around his waist. "Harrison has absolutely no problems in that department."

Marguerite gasped. She took a step closer, trying to gauge Harrison's reaction to the touch. He looked down at the Dancer, his expression unreadable. But he didn't step away. Even a woman he'd been intimate with wouldn't be allowed such a touch. Marguerite's brow furrowed. Damn the Balance for draining her. She couldn't think clearly.

The Dancer's chin jutted out. "Why don't you just get out of Harry's head? You're causing us all a lot of trouble."

Had the draining affected her hearing? Surely this woman hadn't called Le Bilan 'Harry.'"

Harrison stood oddly still, completely motionless. Marguerite braced for lightning, fire, total deforestation of the yard.

Instead, a small smile flicked across his face, and he put his hand over the one resting at his waist. "I can handle Marguerite, sweetheart."

Harry. Sweetheart. Marguerite had been wrong with her first conclusion. There could only be one explanation for this behavior. They were lovers.

"You've had sex and the Dancer's power didn't sever the curse." Relief and jubilation bubbled through Marguerite. The Dancer wasn't a threat. She could go. Rest. She reached out with her senses to touch the earth's energy, gathering herself.

"Marguerite." She paused at Harrison's voice, once again the cold, precise tones she recognized. "Why? Cursing the Balance is suicide. I won't let you succeed."

"You have no choice." Marguerite forced herself to meet his gaze, wishing for a different fate. She inhaled the sweet night air and swayed on her feet, overcome with tiredness.

"Where is your power coming from, Moonflower?"

Harrison's translation of her name made her unaccountably teary-eyed. She damned her weakness, her memories. Nobody called her Moonflower anymore. Not for a long time.

"You are not wielding earth energy alone. Your power has another source."

He took a step toward her, and the part of him that was in her mind vibrated, stretched. She put a trembling hand to her head.

He stopped, his golden eyes seeming to sear through her. His expression became stone, hard and austere. "You've turned to the dark ones, Marguerite. What have you done?"

His gaze burned like cleansing fire, and for a moment she forgot Grand-mère Belle and the horror of the visions. Forgot the mentor who had taught her to strengthen her power, to realize her full potential.

Before she could move toward him and unravel all she'd worked so hard to accomplish, she lifted her hand and used the last of her energy to escape.

"Well, that was interesting." Julie took a big step back from

Harrison and tried to pull her hand from his. Unfortunately, his wouldn't let go. Setting her lips, she yanked hard and then shoved her warm, tingling hand behind her back.

"Thank you for defending my masculinity," he stated gravely.

"She used a common female tactic. Make a slur about a guy's sexual prowess and he'll get angry. Angry men have loose lips."

"I have no concerns about my sexual prowess and I don't get angry, so the tactic wouldn't have worked."

Based on her limited experience with him, Julie had no concerns about his sexual prowess either. His calm assurance about his lack of temper was another matter. "You don't get angry? Then who flashed a few bolts of lightning around the other day when I had coffee with a coworker? Thor?"

He raised an eyebrow. "I was displeased, not angry."

"And the difference is?"

"The difference is a matter of degree," he stated. "I don't get angry."

"Potayto, potawto." She shrugged. "At any rate, it would seem to be in my best interest to let Marguerite think we've slept together."

"I agree. She won't try to neutralize you if she believes you're not a threat."

"Does that mean I'm out of danger now? I can kiss you goodbye and go back to my previously scheduled life?" Okay. Where had the 'kiss you goodbye' part come from? She didn't intend to go anywhere near his fascinating lips. His fascinating, young lips. "Are you really only thirty-five?"

He frowned at the abrupt change in subject. "What does my age matter?"

She had a sudden thought. "Is that in Penumbrae years, or human years?"

He shook his head as if to clear it. "I'm thirty-five. Penumbrae years are the same as human years. We live on the same planet, Julie."

"Well dogs live on the same planet, but somehow their years

are different."

He just stared at her. She rubbed her hands against her arms. "Okay. I'm not thinking clearly." Thank God he'd never seen her naked. A young man wouldn't understand cellulite and stretch marks. "I just didn't know you were so young."

"I've never been young," Harrison said, his voice flat.

"Penumbrae are born fully grown?" Oh. My. God. She put a protective hand over her pelvis.

"Julie, I'm speaking metaphorically." He didn't smile, but she could tell he wanted to. "We're born the same way humans, Walkers and Dancers are. I meant that I've been trained and schooled my whole life. There was little time to be young."

Her heart went out to the boy he'd been, but she was careful not to show him sympathy. "Marguerite said most Penumbrae have children by your age."

"That's true."

"Don't you want kids?"

Harrison looked out into the yard as if searching for something. "I'm expected to have children."

She noticed the tension in his body, wondered at it. "Your child wouldn't have to have the same childhood that you did."

He sent her a sharp glance. "What do you know of the Penumbrae and our ways?"

"Only the little you've told me. I do know about parenting, though."

It was his turn to abruptly change the subject. "Your teacher will be here tomorrow afternoon."

"Can't we postpone training now that the Marguerite threat level is lowered? Maybe I can free up some time in November."

"No. The training is arranged."

"But my time off isn't arranged."

His look ended the argument. "Arrange it."

"What's this about you taking some family leave time?" Joe walked into her office and handed her one of the two cups of coffee he was holding.

Julie took the cup gratefully. "You're my hero." She lifted the plastic lid and blew on the hot liquid. "My life has suddenly become very complicated, Joe. Don't ask questions."

"What about the interviewers you're supposed to re-train on Monday?" He set his cup on her desk, concern deepening the blue of his eyes.

"I'm not dropping off the face of the earth." Hopefully. "I'll come in to meet with them."

"Your timing sucks on this, Julie. What's going on? Is something wrong with Tasha?"

"No. Tasha's fine." So much for hoping he wouldn't ask questions.

"Let's take our coffee and go sit outside on the patio. I want to hear about your complicated life."

Julie glanced out the window at the sunshine. "I don't think so. I'm enjoying the sun."

He looked puzzled. "Julie…."

She stood, walked around her desk and put a hand on his arm. "Thanks for caring. I'm all right, though. Really. I just need some personal time."

A strange thing happened when she touched him. The look of gentle concern in Joe's eyes morphed to determined desire. Before Julie could snatch her hand off his arm, he pulled her against his chest and kissed her. She stood, momentarily numb, while his lips moved over hers.

Obviously she needed to learn the new dating rules. Did having coffee with a guy and touching his arm say "kiss me?"

Once the initial shock passed, Julie decided to kiss him back. For research purposes only, of course. Her working hypothesis was that Harrison had set off fireworks simply because he was the only man she'd kissed in several eons. The same reaction would likely happen with Joe or anybody else who kissed her.

Joe's body felt hard and compact. Her shoulders were level with his, which gave her an interesting sense of equality in the kiss, until he swung her around and pushed her against the wall. Good move. She liked it.

His tongue began tracing her lips, searching for a way in. Very nice. His chest rose and fell at a rapid rate, and his hand reached around her and settled on her bottom. Without any uncertainty, he pulled her tight against him. Wow. Another really good move. She'd give him an 8.7 on technique.

"Do you see fireworks?" Julie whispered.

"No, but I feel an explosion building," Joe whispered back, not missing a beat.

Julie laughed. She pushed against his chest. "Joe. I really don't want to ruin a good working relationship."

"Our relationship doesn't feel ruined to me."

"Yeah? Well that's because you don't know that I was just using you. I wanted to see if there were fireworks when we kissed."

"And?"

"It felt good, but no fireworks."

"Fireworks are dangerous anyway. You can lose a hand playing with them."

"Or a heart," she muttered.

He tilted his head, eyes narrowed. "Your complication is a man," he stated.

"No. Well, maybe in part. Besides, I don't exactly know what to call him. Let's just say he's definitely male."

"You're not making sense, Julie."

That had been a recurring problem over the last few days.

Joe touched her hair gently. "Go and straighten out whatever twist you've gotten your life into. I'll be waiting when you get back."

"Now *you're* not making sense. We're not going to become involved. We work together. Period."

He just smiled. "I'm determined to show you that the slow burn is better than the flashy fireworks."

Julie closed her eyes. What was happening here? She hadn't kissed anyone for years, and suddenly she felt like she was channeling Cindy Lui. She opened her eyes and tried for a stern look. "You're making things much more complicated."

Joe winked and kissed her on the forehead. "Good."

"What do you mean, you're going back to Chicago?" Julie arrived home to find her mother heading out the door toward a taxi.

"Emergency call from the Gigis. I'm needed, ASAP. My flight leaves Metro in two hours, so I have to hurry." Jean paused on the front walk to glance at the sky. "Looks like we might be in for a storm, too. I thought it was supposed to be sunny today."

"It will clear up soon." Julie trailed behind her. "Mom, I still have questions about this Sun Dancer stuff, and energy wielding and Harry and…."

Jean put a finger to her lips as the taxi driver hopped out of the car and opened the back door for her. "I'll call as soon as I can. You'll be fine."

Julie stepped back from the car, surprised by how much she wanted her mother to stay. Tasha had moved back to the dorm this morning since Marguerite was no longer a threat. At least Linda was still around.

The front door banged and Linda, dressed in dull green leather, jogged down the walk. "Sorry, Jean. I had to take a potty break." Linda carried a small duffel bag.

"Wait! You're going with Mom? What happened to 'I'm stuck to you like glue, Dancer?'"

Linda shrugged. "You've been given the all clear. She needs me more."

"Mom needs you?" Julie looked from Linda to Jean. "What's going on? What's the emergency?"

Jean slid quickly into the backseat and pulled Linda in beside her. "No time to chat right now. We'll fill you in when we get back."

"If you're in such a hurry, why aren't you popping instead of flying?"

Linda shot a warning glance at the taxi driver and lowered

her voice. "I'm conserving energy. Got a feeling I'm going to need it for other things. We'll get to Chicago fast enough this way." Linda slammed shut the car door and the taxi took off in a squeal of wheels.

Her mom mouthed the words "I love you" through the rear window.

"I love you, too, Mom," she echoed to the empty street.

Julie turned and went into the house. She'd adjusted to being alone since Tash left for college. One night of a full house wouldn't change that.

There were great things about living on her own. She could blast the volume on her iPod speakers and dance to Eighties music all she wanted. She could eat a whole box of chocolates and no one would know but her. Heck, she could walk around the house naked if she wanted to. Of course, she'd rather eat the chocolate—which is probably why she had no desire to walk around naked.

Silence hummed in her ears. Julie wandered into the kitchen and put on a second pot of coffee. While it brewed she loaded breakfast dishes into the dishwasher.

Being alone gave you plenty of time to consider the compelling questions in life. Like, why had Joe kissed her today at work? Why did Harry do the stormy weather thing whenever she got close to Joe? And why was that owl back in Harry's yard? Julie stretched over the sink, trying to get a better look at the bird that flashed by her window.

The doorbell rang.

She gave up trying to catch a glimpse of the bird and went to the door. A tall, dark-haired young man stood on the front porch. He wore black pants, a black shirt and a decidedly rakish grin. Her pirate from the hotel.

The man held out his hand, grasping hers in a warm clasp. "You probably don't remember me. We met a couple of nights ago. I'm Bascule, your teacher."

Julie waited until he released her hand. Then she reached out, plucked a black and gray feather off his shoulder, and silently handed it to him.

His grin widened. "As you can see, I flew here."

Nine

"BAS, I think my energy channels have closed up again." Julie stood next to the stove, dodging the occasional spit of bacon grease. Frying bacon was such a comforting, normal task. Well, maybe normal wasn't quite the right word. She hadn't actually fried bacon in about ten years. Zapping the pre-cooked slices in the microwave was her no-mess preference. Bas, however, was a purist. "It's been almost a week, and I haven't exhibited a glimmer of power."

Bas cracked another egg into a pink, ceramic bowl, added milk, and expertly whisked the mixture into froth. He moved to her side and poured the mixture into a sizzling pan coated with butter. He opened the drawer next to the stove and quickly found the spatula. "Patience, Julie. Triad children spend years learning to master the craft of energy wielding."

Julie flipped the bacon onto a plate lined with a paper towel. She refused to be a whiner. "You are an excellent cook, Bas."

He grinned. "So are you. That bacon is crisped to perfection."

Julie thought of the crab-stuffed portabella mushrooms he'd whipped up for dinner last night. "I'm not as good as you."

"Nobody is as good as I am. I've had a lot of practice." Bas scooped light, fluffy eggs onto two plates and turned off the burner. "Both at wielding energy and at cooking." He picked up the plates and set them on the kitchen table. Julie followed behind with the bacon and a carton of milk. They worked in tandem like a couple that had been married for years.

"Oh, come on. You're what? Twenty-four, twenty-five years old? You can't have had that much practice." Julie sat down, suddenly depressed. "Good grief. I could be your mother."

Bas laughed as he poured himself a glass of milk. "No, you couldn't."

She didn't want to be that old, so she didn't argue. "How long do we do this?"

"Eat?" He met her eyes, smiling. "For the rest of our lives."

She smiled back. "How long do we pretend like you're teaching me something?"

Bas picked up a piece of bacon with his fingers. He took a bite, watching her while he chewed. "I am teaching you something, Julie. Close your eyes."

Julie sighed, but complied. He'd had her do the same thing every day since he'd arrived. Yesterday, he'd had her keep her eyes closed so long that she'd fallen asleep.

"What do you feel?"

She began the now familiar routine of sifting through her senses. The scent of bacon, the smooth wood of the table beneath her fingers, the tick of the kitchen clock and Bas's even breathing all sharpened into focus. She went deeper, searching for what Bas called her "special sense" but which had so far proven special only in its absence. She was about to open her eyes when a sudden, internal hum brought her to full alert. "Bas!"

"Keep your eyes closed, Julie. Describe to me what you feel."

"A low vibration or hum." She felt something! "I don't know where it's … wait, it's like a string." She mentally gripped the string, holding on to it like a guide. There were other strands brushing her, humming different tunes. She reached out randomly, tugging one here and there. The hum grew into a symphony, filling her. Each note was distinct. She sang when the strands wrapped around her, her blood alive in her veins, and she soared, swirling and twisting to the haunting melody. A joyous laugh, her own, startled her back into consciousness.

"Sun Dancer," Bas murmured.

Julie's eyes flew open. "Where did it go?"

"It's still there." He grinned. "It will become easier and easier for you to feel it. Then you'll learn to grasp the energy—you called it a string?—and pull it until you have enough to transform."

"How do I transform it?"

"That differs for each person. We'll find your path. Learning to wield energy takes time. You've taken the first step. You have to open yourself and feel the energy before you can change it."

"Not always." Julie, suddenly famished, took a bite of egg. "Apparently I sometimes change energy without feeling it at all."

Bas's lazy gaze sharpened. "What do you mean?"

"I may be righting wrongs and changing lives without consciously realizing it." She quickly related what had happened on the studies at work.

A small wrinkle appeared between his brows, and he studied her as if she were a specimen he hadn't seen before. "Remind me of your lineage, Julie."

"My lineage? My mother is a Sun Dancer and my dad was human. Is that what you mean?"

Bas nodded. "And your grandparents?"

"I assume Mom's parents were Dancers and Dad's were human. I never met either set of grandparents. They died before I was born. Why are you asking?"

"Sometimes children who haven't come into their abilities will change small amounts of power unintentionally. But the amount of power it takes to wield the changes you've told me about is immense. To be able to do it without training or without thought is almost incomprehensible. The only ones I know with that kind of clout are the immortals."

"The immortals?"

"God and the lesser immortals—angels and demons."

Julie lost her appetite. "I'm not God."

Bas cocked an eyebrow. "There go my plans to build a Julie temple."

She shot him a look. "I'm not an angel or a demon, either."

He picked up another piece of bacon and chewed, watching her thoughtfully.

He scared her. Power scared her. Most of all, the thought of demons scared her. Once, following hours of lying wide-eyed and board-stiff in her bed after watching an old vampire movie, she'd crawled into bed with her mom and dad. Her mom's chiding voice and her dad's protective arm around her shoulders had finally lulled her to sleep. What would an actual meeting with a demon do to her? She shuddered.

"I'm a working, single mom. Period. I don't want to deal with angels, demons and power. Let me choose the blue pill and lose all knowledge of this."

Bas didn't even smile. He held both hands out, palms flat and devoid of all pills. "You're not Neo in *The Matrix*. This is real life."

"I want my comfortable world back."

"Life has more in store for you than mere comfort, Julie."

"You're sounding like some sort of ancient philosopher, Bas. It doesn't suit you. And don't shortchange comfort. It has a lot going for it." Julie leaned back in her seat, frowning. For no reason at all, because he certainly didn't represent comfort to her, she asked, "How come I haven't seen Harry all week?" She tried to sound casual.

"I don't know. He doesn't keep many people informed of his activities. Heidi, his administrative assistant, only knows enough to schedule or cancel meetings."

Julie hadn't seen him since the night that Marguerite had dismissed her as a danger. Obviously, she'd been a duty that had been discharged.

"You want the last piece of bacon?" Bas held out the plate toward her.

"No. Go ahead and take it."

When Bas picked up the bacon, part of the paper towel stuck to it. He started to flick it off, then stopped and stared at the now-empty plate, a funny expression on his face. He yanked the paper towel totally off the plate. "Where did you get this?"

Still thinking about Harrison, Julie barely glanced at him. "The grocery store. It's the new super-absorbent type."

"This." His voice came out tight and low.

Julie looked more closely. He held the white plate with stars on the border—the one she used to bring donuts to Harrison. "Oh. That used to belong to my grandmother."

"No." Bas looked at her, certainty on his face.

"That's what my mom told me. What's so special about that plate?"

"This is the Sky Plate. It's said the Elves fired this centuries ago as a gift to a favored Shadow Walker king. Shadow Walker royalty has used it ever since to hold the sweet cake and the vinegar shared during the binding ceremony. Fifty years ago it went missing and hasn't been seen since." He picked up the plate carefully. "It was thought lost during the war." Bas gently set the plate down. "Where is Jean Dancer?"

"She's in Chicago," Julie answered automatically. Her mind was still grappling with the possibility that elves were real.

"No school today. We're going on a field trip."

Julie stood on the doorstep of her mother's classic Chicago two-flat and rang the security buzzer that would alert her mom to the fact that someone wanted entrance. After several attempts, she turned to the man beside her. "She's not home."

Bas looked up and down the street, as if she might appear. "Where else could she be?"

"Just about anywhere. The last time I saw her, she mentioned an emergency with the Gigis. But that was when she left Ann Arbor."

Bas's gaze sharpened. "The Gigis?"

"A group mom is involved in."

"That explains her absence. You should be very proud of her."

"I should? I mean, of course, I am." Julie gave up on the buzzer and glanced at Bas. "Uh, how exactly have you heard of the Gigis?"

"Word is spreading quickly about this group. The Gigis are setting an example that all Triad members should follow."

Julie walked down the cement steps onto the narrow sidewalk. Bas loved to cook and he never talked about a girlfriend. Maybe she should have suspected…still, she felt a lingering sorrow for womankind. "I'm glad you feel that way, though I don't know that I agree that all Triad members should follow Mom's example. Everyone has a right to choose their own lifestyle."

Bas shook his head. "In some respects, yes, but being Triad carries with it certain duties."

"Are you saying I have a duty to follow in mom's footsteps?" No one had mentioned this aspect of the Triad before. She looked directly into his eyes, so dark a blue today they almost looked purple.

"That's exactly what I'm saying." His lips curved.

"Bas, are you telling me to become a lesbian?"

His smile froze. "No." He said the word slowly.

"Then what are you talking about?"

"Let's start again. The Gigis are a group of Triad members consisting of Dancers, Walkers and Penumbrae, a rare gathering of Threes. I'm hoping it's a sign that the Rift is closing and our people are starting to trust one another again."

"Are we talking about the Gay Grays—a lesbian support and activist group for seniors?"

"Yes." Bas nodded. "Though they are also warrior protectors, keeping the world free of demons."

"You're not kidding, are you?"

"No."

"My sixty-plus-year-old mother fights demons?"

"The Gigis are gaining in effectiveness as they use their power more."

"Hell." She wanted to use stronger swear words, but her shocked brain couldn't think of any.

"No, right here in Chicago." He must have taken pity on her dazed look. He gently took her arm and turned her to face the deserted street. "What's different about this neighborhood since the last time you were here?"

Julie tried to focus her thoughts—her mom, a demon warrior!—as she looked up and down the block. She frowned and looked again, noting the quiet, well kept facades of the houses and the cars parked bumper to bumper at the curb. Everything seemed normal, except...she narrowed her eyes and looked again. "I can't put my finger on it, but something gives me the creeps."

Bas nodded. "It's the people, Julie. There are no people outside."

"You're right! Nobody's walking a dog. There aren't any joggers. Kids aren't skateboarding or hanging out on the porch steps."

"People are staying inside because they're scared. It's urban warfare on the streets these days."

"I didn't realize things had gotten this bad," Julie whispered. Nightly news stories flashed into her memory, making her aware that she should have been paying more attention. "I need to get Mom out of this city."

"Your mother is needed here. Violence grows everywhere, including Ann Arbor." Bas pulled her toward the alley beside her mother's house. "Come on, let's get back to your lessons. I'll find Jean later."

Julie followed along, though part of her wanted to tear Chicago apart to find her mother so she could yell at her. "Mom ran away from the Triad. Why is she doing this?"

"When you run away from who you are, most times you end up back where you started."

Bas really needed to get a job writing Chinese fortune cookies. "Why doesn't she tell me?"

"My guess is that she wants to protect you." Bas tugged her around the corner of her mother's building, behind a garbage dumpster.

"Keeping someone ignorant doesn't protect her."

Bas drew Julie close as he prepared to pop them back to

Ann Arbor. His bleak expression held none of the easy-going acceptance she'd grown used to. Julie froze, sensing something ancient, something powerful beyond imagination, a will that wouldn't compromise.

Then Bas smiled, dispelling the feeling. "I disagree. Sometimes it does."

Harry showed up bright and early the next morning, just as Julie finished the last of the blueberry crepes Bas had made.

"You two look cozy," he commented as he walked into the kitchen. He was dressed in a white shirt, tie and black pants, as if he'd just stepped out of the office.

"I thought I locked the front door." Julie's heart rate bumped into high gear. She set her fork down.

"You did. How are the lessons going?" The curt question was addressed to Bas, who stood at the sink.

Bas put the crepe pan into the sink and turned. "Fine. Julie is learning to sense energy. It appears she may not wield it in the conventional way of Sun Dancers."

"That doesn't surprise me." Harry's serious gaze turned to Julie.

"We're exploring how her power works." Bas winked at Julie, picked up a towel from the counter and dried his hands.

"What does that mean?" Harry's sharp question raised the hair on the back of Julie's neck. He looked at Bas, eyes narrowed. She could feel a crackling in the air.

"What do you think it means?" Bas asked. He put the towel down and shifted his weight, body square, hands loose at his sides.

Julie suddenly felt like she'd been placed between two bulls and someone had put a red flag in her hand. She gave Bas a warning look, stood up and walked over to Harry. "Hi. Have a tough week?"

He looked down at the hand she placed on his sleeve and some of the tension seemed to leave his face. "Yes." He rubbed the back of his neck and she remembered the curse and Marguerite.

No wonder the man acted grumpy.

"She'll be out of your head soon," she said softly.

He didn't say anything, but the color of his eyes deepened. Her breathing hitched.

Bas cleared his throat.

Harry spoke to him without looking away from Julie. "Bas, are you available to make a trip?"

"I seem to be at your beck and call a lot, recently." A hint of amusement tempered the words.

Julie started breathing when Harry stepped away from her.

He gave Bas a rueful look. "Sorry. I've been in Australia all week meeting with a Walker who lives in Melbourne, Oliver Clayborne. He's agreed to assume the role of Lion of Australia. The Triad there, like everywhere else, is extremely wary of instituting a regional governing structure again, but Clayborne's both charismatic and powerful."

"I've met him. He's a good choice," Bas said.

"You're a legend, Bas. If you show up and give him your approval, his road will be easier."

Bas straightened. "I'm on it. This is very good news, Harrison."

Harry nodded. "It's a start."

Bas walked over and put a casual arm around Julie's shoulders. "Take the day off. Go somewhere with Harrison and have some fun."

Julie glanced at Harry. He had gone still like a predator, his eyes fixed on Bas's face. Bas wore an innocent expression as he gestured toward the window. "You might want to plan something indoors though. Looks like a storm is brewing."

"Good-bye, Bascule." Harry took Julie's arm and drew her out of Bas's hold.

Bas laughed as he popped out of the room.

Harry released Julie's arm and walked slowly to the table. He sat, looking so tired Julie thought about offering him a bed. The image of Harry in her bed sent a frisson of heat through her.

She took a deep breath, walked behind the chair where he sat and touched his broad shoulders with both hands, because she had to. "You work too hard," she murmured, and began a firm massage of the knotted muscles in his back.

His whole body stiffened, and then he dropped his chin to his chest. "No. I need to work harder. There's too much to be done."

"I'm glad you're here now." Somehow it was easier to talk to his back than his face.

He didn't say anything for several long minutes as she gently kneaded his shoulder blades. Then, so softly she barely heard the words, he murmured, "I'm glad I'm here, too."

His words were melted sugar, filling her with sweetness. She had a sudden, fierce desire to ease the load this man carried, if only for an afternoon. "What do you say we do something wild and crazy?"

Harry turned his head and gave her a speculative look. "What have you got in mind?"

Tasha waved good-bye to her three friends, her tennis racquet slung over her shoulder. She always played tennis on Tuesday mornings after her first class. Her muscles felt loose and limber from the energetic game. She walked across Palmer Field and up the gentle incline toward the group of brick buildings known as the Hill dorms. Scents from the lunch preparation wafted out of the cafeteria in Mosher-Jordan, the dorm where everyone who lived on the hill met to eat.

"Natasha." Luc was suddenly beside her, keeping pace with her slow stroll.

Tasha's heart seemed to pause in her chest before resuming its steady beat. "I thought you'd left town."

"I did. I'm back. I want to talk to you." He took her arm and drew her onto the grass, off the paved walk.

"You tried to hurt my mother." She yanked her arm out of his hold. Her voice sounded more hurt than angry, which pissed her off. She cocked her tennis racket in a vaguely threatening manner to make up for it.

His eyes softened. "No. I wouldn't hurt your mother. I wouldn't have let my sister hurt her, either."

She studied his face, looking for the truth. His eyes were clear and unwavering. His lips formed a tight line, with a slight droop that might be tiredness. The tilt of his head indicated pride and the thrust of his chin spoke of stubborn determination.

A tension in her chest relaxed. She had no logical reason to believe him, but she did. She lowered the racket. "What's wrong with your sister? Why does she want to hurt my mother?"

Luc held out a hand. "Come have a drink with me. I'll explain what I know."

Grandma Jean would have a fit if she found out Tasha had gone anywhere with a Shadow Walker. And despite that fact that Tasha inexplicably trusted this man, she fully intended to keep to public places when with him. "Stay here while I run up to my room and stash my racket. Then we can head over to the League and grab something at the food court."

At his nod, Tasha quickly covered the remaining distance to her dorm. Leslie, her roommate, was out. Tossing her racket on her bed, she grabbed a brush from her dresser, pulled out her ponytail and ruthlessly smoothed her hair. She frowned in the mirror as she put on lip-gloss and mascara. What was she doing? This wasn't a date. To prove it to herself, she pulled on a fresh T-shirt that clashed with her hair and changed her shorts for a pair of worn jeans. She pulled out her phone and texted Leslie to let her know where she was going, their safety system when out with new people, and left the room without looking in the mirror again.

Harry sat in the back of the two-person kayak, an orange life jacket snapped around his chest. A paddle rested across his strong, muscular thighs. He wore a pair of beige shorts and a navy blue collared polo shirt. His hair was ruffled from the light breeze and his golden eyes were lit with anticipation. Standing on the dock next to the sleek, narrow boat, Julie felt unreasonably happy that Harry seemed to be enjoying himself.

The kayak bobbed gently in the quiet pool of water at the head of the Argo Cascades, a boat bypass around the Argo Dam on the Huron River. The Cascades were a man-made series of nine water drops that led back into the placid waters of the Huron. During summer, the Cascades were a popular spot, crowded with people navigating the white water drops in over-sized inner tubes and kayaks. On a school day in early fall hardly anyone was on the water.

"You do know how to steer one of these, right?" Julie asked. Harrison had insisted on sitting in the back. The man obviously had control issues.

"I've read about it and understand the basic physics involved." He studied the water rushing through the opening in the limestone rocks that marked the first drop.

"Let's trade places."

"No."

She should have suggested bowling or tennis, neither of which would have ended with her in the water. "Okay, but steer straight into the drop and then just let the current take us over."

His brow lifted. "Bossy."

"Pot. Kettle. Black." She wrinkled her nose at him, entranced by this relaxed and teasing side of Harry.

He smiled. The mischievous, heart-melting smile of a boy about to start on an adventure. She smiled back. The attendant cleared his throat and she stepped into the front of the kayak, taking the oar he handed her. The attendant gave them a push, and they were off. The first drop went smoothly. The kayak shot down the fall, white water spraying Julie's face. She laughed and bounced on her seat when the kayak hit flat water.

"Paddle on your left." Harry commanded.

They made it down the next seven falls quickly. Their oars worked in perfect harmony, as if they'd been kayaking together for years. As her muscles pumped, Julie let her imagination fly free. *This was the final race in the Cascade kayaking competition at the Olympics, and she was going for the gold. The current winning time, set by the French Polynesian team, was a moving yellow line in front of her. The camera zoomed in on her face, intent and determined. Then the shot switched to Bob Costas, who introduced an emotional video montage of her life. Several heart-wrenching moments later, they were back to the race. She dug deep with her oar, determined to cross that moving line. Pull, pull. Closer, closer. Her arms strained. The crowd roared her name. Julie! Julie!*

"Julie!" Harrison roared. "What in bloody hell are you doing? Pay attention."

The final fall that would dump them into the Huron required a sharp right turn as the water curved under a stone pedestrian bridge. Because she'd been gunning full speed ahead, the current caught them before the nose of the kayak could complete the turn.

"We're going sideways!" Julie yelled.

"I noticed." Harrison sounded calm again while she paddled frantically and shouted instructions. The current was too strong. They were going to hit the side of the bridge and flip. Good-bye gold medal. Suddenly, impossibly, the kayak straightened and shot nose first down the fall and out into the serene, tree-lined Huron River.

"Whoo Hoo!" A young woman, watching from the bridge, clapped. "Awesome!"

Julie looked over her shoulder at Harrison, incredulous. "How did you do that?"

Harrison grinned and wiped water off his face. He looked young and carefree. For a moment she could only stare at him, a funny, warm feeling building in her chest.

"I can move from London to Ann Arbor in the blink of an eye and you're shocked when I turn the nose of a kayak?"

Good point. "I agree with our audience. That was awesome. You can be on my Olympic team anytime."

"Is that why you were thrashing water like a mad woman?"

He gave her an interested look. "I hope we won."

"We had to forfeit due to illegal use of magic." Julie turned and began paddling at a more sedate pace. She heard Harry's oar enter the water and felt the boat surge forward.

She relaxed with each slow stroke. The Huron wound through Ann Arbor, but at times it seemed as if they were in a wilderness. Trees crowded the shores, and the sounds of birds chirping replaced the hum of traffic.

"I don't generally do that," Harry said, several minutes later. "Break the rules," he clarified.

"That doesn't surprise me. You're in a job where you see the consequences of that. I, on the other hand, do sometimes break rules." Julie pointed toward the shore. They were floating past the Nichols Arboretum. "When I was a student at Michigan, we'd borrow trays from the dorm cafeteria to use for sledding, we called it 'traying', on the hills here in the Arb. That was totally against the dorm rules."

"Obviously you have a dark side, Ms. Dancer. I'll have to keep an eye you."

Julie laughed, mostly to cover the shiver she'd felt at the promise in his statement.

"I've never been on a sled," he remarked.

Julie glanced back. He was studying the hills with a thoughtful expression, as if imagining what it would be like to zip down them on a snowy winter day. He'd never been in a kayak before today, either. What kind of man spent his life studying and working? She watched the smooth pull of his muscles as he moved the paddle through the water. Okay, he had to spend some time at the gym, too. That body could not just be the result of good genetics.

"You enjoyed yourself." His words were a statement.

It took her a moment to realize he was talking about sledding and not about watching him. She looked toward the shore. "Yeah, it was all fun and games until I'd tip over and end up wet and shivering." She shook her head, remembering. "I'm not a big fan of the cold. I met Jack when he pulled my face out of the snow and offered to share his thermos of brandy-laced hot chocolate."

"Jack was your husband?"

""For about thirteen years. Tash was twelve when we split." Julie pulled hard on her paddle.

"Tell me why you loved him."

Panic fluttered in her stomach. Her muscles tightened, no longer relaxed. "What?"

"Why did you love Jack?" He asked the outrageously difficult question as if inquiring about the weather, with a mild note of curiosity.

People sometimes asked why her marriage had broken up, but no one had ever asked why she'd loved Jack, not even Dorie. "Why does anyone fall in love?"

"I don't know. That's why I asked."

"You've never been in love?"

"Of course not."

The way he said it, as if love wasn't a possibility for him, angered her. She quit paddling and turned. "Balances aren't allowed to fall in love, either? Harry, you need a new job."

He didn't respond, a patient expression on his face.

She sighed. "Jack was so full of energy and enthusiasm that being around him was like getting a shot of caffeine. Nothing got in his way when he had an idea." Julie looked up at the sky, gathering her thoughts. "Back then, we were all trying to figure life out. Jack was different. He was so focused, so sure of what he wanted." She met his gaze and shrugged. "I think his sense of purpose is what attracted me at first."

"Are you sure it wasn't the brandy in the hot chocolate?"

His dry response surprised a laugh out of Julie. "I never thought of that." She looked at his beautiful, serious face. "Love is an emotion that covers a lot of different feelings."

"Yes. I've recently made a study of it. The Greeks identified four different types of love—family, friendship, romantic and divine."

"You studied love?" Like kayaking. Gathering knowledge

about things he'd never experienced. She wanted to find his parents and shake them. What were the Penumbrae thinking? This man should have been surrounded by love as a child. They were just lucky their Balance was as balanced as he seemed to be.

"Do you still love him?" His voice sounded different, darker.

"No." Julie turned back to face the bow and pulled a stroke through the water. "Well, maybe the family kind of love, just a little bit," she admitted, trying to be perfectly honest.

There was another pause before he spoke. "One's mate should be family, friend and lover."

Julie felt his gaze on her back. She turned her head again, and her breath stuck in her throat. His eyes held a mix of emotions that she couldn't begin to interpret. "That would be the ideal, wouldn't it?" The words whispered out of her tight throat.

Then, as if he'd firmly shut a door, his gaze cleared. "I'm getting hungry. Let's find a place to eat the food you brought."

"I like your T-shirt." Luc had opted for a chocolate milkshake, but hadn't started drinking it yet. He held it between his hands, slowly rotating the paper cup.

"Orange does not look good with red hair," Tash informed him, glancing up from her iced tea. She'd been trying not to stare at him. Most of the women in the lower-level food court at the Michigan League weren't showing the same restraint. Luc was the focus of a lot of female eyes.

"Red?" His gaze moved over her hair. "Wasn't it your own Mark Twain who said that when red-haired people are above a certain social grade, their hair is auburn?"

Tasha laughed. "Yes, he did. I love Mark Twain, but I don't think I qualify for the auburn upgrade."

"In your case, social status is irrelevant. Even if you were a pauper, people would struggle to find a word that describes the rivers of honey, fire and gold that flow through your hair. When you move your head, it's as if the last finger of the sun releases the earth, waking its power." His accent sounded thicker than usual.

Tasha swallowed. The guys on campus didn't talk this way. Nobody talked this way. She recognized absolute bullshit when she heard it, but she couldn't even begin to form a cynical comeback. Her heart beat too quickly. She gathered her sunrise/sunset hair together and yanked it behind her shoulders. "Stop being so French," she managed to say, her tone sounding remarkably practical, considering. "Tell me about your sister."

The intensity in his blue eyes notched down to a bearable level. Tasha took a deep breath. Luc looked down at his chocolate milkshake for several seconds before responding.

"We were children when Marguerite first began having bad dreams. She never told me about them, but sometimes I would hear her wake, sobbing."

"Didn't you ask her about them?"

"Yes. At first I did. She said they were nothing." He shrugged. "Marguerite has always needed to be the strong one, the one in control. I didn't push her on this, because I knew she viewed the dreams, and her reaction to them, as a weakness."

"What do these dreams have to do with her wanting to hurt my mother?"

"I don't know exactly. But they have gotten worse. And Marguerite is no longer the sister I knew. She has become secretive and arrogant. Her powers have changed, become stronger. They are no longer drawn only from the earth. I am afraid for her."

"You're afraid for *her*? She's the one acting like a bully. You should be afraid for my mother."

Luc nodded. "I am. That's why I sought you out." His lips lifted in a self-mocking smile. "Well, one of the reasons I sought you out. I want to find out what is happening to Marguerite, and I think your grandmother may be able to help me."

"Grandma? How could Grandma help? Besides, I don't think she'll talk to you." Tasha grimaced. "For a woman who is open-minded and accepting of everyone, she has quite a prejudice against Shadow Walkers."

"That's why I need you. If we go together to see your

grandmother, perhaps you can convince her to see me."

"Perhaps." Tasha doubted it. "What do you want to talk to her about?"

"I want to ask her about my grandmother, Belle. Marguerite has been calling her name out in her sleep. I know our families had a connection before the war. I'm hoping Jean can tell me something about her."

"Our families had a connection?"

Luc gave her a small smile. "Of course. As two of the most powerful families in the Triad, the members worked together frequently in the old days, two sides of a Three."

Huh? "What are you talking about?"

"You truly know nothing of your heritage, do you?" Luc shook his head. "How does Jean expect you to blossom, when she gave you no roots?"

Very good point, but she was the only one allowed to criticize her grandmother. "My roots might not be as long as your roots, but they work. I'm blossoming quite well, thank you."

Luc's eyes darkened and the breath caught in her lungs. The atmosphere between them changed as quickly as a cloud scuttles over the sun. She knew, without a doubt, that he wanted her. Not in the knee-jerk way most of her dates did, hoping an evening would end in sex but philosophical if it didn't. No. This man *wanted* her. The depth of his desire and the possessiveness in his eyes scared her. She couldn't breathe.

"Tasha." He spoke softly, and she thought he took a piece of her when he named her. "Don't be frightened. I won't hurt you."

"Stop," she ordered, not sure what she was asking him to do.

Something flashed through his eyes. His lips curved in a wry smile. He lowered his head in a nod of acceptance.

She took a sip of her drink, her hand trembling. Her brain, her nerves, her world, felt short-circuited. "Does everyone in France talk like you do?"

"Not to you, if they wish to stay healthy." He stated the words simply, yet she read the intent on his face.

Her eyes widened. His lips twisted in another self-mocking smile. "Ignore me, Tasha. This has been a difficult week." His eyes cleared, no hint of the dark possession clouding them. "I believe talking with Jean may provide a clue to Marguerite's behavior, which will help us to protect your mother. Will you come to Chicago with me and convince your grandmother to at least listen to my questions?"

She should say no. She wasn't like her dad. She found her adventures in her books. She had to study tonight. Her schedule was planned. And yet....

Luc's face was carefully expressionless as he waited. This man could hurt her. Not in a physical sense, she had no fear of that. But he touched her deep inside, in a place she didn't recognize, a place no one had ventured before. She understood, with soul-deep certainty, that such a touch was capable of bringing both amazing joy and unimagined pain. Going with him might provide a clue to the behavior of crazy Marguerite, but it was also taking a big risk, a definite step away from the safe and familiar world that she cherished.

Of course, that safe and familiar world had already become just an illusion. Her mother was in danger. Really, there wasn't a choice.

She stood. "Okay. I'll go with you. How do we do this? Plane, train or automobile?" While she waited for his answer, she began putting together a mental To Do list: Call her mother to let her know where she was going, call Grandma to beg her to talk to Luc when they arrived, send another text to Leslie, stop by the dorm to pack an overnight bag and grab her books, and reconfigure her study schedule so she'd still be on target for the art history test.

Luc rose and took her hand. "It will be quicker to travel with earth energy."

Tasha frowned. "That's not a new kind of car fuel, is it?"

He laughed and led her out of the brightly lit food court and into a shadowed corner beside the wide stairs leading to the main floor.

"Luc?"

He turned and firmly pulled Tasha against his chest. The strength in his arms surprised her. Before she could analyze how his lean hardness felt against her softness, an odd tingling suffused her body. Her head began to whirl like when she was little and had spun in endless circles, arms held wide to embrace the world. This felt different than the time she'd popped through space with Harrison. She closed her eyes tightly, concentrated on keeping the contents of her stomach in her stomach and prayed for a quick trip.

Ten

JULIE UNLOCKED her front door and walked into the living room. "That was fun, wasn't it?"

Harry followed behind carrying a now-empty picnic basket. "It was one of the best days I've ever had."

She tried not to read more into the words than he might mean. After the discussion about Jack and love, they'd talked about nothing serious, as if both had needed a break from the real world for a while. Several times, Harry had grown quiet and she'd known he was fighting some internal battle not to let the curse and Marguerite's presence ruin their day. Thursday night was the full moon. He only had two nights before he'd be rid of the curse.

Julie found that she was strangely comfortable with him, able to relax in a way she hadn't been able to with her ex-husband. Jack got bored easily, and she'd always felt like she needed to amuse or interest him. With Harry, she could be herself. Jack had thought her flights into fantasy were odd and irritating; Harry had taken the whole Olympic thing in stride.

She took the basket from him and set it on the kitchen counter next to the phone. "I'm going to try calling Mom again. I'm worried about her." Julie punched in her mother's number, unease settling over her when she heard her mother's recorded voice: *This is Jean's answering machine. Leave a message, if you dare. I'll call back, if I care.*

Julie lifted the phone from her ear and stared at it. "I hate phones."

"Nasty buggers," Harry agreed solemnly. He sat at her kitchen table, long legs stretched out before him.

"Maybe Tasha has heard from her." Julie suddenly wanted to touch base with her daughter to assure herself she was all right. Unfortunately, Tash didn't pick up her dorm room phone or her cell. "I really hate phones."

"Alexander Graham Bell has a lot to answer for." Harry stood from the table and walked behind her, standing so close she felt his warm breath on her neck. "Relax, Julie." He echoed her words from the morning. His hands slowly rubbed her shoulders.

Julie knew that Harry had probably never rubbed anyone's shoulders in his life. The fact that he was trying to comfort her, to give her what she'd given him that morning, almost undid her. Of course, Harry's hands on her body were anything but relaxing, as he might guess if he could see the nipples poking against her shirt. She could, however, barely remember why she'd been tense. Oh, her disappearing family. Right. She wasn't usually such a worrier, but Bas and his talk of demons scared her. "Where do you think everyone is?" The words were embarrassingly breathy.

"It's Tuesday evening. Your mother is out playing bingo, and your daughter is at the library, her phone on mute," Harry murmured.

"Mother does play strip bingo," Julie admitted, her bones melting under his touch even as her nerve endings hummed to attention. She turned her head to the side and her breath caught at how close he was.

"The Council advised me to stay away from you." He leaned in closer, as if to physically to negate the words.

"They did? Why? They don't even know me." How stupid that she felt hurt by a bunch of people she'd never met. She shrugged out of his hold and turned to face him. She wanted to take a step forward. Instead, she took a step back and leaned against the kitchen wall, arms strategically crossed over her breasts.

He narrowed his eyes at her move. "They believe you're

dangerous."

"Just because I took your shirt off in a meeting? That was an accident. It could happen to anyone."

"Your contribution to my lack of proper attire is not the problem."

"Then what is?"

"We're working hard to put back the governing structure that used to guide and organize the Triad before the Rift. You're viewed as a potential distraction and danger to me. The Council is concerned about the possibility of our bonding."

"That's ridiculous. I'm not a distraction to you, and you have no intention of allowing a bond."

"You're right. I don't." His brooding gaze lingered on her lips.

"I think it's wrong that a Balance doesn't bond or get married. Not that I'm a marriage advocate, but some people, like Mom and Dad, or like Dorie and Jim, have great relationships. I'm sorry you don't have the possibility of that, too."

"You're a romantic or an idealist," he said, with amused condensation.

"I'm an American." Where was her red, white and blue flag when she needed to wave it?

"Which means—what? You believe in personal freedom at any cost?" Harry looked suddenly older, cynical. "The Balance doesn't bond for the protection of the Triad. The position loses the perception of impartiality if he or she is mated."

Okay. She could see the logic in that. It helps to stay out of bed with the people you have power over. But who actually did that, except maybe the Pope? "What about Walkers, Dancers and other Penumbrae? Can they have a mixed marriage?"

"There's no law against it. Most of the resulting children are powerless, as if the different energies cancel each other out. But not every mixed couple gets lucky. Some of the children have wild powers. We have to banish those offspring."

"Banish the offspring?" That sounded ominous.

"Yes. Their very lack of control threatens our safety and

anonymity." He didn't go into detail.

Julie took a deep breath, suddenly understanding the fear he could generate. Had he been the one to send the children away? "That's inhumane."

"No. What's inhumane is to allow the slaughter of our people, which is what would happen if our true nature were exposed to normal humans."

"Harry, get real. You guys are much stronger than we are."

"Julie, you're not one of the normal humans."

She narrowed her eyes. "Psychologically I am. I was raised normal." She thought of her mother. "Sort of."

He apparently decided not to argue the point. "We're different, but not necessarily stronger than most humans. Humans wield their own kind of power, and there are many more of them than there are of us. We have no wish to fight. We've experienced what fear can do to us many times in the past."

"Witch trials?"

"Yes. That's one example."

Julie frowned. "No one should have to hide who they are. I don't think you give humans enough credit."

"Do you read history books or even yesterday's news?" Anger flashed in his eyes.

"We don't have to repeat mistakes of the past. You underestimate human nature's ability to change."

"And maybe I don't." he said, his anger now morphed into a look of weariness.

"I'm not out to change anything. I just want to—"

The tension in his face eased into a smile as he finished her sentence, "enjoy your quiet middle years."

"Right." She nodded. Her hip shifted and brushed against him. "Not to change the subject or anything, but why are we standing so close together?"

"It's easier to kiss you this way."

"Oh?" She swallowed, forgetting about everything but the golden glow in his eyes.

"Oh." He murmured, intently watching her lips. "I'm waiting for you to stop talking."

"Like that's going to happen." She nervously licked her lips and watched his eyes deepen to bronze. "Aren't you afraid if we kiss we might bond and, I don't know, the known world might blow up or something?"

He smiled. "Not the world, just the Council. They'd remove me as Balance." His smile faded. "I'm not planning to have sex with you." His voice sounded cool and controlled, in direct contrast to the heat of his gaze.

Julie ignored the zip of disappointment that coursed through her. "Of course not. I didn't think you were. That would be stupid. But—"

He kissed her. Apparently he realized the futility of waiting for her to be quiet.

There was nothing cool or controlled about his kiss. He pulled her body flush against his. His lips slammed into hers, hard and hungry. There was no space between them, and still his arms tightened until she thought nothing would ever be able to separate them. His lips moved over hers again and again, like he couldn't get enough of her. Heat pooled in her body, spreading out to her limbs, licking her, fogging her brain. Her hands found his thick hair and she threaded her fingers through the strands, tugging, trying to bring his head closer even though that was impossible.

She heard noises. A thumping heart beat, a ragged gasp for air, a sigh that ended in a moan, soft pings and the chime of shattering glass. She ignored them all as her hands worked Harry's shirt from the grasp of the black leather belt at his waist. Her hands touched the hot skin of his back and for a moment, his whole body stilled.

Then his tongue was in her mouth, his hands against her cheeks, holding her, and he felt good, so good. She wanted to touch him everywhere. Her hands slid over the smooth skin of his back, found the indentation of his waist and lowered to the tight curve of his buttocks. His muscles were lean and rock hard. They clenched tighter beneath her seeking fingers. She spread her legs slightly and moved her hips, gasping at the sensation.

"Bloody hell!" He groaned the words against her neck, his hands clenched beneath her bottom, shifting her angle. The piercing pleasure stole her breath. "Where are our clothes?"

"Hmmm?" She rubbed the tips of her breasts against him, feeling the soft scrape of his hair against her skin.

"Julie." His teeth found her earlobe, and he nipped it gently, the tug sending a thick spiral of pure heat through her core. "We're naked. Help me."

Her hands moved between them. The air stilled in her lungs when her fingers wrapped around the hard length of him. He pulsed and his body jerked. With a smooth, swift motion, he pushed her back against the wall. Her hands came up and gripped his shoulders, hanging on tight. His hands slid beneath her thighs and a strong tug brought her legs around his waist. One slight shift of her pelvis and he'd be inside her.

"Not that kind of help." His normally calm voice sounded desperate. He gritted out the words between clenched teeth. "We. Can't."

The cold wall against her heated back, the realization that he was actually lifting her and now knew how much she weighed and the fact that this was the first time she'd seen Harry out of control brought reality crashing back.

She squirmed.

"Don't. Move." Warm puffs of air brushed her nipple with each word.

Her body stilled. The tip of his penis slid smoothly against her dampness, feeling so damn good. Why couldn't they make love? Was spending the rest of her life connected with this fascinating, complex man really such a nasty proposition? Was she really considering this?

Wait. The rules. Harry couldn't have her and be the Balance. There were many things she didn't know about him, but the one thing she was certain of was that Harry was the Balance. The two couldn't be separated. She closed her eyes and leaned her head against the wall, holding her breath, willing herself not to shift forward and take him inside her. A sheen of sweat slicked Harry's shoulders as he fought for control. Her fingers gripped the damp muscles. She didn't want to let him go.

But above all, she didn't want him to do something he would regret, something he would hate them both for later.

She kept her eyes closed and reached for her special sense. The power was there, surging inside her. What was she supposed to do with it? She felt something, a small tickle inside her. Then the soft weight of her clothes brushed her skin. The crisp cotton of Harry's shirt appeared beneath her fingers, the rough chill of denim rubbed against the sensitive skin of her thighs.

Harry gently lowered her to the floor. She noticed then that the house was dark. Something crunched beneath Harry's shoes as he backed away.

"Thank you." His voice sounded different, more distant. "The light bulbs broke."

"Did I do that?" She nervously brushed her palms against her jeans, trying to make out his expression.

"I don't know. It might have been me."

"Who got us naked?"

"That was you." He sounded sure of that.

"I'm sorry." She knew she was blushing. How positively crude can you get? She kept stripping the poor guy.

The phone in her pocket buzzed, startling her. Julie dug it out, still trying to see Harry's face.

"Are you okay?" Dorie's voice sounded blessedly normal.

"Why wouldn't I be?" Julie answered cautiously. Was Dorie psychic or something?

"The electricity is out." Dorie announced. "I called the electric company. They expect to have power back within a few hours."

"Oh. Thanks for the information."

"Julie, are you all right? You sound funny."

"No, I'm okay. Harry's here."

"Ahhhhhh. Harry's there. Sorry if I interrupted anything. But use protection. I read there's always a mini baby boom after a major blackout."

"I don't think it counts as a blackout if it's in the afternoon. Anyway, we're just talking."

"Right. Details later, okay?"

Julie decided to move to safer subject. "Did the whole neighborhood lose power?"

"Yep. The guy said there was some big electrical surge that blew the circuits. They have no idea what caused it. Anyway, I've got to go. I'm on my way to the school to pick up the boys."

"Drive carefully. The traffic lights will be out," Julie cautioned, then disconnected the call and shoved her phone back in her pocket. She looked toward Harry, who now stood the length of the kitchen away. "One of us blew the local power grid."

"I'm not surprised." His voice still had that distant quality.

"Really?" She tried to remember recent power glitches. "Does this happen often when energy wielders kiss?"

"No."

Then why wasn't he surprised? She started to ask when the phone rang again. Hoping it was Tasha, Julie picked up.

"Mrs. Dancer?" Julie recognized the voice of Tasha's roommate, Leslie.

"Leslie! Hi! Is electricity out at the dorm? Is everything okay? I've been trying to get in touch with Tasha."

"Oh, that means she's not with you." Leslie hesitated. "Tash wasn't in the history class we have together after lunch. I can't reach her on her cell. I thought maybe she went to your place after meeting with that guy."

"What guy?" Tasha didn't currently have a boyfriend.

"She texted me earlier today that she was heading to the food court at the Union with someone."

"Luc Deschamps." Tasha wouldn't be so stupid. Would Tasha be so stupid?

"That's the name. Look, I'm sorry to bother you." Leslie tried to backpedal, obviously realizing Tasha might not want to be found if she had her phone off and was with a guy. "Her phone battery is probably just dead. I'm sure she's fine."

Tasha finished retching into the tall weeds that sprouted around a fire hydrant and took the handkerchief Luc handed her. She wiped her mouth and crumpled the cloth in her hands. She straightened, embarrassed beyond words. "Thank you. American guys don't carry handkerchiefs."

"They're all heathens," he said mildly. "Are you okay now?"

"Yes, thanks. Next time I'll take some Dramamine before we travel that way."

He smiled. "Your system will become accustomed to it."

Tasha gave him a doubtful look and tucked his handkerchief in her pocket. She finally took in her surroundings. The neighborhood they stood in looked familiar, and yet it didn't.

Rows of gray stone buildings crowded the sidewalk. Trees grew in the tiny patches of grass tucked between the walk and the street. Cars hugged the curb, jammed fender to fender. Tasha frowned and looked down the block. A small park occupied the corner, currently deserted. "I think we're on the wrong block. Grandma lives on the other side of that park."

Sometime during the trip here, she'd heard Luc asking her for directions. How a mass of molecules—or whatever she'd been on the way over—could hear something was beyond her. Maybe it was more accurate to say she'd become aware that he wanted directions and somehow she'd relayed them to him. She looked around the neighborhood. She'd obviously been a bit off. Not like her usual precise self at all.

Luc took a step toward her and Tasha backed away. "Let's just walk there."

He nodded. "I'll need time and food before we travel by energy stream again"

Good. Tasha started off a brisk pace toward her grandmother's.

Her steps slowed, however, as her she looked around. The afternoon was cloudy, the atmosphere somber.

Every house they passed had a bright light gleaming from the porch, even though there was still daylight. Shades were drawn tightly against windows. No toys or bikes littered the tiny lawns. Not a single person sat on their steps, or loitered on the sidewalk talking. "There's nobody around. This feels a little creepy. Grandma talked about an increase in crime. I wonder if that's why everyone is tucked in their houses."

Luc took her arm. "There's no need to worry. I won't let harm come to you."

The confidence in his voice was comforting. He might even be telling the truth. Maybe Luc could put a force field around them, or something.

Tasha slowed even more as they skirted the park. There was something sad about the empty playground. Young trees draped in shadow stood like sentinels on the far edge of the park. A swing set and slide rose from faded woodchips. Angled to the side was a picnic table, where parents would sit and chat while their children played. The faint, decaying scent of leaves, mixed with the bus fumes and sewer smells of a big city, brushed against her. Her neck tingled with an uncomfortable feeling she couldn't ignore.

"Luc," she whispered, tugging his arm when he came to a standstill in front of the park.

He scanned the grassy area, an intent look on his face. "I sense it, too." He spoke more to himself than Tasha. "Not Penumbrae, Walker or Dancer." He bent and scraped up a handful of dirt, cradling it in his palm. "Something more akin to earth energy, than light." He blew gently on the dry scrabble in his palms.

The dirt suddenly burst forward out of his hand, billowing and growing into a large swirling cloud before transforming into soft crystals of light. The park lit up, as if the clouds had parted, letting through the rays of the setting sun. For a moment, Tasha didn't see anything, dazzled by the spectacle, amazed by what Luc had been able to do. Then the tall shadows at the opposite end of the park began to move. Six men, dressed in black, walked slowly toward Luc and Tasha.

"Gang members!" Tasha tugged on his arm. "Run!"

He didn't budge. "Go. Quickly. Find your grandmother. Tell her the Skaven are here."

She tried to tug him with her but Luc removed her hand from his arm, put both hands on her shoulders and gave her a push in the direction of her grandmother's. "Get Jean Dancer."

Obediently, Tasha ran half a block before she stumbled to a stop. She couldn't leave him to face six men alone. God knew if her grandmother was even at home. He could be dead by the time she found help.

She turned back toward the park. Luc stood where she'd left him. In the odd light, she could see that he watched the approaching men with an expression more curious than scared.

Knowing it was the height of stupidity, she ran back to his side and stood with him, shoulder to shoulder. She dug the cell phone out of her pocket and flicked it open. Damn, she had it off. She fumbled for the "on" button and waited impatiently as the face lit up and icons appeared on her screen.

"Get out of here, Natasha." Luc's voice held a firm command. "Now!"

"'Come when they may, they shall not find us skulking and hiding.'" She apparently channeled Dickens in times of crisis.

"'Be where your enemy is not,'" Luc shot back, adding "Sun Tzu, *Art of War*."

Excellent advice. Tasha was definitely going to read that book when this was over. She dialed 9-1-1 and looked up as the men circled them. Luc put his arm around her shoulder and pulled her close.

The men appeared to be in their late twenties or early thirties—much too old to be strutting around Chicago streets dressed in black sleeveless T-shirts. Two were black, one was Asian, three were white. They all had different builds and yet there was something about them—besides the T-shirts—that marked them as similar.

Tasha gasped when she realized what it was. Their eyes were all ice blue, and they all held the same expression of cold malice.

The 9-1-1 operator's voice squawked into the air between them. Eight pairs of eyes riveted on the phone in her hand.

"Excuse me." Tasha held the phone to her ear and spoke calmly. "Officer down. Please send every available squad car to—" The phone flew out of her hand and crashed into the sidewalk, splintering into several pieces.

Tasha pressed herself against Luc. "Okay, now's the time to do your energy thing. Beam us out of here."

The circle of men closed on them as the six took a single step forward. A frown appeared on Luc's face, and one of the men grinned.

She felt the movement of…something. A kind of hum in her bones that was there and gone. "Too soon," he murmured, his quick glance at her calm and reassuring.

He turned his head and looked directly at each of the six men. "You cannot do this." His voice roared out, forceful and commanding.

"Tell that to your Triad Council, because we don't care." One of the white men spoke. "One lone Walker boy against six Skaven." He shook his head. "Destroying you will be a walk in the park." He gestured to the park and all six of the strangers snickered, as if he'd said something really clever.

Skaven? Tasha tried to make her brain function through the fear. Was that the name of a multicultural street gang? And how did they know Luc was a Walker?

"Except it's not just one lone Walker boy, Frankie. The Gigis are here."

Tasha swung her head so hard she almost fell over. Grandma Jean strode quickly down the sidewalk toward them. A posse of about fifteen women, all wearing pink shirts with 'Gigis' written in script across a breast pocket, marched behind her. One pushed a walker and several carried canes.

They were going to get killed.

"Grandma! Run!" Tasha screamed out the words.

Jean hurried to the circle surrounding Tasha, breathing heavily. "Nice idea, sweetheart, but a brisk walk is all I can manage these days." She turned to the man whose grin had been wiped off his face. "Frank, I'm getting very angry. I thought we banished you."

"This is your granddaughter?" Frank looked at Tasha, a gleam in his too-blue eyes.

Jean didn't even glance at Tasha. She held out her arms. "Gigis, form your Threes and send Frank and his fellows back to their dark alleys."

The women moved quickly, each holding out a hand, forming groups of three. As their fingers connected, a surge of energy coursed through Tasha's body, like a sharp, biting wind.

Frank tensed, and then laughed as his shoulders relaxed. "You are still weak from banishing the demons in Lincoln Park. Victory will be ours."

"Stuff it." Grandma didn't look impressed. "We may not be at full strength, but we still have enough power to send dirty Skaven back to their nests." Grandma stood up straighter. "Ladies, again!"

Luc spoke. "These really are Skaven?" He looked fascinated, like he wanted to interview the scum.

Frank ignored Luc. His face wrinkled in concentration, and the muscles in his arms bulged. He appeared to be battling an invisible foe. Four of the Skaven suddenly disappeared, and four large rats appeared in their place. One of the women limped toward them, swishing her cane with terrifying force. The rats scattered.

"A prize so precious as your granddaughter cannot be lost." Frank gasped the words, his teeth clenched. He jerked his head toward the remaining man—Skaven, rat, whatever—beside him. The man's eyes widened, but he pulled out a small flat silver rectangle from his pocket. Frank took it from him and nodded toward Jean. "For emergency use only," he wheezed. He flipped open the lid of the rectangle with a shaking hand and pressed a button.

Tasha groaned, hit by the immediate wave of pure, sharp power. She heard Luc swear and felt him turn her into his chest, both arms wrapped tight around her. Night shredded into a million silver molten drops that pierced her skin. Her bones began to melt. Grandma yelled her name and then there was nothing. Nothing but endless pain and the insistent sanity of Luc's strong grasp.

Eleven

SUN TINTED the horizon when Julie finally fell asleep on the couch. Harry took a folded wheat-colored afghan off the back of a chair and shook it out. A single kernel of popcorn skittered across the floor. This must be Julie's movie-watching afghan. He tucked it around her, arranged a throw pillow under her head and gently removed the phone from her fingers. He went into the kitchen and plugged it into a charger. Then he returned to the living room and sat in the chair across from her.

Even in sleep, a worried furrow marked her brow. He stared at the wrinkle and willed himself to stay in his chair. He wanted to rub his thumb over the small crease to smooth it out. He wanted to comfort her. Hell, he wanted to get naked with her and pump himself into her body.

It wasn't like him to want what he couldn't have.

Harrison leaned his head back and closed his eyes to shut out the image of Julie. He'd avoided sleep for much of the three weeks that Marguerite had been in his head. When external activity ceased, her presence inside him seemed to grow to boulder size, a dead weight dragging at his consciousness. And this was nothing compared to what would happen if she succeeded with the second tie. She wouldn't be merely an irritation; she'd know his thoughts, and he'd know hers.

The thought of such forced intimacy repelled him.

His eyes opened, and he stared at the woman lying on the

couch. How would he feel if Julie were in his head? He waited for the sour curdle of distaste. Instead, warmth grew, hard and solid, in his chest.

Being close to this woman didn't repel him, not in the least. He was drawn to her, to the circle of light that she broadcast, not through her power, but through her personality. She brightened his world and drew feelings to the surface that he'd long ago buried. Feelings like that ridiculous thing he'd do when he was four years old. As soon as the nanny would shut off his bedroom light, he'd dive under the covers and pretend that she had stayed in the room and he wasn't alone. He'd imagine he could feel her weight as she sat on the side of the bed and he'd hum himself to sleep, pretending it was her. The fantasy game had stopped when he moved to boarding school at age five and began to fully understand his role and his duty.

Now here were those feelings of not wanting to be alone again. He wanted Julie in his bed at night. He wanted to delve into both her mind and her body. He wanted to belong to her, be part of her golden circle.

She scared the hell out of him.

A quiet knock sounded on the door. Bascule stood on the porch when Harry opened it.

"You don't knock on doors." Harrison stood back to let him in.

"Julie doesn't like it when I just pop into a room." Bas shrugged and handed Harrison a leather-bound book. "You left your copy of the *Mots de Sagesse* in Australia."

Harrison frowned at the book. "So I did. Thank you for bringing it to me. How did your trip go?"

"Well enough, though I cut it short when news reached me of what is happening here. How's our Jewel doing?" Bas lowered his voice when he saw the sleeping Julie.

"She's worried about Natasha."

Bas nodded, his expression grim. "And so she should be."

"What do you know, Bas?"

Bas walked quietly through the living room to the kitchen and began gathering what he needed to put on a pot of coffee. He wore a pair of khakis this morning, and an untucked button-down shirt decorated with koala bears. His bare feet were stuck into a pair of leather loafers. "I know that change is painful." The scent of ground coffee filled the kitchen as Bas took a foil bag out of the cabinet and opened it. "I know that the chrysalis becomes nothing more than a coffin if the butterfly doesn't have the strength and courage to struggle free."

"Jesus Christ, Bas." The soft words exploded from Harrison. He didn't have patience for obscure analogies.

Bas put the empty carafe under the faucet and filled it with water. He turned and stared calmly at Harrison. Bas didn't hold with taking God's name in vain, any god's name for that matter.

Harrison took a deep breath and tried not to feel like a chastised nine-year-old. "Sorry," he mumbled. "Let me rephrase that. What the fuck are you talking about?"

Bas didn't say anything until he'd pressed the button that started the coffee maker. Then he leaned against the counter and folded his arms across his chest. "You must know she's special."

"Of course she's special. She's a Dancer from a powerful family."

"Untrained Dancers don't wield energy without intending to. They can never change a person's luck or their destiny. It takes Triad children years of practice and concentration to effectively wield energy."

"Is she a wild power?" Harrison forced himself to ask. He would be required to banish Julie if she were.

"Understanding Julie's heritage is only the beginning," Bas responded, not answering the question.

Harrison didn't push, but changed the subject. "Why did you say the chrysalis could become a coffin? Is Julie in danger?"

Bas turned and jiggled the coffee pot, as if that would speed the rate of dark liquid dripping into it. Harrison curbed his impatience, having learned the futility of trying to rush Bas.

When Bas finally looked at Harrison, his lips had curved into a small, sad smile. "Why do you assume I was referring to Julie? She is not the only one who faces darkness if she doesn't have the courage to change."

Julie heard muted voices in the kitchen. Pushing herself up, she swung her feet to the floor. What was she doing on the couch? Who was in her kitchen? With a rush, the past evening came back to her. Tasha had gone missing with a Shadow Walker.

Julie jumped to her feet and ran into the kitchen. Both Harry and Bas turned to look at her.

"Is there any news from Tasha?" She propped herself against the doorjamb, still not entirely awake.

Bas poured her a cup of coffee and brought it to her while Harry shook his head. "I've been calling Tasha's cell every hour."

"We need to call the police."

"No." Both Bas and Harry spoke the word together.

Julie straightened. "My daughter is missing and in the company of a potentially dangerous man."

"In spite of what Marguerite has done, I don't believe Luc Deschamps is a danger to your daughter." Harry's jaw set in an implacable line. "The Guardians are searching for Tasha as we speak."

"Don't call the police?" Julie walked slowly into the kitchen and set her cup down on the maple kitchen table. She sat in one of the chairs. Her mind wasn't functioning yet, but not calling the police seemed wrong. Having a lot of Linda-type people looking for her daughter seemed wrong. Harry seemed to read her mind.

"The Guardians aren't all like Linda. Most of them blend well with the human population. You can't tell them from anybody else."

"And I was just lucky to get assigned a six-foot Wonder Woman?"

Harrison's serious expression shifted with the hint of a smile. "I thought a visible reminder that you're protected by the

Penumbrae might act as a deterrent to Marguerite."

"That didn't work."

Harrison's face lost the smile. "No. That didn't work."

Julie sighed. Accepting the reality of the Triad when it meant taking classes from Bas and jumping around through space with Harry was easier than when it meant placing Tash's safety in their hands.

Harry suddenly stood in front of her. He reached out as if to tuck one of the wayward strands of her hair behind her ear. His hand dropped to his side before he touched her. "Trust me, Julie. I will do everything in my power to find your daughter."

Julie looked up and met his eyes. She nodded her assent slowly. He nodded back a thank you. A promise.

His hand reached out again, this time briefly touching her cheek. "Marguerite will know where her brother is. I'll go to her first. I'll keep you updated." He paused as if he wanted to say more. He looked over at Bas, who nodded at him. Then he was gone.

For a brief instant, a well of emptiness so vast it seemed to suck her into its hole filled the kitchen. Bas's voice snaked into the loneliness.

"Do you want pancakes or eggs for breakfast?"

Julie blinked and gripped her coffee cup. "Cinnamon toast would be great. I've been eating a lot of it lately."

Bas reached down into a cupboard and pulled out a yellow ceramic bowl. "Then you'll love my apple-cinnamon French toast."

Julie leaned her tired head on her hand and watched the lithe, graceful figure bustle around her kitchen. Bas was the type of man who would fit comfortably into any environment. She had a brief vision of him controlling a prancing horse, exhorting his battalion of troops to fight, Gladiator style. She had a feeling she'd go to battle for him, just as easily as she'd eat his apple cinnamon French toast. There was just something about him. She trusted him.

Just like she trusted Harry.

More than anything, she believed in Harry's integrity. He would do everything within the rules of the Triad to find her daughter and keep her safe.

The only problem was, Julie would do anything, rules of the Triad be damned, to find her daughter and keep her safe.

She sat up straighter. "I'm going to call my mom again and Jack, Tasha's dad, to see if they've heard from her."

Harrison stood on the graveled drive of the ancient chateau nestled in the foothills of the Montagne Noire, the Black Mountain range, in Southern France. The scent of pine blew off the wooded slopes of the mountains. Cheerful chirping filled the air as birds fluttered to and fro in the early afternoon sunlight.

Marguerite would be sleeping at this time of day, gathering strength to place the second tie. The next new moon rose on Thursday, tomorrow.

He controlled the anger that threatened to roar free at her audacity. For now, he needed information. He would wake her from her sleep and question her before she had her defenses fully in place.

Still, he stood on the drive. Ahead of him, the warm sun barely penetrated the dark gloom of Les Quatre Horizons, the massive stone residence that had belonged to the Deschamps family for countless generations. The earth wards placed around the home, guarding the occupants, nudged him. He owned both sun and earth energy. They held no power over him.

For a moment, he thought he felt Julie's desperation touch his mind. Impossible, but enough to push him off the drive and into Marguerite's bedroom.

The Moonflower did not sleep easily. She tossed and turned in her plain white cotton sheets, wrapping them tightly around her like an Egyptian mummy. Large tears of sweat beaded her brow and dampened the silver strands of her hair. Her lip trickled a thin line of blood where her teeth had clamped it. She twisted again, muttering "Belle, Belle."

Harrison paused, surprised by her distress. He put a hand on her shoulder and immediately felt a swirl of dark evil, a tightening of the first tie. He yanked his hand away as her eyes flew open, a frantic, searing blue.

She jack-knifed to a sitting position, and Harrison took a step back. Her eyes searched his and then skimmed the room, as if reorienting herself to where she was.

"Balance," she murmured, pushing at her damp hair. "What are you doing here?"

"Where's your brother?"

She rubbed at her mouth and winced, grimacing when she saw the blood on the back of her hand. "Luc? I imagine he's in the study."

Harrison assessed her expression carefully. "He's gone, last seen with the young Dancer, Natasha."

Shock crossed her face. "Why would he be with a Dancer?"

"You tell me, Marguerite. Why is he with Natasha, and where have they gone?"

"You must be mistaken. Have you checked the study? If he's not sleeping, Luc is usually there reading at this time of day." She shook her head as if to clear it. "You're wrong. He would not be with a Dancer."

She didn't know where her brother was. That was unusual, as the Moonflower kept close tabs on her twin. Luc had slipped her leash.

Harrison took in the circles beneath her eyes, the hollows of her flushed cheeks. This was not the confident, brash Marguerite he knew. "What troubles your sleep, Moonflower?"

She closed her eyes. "You are the only one who calls me that anymore."

"Talk to me. Tell me what's wrong and why you're destroying your future with this curse."

She shook her head, not meeting his eyes. "I'm righting a wrong. Sometimes the cost of that is high."

"You can't use evil to right a wrong. It always backfires in the end."

She lifted her chin, the defiance and anger stamped on her face her only answer.

"This action sets you on a dangerous path," Harrison warned. "Your people will suffer Triad-wide sanctions if they don't bring you for judgment to the Council. Turn yourself in, Marguerite. End the curse. Your punishment will be less severe if you voluntarily release me from the first tie."

"I won't do that. I'm not going to release you." She stared at him, so certain of her power that Harrison felt the first twinge of unease.

"Why?" he asked again.

"You'll know on Thursday, when the second tie reveals our thoughts to each other." She stood, and the sheet slid slowly from her body, revealing milk-white skin and lush curves. "There will be no secrets between us then. We will be of one mind. We can also be of one body, Balance." Her voice became sultry. "I will know how to perfectly please you. How each touch feels, how to build your desire." Her hands traveled up her flat stomach and cupped her breasts, as if offering them to him.

Harrison quietly met her gaze until a red flush touched her cheeks. Without a word, he left the room.

Julie walked out of the heavy, wooden double doors of the church. After checking out all of Tasha's favorite places in town, she'd stopped at Zion Lutheran Church. She sometimes went and just sat in the quiet sanctuary when she was particularly anxious or stressed about something. She always felt soothed afterwards. Today, though, not so much.

She turned to Bas who had gone with her. "I'll drop you off at my house if you're sticking around. I want to head into work for a couple of hours. I doubt if I'll get much done, but maybe if I keep myself busy, I won't go crazy waiting to hear from Harry or Tasha or Mom."

Bas opened the driver's side of the car for her. He kept an arm on the door, leaning toward her after she slid in. "You don't have to drop me off. I can get to your house on my own."

"Not too many owls out and about during the daytime."

Bas raised an eyebrow. "I'm not limited to owls, you know. I just prefer them." He started to shut the door for her.

Julie held up a hand to stop him. "Bas, wait a minute. I have a question I've been wanting to ask you." She didn't quite know how to phrase it.

Bas smiled slightly. "What do you want to know?"

She took a deep breath and held it. "What am I? I'm not a normal Sun Dancer, am I?"

"That's not the right question. What you are doesn't matter. What you do is more important."

Julie frowned, exhaling. "There are no wrong questions. My fourth grade teacher said so. Just answer what I asked."

"You know why I like cooking?"

Julie narrowed her eyes at him. "Tell me later."

"You mix separate ingredients that by themselves don't have much going for them. Have you ever eaten plain flour? Taken a taste of vanilla extract?"

She sighed, seeing no way out of this conversational tangent. "As a matter of fact, I have. Yuck."

"Right. But mix them together with a little sugar, butter, eggs and some chocolate chips, and you have a great-tasting cookie."

"And your point is?"

"I'll have cookies waiting when you get home from work this afternoon."

"That is not your point."

"I know. But you already know what my point is."

She did? Julie tried to unravel the conversation in her head. "You're very Gestalt," she said tentatively. "The whole is greater than the sum of the parts."

"No." He beamed like a teacher with a very bright student. "You're very Gestalt."

Julie sighed and started the car. This conversation was starting to sound too much like psychotherapy. Why didn't he just tell her the blasted answer to her question? "Step back and close the door, or I might clip one of your wings." Bas laughed and did as she said. She put the car in gear and rolled down the window. "It's very irritating when a person won't answer a direct question."

"I'll answer it when you're ready to hear the answer."

"You don't have a girlfriend, do you?"

"No," he answered, giving her a curious look. "How do you know?"

"She would have killed you by now." Julie scowled at him. "I like a little peanut butter in my chocolate chip cookies."

His smile widened. "You've got it."

Twelve

"YOU'RE LATE this morning. And where's the Purple People Eater?" Joe stood in Julie's office doorway. Gray hair ruffled, wearing running shorts and a T-shirt, he looked like he'd just come in from jogging.

"Looks like you're running late, too." Julie pushed aside the modified Bad Luck questionnaire that she wasn't really reading. She couldn't even muster a smile for her pun. "And Linda is busy doing important work." Hopefully finding her mother and daughter.

"Aha." He twirled an imaginary mustache, a dimple creasing his cheek. "Then I've found you without your chaperone."

"You better leave before you compromise me."

"What would be the fun of that?"

"Compromising me?"

"Leaving before I did."

She shook her head at him and smiled at his nonsense, despite her worry. She eyed his running attire. "What's with the outfit?"

He put a hand on her doorjamb. "I've been running to work lately. I enjoy being outside." For a moment his face looked wistful and then the expression was gone. "I have a change of clothes in my office. I thought I'd stop by here first, though, and show you what a jock I am."

"Stop flirting with me."

"Can't." His grin turned mischievous. "I've never been good

at resisting temptation."

"Oh, good grief." Since when had she become a femme fatale? She considered hunting down a mirror to see if her hair had suddenly straightened and picked up some golden highlights. She touched her head and felt the soft bounce. Same old, same old. She fixed her sternest look on Joe. "No fireworks, remember? We're just colleagues."

Joe held up a finger. "Wait. Be right back." He disappeared down the hallway and returned less than a minute later. He held up a slim, silver stick.

"Is that what I think it is?" Julie felt a reluctant smile form.

"A sparkler. I decided to provide my own firepower."

She almost laughed. He looked so sweet, standing in her doorway with a sparkler and a hopeful expression.

The diversion had actually helped to take her mind off Tasha for a few minutes. Tasha. Her smile died. "Go away. Joe. You're not going to get lucky."

He walked into the room, frowning. "What's the matter?"

Julie sighed and leaned back in her chair. "Tasha's been gone overnight, last seen with a man I'm nervous about. My mom is not answering her phone either, though that could just mean she's lost it."

Joe sat down across from her. "Have you called the police?"

Okay, this is what she got for giving in to the urge to confide. How the heck was she supposed to answer that question? No, I can't call the police. The Penumbrae Guardians are taking care of it.

"They probably require someone to be missing twenty-four hours or something before they'll take a report, right?" Joe said, providing her with the perfect excuse.

"Something like that," Julie mumbled. "I have some friends out looking for her. I'm sure she'll be all right."

"Have you called your ex-husband? Could she be with him?"

"Jack is in Spain. I called him this morning. He hasn't heard from her. He'll call if she shows up there or calls him. She won't, though."

Joe nodded. Julie was thankful he didn't probe for more information about Jack. Tash and her dad hadn't been close since the divorce. To be honest, they'd never been close. Jack always said he wasn't a "kid person"—whatever that meant.

"Who's the guy Tasha is with?" The concern on Joe's face comforted her.

"He's not a student here. He's not even from this country."

Joe straightened. "He's not a student? What's his name?"

"You wouldn't know him."

"His name." The words were an order.

"Luc Deschamps. He's from France." Julie gave him the information slowly, amazed at the change that had come over the usually mild-mannered statistician. "Why do you want to know? Do you know him?"

Joe stood abruptly. "No. I don't. Listen, I'm going to work from home today, but let me leave you my cell number. Call me if you need anything."

Julie nodded, bemused, and watched as he scribbled his number on her note pad. He paused at the door on his way out. "I'll talk to you soon."

"Okay."

He left in a swish of muscled leg and squeaky running shoes. What was that all about? Julie rubbed her forehead and wished that just one person in her life would act normally. When the rain began pelting her window, she put aside her work.

She got out her phone and tried calling every friend of Tash's that she could remember from high school. She knew Tash had stayed in close contact with most of them. None of her friends sounded as if they thought it particularly strange that Tash would be out all night and not home yet. "She's probably sleeping at a friend's, Mrs. Dancer, or her phone needs charging. I'm always forgetting to charge my phone," one of Tash's friends assured her.

Julie even went to Tash's Facebook page, though she knew her daughter rarely used it. Then she got in her car and drove around campus and town.

"Why are you eating directly out of a carton of chocolate ice cream?"

Julie took her spoon out of her mouth as Harry walked into the kitchen the next morning. "Because I've finished off Bas's cookies. What did you find out from Marguerite?"

"Nothing, but the Guardians have determined that Tasha and Luc were in Chicago with your mother."

"Chicago? Why? How do they know that?"

"Powerful Sensitives." Harry walked up to her, took the carton out of her hands and put it on the kitchen table. She let him, her mind busy with trying to figure out why Tash was in Chicago. "Is she still there? Can those Sensitives find her?"

"I'll tell you everything in a moment." Harry pulled her into his arms and Julie felt some of the tenseness drain from her muscles. Her ear rested over the steady beat of his heart, and she breathed deeply, the scent of him filling her.

"I'm going to smear chocolate on your white shirt."

"I don't care."

The phone rang, and Julie jumped back out of his arms and grabbed it from the table beside her. Since Tash had disappeared, she was never without it.

Her mother's number flashed on the face. "Mom!"

"Julie, honey." Her mother's blessed voice rushed through the phone receiver.

"Where are you? Are you okay?"

"I'm fine. I'm sorry I've been out of touch. Everything has been chaotic here. I'm at my apartment but only for half a second. Is Harrison with you?"

"Yes. Mom, Tasha's missing. Have you seen her?"

"The Gigis have been looking nonstop for her. I just got a call from Phyllis, who thinks she's finally located the local Gate of Gehenna. I'm heading there now with the rest of the Gigis. We're going to bust that Gate wide open." Julie could hear an excited buzz in the background. "I wanted to keep you and Harrison in the loop. I'll call as soon as I can." Her mother hung up.

"She hung up." Julie stared at the phone in disbelief and hit the redial button. "She said something about searching for Tasha, gates to Gehenna and getting Tash out." The phone clicked to her mother's answering machine.

Harry's calm voice broke through her confusion. "I spoke with Linda, who's with your mom. Tasha and Luc have been kidnapped by Skaven—rat people who work for the demons—and taken to Gehenna. Jean has sent out a message to all Triad in the area to gather. She's going to attempt to meld power and wield enough energy to break through to Gehenna."

At Julie's confused look, he clarified. "Gehenna is a name for Hell."

Julie sank down into one of the chairs at the kitchen table. "Rat people?" She jumped up again. "Demons want Tasha? Why?"

"Linda thinks it was a mistake on the part of the Skaven. The demons aren't stupid enough to totally flout all laws by taking a living Dancer and Shadow Walker. The entire Triad is up in arms. This kidnapping is uniting us in a way we haven't been since the Rift."

She frowned at his positive spin on the whole nightmare. Then his words sunk in. Her baby was in Gehenna. For a moment she couldn't think, she couldn't move, she couldn't breathe. "Will they hurt her? How can we get her out? Should I call my pastor?"

Harrison stepped close to her, his body warmth a comfort. "She's okay, Julie." His voice reassured her. "I met with the head demon's lieutenants last night, trying to negotiate a release. I meet with them again this afternoon."

"There's a head demon?" She rubbed her forehead. This was too much, but she refused to lose it. Tash needed her.

"His name is Abigor."

The bad guy had a name. "When did you find out she'd been taken?"

"Right after I left Marguerite."

"And you didn't let me know?" Fear and confusion switched into fury. He backed up a couple of steps, a wary look on his face.

"I believed if I could get Natasha released quickly, you wouldn't have to live with the fact that she was in Gehenna." His chin set in a firm line. "I didn't want you to worry needlessly."

"You didn't want me to…" She closed her eyes, counted to ten and reminded herself that he didn't have children. "I have been worried out of my mind. I thought my daughter might be dead. How could knowing the truth possibly be worse than not knowing where she is?"

"No mortal has ever left Gehenna."

She opened her mouth, took a deep breath, closed it. His expression made her very nervous. "Ever? In the whole history of the world?"

"Ever."

"But Linda thinks they were taken by accident."

"For which the demons are duly apologetic. They just don't want to give them back. But they will. Abigor will be forced to release them."

Julie nodded. "Yes, he will." She calmly walked over to the table, picked up the melting ice cream and tossed it in the sink. She carefully rinsed her hands, wiped them on a piece of paper towel and then turned back to him. A fire built in her chest. "I want my daughter. Take me to the Gate of Gehenna."

"No." His expression was implacable.

"Why?" Her voice remained absolutely level.

"The demons are unusually curious about you. I won't allow it."

"My daughter is in danger." Was the man totally clueless? She'd spent eighteen hours of hard labor to bring this child into the world. Okay, maybe she should have used an epidural. But she'd bought into the whole natural childbirth thing (thank you, Mother) and had felt every single second of her body's struggle to birth her baby. She'd gone without sleep countless nights because Tash ate on a two-hour schedule. Later she'd gone without sleep countless nights because she'd worried about the effect the divorce would have on Tash, or because Tash stayed out late with friends, or because Julie had to figure how to squeeze out extra money for band trips or music lessons or soccer camps. She'd laughed, battled, cried and triumphed with her daughter. Part of her heart and soul lived in that child. Did Harry really think she'd let a few demons take her away?

"I will get my daughter back, even if it means blowing the Gates of Gehenna off their hinges."

"No energy wielder has ever crossed into Gehenna of his own accord. The way is barred to all but immortals."

"So I'll get an immortal. They can't be all that hard to find. God, angels and demons, right?"

Harry waved his hand in a vague gesture. "And one or two others."

"What do you mean—'one or two others'? Who are those one or two others?" Julie stared at him, thinking. "Bascule! Bas is an immortal, isn't he?" She almost hopped up and down in excitement. Bas could get her into Gehenna and help her rescue Tash.

"I don't know if Bas is immortal. I know he's been around for a very long time." Harry watched her, concern on his face. "He doesn't talk much about himself."

"Where is he? I'll ask him."

"I don't know where he is."

He could find out, but obviously he wasn't going to. Julie folded her arms across her chest. "Okay. Then you take me to the Gates. I'll figure out what to do when I get there. Maybe Mom will be successful with her group energy thing."

"Julie, I'll negotiate for Tasha. Triad members are expressly forbidden to enter into any kind of contracts or bargains with demons. They always work out badly. The Balance and the Council are the only Triad members empowered to deal with Gehenna."

"Where is this negotiating taking place? In some time-warp neutral dimension?" Bas had mentioned those.

"Actually, we're scheduled to meet at a Starbucks in Chicago at five this evening."

"Demons like coffee?"

"Lattes. They're addicted. Abigor doesn't allow any coffee in Gehenna."

"Must be hell—ha, ha." She cleared her throat at Harry's raised eyebrow and went on. "Take me with you. I promise to sip my house blend and not say a word."

"No. It's against the rules."

"If you don't take me with you, I'm going to go stand at the Gates of Gehenna and join with Mom," she threatened.

"No."

"You're the Balance. I'm giving you two choices. You have to weigh the respective merits of each and choose one."

"No, I don't."

"Harry, I'm deadly serious about this. You can't leave me out of the loop when it comes to my daughter. I'm going to go with you when you negotiate for her."

"No, you're not. I am the Balance, Julie." He stood straighter and his voice filled with confidence and authority as he eyed her, his face grim. "You are not going. My word is final."

"What's she doing here?" The handsome young man dressed in jeans and a white T-shirt juggled two paper cups of mocha latte and nodded toward Julie as he slid into a booth at Starbucks.

"I brought her." The tone of Harry's voice didn't invite further questions.

The man blew on his coffee and regarded her thoughtfully. With his shaggy brown hair, snub nose and open expression, he looked like he just stepped out of a Norman Rockwell painting. There should be a law against demons looking so nice. An equally attractive young woman squeezed in beside him, also carrying two cups of latte. She smiled sweetly at them both, settled back in her seat and raised one of the cups to her lips.

The young man broke the silence. "Abigor wants free

communication between demons and Triad members. No restrictions on contracts or bargains."

"No." Harry didn't even pause to consider the terms.

Julie nervously fingered her cup filled with plain black coffee. Surely Harry knew what he was doing. The outrageous demand was probably just an opening gambit on the part of the demons. Soon they'd settle into the real negotiations.

The woman shrugged and looked at her companion. "At least we got the latte." She slid back out of the booth, grabbed both of her cups and sauntered out the door. She turned back, a smirk on her face. "Guess we've got ourselves a Dancer and a Walker, too. They'll be so fun to play with."

The man grimaced an apology. "Stephanie isn't very polite." He held out his hand, which Harry ignored. When Julie's right arm jerked out of habit, Harry's left hand clamped down hard on it, holding it at her side. The man's grimace became an evil-looking grin. "I'll give your response to Abigor." He stood and reached for his cups.

"Wait." Julie couldn't let him leave. "Can we make a counter offer?"

The man paused and turned his blue-eyed gaze on her. He didn't look quite so much like a wholesome midwestern boy anymore. "Who are you?"

"Nobody." Harry interjected, firmly. "Goodbye, Jeffrey. Tell Abigor we'll talk when he's willing to quit playing games with us."

Jeffrey waved an impatient hand, his eyes still watching Julie. "What is your counter offer, woman?"

"I'll trade myself for Tasha." Julie hadn't thought it out, but once she said the words, they made perfect sense.

"You would come to Gehenna?"

"Yes." She would do anything to free her daughter.

"You would come of your own free will?"

"Y—" Harry's hand clamped over her mouth. Julie felt his sudden tension.

"No. We offer you nothing, Jeffrey. You'll have a war with the angels on your hands if you don't release both Natasha and Luc. Abigor knows this. He's putting off the inevitable in the hope of gaining something out of this mess."

"The woman has offered of her own accord to come to Gehenna. Free will decisions are allowed."

Harry released Julie's mouth, which was a good thing since people were beginning to look concerned. This was Chicago and a certain amount of odd behavior was ignored out of good manners, but the hand had been over her mouth long enough to look serious. Just before it slid away, a command echoed in her head. "Quiet!"

Julie licked her lips and then kept them shut. If angels were willing to go to war for her daughter, maybe she should sit and listen.

Harrison pushed out of the booth and stood to his full height. Today he wore a black silk shirt and black pants. He stared down at the demon, taller by at least two inches. He radiated power. "She has offered you nothing."

Julie felt the hair on the back of her neck rise at the authority in his voice. She, and everyone within hearing range, believed him.

The demon was obviously not similarly affected. Jeffrey snapped his fingers, and Julie's desperate voice floated between them.

"I'll trade myself for Tasha."

"You would come to Gehenna?"

"Yes."

He smiled and shrugged. "She offered, Harrison. She's fair game. Even Gabriel can't argue with that." He picked up his latte cups and let his gaze rest on Julie. "I'll give you three hours to get your life in order." He glanced at Harry. "See, I'm not a monster."

Harry didn't respond.

"What is your name, woman? Abigor will want to know who he has traded for."

Harry's sharp "No!" in her head didn't stop her. She wanted

the damn demon to know who she was. "My name is Julie Dancer."

Her mother's small living room always made Julie feel like she'd stepped into a crowded, magical jewelry box. Bright colors glittered around the room, taking the form of pillows, planters, sun catchers and assorted knick-knacks. Harry stalked through the gems likes a shadow. He filled the room with his presence, seeming to suck in all the brightness. He picked up a large crystal sitting on a stack of books and held it to the window as he spoke. Light danced around his blond hair, making a halo. "Abigor will release Tasha and Luc. He isn't stupid. You didn't need to sacrifice yourself." He turned to her, lowering the crystal. "I shouldn't have brought you with me."

Julie sat curled on the couch. "That was my decision. Is there a book called *Things You Should Never Say to a Demon*? Because if there is, I really need to get a copy."

She felt strange, like all of this wasn't really happening. How did she go about putting her life in order in three hours, when she hadn't managed that in a lifetime? She looked at the ruby red and blue clock on the wall. Make that two and a half hours.

When Tasha was released, she might not even have a chance to talk to her. Maybe she should write a letter—one that could be read at her memorial service—saying good-bye and promising to be there in spirit at all the major life events she would be miss out on. Things like Tasha's graduation, her wedding day, and the birth of her three darling children. Julie frowned. Those things she'd be missing all had to do with Tasha. Didn't she have any dreams for herself that she wouldn't get to experience? Of course she didn't. She'd been gliding through middle age, waiting for the slide into old age. Now that death—or life in Gehenna, whatever that could be called—was staring her in the face, she began to think that had been a pretty wimpy attitude on her part.

If she had her life to live over, she'd go back to college, paint a famous picture, climb Mt. Everest, swim the English Channel or maybe do a slow striptease until Harry couldn't control himself and went mad with lust.

"What are you smiling about? Don't you realize the trouble you're in?" Harry stood in front of her, looking down at her in much the same way he'd looked at the demon in Starbucks.

"Harry, have you ever been mad with lust?"

His jaw went rigid, and his gaze seemed to burn like molten gold. For a long time he just stared at her. Then silently he nodded.

The air poofed out of Julie. She actually felt herself shrivel and deflate. She'd wanted him to say no. She didn't want there to be a woman in the world who drove him crazy with longing. "She's not dead by any chance, is she?" she asked hopefully, despising herself. What kind of sick person was she turning into?

His lips twitched. "No. But she's currently driving me insane because she won't focus on the problem at hand."

She closed her eyes for a moment, savoring the hot flow of joy that coursed through her. She wanted to be honest with him, since she might not see him again. "Sometimes I can't stop thinking about you, Harry. You're in my head like Marguerite is in yours, only I don't want you to leave. Will you be all right when I'm gone? You're sure that you'll be able to stop Marguerite from placing the second tie?"

His jaw worked for a moment, and then he nodded stiffly. "The Council is set to gather and weave a protective ring. I'll simply stay in the circle from sunset to sunrise tonight and Marguerite will not be able to place the second tie. The spell will be broken."

"Tonight! With everything going on, I'd totally forgotten the new moon was tonight." How could she have done that? "What time is sunset?"

"7:32 pm here in Chicago."

"You should go to the Council circle, now! What if she travels somewhere in the world where sunset is a different time?"

"This is a powerful spell. Distance will weaken her ability. She'll want to be as close to me as possible."

Julie glanced at her watch. "We have about ninety minutes

until you need to get in the circle." She would know he was safe before the demon came and got her. "After, when the curse is blocked, will you keep an eye on Mom and Tasha for me, make sure they're all right?"

"Stop talking like you're actually going to go to Gehenna. That is not going to happen."

"Okay, but in case it does, I need to do three things. I'm going to call Joe and let him know I might not be at work for a while—okay, for eternity. Then I need to call Dorie and tell her what's happening. Otherwise, she'll have my face on milk cartons and every social media site around the world. Then I want you to take me to whatever Gehenna Gate Mom is at so I can say goodbye to her."

He lifted her off the couch, his grip hurting her upper arms. "You are not going to Gehenna. The very fact that demons hold your daughter constitutes duress. Your statement was not made with free will."

She blinked at him. "That argument makes a lot of sense."

"I'm the Balance." He reminded her, voice dry. "I always make sense."

"So how do we keep Jeffrey from transporting me to the hot place?" The hands on the clock seemed to be moving abnormally fast.

"We go directly to his boss, Abigor."

"And how do we go directly to Abigor?"

"Through the silver phone, his private line."

"You have a silver phone?"

"No. Bas does."

"Why don't you have your own phone?"

Harry took a deep breath. "I have never heard anyone ask as many questions as you."

"How else am I supposed to figure things out?"

He seemed to gather his patience. "The Balance has never had a direct link to the immortals. We keep separate as much as possible."

"That's a great non-answer. Right along the lines of my favorite parental response—'Because I said so.'"

"We'll get into the history of the Triad and its relations with immortals another day." His patience hadn't lasted long. "I need to find Bas. Now."

"He left after the last batch of cookies came out of the oven. He didn't say where he was going."

"Bas comes and goes as he pleases. Sometimes years elapse between visits." His grip had loosened, but he still held her securely. His gaze seemed riveted on her mouth.

"Will you be able to find him before you need to get in the circle?" She found it difficult to focus with him watching her. She licked her dry lips.

"Yes," he answered absently, as if his mind were already flitting toward Bas. Not a shred of doubt marked his face.

"Will Abigor release Tasha and Luc today?"

"Probably. He's played his game. He'll let them go before there are lasting repercussions." Harry's gaze shifted to her eyes. "I have to leave." He didn't move.

"I know."

"If Tasha and Luc aren't returned before, Bas will deal with Abigor while I'm in the circle."

"Good. That's good."

"Yes." Still he didn't leave.

"Well, bye. See you soon." She didn't move, either.

"Did you mean what you said?" The question pushed out from him, like he hadn't wanted to ask, but couldn't hold back the words.

She crinkled her brow, not sure what he meant.

"About me being in your head. About not wanting me to leave."

She lowered her eyes to his chest level, embarrassed that she'd let him know how much she cared. He'd already told her that they didn't have a future because he was the Balance, not to mention she was a Dancer. If she were of a romantic nature, she'd envision them like Tony and Maria from *West Side Story*, kept cruelly apart by a bigoted society. Except, of course, Harry was a leader in that bigoted society, so the comparison didn't fit. And they were a lot older than Tony and Maria. In fact, she could be their mother, which was a sobering thought. And she didn't want to think about the tragic end of the movie, even though she didn't believe in happily ever after.

"Where do you go when your eyes glaze over and you seem to sink inside yourself? I want to know what's going on in your head." Harry pulled her closer, bringing her back to reality.

"No you don't. I was thinking about *West Side Story*."

His lips touched her neck. "I'm talking about our relationship and you're thinking about *West Side Story*."

Her pulse skipped. "Great movie. I have it on DVD—"

His lips silenced her, making her forget all about Tony and Maria and causing beautiful music—of course by Leonard Bernstein—to fill her.

He lifted his head. "Did you mean it?"

"Yes." She could barely speak.

His muscles relaxed and he just held her, enveloping her in his arms. A bird tweeted six times in the kitchen.

"That's Mom's bird clock." Julie didn't want to be reminded of reality, or of how fast time was zipping by. "You only have an hour and a half until sunset."

Harry took a step back, his arms dropping slowly. "I'll find Bas," he said. Then he smiled slowly. "I liked the music."

He popped out of the room, quicker than a heart beat.

At least it hadn't been fireworks. Mom would have been upset with scorch marks on the ceiling. Julie sighed and looked around. Even with all the warm, familiar clutter, the room felt empty with Harry gone. She picked up a green and yellow knit afghan from the back of the bright red couch and wrapped herself in it. What if something happened, and Harry couldn't find Bas? What if he didn't make it to the circle in time? What if the demon came and whisked her away?

She headed for the purse she'd left on the small lacquered table just inside the door. She pulled her phone from the outside pocket and searched inside the purse for the note Joe had handed her. Surprisingly, given the internal state of her purse, she found it.

Sitting back on the couch, she covered as much of her body as possible with the afghan and dialed Joe's number.

Thirteen

"YES?" JOE answered, his voice distracted. The noise in the background made it very hard to hear him.

"Joe? Where on earth are you?"

There was a pause on the line, then "Julie?" The background noise, it almost sounded like a lot of people moaning, dimmed as if he'd walked into another room.

"Are you at the scene of an accident, or did I interrupt something I shouldn't be asking about?"

"No, that's just the, uh, wind. I stepped in from outside. We should be able to talk now."

Writers have described the wind as "moaning" since the first rock scratches on stone. Not until today had Julie understood why. "Sorry to bother you, Joe, but I don't have Phoebe's phone number with me and I want to let you both know that I may not be able to make it into work for a while."

"Does this have to do with your daughter?" Joe's voice sharpened.

"I've found out where Tash is. I think she'll be okay, but I may have to leave the country," not to mention the known world, "and I'm not sure when I'll be back."

"Don't go anywhere with anyone but me!"

"Why not?" That was a weird thing to say. Was he going all alpha male possessive on her after one kiss? When he didn't respond, she continued. "I'll be okay. It's not a sure thing that I have to go, but if I do, would you please explain to everyone at work that I need to take some time off?"

"Julie, I think I can smooth things out."

What was he talking about? "What are you talking about? And answer my question this time."

Silence on the line. She could almost feel the air shimmer with his emotion. "I know who took Tasha. I'm trying to help get her free."

Whoa. "Joe, have you been drinking?" She'd never once seen him with alcohol, even at the winter holiday party at work (formerly known as the Christmas/Hanukah party, until Kwanzaa came along and the combined name became much too unwieldy. Some enterprising soul had tried to get everyone to call it the Kwistmaskah party, but that had just offended everybody). In fact, the only drink she every saw him with was his ever-present cup of latte.

Latte. Oh. My. God.

"Joe." A horrified whisper dribbled from her mouth. "You're a demon."

She hoped he'd laugh and accuse *her* of drinking. Instead, he said nothing, though she could still hear the faint howls of the wind, so she knew he was on the line.

Moans and howls. Oh. My. God.

"That isn't the wind, is it? Joe, you're in Hell!" Goosebumps formed on the back of her neck and she almost dropped the phone. Then she remembered. This was a good thing. Tasha was in Hell, too. "That's not Tash making that noise, is it?"

"No. Tasha is in a holding area. She's fine."

She closed her eyes, thankful for that brief bit of news. A totally tangential question occurred to her. "They have cell phone towers in Hell?"

"We don't need towers to make the phones work. And we call our home Gehenna." Did his voice sound more menacing now that she knew he was a demon, or was that her imagination?

A shiver worked its way down her back. Joe was a demon.

She'd kissed a demon. That couldn't be good. She cleared her throat. "I have several questions I'd like to ask you."

Her voice sounded calm and in control, which worried her. Any normal person would be either catatonic or screaming like a banshee. She felt icy, and angry. "But first I'd like to warn you, if you don't get your butt over to that holding area and get my daughter out of that place, you are dead meat."

"I'm immortal, Julie. You can't kill me."

"Okay. I'll do something even worse." Like what? Think, Julie, think. "If you don't bring Tasha to me, I'll make you regret every day of eternity. I'll make you suffer in ways you've never imagined."

"I'm in Gehenna, Julie." He said the words almost gently. "How are you going to top that?"

Okay, gloves off. What's the worse that could happen to an evil demon? "I'll petition God to have you sent to Heaven."

"Like that will ever happen." He didn't sound worried.

"I'll tell everyone at work who you really are."

"Will that be before or after I tell them who you really are?" Now he sounded amused.

"How about bamboo under the fingernails or rolling you down a hill in a nail-studded barrel?" She knew the threats were weak, even as she said them.

"Baby leagues, Julie. You've been watching old movies haven't you? Modern human torture techniques are much more sophisticated."

"Okay, look. So I'm lousy at torture. Joe, please. For the sake of our friendship. Get Tasha out of there. And that Luc person, too," she tacked on, not wanting to leave anyone in Hell who didn't belong there.

"It's not that simple, Jules. There will be a cost to you if I do."

Julie went on high alert. Harry's warning about deals with demons made her wary. "Abigor doesn't have a choice. The angels will attack if he doesn't let Tash and Luc go. He's not allowed to take Triad members."

"Oh, he'll let them go. But what condition will they be in? Make no mistake, Abigor has bargaining power in this game."

"I don't understand, Joe. What does he want to bargain for? Why is he risking war?"

"Abigor tires of the old rules. Now that he's vanquished his archenemy, Ashakarin, he's turned his focus toward earth. You've heard of the increase in crime and gangs? That's our crew. People are afraid. That is the first step. Abigor wants dominion over the earth."

"How evil!" But clever. Even she locked her doors now.

"He's planted the seed, Julie. He'll slowly turn fear to chaos. More and more, we will walk the earth until we control it."

"What's your role in all this? Are you on earth to create chaos in the research lab?"

He laughed. "You seem to be doing that job yourself."

She gripped the phone tighter, but said nothing.

He sighed. "My sole purpose on earth is to seduce you."

"Ha! Like I haven't heard that line a few times." He didn't laugh. She swallowed hard. "Okay, say I take that statement at face value. Why would a demon be sent to earth to seduce a social worker?"

"Abigor wants you in Gehenna, willingly. I thought making you fall for me would be the easiest way to convince you to come to Gehenna."

"Bad choice and big ego, Demon Boy. Kidnapping my daughter works better. Why does this Abigor fellow want me in Gehenna?"

"The prophecy, Julie."

"What prophecy?"

"'A daughter shall be born in light and shadow, a guardian who rises out of evil. Wild power circles her and chaos follows her footsteps.'" Joe recited the words. "That's from the Triad book of prophecy, *Words of Wisdom*."

"So what has it got to do with me?" Julie shifted, uneasy.

Joe didn't answer her directly. "The demon prophecies are

remarkably similar to yours, only they make a bigger deal about the mayhem and destruction part, as you might expect. They speak of the One who will usher in an age of chaos."

"I repeat, what has this got to do with me?"

"Let's just say that Abigor considers you a 'person of interest'. He's been waiting for you to come into your power. He believes you might be the Queen of Chaos, the One."

She did not need this right now. "I may only clean my bedroom once a week, and, okay, my junk mail pile is out of control, but that hardly qualifies me to usher in an age of chaos." A thousand questions floated in her brain. How to free Tasha kept rising to the top. "Here's the deal. Free Tasha, and I'll come with you to Gehenna.

"No." Joe's voice hardened. "This is the deal. Come with me to Gehenna and I'll free your daughter."

"Stop talking this way!" Her semi-calmness evaporated. Her brain couldn't handle any more. "Just get Tasha and Luc, and come back to work and we'll pretend like none of this ever happened."

"Don't start making up a fantasy world for yourself, Julie. If you want to see your daughter again, meet me at the Gates of Gehenna at 7:30 pm."

"Joe, how can you threaten me and my daughter like this? You're a statistician. A thoughtful, reasonable…demon."

"One hour, Julie. Be there at 7:30 pm., or your daughter will be sorry." The phone cut off.

Julie stared in disbelief at the phone in her hand. She pushed the redial button, but got a non-working number.

Okay. Think. She took a deep breath. She couldn't think. Her mind just whirled like a mini-tornado inside her head. But what was there to think about anyway? She had no choice. When Jeffrey came to get her, she'd already be gone. Call her crazy, but she'd rather go to Gehenna with a demon she knew than one she'd just met in a coffee shop.

She was halfway out the door before it hit her. She didn't know where the Gates of Gehenna were located.

"Dorie, I don't have much time, so I need you to hurry. Get on the Internet and plug Chicago Gates of Gehenna, Chicago Gates of Hell, anything like that, into a search engine." Her mother's laptop was nowhere to be found, so Jean must have taken it with her.

"Jeez, Jules, it's almost seven. I need to give the boys a bath and get them into bed."

"Tash's life depends on it."

"Jim, get the boys started in the tub!" Dorie yelled to her husband. "Okay," she said in a more normal voice, "I'm heading toward the office. Logging on to my computer. Clicking on the Internet browser...."

The play-by-play comforted Julie. She closed her eyes and waited, seconds ticking off in her head.

"Hey, did you know that in 1880, Rodin created models for something he called the Gates of Hell?"

"Are they currently in Chicago?" She somehow managed not to yell.

"No, doesn't look like it."

"Dorie! Focus. Did I not make it clear that time is of the essence?"

"Sorr-eeee." There was a pause. "I'm scrolling through the hits. While I do that, fill me in on what's happening."

Talking was better than biting her nails. Julie quickly brought Dorie up to date.

"Okay, so Tasha is in some holding cell in Hell. And in order to save her, you have to trade yourself for her?"

"Yes."

"Why do they want you?"

Dorie always had very good questions. "I might be the prophesied Queen of Chaos."

"Is there a King?"

"Joe didn't mention that." Julie could hear the rising note of hysteria in her own voice.

"Forget the prophecy, Julie. You know who you are." Dorie

sounded remarkably calm, an anchor in the midst of madness.

"I do?"

"You do," she replied firmly. "I'm almost through the first ten screens. There's nothing, Jules, nothing useful."

Julie stomped down the panic that wanted to explode through her body. "Thanks anyway."

"I may not have any super powers or anything, but if there is anything I can do—anything—just let me know. Humans can be pretty resourceful people."

Julie swallowed the lump in her throat. She wished Dorie were with her right now. But she had a husband and two kids and needed to be kept safe. "I'll be in touch as soon as I can."

She clicked off her phone and looked at her watch. Thirty minutes to go. Unless Harry and Bas showed up, there was nothing to do but hop into a cab and drive around the city. If her mother had amassed the local Triad members, surely a crowd at this time of the evening would be noticeable. Her mother never did anything quietly.

She picked up the pad beside the phone, intending to leave a message for Harry. Something along the lines of: *Off to save daughter through trade-off with demon. Hope your curse is broken and you have a happy life. Affectionately, Julie.*

She paused, pen to paper, trying to think of something more personal to write. Nope, she couldn't come up with anything. She tapped the pad in frustration and noticed the small indentations on the pink paper. Suddenly, a scene from *North by Northwest* clicked into her head—the one where Cary Grant is in Eva Marie Saint's hotel room, trying to figure out where she's gone. Eva receives a message on the telephone, writes it down on a pad of paper and then tears off the top sheet and puts it in her purse. After she leaves, Cary runs a pencil over the sheet that had been beneath it, and is able to read the message.

Mom had gotten a phone call from Phyllis about the location of the Gates of Gehenna. Had she jotted it down on her note pad? Holding her breath, Julie traded the pen for a pencil and rubbed it sideways, firmly, across the paper. A phrase appeared in white: Devil's Brew Coffee Shoppe.

The portal to Gehenna went through a coffee shop. How diabolically clever.

Grabbing her purse, she headed out the door. She had twenty minutes to find the place.

"Here you go, lady. Devil's Brew. Best damn coffee in Chicago." The taxi driver, who drove like he was permanently wired on caffeine and therefore should know, pulled up to a trendy brick coffee shop just off of Michigan Avenue in an upscale shopping area. An extra twenty had gotten Julie there in fifteen minutes. She threw more money at the driver and got out, barely noticing when he drove away.

Everything else on the block, mostly boutique clothing stores, had already closed. A red, neon "Open 24 Hours" sign blinked in the coffee shop window. Next to it, painted directly on the glass, was a figure of a red devil with horns and a pointed tail, drinking a cup of coffee that had a little flame on it. The word "Heavenly!" floated in a thought bubble over his head. Too cute.

The coffee shop was lit, but looked deserted from her position on the street. Where were Mom and her entourage? Was she at the right place? Was Devil's Brew a franchise and she'd picked the wrong one? Had her mother just written that word on her phone pad because she liked the coffee?

A thousand questions and doubts bombarded her as she pushed her way through the door. A little bell jingled, announcing her entrance. Round, wooden tables were scattered around the room, interspersed with overstuffed chairs pushed together in cozy seating arrangements. Plants and oak abounded, as well as the scent of strong, rich coffee. A polished oak counter ran along the wall to the left. A young woman emerged from a door behind it, a welcoming smile on her face.

"Hello. Can I help you?" The woman appeared to be in her mid-twenties. She wore jeans and a white T-shirt, covered with a bright, orange bib apron. The same coffee-guzzling devil from the window decorated her oversized pocket. Her brown hair was pulled back in a neat ponytail, and her blue eyes sparkled with more energy. Julie glanced at the big clock on the wall behind the woman—7:25 p.m.

Five minutes until her deadline. She marched up to the counter. "Excuse me, are you a demon?"

The woman's smile took on a wicked edge. "Some of my boyfriends have called me that. Who wants to know?"

"Julie Dancer."

"Ah, Ms. Dancer. We've been expecting you. Have a seat, and I'll be right back."

The woman went back through the door behind the counter. At least Julie had the right place. She gripped the counter, trying to still the tension thrumming through her. She couldn't run. She had to do this. She had no choice.

At first she thought the loud noise pounding in her ears was her heart. Then she realized it came from the street. She ran back to the door and looked out. Mom marched down the sidewalk, followed by a group of elderly women in pink T-shirts. Behind them followed a crowd of people that extended halfway down the block. But what caused Julie to almost sink to the floor with relief was the sight of Harry. He strode on one side of Mom, Bas on the other. The cavalry had arrived. Too late, but she would have a chance to see Harry and her mom one more time.

She ran out the door onto the sidewalk. Harry did not look as happy to see her, as she was to see him.

"What in bloody hell are you doing here? You're supposed to be safe at your mother's." He stopped in front of her and barked out the question.

"She made a deal with me." Joe's voice came from behind her shoulder.

A collective gasp arose from the group now forming a large semi-circle around the coffee shop. The round, accusing eyes of the Triad members focused on her. She looked over her shoulder at Joe. His expression held a possessive quality as he smiled at her. Yikes.

"No." Harry's clipped voice brought her attention back to him. He stared calmly at her, waiting for her to deny it. "I told you it's forbidden for Triad members to enter into deals or contracts with demons."

"Harry, normally I wouldn't. But this is about Tash's life." Julie didn't want Harry to think less of her for breaking one of his precious rules.

"No matter what the cause, you do not make deals with demons. You're Triad."

"Is she?" Joe put his hand on her shoulder. "I don't think so." Harry's gaze sliced to the hand on her shoulder. He looked back at her, as if waiting for her to shrug it off. She stood quietly.

"Get your paws off my daughter." Jean rushed forward and pushed Joe backward, severing his connection with Julie.

"Mom!" Julie quickly glanced at Joe, but he seemed more amused than angry.

"Julie." Harry's hand reached out to her. "Come here."

She stared at his hand, imagining how it would feel in hers. Hard, warm, safe. With a sigh, she asked him the one question that mattered, studying his face as she did so. "Can you get Tasha out?"

"Yes." He responded with no hesitation. Honesty and determination were stamped on his features. "We've been in contact with Abigor."

"Can you guarantee that Abigor won't hurt her?"

"Can he?" He nodded toward Joe. She noticed he hadn't answered the question.

"Yes."

"Did you specifically ask him if Tasha would be returned to you unharmed?"

She racked her brain, trying to remember the conversation. "I guess I didn't, but he implied he could get her out safely if I made his deadline."

Harry rubbed a hand over his face, an unusual show of emotion for him. "Ask him, Julie," he growled the words.

Julie turned to Joe, aware of the hushed silence of the crowd. "Joe?"

Joe didn't look at her. He stared at Harry, his eyes cold and dead. "She may be released unharmed. That hasn't been negotiated yet."

Julie stepped away from him. Joe put a hand on her arm. "I'll talk to Abigor, Julie. He has no reason to harm your daughter or the boy. Come with me. I'll take you to Tasha and Luc now. You can see your daughter for yourself."

"What are the terms of your agreement?" Harry's voice broke the spell Joe was weaving.

Julie tried to remember the exact words. "I said almost exactly the same thing that I did in the coffee shop. I agreed to go to Gehenna with him for the release of Tash and Luc."

The crowd gasped, and her mother swore. Harrison's expression didn't change. He watched Joe with focused intensity. Julie felt unaccountably guilty, so she turned to Bas, who had been surprisingly silent through all this.

"Bas?" Her teacher usually had something to say about everything.

"This choice is yours alone, Julie." His expression was serious.

"The choice may be hers alone," Harrison interjected, "but she should know the consequences of any decision she makes. Julie." His commanding voice brought her gaze to his. "If you make a deal with this demon, if you survive and return from Gehenna, you will be brought for judgment before the Council. This is one of the most serious crimes you can commit."

"And if I don't make a deal with a demon? What happens to Tash?" And if she did, was there such a thing as a Triad lawyer?

"Abigor can't hold her. I'll not rest until your daughter is free," Harrison said firmly. His golden eyes, warm and steady, willed her to believe him, to trust in him. "Don't go with the demon. Stay."

"Come with me now." Joe touched her arm. "You'll have Tasha back home almost immediately, with none of the delays of negotiating with Abigor."

The clock struck the half hour and stilled. The last glimmer of light from the sun danced on the horizon. The world seemed to pause, waiting for Julie's decision.

She trusted Harrison with her life. With her daughter's life. She knew he would negotiate with Abigor, pull whatever strings he had to pull and free her daughter. She also knew he would not go into the protective circle of the Council while he did so. He would stay and fight for Tasha, and Marguerite would place the second tie. The tie he said would drive him insane.

She couldn't let him do that. Not when she had another way of saving Tash.

"Julie." Joe tugged at her arm.

She ignored him, her gaze still on Harry. "Harry, go home. Get into the circle. I'll get Tasha."

Emotion, stark and raw, flared in Harry's eyes. Julie stepped back, pushed by the anger on his usually impassive face. What had happened to the unemotional, cool-headed Balance? He looked livid with rage.

"I don't want you hurt," she whispered, as Joe pulled her back into the Devil's Brew. She turned toward the interior of the coffee shop, then took one last look behind her. No one followed. Her mother stood in front of a veritable army of Triad members, unmoving, looking older than Julie had ever seen her look.

Harry stood off to the side of the crowd, tall and alone. Despite the power etched in his bearing, she felt his vulnerability. He watched her with a terrible gaze that hurt. Bas stepped to his side and put a hand on his arm. Julie wasn't sure if the hand was meant to comfort or restrain Harry.

"Julie." When Bas spoke, even Joe stopped to listen. "Abigor and his demons will try to trick you. The trade is one thing, but after the trade is made, if you verbally agree to remain in Gehenna for any length of time—even a moment—it will bind you forever.

No one will be able to get you out."

Julie nodded, feeling more frightened and alone than she could ever remember. Joe tugged on her arm again, pulling her through the door into the coffee shop. The lighted room seemed too cheery and comfortable to be a reception area to eternal damnation.

She followed Joe behind the counter and went through the swinging door that led into the back room. The door closed behind them, locking out the light, leaving them in total darkness. Joe didn't falter, easily moving through the room. Julie's panic grew when she realized he didn't need the light to see.

What exactly had she gotten herself into?

Fourteen

TASHA SAT on a gleaming white floor, her back against a solid white wall made of some material she'd never seen. The wall had no seams and felt smooth and hard, like marble. The room's harsh lighting sprang from nowhere. The temperature felt slightly warm, but not uncomfortable. A faint scent of lemon tickled her nostrils, as if someone had just finished cleaning the room. She stretched out her legs, pointing her toes. Her white tennis shoes almost faded into the floor, making it look like her feet disappeared at the end of her blue jeans. Great. The all-white room must have caused sensory deprivation and she was now having hallucinations.

Luc hadn't spoken much since they'd been popped into this room from the park in Chicago. They had both worked slowly around the room, examining the smooth surfaces closely. There was no apparent means of escape, or even any vents for air to circulate, for that matter. But since she was breathing quite easily, that didn't seem to be a problem.

"How long do you think we've been here?" She looked over at Luc, who was sitting next to her.

He shrugged. "Perhaps several hours, perhaps several days."

Tasha tapped the face of her watch. "My watch isn't working."

"Time doesn't exist on the immortal planes. Your watch won't function until we return to our world."

"I wonder if that's why neither of us has had to go to the bathroom since we got here. Wait, we're on an immortal plane?"

Her brain screeched to a halt. She had no way to process that information. "I really should have taken more physics, or philosophy or maybe even Greek mythology in school."

"Nothing you could learn in a human school would help in this situation. You should have attended a Triad boarding school."

She turned her head to look at him. He was close to her, and she could see the faint, blond stubble on his jaw. She wondered if it felt as soft as it looked. His eyelashes, a deep brown at the base, became lighter along their length until the tips seemed to shimmer with silver. He appeared unaware of her fascination with his features. He stared straight ahead at the wall opposite them, his brow slightly furrowed.

She cleared her throat. "You went to a Triad boarding school?"

"Yes."

"Good. What do we do?"

"Nothing."

"I see I missed out on a great education."

"We're in a holding cell awaiting judgment. Nothing can be done until the demons decide what to do with us."

"Demons? When did they enter the picture? What do they have to do with Chicago rat gangs? Oh my God. Isthislike Purgatory?" Her words tripped out, her heart raced and black dots flashed in front of her eyes.

"You're not Catholic, are you?" There was a thread of amusement in his voice. "Demons aren't in Purgatory. They're in Hell. Or as they like to call it, Gehenna."

His arm wrapped around her shoulder. The weight of it felt like an anchor, holding her to reality. She drew in slow, measured breaths and stared resolutely at her denim-covered knees until her heart rate slowed to a brisk trot. "So what are their options?" she asked.

"Whose options?"

"The demons. What could they do to us?"

"They have two choices. They keep us here or they send us back."

"What are the chances they'll send us back?"

"I've never heard of it being done."

Tasha shivered, despite the warmth. She shifted out of his hold and half-turned so she could see his face. "The Skaven called me a prize."

"For once they have it right. You are a prize."

Tasha managed a small smile at that. "Do demons kidnap humans often?"

"No." He held her gaze. "But then, we're not truly human, Natasha."

She swallowed. "Maybe you're not, but I can't do what you do. I feel very human."

He touched a strand of her hair, his finger grazing her cheek. "You feel like you. You just thought that was human."

Whatever she was, she liked the way he made her feel. She leaned into his hand.

"I'm sorry," he said quietly.

"For what?" She lifted her head to look into his eyes.

"For bringing you to Chicago and placing you in a dangerous situation. For not being able to save you from this."

"It's not your job to save me. I'm a big girl. I made my own decision to go with you." Which, in retrospect, was looking pretty stupid. Why hadn't they just called her grandmother?

"Since you don't have all the information about this world you live in, you can't make truly informed decisions." The man was stubbornly determined to shoulder the responsibility for this mess. "You trusted me not to place you in danger."

"I guess I did. But, come on, we were going to visit my grandmother. Who would expect that we'd be attacked and sent to an immortal plane? Give yourself a break." And ditto that for herself.

A faint noise intruded into the room, the first they'd heard since arriving. She jerked, caught by a familiarity to the sound, and put her ear to the wall. All of her practical, rational thought processes gave way to hope.

"Do you hear voices?" She scrambled to her feet. "I hear voices."

"I believe that happens a lot here, low rumblings and moans, occasional screams."

"No, I hear my mom." She had to make noise, let her mother know she was here. She began beating the wall with her fist. "Mom. Mom! I'm here. Mom." She paused to listen. The voices, almost inaudible to begin with, grew fainter until they disappeared.

She slugged the wall repeatedly with hard, angry punches, calling out as loudly as she could. Her arm muscles hurt. Small smears of blood marked the whiteness from where her skin split against her knuckles. Her throat dried, and her chest heaved. Then Luc stood behind her. He pulled her away from the wall, turned her and dragged her against him.

"Shhhh." He whispered softly into her hair.

"That was Mom. I know it was." Tasha never cried, even the day her father moved out. She sagged against Luc, eyes dry and burning.

Luc tightened his arms but said nothing. He held her for what felt like hours, his hand rubbing her neck and the base of her skull, soothing her.

"All of my life, no matter what happened, I always knew mom and grandma were there for me. My safety net." She pushed away from his chest and looked up into his clear, steady eyes. "Do you have anyone like that?"

"Yes." His response was immediate. "Marguerite. Our parents died when we were young. Marguerite has always been there for me, and I for her."

"You understand then." Tasha took a shaky breath.

"Yes."

"Mom's not here, is she?"

"Her presence in this place is highly unlikely," Luc confirmed.

Tasha wrapped her arms around her body. "Then this really is Hell."

Joe pulled Julie quickly through the back room of Devil's Brew. Nobody was around, not even the young female demon who had waited on her when she arrived. Julie got a brief impression of shadowed counters and boxes that probably held pastries ready to be put in the display case out front. The smell of coffee weighted the air until taking a deep breath almost felt like taking a sip.

The rich scent triggered a memory that caused her panic to subside. She flashed back to school mornings when she'd wake to the smell of the coffee her mom always made for Dad. She'd lie in bed for precious extra minutes, knowing Mom would be making her a sack lunch while Dad cooked the one and only thing he knew how to make—oatmeal. She'd rush to get dressed and then run downstairs where all three of them would have oatmeal sprinkled with brown sugar and milk.

Then Dad would drop her off at school on his way to work. "Knock 'em dead, today, Princess," he'd say every morning as she got out of the car. She'd groan at his corny phrase, but she'd feel like a princess for a few seconds, forgetting her frizzy hair and the fact that she hadn't understood the last three math problems on her homework.

Joe tugged her hand, and she almost fell as she came back to the present. Her father's words stayed with her. She'd knock 'em dead today, and she'd get her daughter back.

Joe dragged her toward two large stainless steel doors. When he opened one, a frigid rush of air greeted her.

"The Gate to Gehenna is a walk-in freezer?" Julie asked in disbelief.

"Abigor has a sense of humor," Joe said flatly, not a hint of amusement in his voice. "A frozen entrance to the fiery place—get it?"

"Funny guy, that Abigor." The freezer was pitch black. Julie couldn't tell how big it was. The cold assaulted her nose, freezing her nasal passages with each breath. Joe walked into the dark cavern, and Julie followed. Joe pulled the inside handles of the freezer door, the room growing even darker as he closed them.

Suddenly, a small shadow squeezed through the door.

"You're not going without me." Her mother's voice, breathless but resolved.

Joe swore. "How did you get past the wards I placed?"

"There are Shadow Walkers and Penumbrae outside, along with the Dancers. Tonight is the beginning of the full moon. Your wards won't hold against their combined power on a night like tonight."

"Go away, Jean Dancer."

"Like I'm going to listen to you? My daughter is not going to Gehenna to rescue my granddaughter while I sit on earth twiddling my thumbs. Take me, or I'll gather enough Triad members to split your Gates wide open and give every human in Chicago the grand tour of your stinking homestead."

Joe sighed. "You are trouble, Jean Dancer. You may come, but I have a feeling I'm going to regret this decision."

"Mom." Julie rushed to her mother. "Stay here. I promise I'll bring Tasha back."

"No arguing!" Her mom used a tone of voice Julie was very familiar with. She then turned to Joe. "Now get on with it before I turn into an ice cube."

Joe gave Julie the look that a lot of people gave her after talking with her mom. Sort of a combination of frustration and disbelief. Julie did what she always did in response. She shrugged.

Joe grimaced and locked the freezer door from the inside, muttering something about how he should have done that sooner. Dim light, seemingly coming from nowhere, filled the room. A brief humming noise surrounded them, and then Joe opened the doors again. White light spilled into the freezer, the glare so bright Julie couldn't see beyond the door.

Joe stepped forward and took her arm in a courtly gesture. He placed her mother's hand on his other arm. "Ladies, we've arrived in Gehenna."

With that brief announcement, he stepped with them into the light.

Harrison turned to glare at Bas. The man still had a hand on his arm. "Let me go." He spoke with a quiet ferocity.

"She chose to take this journey without you to keep you safe," Bas said. "Don't negate her sacrifice."

"No." He wanted to deny what she'd done, the danger she was in.

"You can't stop her." Bas released his arm but Harrison knew it was too late to follow her.

"Get to the Council circle," Bas ordered. "Now."

Harrison didn't move. Julie was gone. She'd made a deal with a demon and entered Gehenna, in part to keep him safe from Marguerite's spell. If, against all odds, she returned, he would have to answer her sacrifice by sitting in judgment on her. There was no doubt that with all the witnesses tonight, she would be brought before the Council for breaking Triad law.

For the first time ever, Harrison considered walking away from the Triad, from his calling to be the Balance.

He heard Bas make a sound almost like a growl beside him. "Harrison. Now is not the time to act like a man in love. Move it!"

A man in love? Harry was still framing a suitable retort when Bas impatiently grabbed him by the shoulders and whisked him into the circle.

Neither noticed the silver-haired woman standing a half-block away, hidden in the shadows of an awning-covered door.

"Shouldn't Gehenna be hot and reddish with a lot of flickering shadows? I thought stepping into the light would happen in Heaven," Julie whispered across Joe to her mother as she blinked rapidly, wishing for a pair of sunglasses. She felt like she'd stepped into the sterile spaceship of *2001, A Space Odyssey*. Everything looked post-modern and much too white.

"I like to think of Heaven as having ambient lighting," Jean whispered back. "Warm and kind of cozy."

"Oh, nice. I like that too."

Joe rolled his eyes and quickened his pace.

Julie broke into a trot to keep up. For a guy with short legs, he was quick. Her mother had trouble with the pace, breathing heavily. "Slow down or you'll be dragging Mom."

He glanced at her mother and slowed. "Sorry."

A voice from behind made her jump. "Being a demon means never having to say you're sorry. You've been on earth too long, Josephius, if you're apologizing."

Joe came to an abrupt halt, and all three of them turned toward the voice. It was Jeffrey, the Norman Rockwell demon from Starbucks.

He frowned when he saw Julie. "Does the Big Guy know you brought this one with you, Josephius? He wants all contracts cleared through him, first."

Joe's lips thinned. "I'm heading to speak with Abigor now."

"He wouldn't approve my free-will contract with this babe earlier today. He refused to let me hold her to her word and bring her here."

Babe? Julie felt a small glow that anyone would consider her a 'babe.' Then the rest of what he said sunk in. "What? Abigor wouldn't have let you take me here? Why didn't you tell me? I thought you were going to come and snatch me away."

"Oh yeah. Sorry." He smirked as he put exaggerated emphasis on the last word. "What was I thinking? We demons don't like to worry people."

Joe ignored the demon's words, but he didn't look as confident as he had.

Jeffrey looked her up and down and then shook his head. "Abigor's not big on mistakes. You remember what he did to the last demon who messed up? Oh yeah, that was you."

Voices could be heard approaching from down the hallway. Jeffrey laughed maliciously. "Here he comes now. Guess we'll find out what he thinks of the company you brought."

Julie, watching Joe, shivered as the blood dropped out of his face. He went completely white. Curious as to what could cause a demon to be so scared, she looked toward the group approaching them. Seven men walked quickly down the hallway, their dark suits smudges against the seamless white of the walls and floor. As they got closer, she heard her mother gasp and glanced quickly at her. Jean put out one hand to steady herself against the wall, her face as pale as Joe's.

Julie's gaze swiveled again to the men, seeking out the reason for her mom's shocked expression. She met the eyes of the tallest man, striding in front of the group. Everything inside her stilled.

Seconds, maybe years, passed. As if in slow motion, her heart started beating again, and joy pulsed through her with each pump of blood. Then she realized the significance of what she was seeing.

"Daddy," she wailed. "You went to Hell!" She wanted to run to him, to hug him, but her legs wouldn't move. Joe's hand had tightened painfully on her arm.

"Daddy?" Joe hissed in a croaky voice.

Her father came to a halt several feet in front of them. His eyes traveled from her to her mother. He stood slightly over six feet tall, as strong and powerful as she remembered him. His black suit didn't have a single crease and his shoes reflected the light as if they'd just been polished. A salesman by trade, he'd always been meticulous about his clothes, very unlike her mother. A thought struck her. Was this the outfit he'd been buried in? She tried to remember, but couldn't. The memories of that day were locked in a haze of sorrow.

She'd slipped two pieces of paper into his pocket while he lay in the casket. One had been written by her and one was a picture drawn by Tasha—their personal goodbyes to the man they had loved. Had he seen them?

He hadn't said a word yet. His hair was combed back from his widow's peak, immaculate, the same thick mix of silver and black that he'd had even when she'd been small and he'd been younger. His thin face looked the same, with the high forehead and sharp cheekbones. His blue eyes lit with some emotion that she couldn't read, but he didn't look happy.

Julie shook her head, confused. What was Daddy doing in

Hell? Okay, so he lost his temper sometimes, and he and mom constantly "debated" (her mom's word) about every debatable thing, including whether to go to church on Sundays (Mom went, Dad didn't), which had obviously been a big mistake on Dad's part. But Dad was basically a good person—wasn't he? Her mom and dad had loved each other with a passion that she'd never found in her marriage, with the kind of passion she'd begun to feel for Harry. Dad didn't deserve to be in Hell.

Her anger started to build, growing and stretching. She wanted to have a word with God about the whole final judgment process. Heat crackled along her skin, a heat she hadn't felt since her powers first released.

Her father's eyes flashed to her, alert. The men with him took a step back. Good. She hoped they could see how upset she was. She'd negotiate with Abigor for Dad's release as well as Tasha's. She wasn't leaving her father here.

Her mother suddenly sagged, leaning against the wall. Julie broke Joe's hold and went to her, holding her arm. Her skin felt like ice. "It's Daddy, Mom," Julie whispered, her eyes still on her father. She didn't doubt that her mother recognized him; she just needed to say the words out loud.

Her father made a sharp movement with his hand, and everyone, Joe included, melted away. Just the three of them stood in the quiet hall.

"Abe?" Her mother's voice didn't sound like her.

"You always were a foolish woman." He stared at her mother as if he couldn't stop looking at her. He'd watched her that way when he'd been alive. "You shouldn't have come here."

"What are you doing here?" Jean struggled to stand straight. Dad didn't step forward to help her, the way he would have when he was alive.

"This is where I am."

The phrase struck Julie as odd. "You mean you were damned after you died." Julie clarified slowly, hanging on to her mother's arm.

"No." Her father's eyes seemed to slice through her. "That's not what I mean."

Julie frowned, too confused to try to sort it out. "Have you seen Tasha? She's here, too." How bizarre was that? Her whole family in Hell. "Don't worry, Dad. I'm going to hunt down this Abigor guy. I'll get you, Tash and Mom out of here."

"How are you going to do that?" her father asked.

She didn't want to tell him that Abigor might be willing to trade them for her, because it didn't make a whole lot of sense. Maybe he needed a social worker, or wanted some research done. "I'll think of something," she finally said, when one of her father's thin eyebrows rose in question.

He regarded her steadily. "I'm Abigor."

"No." Julie shook her head in denial, aware of how still her mother stood. "Abigor is this master demon guy. You're Abe. My dad. An insurance salesman. A dead insurance salesman."

He continued to watch them, not saying anything more. Abe. Abigor. Julie refused to allow her mind to make the connection. Her father was not a head demon. That would make her part demon. No. No. No.

Her mother took a deep breath and then finally spoke. "Why?" Jean asked quietly.

"A great war waged in Gehenna. The battle for dominance was not going well. Ashakarin, my enemy, had gained ascendancy in the war. He would not look for me in the home of a powerful Dancer while my forces regrouped."

"You ran and hid on earth and duped me into marrying you so you could hide from Ashakarin?" Her mother sounded outraged, more like her normal self. "You lying, gutless demon spawn!"

Julie stiffened at the insult. Hey, she was demon spawn herself.

Abigor's face remained impassive. "You were…unexpected," he told Jean. "I stayed much longer than I should have, against the advice of my generals. I left only as the final battle began because my personal leadership was needed."

"You lied to me."

"Yes."

"I loved you with my whole heart. I grieved for you. I still grieve for you." Julie felt her mother's pain and sorrow. Her betrayal.

Abigor nodded. "I know."

"You've damned our daughter by fathering her. That's the worst sin of all, Abe."

Julie froze. She was damned?

"Our daughter makes her own choices. She alone among us has that power. I have given her that much."

"What do you mean?" Jean asked.

Yeah, Julie silently echoed. What did he mean?

"Our daughter is the product of the most powerful demon family and the most powerful Dancer family. She also carries powerful Walker blood."

"What are you talking about?" Jean asked.

"Your mother wasn't kidnapped, Jean. She went to be with Timothy Walker, your true father, the ruling Lion of Great Britain."

"No!" That came from Julie. Her mother was strangely silent.

"They couldn't marry because their families wouldn't allow it, but he gave her the Sky Plate as a pledge of his love. Their children would have been banished as wild powers."

"Did my father, my mother's husband, know that he wasn't my true father?" Jean asked, finally speaking.

"No. Your mother couldn't tell him and risk your banishment. Your mother refused to send you to boarding school, afraid you might exhibit the wild powers of a mixed child. She negated your powers as much as possible."

"Until recently, I thought my only power was that of a Sensitive. When I began working with the Gigis, they showed me that I, too, could wield energy in other ways."

Abigor nodded. "Your mother met your father again at a

Triad gathering when you were fifteen. Once they saw each other, they decided they couldn't live apart. Your mother ran off with the Walker, planning to come back for you later. Instead, she and the Walker were killed in an accident, and their deaths started a war that almost destroyed your Triad."

"Oh my." Julie put an arm around her mother, feeling the tremor that went through her.

"Love can make people do stupid things." Abigor watched Jean as he said the words. Then he turned to Julie. "I want to talk to your mother alone." He moved his arm. In the blink of an eye, Julie found herself in a white-walled room.

Damn him! Oh, wait. That would be redundant. Julie slowly sank to the floor, leaning her back against one wall as she stared at the one opposite.

She trusted her mother to be able to hold her own against her father. That had never been a problem in the past. She pinched herself, hard, hoping this was some bizarre nightmare and she'd wake up in her bed. She broke the skin on her arm, but remained in the silent white room.

Her dad was a demon! And not just any two-bit demon. He called the shots in Gehenna. She closed her eyes and let that truth sink into her reluctant psyche.

She was the offspring of evil. A bad seed. Demon genes, if demons had genes, were part of the building blocks of who she was. What exactly did that mean? Did she have the genetic disposition for evil? When under stress, would she suddenly do something like hang her crucifixes upside down or sacrifice virgins?

She jumped up, unable to even think about it. No. No. No. She didn't want to be a demon. Aside from any other ramifications, there was no way she and Harry could ever have any kind of relationship. If the rules didn't allow him a relationship with a Dancer, they sure as hell wouldn't allow one with a demon/Dancer/Walker hybrid.

She put up a big red stop sign in her head, a neat little trick that a cognitive psychologist had taught her to use when she wanted to quit thinking unhealthy thoughts. Thinking about her relationship—or non-relationship—with Harry led her down a dark tunnel with no light at the end of it.

She straightened her shoulders and reviewed her choices. She could succumb to Post Traumatic Stress Disorder, or she could tuck this trauma into her subconscious—to be dealt with later in intensive therapy—and figure out how to accomplish her original mission to save her daughter. Of course, after saving Tash, she'd have the hard job of explaining to her that Grandpa was a demon. And that she better compare family trees with the cute hunk of a Walker she was dating to make sure they weren't related.

Julie leaned her forehead against the smooth wall and groaned. The red stop sign wasn't working. She had a feeling that orange barrels and wooden roadblocks wouldn't stop these thoughts. She could almost wish for the good old days when she'd found out her husband thought she was boring, and she would have to raise her daughter as a single parent.

A thin thread of something trickled through her pity party, tugging her out of her funk. She sucked in her breath and lifted her head, trying to capture it again. That something felt like Tasha. Tasha was near.

Both her hands came out and touched the wall. She felt energy flowing like static across a television set. She jumped, snatching her hands away. Slowly she put them back, wonder building inside her. In the midst of the chaos, she felt the familiar thread. The life force that she recognized as her daughter.

She took a step away from the wall and considered her options. Somewhere inside her, if she could only access it, she had the power to get out of this room and follow the energy trail to her daughter. She knew this with a deep certainty.

She tried to remember what Bas had taught her. "You don't need to look at something to see it," he'd told her one day in her kitchen, when he'd been trying to teach her to transport a book from her bedroom into the kitchen. She hadn't known what he meant then, and she still didn't know, but the words kept running through her head as if they were a key.

An hour later—at least she thought it was an hour later, her watch had stopped working—she kicked at the wall in frustration. She really, really hated cryptic phrases. Why couldn't people just say what they meant, straight out?

She'd tried closing her eyes and letting her senses "see" how to get out of the room. All she had to show for her efforts were several large bruises from walking into the wall. She'd tried looking through and beyond the wall with some magical inner sight, but she didn't seem to have a magical inner sight. Then she'd thought about strangling Bas, a much more rewarding endeavor, which had taken most of the elapsed hour.

What good is power if you don't know how to control it? It's kind of like dying of thirst in the kitchen because you can't figure out how to turn the water faucet on.

She slumped on the floor, dejected. Maybe if she fell asleep, she'd dream the answer. Her unconscious would release it into her relaxed dream state mind. Okay. So it was a stupid idea. But she didn't have any better ones. She closed her eyes and tried to will her body to sleep. Instead, she felt a surge of energy rush through the room. She sat up straight and opened her eyes.

She was no longer alone. She blinked, wondering if she had fallen asleep and was dreaming. The vision remained, staring at her with a grim expression.

Harry!

Fifteen

JULIE RUBBED her eyes. Harry was still there, though he looked like he'd been through hell and back (or not back, as the case may be). His blond hair poked up around his head, giving him an interesting punk look. Stains and creases marred his white shirt, and his shirttail was half in, half out of the back of his pants. He wore no shoes; his black socks were torn and gray with a layer of dust coating them. "Are you okay?" She scrambled to her feet. "What are you doing here?"

He ran a tired hand through his hair and gave her a steady look. "You're here," he said simply.

His words stopped whatever she'd been about to say. For a moment, she'd have sworn her heart stopped too. Then she ran to him, and his arms closed around her so tightly she couldn't breathe. She didn't care. She could die now, right here in his arms, and be happy.

"I've been so scared." The words poured out of her, tumbling over each other. "Everything is so confused. Abigor is my dad, Harry. I'm part demon. I'm like those things that slither up from the Hell Mouth on *Buffy the Vampire Slayer*. Oh no! Will I go poof if someone puts a wooden stake in my heart?"

"Slow down. I have no idea what you're talking about," he said above her head. "No one is going to put a stake in your heart."

"Harry, did you hear me? I'm part demon."

"Bas told me before I came."

"Bas knew?" She would kill him. "Why didn't he tell me?"

"Something about the learning process being important."

She hated Bas. To withhold important information because he thought she should learn it on her own was arrogant and... arrogant.

"I think he just found out recently," Harry offered, his hand rubbing her back.

"I don't want to be a demon." She whispered the words, trying to burrow into him and make this night go away.

"Everything will be all right."

The standard comfort phrase socked her in the gut. She loved him for saying such a totally stupid, untrue thing. Tears pressed against her lids, and she sniffed. He held her, just rubbing her back.

Then she remembered. He should be safe in the protective circle of the Council. She didn't know how much time had passed, but surely not enough for the moon to have risen and set. She pulled against his arms. "Harry. You have to get in the circle before Marguerite succeeds with the second tie."

His gaze remained calm as he fished a handkerchief out of a pocket with one hand and wiped the tears dribbling down her cheeks. "Too late. She already has."

"What did you say?" Surely not what she thought he'd said.

"Marguerite placed the second tie before I made it to the Council circle." His eyes were carefully blank as he tucked the handkerchief back in his pocket.

This was all her fault. He'd put himself at risk because of her. The idiot man. Julie looked hard at him, expecting to see a change somewhere. He looked the same—golden, hot and British, even in his current untidy state. "She's in your head right now?"

"Yes. She's searching for something. Some kind of information she hasn't found."

"She knows what you're doing and saying?"

"Yes."

"Does she know what I'm saying to you?"

"Yes."

"Marguerite—you're an ugly, nasty toad and nobody likes you."

His lips twitched. "I've always admired your maturity."

"Ha. She's lucky I don't steal her soul and lock it in some back room in Gehenna." She frowned and then slowly mouthed the next words. "Can I do that?"

"I don't know," he mouthed back. "If I know what you're mouthing, so does she," he continued in a normal tone of voice.

"We can't have secrets? Small, intimate moments between the two of us?"

"Do you want small intimate moments between the two of us?" His voice deepened, and he regarded her with interest.

"I want much more than that, Harry," she finally admitted, probably letting the devil in her overcome her common sense. "So owhay oday eway etgay idray ofway Argueritemay."

"I have no idea what you just said."

"You don't have Pig Latin in England?" No wonder they lost world dominance.

He frowned. "It wasn't taught at the boarding school."

She sighed. "Your education is lacking. So does this work both ways? Do you know what Marguerite is doing and saying?"

"Yes."

"What's she doing now?"

"Looking up a Pig Latin translator on the Internet so she can figure out what you said."

"The itchbay."

He looked confused and then a smile broke on his face. "She found the translator."

"Okay. Enough fun and games. Let's just ignore her like she deserves." Julie stepped away from him so she could pace. "My father popped me in here so he could have a private discussion with my mother. If past history is anything to go by, I could be here for a very long time. How did you get here?"

"The Triad. Your mother's determination and your daughter's

kidnapping have united the community much more quickly than my speeches could have. Their combined power opened the gate enough for me to slip through. I stepped into the freezer, visualized you, and stepped out into this room."

"Can they get us back out?"

"Bas doesn't think so. Apparently it's easier to get into Gehenna than out of it. I think we're on our own in finding our way back."

"Why did you come?"

He spoke patiently, as if to a slow child. "I already told you."

"Harry, you've let Marguerite place the second tie. You've put your soul in mortal danger. You've probably broken a few Triad rules—travel to Gehenna can't be allowed for the Balance. Why? Being with me doesn't seem like enough of a reason."

"It's enough of a reason." He met her eyes.

She would have done the same stupid thing. She would slay giants to get to him if she thought he needed her. At least she'd try to slay giants. She frowned. "I know I have the power to get us out of here and rescue Tash. I just don't know how to access it."

With one swift movement, Harry shoved her against the wall. His body came against her, hot and hard. She felt the energy from the wall sizzle through her back and the energy from the powerful male sear her front. His head swooped and he found her lips, taking them without hesitation. Taking them as if he owned them.

Sunbursts exploded behind her eyes. She felt as if her feet floated off the ground. She pushed into Harry, her mind firing at the feel and taste of him. Just when she thought she couldn't take any more without going up in flames, he gentled the kiss. His hands softened and moved to frame her face. He lifted his mouth from hers and brushed them against her forehead.

"The wall is gone," he whispered.

She blinked, and turned her neck, looking up and down the long, white corridor that flowed past where the wall had been. "Did I do that?"

"Yes. You seem to have no trouble finding your power when we kiss."

"How weird is that? I might have to keep you around."

"Yes. You might."

She glanced at him, his serious voice pulling her from her study of the hallway. "You told me we can't be together. What changed? Has someone added a Bill of Rights to your rule book?" Her heart beat faster than her flip tone indicated.

He smiled. "No. The rule book hasn't changed." He abruptly switched the subject. "Do you know where Tasha is?"

Julie closed her eyes to block out the distraction of his face. She felt the insistent tug of her daughter's energy force. "Yes, I know where Tash is. Follow me."

Julie followed the thread of her daughter's energy as easily as if she were following crumbs on a forest trail. There was a sameness about the white walls and endless halls that could be disorienting, and Julie knew if she hadn't latched on to Tasha's life force, she'd be wandering aimlessly in circles. Harry silently followed her, his gaze alert and constantly scanning. No one appeared, however— no demons, gargoyles or minions of Hell. The whole thing was really pretty bizarre. Julie came to an abrupt halt in front of a blank wall. She looked at Harry.

"Tasha is in there." She knew it with absolute certainty.

Harry studied the wall and moved his hand in a quick, sharp motion. Nothing happened. "You'll have to get us in. Only the immortals can wield power inside Gehenna."

Julie sucked in air at the calm statement. "I may look young for my age," at least she liked to think so, "but I'm not immortal."

Harry leaned a shoulder against the wall and crossed his arms over his chest. He looked very relaxed, considering they were in Gehenna in the midst of a rescue mission, and he had some psychotic Shadow Walker in his head. "You've got demon blood," he reminded her.

"I don't have much of the stuff." She rubbed her hands

nervously up and down her thighs. She felt nowhere near as calm as he looked.

"You're half demon," Harry pointed out with maddening accuracy.

"I know." Julie whispered the words. "I'm all for diversity, but I'm thinking this demon thing cannot be good."

"Every one of us has the capacity for evil."

"But we're not all half demon. I have one heck of a dark side. If this were *Star Wars*, I'd be a female Anakin Skywalker."

To give him credit, Harry didn't even attempt to tear his hair out at her movie analogy. "No. You're a female Luke Skywalker, or his sister Leia, and you will not succumb to the evil lure of your father."

Julie looked at him, surprised. The man was a *Star Wars* fan. Hidden depths.

He shook his head, as if he realized what he'd said. "You make your own choices." Harry looked up and down the empty hall and then back at Julie's face. He seemed to come to a decision. "Your daughter isn't going anywhere. We have a minute. Do you know the story of how the demons were created?"

"There's a story?"

"There was great war among the angels in Heaven. The losers were cast down to Gehenna. Demons are angels who revolted against God, but they were created as angels—glorious, powerful beings. They chose the dark path. You can choose light."

So she had the same make-up as the angels? Maybe he was just giving her a positive spin on a bad situation, but she'd take it for the moment.

A fine tension built in her to get Tasha out now. "Angel or demon, we know I can wield magic here. Let's see if I can do it without the kiss." She looked at his beautiful face. "Not that I'd normally want to skip that, but I'm not into threesomes." The fact that Marguerite had shared in their previous kiss gave her the willies.

He merely nodded and stepped back, giving her room.

Julie looked at him for a second longer and then turned to face the wall. She cracked her knuckles and stood with her feet apart. Taking a deep breath, she put both hands flat against the smooth surface.

"I don't think you can push it down," Harrison commented after a few moments of silence.

"I know that." She tried to look confident. "I'm taking a moment to gather my power." So, exactly how did she do that and get rid of the wall?

"Mom?" Faintly, she heard the whisper of Tasha's desperate voice.

Tasha needed her. Just like that, the wall was gone.

"Mom! I knew I heard you!"

Tasha stood directly across from her, her orange T-shirt rumpled and her cheeks red. She looked like a warm flame against the unrelenting white. Behind her stood the Shadow Walker, a look of surprise on his face.

Julie was still frozen with the shock that she'd gotten rid of the wall when Tasha catapulted into her arms, pushing her back into Harry. He steadied both of them.

Julie hugged her daughter close, savoring the familiar scent and feel of her. Then she pushed her back a step so she could look her over. "Are you all right?"

Tasha nodded. "We've been stuck in that room ever since the Skaven brought us here."

"Skaven?" Harry had mentioned them earlier.

"Rat creatures, controlled by the demons." Luc explained.

Wonderful, but unfortunately they weren't the worst of her concerns. "Have you seen…anyone while you've been here?" she asked carefully.

"No, just Luc. Do you know how to get out of here?" Tasha jumped as they all heard a sound, and she gave Julie a frightened look. "Someone's coming! We have to run."

Julie winced at the sound of approaching voices. Loud, arguing voices. Actually, only one voice was loud and arguing.

Her mother's. The other was a faint, conciliatory murmur.

"Tash, I need to tell you something." She put a hand on her daughter's arm to stop her mad dash in the opposite direction from the voices. No time to soften the blow. "Your grandfather is here."

Tasha stopped tugging on her arm. "Grandpa's here? In Hell? My sweet Grandpa Abe?" Tasha stared at her mother, slowly shaking her head. "No!"

"Grandpa may not be quite as sweet as we thought. In fact, he might be one of the most powerful demons in Gehenna." She ignored the soft snort from Harry. There might have been a more tactful way to tell Tasha, but Julie's mind wasn't firing on all cylinders at the moment.

Tash vehemently shook her head, her red hair slapping her cheeks at the force of her denial. She took a step away from Julie and reached for Luc's hand. Julie felt a brief pang in the region of her heart.

"I don't believe you," Tasha said calmly.

"I don't want to believe it either." Julie wished she could make it all go away, make her daughter's world normal and sane.

The voices grew louder. Her mother's voice drifted to them. "All those times you told me you were traveling on business, just what were you up to, you conniving devil?"

Tasha's face tightened, but she stubbornly ignored what she heard, her eyes defiant. Tasha's whole body began trembling like a slender tree in the midst of a huge windstorm. Luc put an arm around her shoulders and tugged her close.

Julie looked frantically over her shoulder at Harry, who still stood at her back. Her daughter's reaction worried her. Tasha didn't like change, to the point where she even had trouble getting rid of old furniture and chipped dishes. She'd recently found out she wasn't human, she'd been kidnapped by rat people and brought to Hell, and now her mother was telling her that her beloved grandfather was a demon. Apparently acknowledging that Abe was Abigor was one change too many.

Harry leaned down and whispered in her ear. "She's your daughter. She's strong."

Julie nodded, needing to hear the words, but also knowing that no one, including herself, could deal with the shift in reality they'd experienced without some repercussions. She touched his arm in thanks and immediately felt the tension. Every muscle in his body stretched tight, as if it took all his control to maintain his physical integrity in the face of Marguerite's invasion. She met his eyes in mute apology.

"Balance!" Luc's voice brought them both around to face him. Tasha was bent over, breathing quickly, her whole body shaking. Panic attack.

Julie stepped to her side. "Deep breaths, baby," she commanded.

"Get her out of here, now," Harry commanded.

Julie saw her mother step around a corner in the white hallway. She had to act fast. She had to find a way to get Tasha out of Gehenna, away from the unacceptable reality that was about to be shoved irrefutably in her face. Before she even had time to formulate an escape plan, a rush of power flushed through her.

"Ouch." Julie landed on her bottom, which cushioned her fall more than she would have liked. Tasha tumbled onto the carpet beside her, dragging Luc along with her. Julie raised herself up on her elbows and looked around. She was in her living room. Back on terra firma. Somehow, she'd done it. She'd pulled them out of Gehenna. Maybe having great power wasn't so bad after all.

Suddenly, her budding euphoria vanished. She counted heads again. Then she stood and searched behind the furniture. Harry was nowhere to be seen. She hadn't quite pulled them all out.

"We're home!" Tasha stayed on the floor, gulping in huge mouthfuls of air.

"You can't leave Gehenna without going through a Gate! Not even Abigor can do that." Luc sat up, his expression dazed.

"Harry?" Julie raised her voice. Maybe he'd landed in another room. She dashed quickly through all the rooms. Nothing. "Crap. We left Harry behind."

"Who are you?" Luc was on his feet, a hand pushing through his silver hair.

"How could we have left Harry?" Julie glanced impatiently at Luc. "What's wrong with you? Why are you looking at me like that?"

His expression bordered on awe.

Julie narrowed her eyes at him. "Don't get crazy on me. We need to find Harry."

"He's probably where we left him," Tasha offered, sitting up. "Don't even think about going back, Mom."

Julie couldn't believe her ears. Tasha, of all people, knew what if felt like to be left in Gehenna. Harry had sacrificed his sanity to help them. And Julie had just popped out, leaving him. She felt sick to her stomach. "No man left behind. That's my motto."

"Mom, you're not a Navy Seal. You're a researcher. And I didn't mean we should just leave him there. Let's go talk to Bas, he'll know what to do."

Finding Bas would take too much time. Besides, they didn't need him. "I know what to do. I know how to get back the way we came."

"You do?" Tasha looked surprised.

"I do have a reasonable brain. And the more that I use my power, the more I'm able to recognize flow and direction. I think I can get back along the same path we came on." Except she felt like she was running on an empty tank. Maybe food would help.

"You need to wait until the sun rises to gain enough power for something such as this," Luc said, and all three looked at the clock on the living room wall. Five o'clock. Judging from the darkness pushing against the windows, that would be in the morning, not the afternoon. The sun wouldn't rise for a couple of hours, at least. She couldn't wait that long. She didn't need to wait that long.

"I'm not just a Dancer. I tap sun power, possibly earth

power and definitely whatever power source the demons have." Julie paused and looked at Luc. "Just what power source do the demons have?"

He shrugged in the way only the French can. "I've never met one before," he said. "I always believed they had access to the power matrices of the universe." He looked apologetic. "But I don't know that for sure."

"I guess it doesn't matter. I'll just suck power from wherever I can and point it back the way we came. You two stay back so that I don't accidentally take you along with me. This will work," Julie said with more confidence than she felt. "I just need to find the internal trigger that will allow me to access power and wield it."

"Most of us focus on a specific item. Sometimes it is a word, sometimes a phrase, sometimes just a picture in our mind."

Julie frowned, wondering why Bas hadn't told her that interesting bit of knowledge.

"What did you do to trigger the power last time?" Luc asked.

"Nothing. I wanted to get Tasha out before my mother and Abigor came down the hallway."

"And before that?"

"I heard Tasha's voice. I wanted to get to her."

"So your power is most easily triggered by strong emotion, the need to save those whom you care about."

Julie nodded slowly. That made sense. She had panic power. "Why didn't I bring Harry out with me when we left Gehenna?"

"My guess is that Abigor became aware of what you were doing and countered your power. The fact that only the Balance was blocked from leaving is surprising."

Her father was really starting to make her angry. What was his problem? Whatever. She needed to focus. She would bring Harry out of that hellhole, no matter what games her father wanted to play.

"Think of the Balance," Luc instructed. "Bring his face, his body into your mind. Imagine that he is calling for you. Needs you."

Julie closed her eyes. She had no trouble imagining Harry. His features were stamped on her brain. She placed him in the white room where they'd found Tasha. The wall was up again, and he was alone, standing still in the center of the room. She smelled the faint scent of lemon and the warm, masculine scent that was Harry.

She watched as without warning, he collapsed onto the cell floor. Her hand reached out before she realized she was still just seeing him in her mind. He rolled into a fetal position, his hands holding his head. Small sounds of distress split the pristine silence of the room while Julie watched him struggle in helpless horror.

Suddenly, Harry's face melted into Marguerite's, and Julie saw the woman on a wide bed in a darkened room, tossing and turning. Marguerite appeared in the throes of a nightmare. She thrashed in her covers and large drops of sweat beaded at her brow before trailing down her face. She mumbled words Julie couldn't understand.

And then Harry was back, standing again. Alert and in control. His gaze swept the room, as if searching for something. She swallowed, nervous as stalked prey. His eyes found hers.

"Do not come back to Gehenna." He spoke the words out loud with grim force.

I'm not leaving you there. You came to me. I can only do the same.

"The risk is greater for you. Find Bas. He'll get me out."

Finding Bas was undoubtedly the smart thing to do. Harry could be right. She didn't know what she risked, being half-demon and hanging out in Gehenna. But she couldn't walk away. She couldn't cut the connection and hope Bas would be able to rescue him.

I'm going to get you out.

"No. I forbid it." His tone commanded, the voice of a male used to being obeyed. The voice of the Balance.

My mom is there, too.

Julie used that as an argument, even though she didn't think her mom would leave Gehenna until she was good and ready.

"Your mother doesn't need rescuing." Harry's voice was dry. "Though Abigor might."

Be quiet a minute, Harry.

The fact that she was communicating with Harry meant she was accessing some power source, but she needed to mainline into the mother lode if she wanted to get back to Gehenna. Julie tried to send her mind deep into the earth, then into some imaginary power matrix that surrounded the earth. She couldn't touch even a sizzle of energy let alone wield it. Too bad she didn't have a simple word she'd been trained to that would open the door to her power. How cool would that be? She tried several of her favorite words on the off chance they'd work.

Hot fudge. Chocolate. Mocha.

No wonder she couldn't get that pesky ten pounds off. The words triggered a few cravings, but that's all. She'd have to go with strong emotion as a trigger.

The problem was that Harry was so damn calm and competent. Now that she could see him, she wasn't feeling panicky or desperate. Since that brief moment of vulnerability on the floor, he appeared well able to take care of himself. Damn... she bit her mental tongue before she could complete the thought.

Saying "damn it" took on a whole new significance when you were part demon. "Darn it" would have to be her expletive of choice from now on. If it turned out her words had some kind of special power, the worst that could happen with that phrase is that the hole in someone's sock would get fixed.

Harry cleared his throat and lifted an eyebrow. "Gehenna to Julie," he called. "Focus. I want you to go find Bas."

Would you mind calling out for help? Maybe that would trigger her power.

"Yes." He looked affronted by the request.

How about just saying that you really need me?

"What are you up to?" He stared thoughtfully at her.

Harry, please. Just do it.

She heard the whine in her thought and hated it. Suddenly he turned and held up a hand, as if to silence her. He wasn't alone anymore. A woman appeared in the room.

She stood about as tall as Julie, with sleek, shiny mink-colored hair that had a tendency to curl. On her, the hair looked adorable. Her eyes were large and wide-set, a deep, warm brown, richer than the brown of Julie's eyes. She had the same oval face and high forehead as Julie, but her cheekbones seemed more defined, her nose straighter, her lips more perfectly formed than Julie's.

Julie blinked in astonishment. The woman looked just like her, only better. Younger, skinnier, prettier—the Photoshop image of her.

Julie's gaze flew to Harrison. He was watching the woman, his gaze focused, his expression intent.

Harrison. That's not me. I'm still here in Ann Arbor.

He ignored her, if he even heard her anymore.

"Harry." The woman had her voice, only deeper and more melodious. She walked up to him and put a hand on his arm.

"Who are you?" Harry asked, which was exactly the question Julie would have asked. Unfortunately, he didn't jerk the woman's hand off his arm, which was exactly what Julie would have done.

"Abigor thought you might like some company. I hope you don't mind." The woman smiled at Harry.

"Abigor was wrong. I don't need company." Harry's voice was flat. Good, the little hussy wasn't succeeding in charming him.

"Abigor can be a bit of a bastard if one doesn't do what he says." The woman dropped her hand and backed up a step. "If you don't mind, I'll just sit in a corner. You don't have to even talk to me if you don't feel like it." She walked backward until she hit the wall and sat down with a lack of grace that was, unfortunately, too familiar.

Julie could feel hands on her shoulders as she twisted in agitation. *Harry! She's a demon. She's been sent to tempt you! Be strong!*

Julie's channel to Harry must have been switched off. He

didn't even blink when she called out to warn him. The expression on his face was unreadable, which irked her. Harry often looked at Julie, the real Julie—her!—in that same inscrutable way. Okay, so maybe she really didn't want that aloof, detached look to be her special look from Harry, but still.

She was going to shake Harry. Then she was going to kill her father. Who did he think he was, sending a Julie Deluxe to Harry? Did he want to torture her, his own daughter?

The hands on her shoulders began rocking her roughly. "Mom!" Tasha's sharp voice snapped Julie back into her living room. "Mom, are you okay?"

Julie opened her eyes and looked at her daughter's worried face. "I'm okay, Tash. But Harry could be in big trouble." She looked at Luc. "We've got to find Bas."

Sixteen

HARRY CONSIDERED the beautiful woman who sat against the wall. Her resemblance to Julie was so striking that he felt odd in her presence, pulled toward her yet repelled at same time—his Julie, but not. On an intellectual level, he was tempted to ask her questions, to see how far the replication went. The ability to take on the form of another person was a rare talent. So rare, he'd only heard tales of one other with that power.

"Who are you?" he asked again, wanting to get her to speak, telling himself he needed to learn what he could about the limits of this talent.

She tilted her head and met his gaze. Her eyes, the golden brown of aged sherry, were filled with intelligent acceptance. He felt a twinge of admiration at the same time his right fist clenched with anger and other emotions he wouldn't name. The look was spot-on Julie.

"It's really great what you did—coming to Gehenna of your own free will. We don't get many heroes around here. None, actually." Her voice, just like Julie's, slid through him and warmed him. He set his jaw. "All that risk and she didn't even care enough to take you with her." She leaned forward a little. "Nobody ever cared enough to take you with them, did they? Not your mother, your father or even Bas."

An old sorrow rose to the surface, quickly followed by anger at himself. The Julie clone unsettled him, even when he knew that was her purpose.

Marguerite, who'd been blissfully quiet up to now, laughed. The sound scraped like a cheese grater against his skull. "She thinks you have emotions like the rest of us, le Bilan. She hasn't seen you sit in judgment on someone. And truly, don't you have to want to be taken by someone to be left behind?" Marguerite's presence moved and he felt as if his brain twisted. For a moment, dots appeared before his eyes. He took a deep breath and put a hand against the wall until his vision cleared.

Perhaps he should knock his head against this wall until he either drove Marguerite out or lost consciousness. At least he'd be doing something, taking some action. Not being in control drove him mad. He took a closer look at the wall. The sheer idiocy of the idea appealed to him.

"You're not an idiot and never will be," Marguerite murmured. "You've been carefully trained since birth. You're the Balance. You'll deal with me and you'll deal with this situation in a cool, logical manner. That's your way."

Marguerite wiggled like a worm in his brain, slithering into dark places, nibbling at and exposing essential parts of him. But she was right. She knew him. At least the parts of him that were easily accessible.

He knew her too, though he had no wish to. Her willing participation in the curse had opened the floodgates of her mind. Her strengths and her weaknesses, her fears and her dreams rolled through him. He knew her love for her brother, and the nightmares that drove her to save her grandmother. He also knew what she searched for in the hidden recesses of his brain and why she'd risked so much with this curse. He would do his utmost to keep the knowledge she sought hidden, but given enough time, she would burrow through his shields and find it.

And he knew, though she refused to accept it, where her power came from. She was nothing more than a pawn for a master demon.

Julie stood and took a step toward him. She studied him, her expression serious. No. Not Julie. This woman was not Julie.

He studied her as well, at first looking for the differences, the elements, that this clone hadn't matched correctly. But soon he felt his hands actually itch to touch her, to run his thumbs over the smooth skin of her cheek, to let go and lose himself in this fantasy of Julie.

He wanted to blame Marguerite and the curse for his weakness. He suspected, however, that the demons, for the first time in all their years of attempted temptations, had finally discovered his weakness.

"Who are you?" He asked for the third time, truly curious.

"You know who I am."

"No, I don't."

Her lips curved in the small, patient smile Julie wore when she thought he was acting crazy. "Yes, you do, Harry. I know who you are, too." She took another step toward him. "You are strong and good, a man who I truly admire. You have given up your family and your life for your people, to be the Balance. Things are different now. I'm here. You don't need to be separate and alone anymore. You can trust me not to leave. Let me in. Let me be your family." She held her hand out.

Harry stared at her hand. Family. He had never really thought much about the concept in relation to himself before. The ties that bind families together came in all different strengths—some easily broken, some forged with the strength of steel. One could almost see the strong cables linking Julie to her daughter and her mother. Which made the yearning he felt to take her outstretched hand all the more confounding. Before Julie, he'd never considered the possibility of sharing his life with someone. Yet this simple offer of family, to be part of Julie's family, was seductive, tempting. He flexed the fingers of one hand, and a searing bolt of pain crashed through his temples.

Nails in his head. Marguerite in a towering rage of fear.

"The Dancer is not here." Marguerite's urgent voice jabbed him.

"Be still, Moonflower." He issued the command in a firm tone, despite the pain rippling through his skull. "I am aware of that."

"Harry." The Julie clone smiled with uncertainty, her hand still outstretched toward him. "Harry?"

"Harrison," he said. "My name is Harrison."

She watched him for a moment. The edge in her smile as she dropped her hand iced his backbone. "You're going to cause me problems, Harrison Chevalier. But we've got time. Lots of it."

Harrison didn't bother to respond. He turned his back on her and moved to the corner of the room farthest away from her. He took a deep breath, searching for his calm, balanced center. He took another breath and felt his muscles tense. The simple exercise was now impossible.

There was no calm center in his head, only endless noise and chaos.

Marguerite chattered like a magpie as she paced the cool stone flooring of her bedroom. "Stay as far away from the demon as you can, Balance. You're not thinking clearly. I will find le Hibou. He'll get you out."

Her fear fluttered wildly, battering against his consciousness like the wings of a trapped moth. She had reason to worry. He wasn't thinking clearly. He wanted Julie. He wanted her to hold out her hand to him and ask him to be part of her family. Bollocks. He'd gone mad as a hatter. Le Hibou, Marguerite had said. The owl. Where the hell was Bascule?

"Where the hell is Bascule?" Julie grumbled and slammed down her phone on the end table next to the sofa. Heidi, Harry's secretary in London, hadn't seen him and didn't know how to contact him. She'd hinted that Julie should let Bas know that she was available for lunch anytime if Julie found him. Good grief! What was wrong with that woman? Harry was in danger, and Heidi wanted a date? "Hell, hell and hell again!"

"Mom!" Tasha wasn't used to hearing her swear.

"Tash, I'm a demon now. You have to expect these kinds of words are going to start to slip out with increasing frequency. Before you know it, I'll be using the F word as often as John Travolta in *Pulp Fiction*. I'll probably forget to say 'please' and 'thank you,' and I'll never apologize for anything again, even if I think nasty thoughts about a certain hormone-crazed secretary in London." Inexplicably, Julie sniffed back tears. "Being a demon means never having to say you're sorry."

Tasha exchanged a worried look with Luc. "When she starts misquoting movies, especially *Love Story*, something is seriously wrong." Tasha walked to her mother, grabbed her shoulders and shook her. "Get a grip, Mom. You've always been a demon. Finding out about it isn't going to change you—unless you let it."

Out of the mouths of babes. Well, out of the mouth of a nineteen year-old, at any rate. Wise as the words sounded, and as much as Julie wished them to be true, she was afraid that sometimes finding out your heritage did change you. Or at least changed the way other people viewed you. But Julie just smiled, closed off the tears and gave her daughter a quick hug.

"You're right. Sorry." She pulled herself together and turned to Luc. "Any ideas where Bas might be?"

Luc shook his head. "No, but I'm good at research. I'll find him. First, I must contact Marguerite. She may have tried to reach me while I was in Gehenna and she'll be worried."

Oh, cripes. "I think your sister knows you're okay," Julie said.

"How could she know that?" Luc frowned.

There was no way to break this news gently. "She placed the second tie of the curse on Harrison. She was in his head when we found you in Gehenna. She saw you, in a manner of speaking."

Luc stood. "She shouldn't have done this," he finally said, which Julie considered to be a massive understatement. "I must talk with her."

"I think Bas is our first priority." They had to get Harry out of Gehenna, fast. She had a really bad feeling about Julie Deluxe, and not just because she'd managed to do things with her hair that Julie could only dream about. "Heidi told me that the Triad Council is in emergency session. A Balance has never been trapped in Gehenna before."

"He chose to go to Gehenna of his own free will. I don't know if he can be considered trapped," Luc pointed out.

"He went to save me. Of course he doesn't want to stay there." Julie frowned at Luc.

"He entered the Gates of his own volition." Luc seemed stuck on that point.

"Can't he be treated like an ambassador from a foreign country?"

Luc looked intrigued. "Now, that's an interesting concept. As Balance, one could certainly argue that his presence in Gehenna has a diplomatic purpose since Tasha and I are Triad members who were taken against our will. I believe the Council keeps several demon lawyers on retainer. They could certainly present this argument to Abigor."

"The Council retains demon lawyers?" She absolutely refused to make a bad joke about lawyers. "How do they differ from regular lawyers?"

"They don't," Tasha and Luc deadpanned together, stealing her punch line.

Julie laughed for the first time since finding out she'd left Harry in Gehenna. Luc shot Tasha a worried look. He'd probably picked up on the note of hysteria.

"Mom's sense of humor gets weirder the more stressed she is. Think of it as her nervous tic. You'll get used to it."

"Ah," he said, as if the nervous tic thing explained it all. "It is important we get to the Council and have them send the demon lawyers to Gehenna immediately. The longer the Balance remains, the greater danger he is in."

"Is Julie Deluxe dangerous?" Julie had described what she'd seen to Luc and Tash.

"The female demon will attempt to trick the Balance into the one contract which cannot be broken."

"And that would be?" Tasha asked.

"If Harrison verbally agrees to stay in Gehenna, for any reason, he is bound there. Nothing can get him out."

Julie shivered at the words. She remembered Bas calling the same warning out to her as Joe dragged her into the Devil's Brew. But this was Harry they were talking about. Harry would never agree to stay in Gehenna. He was clearheaded and logical.

Unbidden, a memory of Julie Deluxe flashed into her head. Darn it all, her father was good. Julie knew Harry had feelings for her, and she knew Julie Deluxe would play on them.

"I need to think," Julie said. "Just give me a few minutes to sort this out." Tasha and Luc exchanged glances again, reminding Julie she really needed to find out if they were related. Tasha nodded.

Worried over Harry and not knowing what to do next to find Bas, Julie walked into the silence of the kitchen. The room felt warm and welcoming. She ran her finger across the smooth wood of her kitchen table. Forever had passed since she'd been in here, cooking a Sunday dinner, looking forward to a visit from Tasha.

Of course, the very last time she'd been here, Harry had been with her. Harry, who might be stuck in Gehenna forever, just because he'd wanted to help her.

She had to do something. Guilt and grief built inside her, driving her out of the comfort of her kitchen and into her backyard. The sharp October morning brushed against her, dark and cool, tinged with power. She felt like she could reach out and grasp the energy, mold it, use it.

Her fingers closed against her palm, nothing but air trapped inside them.

No lights shone from Harry's house next door. No golden owl eyes peered at her from the black canopy of the trees. Where was Bascule? More powerful than any of the non-humans she'd met, with the possible exception of the demons, she knew he would help her. He loved Harry.

She didn't know where he'd gone, but if she could let him

know Harry was in trouble, he would help. Standing in the middle of her yard, she placed her hands on her hips and turned a slow circle, considering how best to summon him. Lightning flashed repeatedly in the sky and the distant rumble of thunder broke the silent hush of early morning.

She didn't have his phone number or his email. Transporting to him wasn't an option since she didn't know where he was, and she hadn't learned yet how to transport when not in a state of panic. Out of options, Julie arched back her neck and pushed out a mental call so powerful she fell to her knees. "Bascule. I need you."

She put a hand to her throat, dismayed. That was a mental call. She didn't just scream at the top of her lungs. Did she?

Dorie's bedroom light flashed on and a silhouette appeared in her window. Several other lights splashed into backyards farther down the block. A minute later, the distant wail of a police siren answered the question definitively. With a groan, Julie rested her forehead in the damp grass.

According to the news, the world was full of people who were afraid to get involved, who would turn their backs on scenes of murder or rape. Here in Ann Arbor, she screamed one little scream in her own backyard, and someone called the police. Thank you, Neighborhood Watch. Nothing got by Cindy Lui, block captain.

Julie stood and bent to brush off her damp knees. Then she went back into the house to put coffee on. This could be a very long morning.

The Demon-Who-Wasn't-Julie kept up a monologue that was soothing, beguiling, and that had several times rung a reluctant chuckle out of Harrison. He sat on the floor, back against the wall, his legs stretched out in front of him, ankles crossed.

She sat across the room from him. Dressed in a pair of jeans and a tucked-in top, she shouldn't appear particularly alluring. She did, however. She was also bloody amusing. He knew she wasn't Julie, but the longer he spent here, the stronger the illusion became.

The longer he spent here, the more he also began to contemplate the dividing line between reality and illusion. Could one move easily back and forth over it, or once crossed, was the way back closed forever? And if one were trapped in an illusion, would one know?

Despite his effort to distract himself, only Marguerite's constant prodding and her pointed references to his idiocy kept him from stepping forward and shutting the mouth of the Demon-Who-Wasn't-Julie with his own.

"This is what happens when you don't have a woman for awhile, Balance. It unbalances you. You're letting a minor demon get under your skin." Marguerite's words poked him.

"This demon is not minor," he mused aloud, watching a frown furrow the brow of the Demon-Who-Wasn't-Julie. "In fact, she has an enormous amount of power. I wonder why I haven't heard of her before."

"Perhaps you have. You could be looking at Abigor, for all we know."

"This is a female." He knew that, beyond a doubt.

"Are you speaking with the Walker in your head?" The Demon-Who-Wasn't-Julie stopped whatever she'd been saying to ask.

"Yes," Harrison responded.

She smiled, obviously pleased Harrison finally answered her. "I can poof her out of your head if you'd like."

"How can you do that?"

She waved her hands in the air. "It will take a little while, but it's not all that complicated. Will you stay here while I work on it?"

"Why are you pretending to be Julie?" He ignored her question.

The demon looked down at her body and pressed a finger into the flesh of her thigh. "I could be whoever you want. I could be a little thinner if you like." She looked up hopefully.

"Answer me, demon." His tone was mild, but he put the weight of command behind his words.

"She can't do that, Balance. I wouldn't like it." Abigor suddenly stood in the room with them. He was tall, as tall as Harrison, but more slender. He looked like Julie through the cheekbones and mouth, but his eyes, ice-shard blue, held none of her warmth and humor. The Demon-Who-Wasn't-Julie pushed against the white wall, trying to make herself smaller.

"What game are you playing, Abigor?" Harrison rose to his feet.

Abigor ignored Harrison, his gaze focused on the shivering demon. "I am not pleased with you. You have not completed your task."

"Give me more time. He's weakening. I know he is." The Demon-Who-Wasn't-Julie threw Harrison a desperate look.

Part of her illusion or real?

Abigor folded his arms across his black shirt. He said nothing, but the Demon-Who-Wasn't-Julie disappeared as silently as she had appeared. He sighed and turned to Harrison. "My daughter is obviously not the temptation I thought she would be."

"That wasn't your daughter." The hair at the nape of Harrison's neck stood straight up. The power in the room crackled against his skin.

"Of course, you're right." Abigor stood completely at ease, his legs spread slightly, his arms still crossed. The stark contrast between his black attire and the white room hurt Harrison's eyes. "My daughter is a very special creature."

Julie wasn't a "creature." Harrison, however, said nothing.

"Immortals don't reproduce," Abigor continued, in a musing tone of voice. "We don't die, so there's no need to continue the species, so to speak. I never expected to have a child."

Again Harrison said nothing, waiting for Abigor to get to the point.

"He would never have allowed such a thing, you know, unless

there is purpose to her birth. I've thought much about what that might be."

He referred to the Great Architect, the One Over All—God. Harrison took a deep breath. "He allows us free will, Abigor. That takes us along many undetermined paths."

Abigor stared at Harrison long and hard. "Free will? You think so? I wonder." Then he shrugged. "She is spoken of in the prophecy," he said abruptly.

"A demon prophecy?" Harrison hadn't known demons had prophets.

"Yes. Your Wanderer has also foretold her coming."

The fact that Abigor was familiar with the Book of Wisdom made Harrison uncomfortable, especially since he'd never gotten around to rereading the book, despite Bascule's urging.

"Do you know what the Book of Wisdom says about my daughter?" Abigor smiled slightly.

"No." Harrison bit the word out.

"It says that she has power beyond imagining. I have been watching her, waiting for her time. She has followed the path of the prophecy so far."

Damn, what path was he talking about? Bascule could have stated more strongly the need for him to reread the blasted book. "How do you know the prophecy refers to Julie? If I recall, prophecies are usually obscure enough to be open to many interpretations."

"'A daughter shall be born in light and shadow, a guardian who rises out of evil. Wild power circles her and chaos will follow her footsteps.'"

Harrison frowned. "Is that from the demon prophecies?"

"No." Abigor looked smug. "That comes from your own *Words of Wisdom*. Whom could it refer to but my daughter?"

"I have no idea, but those words do not describe Julie." Harrison knew that with certainty. "Did you stop Julie from taking me with her?"

"My daughter may be powerful, but she is unschooled. It was

not difficult to grab you from her hold and keep you here. The other two were a political liability and should never have been brought here in the first place. The Skaven should never try to think for themselves."

"You let Julie leave."

"Julie can not be held where she doesn't wish to be." He smiled proudly. "However, I have much to teach my daughter. She must willingly make Gehenna her home. I thought to use Josephius as a lure, but he didn't appeal to her. You do appeal to her. If you are here, she will stay." The simple logic sent a chill through Harrison.

"She won't. Gehenna will never be her home."

Abigor smiled again. "There's a human saying that applies to my daughter. Something about home being where the heart is. If you are here, and her mother is here, Julie will be here also."

He might be right. "I came here in my role as Balance to protest the kidnapping of two members of the Triad and your holding of a third. If you don't allow my return, your action will start a war far greater than any we've witnessed before."

Abigor didn't look concerned. "Not if you agree to stay here."

"I won't agree." The fact that Abigor had revealed his plan worried Harrison. He must be very sure of his ability to keep Harrison here.

"I'm a demon," Abigor pointed out. "I'm very good at making people do things they never thought they would." He unfolded his arms and stuck his hands in his pockets. He cocked his head slightly as he studied Harrison. "What is the most important thing in the world to you?"

Harrison didn't answer. Abigor knew what mattered to him—justice, maintaining balance and order, keeping the demons in their place. Julie.

"Julie is a wild power," Abigor said, his tone almost gentle. "Your laws demand that she be banished. She could unintentionally bring death and destruction to your people if she can't control her abilities. If she is in Gehenna, I can train her, guide her powers.

We demons have no desire to destroy the Triad or your Balance, we have internal problems of our own to deal with."

He referred to Ashakarin. Even though Abigor had managed to send him to Lobolo, a hidden dimension used to house criminals, Ashakarin refused to stay vanquished.

"Stay here, Harrison. This will be your sacrifice for your people, the ultimate expression of your duty. I promise your duty will not be painful." Abigor spread his arms in invitation, and the plain, white room became the green, sloping fields of England. Harrison smelled the rich air, redolent with grass and wildflowers. How long had it been since he'd walked the hills of Surrey or Kent? A quilt lay on the side of a hill with a picnic lunch spread out, a bottle of wine propped against the basket; a replay of his recent picnic with Julie. A woman—he looked closer—Julie, of course, leaned back on the blanket, her face raised to the sun. She wore a bright yellow, sleeveless sundress that buttoned down the front. Her bare legs were stretched out in front of her, toes cocked to the sky. Several buttons of her dress were undone, and Harrison could see the smooth curve of a bra-less breast. Her bare arms were brown from the sun and looked soft and warm to the touch.

"I can make Gehenna anything you want it to be, Harrison. You will save your beloved Triad, you will keep Julie from banishment and you will have my daughter for as long as you live."

Julie turned toward him. She held out her hand to him in invitation.

"Do you choose to be with my daughter forever?"

As Harrison contemplated that question, his gaze locked with Julie's. He logically worked through the pros and cons, the costs and benefits, of various responses. When he finally looked at Abigor, he knew his answer was clearly written in his expression.

Abigor smiled. "Will you stay in Gehenna, Harrison Chevalier?"

The coffee maker had just spit the first of the rich, dark liquid into the carafe when Dorie burst through the back door. "You're back." Her strong arms immediately engulfed Julie in a hard hug.

She stepped back and eyed Julie carefully, as if looking for signs of injury. "Was that you with the bullhorn outside? You could have set off cannons if you wanted a less obvious way to announce your return." Dorie had on a pair of sweats and an old T-shirt. The shirt was inside out and the tag was in front.

Cindy Lui ran in behind her, wearing red silk pajamas that had definitely come from an expensive lingerie catalog. "I called the police. They're on their way. Are you okay?"

Julie opened her mouth. She paused, not sure how to answer. Her head swiveled toward the kitchen window, drawn by the odd vision of lights bobbing in her backyard like fireflies on growth hormones. She closed her mouth and brushed past Dorie and Cindy to lean over the sink and get a closer look. Several uniformed police officers were in her yard, scanning the bushes with flashlights.

Okay. She could handle this. She'd just go talk to them and explain she'd been sleepwalking. When they asked why she had screamed, she'd say she saw a giant raccoon. No, that wouldn't work. It was hard to see raccoons, or anything really, while asleep. Okay, she'd tell them she had a nightmare. She'd had a nightmare about, oh, something totally preposterous like being half-demon. Of course, the horror of that had caused her to bellow so loudly, most of the city had woken up.

Satisfied she had a reasonable excuse for her behavior, she pushed away from the sink and took a step toward the back door. At that precise moment, someone knocked loudly on the front door. She stopped, unsure which direction to go in. The police were probably at the front, too. Tasha would answer it.

In fact, the police could just take care of themselves for a few moments. Coffee was more important. She brushed past Dorie and Cindy Lui again. Both women were watching her with concerned expressions on their faces. Too bad. If they'd had the kind of day she'd had, they would be whimpering on the floor.

She glanced at them again. Okay, maybe not. Dorie had twin boys and had never whimpered a day in her life. Julie wasn't so sure she'd be able to say the same thing if she had to watch Dylan and Daniel for more than a day. And Cindy definitely didn't seem the whimpering type. She'd probably have half the demons in Gehenna coming to her Halloween party if she'd been in Julie's place.

And neither woman would have messed up and left Harry behind in Gehenna.

Really, could life get any worse? Feeling like a total failure, Julie grasped the handle of her favorite coffee cup just as something silver and slim flashed into her peripheral vision.

Marguerite appeared in the middle of her kitchen.

Which only proved that, yes, things could get worse. Julie's favorite cup slipped from her fingers, Cindy screamed and the police rushed into her kitchen from two directions, weapons drawn.

Julie held up both her hands. She knew it made her look guilty, but it was her first reaction. As her mind scrambled to come up with a new explanation that would cover Cindy screaming and Marguerite materializing, she heard a sound that made her forget everything else.

A soft, echoing hoot, coming from the direction of the open back door, slid through the cacophony of noise. She sagged in relief. Bas had finally arrived.

Seventeen

THE SLEEPWALKING story worked. Sort of. The police looked skeptical but had better things to do than question a bunch of people who swore nothing was wrong when all that had been reported was a scream. Julie claimed that Cindy Lui had shrieked because Marguerite startled her when she stepped out of the shadows. Never mind that the well-lit kitchen didn't have any shadows.

Cindy looked confused and inclined to argue until Bas knocked on the back door. The sight of bad-boy Bascule, dressed in full leather, seemed to wipe everything else from her mind. The police left very quickly after Bascule arrived, as if pushed out by an invisible hand. Cindy followed after them with a promise to get more Halloween party invitations to all the new people.

No doubt about it, Bas was awesome.

"Where have you been?" Julie asked as soon as the door closed on Cindy.

"You need to get back to Gehenna," Bas said, not answering her question.

A muffled sob pulled her attention from Bas. She turned to see Luc folding his sister into a bear hug.

Ah, yes. Marguerite.

Julie marched to the woman and yanked her out of Luc's arms. Marguerite gasped, took one look at Julie's face and cringed. Jeez.

"I'm not going to hit you." Julie held on to both of Marguerite's forearms. "At least, I don't think I am," she amended, impelled by honesty. Squinting, she looked into Marguerite's thick-lashed eyes, trying to see through into her brain. She raised her voice. "Harry, can you hear me?"

"No. He can't." Marguerite blinked, tears welling. "There's been nothing but a wall for the last ten minutes. I don't know what happened."

Julie felt herself soften at the desperation in Marguerite's eyes. The woman couldn't be all bad if she was worried about Harry.

"What happens if the Balance dies while I'm in his head? I'm feeling dizzy and my head is pounding." A tear rolled down Marguerite's cheek. "Will I die, too?"

Julie dropped Marguerite's arms and walked away before she smacked the selfish itchbay. That would not be a good example to set for Tash. "Bas. What's happening? Why has she lost contact with Harry?"

"I don't know. I do know this is a critical time for Harrison. Abigor is tempting him. If he agrees to stay in Gehenna, he's lost to us."

Julie swallowed. "Could Harry be dead? Is that why the curse isn't working?"

"No one in Gehenna will kill him. If he's agreed to stay, he will be kept there until his body dies naturally. When that occurs, his soul will be trapped forever."

Icy-hot chills choked her lungs. Her stomach heaved, and she put a quick hand over her mouth. No. Not Harry. If he got stuck in Gehenna, she'd spend the rest of her life trying to get him out. Her coffee cup was placed in her hands and she looked up at Dorie.

"Drink," Dorie said, firmly. "Pretend there's whisky in it."

Bas turned to Marguerite. The woman straightened and sniffed, but seemed to pull herself together. He spoke gently. "You don't have the power to instigate or sustain this tie on the Balance. I assumed your energy was coming from Abigor, but it's not, is it?"

Marguerite looked uneasy. Her eyes flitted around the room, not settling on anyone.

"Tell me you didn't make a deal with Ashakarin," Bas ordered.

"Okay." Marguerite agreed too quickly.

"You don't know what you've done." Bas sat down on the table.

"Ashakarin's the demon who was at war with Dad, right?" Julie didn't like the look on Bas's face.

"Is at war is more like it. Abigor currently has the upper hand, but the battle is eternal. They're like two pit bulls at each other's throats. The only good thing about it is that they're so occupied with each other they don't cause as much trouble on earth as they could. Abigor managed to weaken Ashakarin enough to send him to Lobolo—the dimension of lost souls. Ashakarin has obviously regained enough power to work through Marguerite."

"I don't know that it's Ashakarin," Marguerite said quickly. "It could be Abigor or…anybody. The demon promised to channel power through me so that I could succeed in tying Harrison to me. As Balance, Harrison has the key to Lobolo. Through him, I can find out how to release my grand-mère."

"For what price, Marguerite?"

"Price? Nothing has been asked." She looked at her toes.

Bas shook his head. Even Julie realized how stupid Marguerite had been. Demons didn't give away anything for free. "You have been tricked, Marguerite. Belle is not with the lost souls. I knew your grandmother and was with her when she died. Her soul is at rest." Bascule spoke softly.

"No. I've had dreams for years. Grand-mère Belle needs me. I have to control the Balance and find the secret of Lobolo to save her. She told me the demon would help me." Marguerite's voice took on a note of panic.

"Ashakarin sent you the dreams. He twisted your mind and your will. He deceived you." His calm tone gave truth to the words. "Ashakarin needs the key to Lobolo to be free."

"No!" Marguerite shook her head, horror on her face.

"Why did he choose Marguerite?" Luc asked, running a soothing hand down his sister's hair.

Julie looked at Bas, waiting for him to say that Ashakarin chose Marguerite because she was morally weak and easily swayed.

Instead, Bas shrugged. "Your sister is powerful, yet the death of your parents at a young age left you both vulnerable. Perhaps it is only chance that Ashakarin happened upon Marguerite in her dream state that first time. He gave her purpose, and he gave her hope when he planted the seed that she could save a loved one."

And perhaps Bas was being way kinder than she would have been by giving the Walkers that explanation. Julie frowned, suddenly uncomfortable. Of course Bas was kinder. She was half demon. To make up for her previous demon-like thoughts, Julie smiled sweetly at Marguerite, which made the woman blink nervously and sidle closer to Luc.

Julie sighed and turned to Bas. "How do I get back to Gehenna?"

"Demons normally use a Gate to travel between worlds," Bas said. "With you, the rules are different. I think you just need to want to be there, and you will be there."

"I tried that and it didn't work. What about a focus or trigger word? Luc told me members of the Triad use them to access power."

"They do. They are trained to their word as children. You don't require one, Julie."

"I require something."

Bas studied her thoughtfully. "Perhaps you are trying too hard. Just say the words, Take me to Harrison. Maybe that will work."

"Take me—"

"Wait!" Tasha pulled on her arm. "I want to go with you, Mom. We need to get Grandma back, too. I want to help you."

No way was Tasha ever setting foot in Gehenna again. Julie hugged her close and whispered in her ear. "Hon, we have company. I need you to stay and play hostess."

"Mom," Tasha whispered back, "cut the bullshit."

"Okay." Julie lifted her head and looked directly into her daughter's eyes. She kept her voice soft so only Tasha could hear her. "I love you more than anything in this world or any other. You are not going to Gehenna." Then she said the words that always signaled to Tasha that an argument was over. "This is non-negotiable."

Tasha closed her eyes. "I love you more than anything in this world or any other, too. How can I let you go into Hell, how can I let you confront Grandpa by yourself? How can you ask me to do that?"

"Easily," Julie said promptly.

"Mom, I never defended you during all those arguments you had with Dad toward the end. I was such a chicken that I hid under the covers. Please, let me help you now." Tash's voice was low and trembling.

Julie frowned. "What are you talking about?"

"I heard Dad say that you were destroying him and his career. I heard him say you were boring and he couldn't hold an interesting conversation with you. He said you just let your mind and your body go."

Dear Lord. She hadn't known Tash heard those terrible fights. Both she and Jack had said horrible, nasty things. Well, mostly Jack had said them. He'd wanted to leave, but hadn't known how, so he'd created a huge rift that had made it impossible for him to stay.

"Your dad didn't mean most of what he said, but I'm sorry you had to listen to those arguments. That must have been scary for you." She closed her eyes for a moment, sad to her soul that she couldn't take that small Tasha in her arms and comfort her. "And what's this about defending me? Children aren't supposed to protect their parents. Besides, I defended myself quite well on my own."

"Mom, I heard you cry," Tasha whispered.

Julie took Tasha's cheeks between her hands and met her eyes squarely. "Honey, I cried mostly because I was stupid enough to think your dad could be something he wasn't. I cried because I wanted the perfect family for you, and I gave you a broken mess."

"No." Tasha shook her head, a quick, agitated motion. "No. You gave me the perfect family. You and Grandma Jean and Grandpa Abe…." Her voice trailed off. "You and Grandma Jean. You were always there for me. Let me be there for you. Please."

How could she deny Tasha's need to give back to her? Julie could see how important it was to her daughter. But how could she let her go back into Gehenna?

She couldn't. Dropping her hands, she took a step back, filled with regret, knowing her refusal would hurt Tasha. "I will come back." She tried to think of something hopeful and upbeat to say, but for once, nothing came to mind.

Tasha stared at her, pale and stricken. Then she turned and, like a homing pigeon, headed toward Luc.

Julie's gaze lingered on her daughter wrapped in the tall man's arms. She forced herself to look away.

She should consult with Bas and plan what to do when she reached Gehenna. But a growing urgency blocked out common sense. Harry needed her. So she smiled at Dorie, grimaced toward Bas, and then said the words. "Take me to Harry." The kitchen disappeared.

Harry and her father stood in the center of one of the white rooms. Neither glanced at her when she appeared in a corner.

"Will you stay in Gehenna, Harrison Chevalier?" Her father asked, with the kind of persuasive enthusiasm only an ex-salesman or game show host can pull off.

"No!" Julie burst out before Harry could answer. "Harry won't stay here."

Harrison turned to look at her, his face remote. "My name is Harrison."

"I know that," Julie said, moving toward him.

"Stay away," he warned, holding up a hand.

She paused, confused.

Abigor laughed harshly. "He doesn't want you, Princess."

She looked at him, a pain in her chest. "Dad, don't. Don't call me Princess and don't laugh at something that hurts me."

Her father's mouth snapped shut, and he watched her warily. "You were always too sensitive. You're a grown woman now, Julie."

"Does that mean I don't need a father? Does that mean you can be cruel to me?" When he didn't answer, she sighed. "What do you want from me, Dad?"

"I want you here, in Gehenna, with me. Now that your powers are fully triggered, you're too dangerous to walk untrained on earth." He nodded toward Harrison. "If you go back, you'll force Harrison to sit in judgment on you. You're a wild power, Princess. You haven't been trained to ignore your heart and wield power with your head."

"Like you? Oh, but wait. You have no heart to ignore."

"You and your mother were my heart."

Julie sighed. "I don't believe you."

Abigor reached out a hand. "Stay and let me teach you, Julie."

Julie ignored his hand. "I don't want to learn evil."

Abigor smiled, a small twist of his lips. Julie felt a rush of emotion so strong that she almost sobbed. She'd watched old movies with this man every Saturday afternoon while curled on the couch in front of the television. He'd helped her build snowmen in the winter and had made her button her coat up to her chin so that she wouldn't get cold. This was the man she still missed with every movie she watched, that man she still mourned years after his death. How could he be evil?

"What is labeled evil and good depends on your perspective." Abigor spoke quietly. "Some call Americans evil, some call terrorists saviors. Demons don't accept the labels others give us. When you know us, know our motivations, neither will you."

He made his argument sound plausible, sane. She looked at Harry, who watched her intently.

"Just stay here for a while, Princess. Learn who we are. Who you are."

The pain inside her grew. "You're trying to trick me."

Abigor shook his head. "You can't be held by tricks or promises. Don't you know that? You're more powerful than any here."

"Where's Mom?" She needed her mother. Desperately.

"She's not leaving."

"Where is she, Dad?"

He flicked his hand, and Jean appeared, holding two small pieces of paper. "Abe, don't do that! Ask before you move me." Then she saw Julie. She dropped the papers and ran to her. Harry walked over and picked them up.

"Tasha?" Jean asked, folding Julie in a hug.

"Safe, at home."

Jean turned her head and scowled at Abe. "Those Skaven are dumb as dirt."

"Dad could have released Tash and Luc immediately," Julie reminded her mom, stepping out of her arms.

"I know. What he's done is unforgivable." Jean wouldn't meet her eyes.

"Yet you forgive him?" When her mother didn't respond, Julie stepped back farther. "Mom, I don't think the forgiveness thing needs to extend to demons. And what happened to being gay?"

"You're gay?" If anything, her father looked intrigued by the idea. Not something she wanted to see. "That must give your church fits."

Jean narrowed her eyes. "Some people in the church have a problem with my sexuality, some don't." Then she turned to Julie. "I've always loved your dad, Julie. It transcends sexuality."

"Does it transcend eternal damnation? Mom, you're being even more nuts than usual."

"Julie Anne Dancer." Her mother skewered her with her gaze. "I know you've had a difficult week. But so have I. I just found out my dead husband is not dead. He's a demon. My father is not really my father because my mother was fooling around with a Walker. And my daughter—who never showed a smidgeon of ability to wield light energy—is actually an immortal of untold power." Jean paused to take a deep breath. "Don't you dare call me nuts, young lady. Not until I've had at least a week to incorporate all of this into my world view."

"Don't speak to your mother that way. Ever," Abigor added in a cold, menacing tone.

Which stopped Julie's movement toward her mother. She turned on her father. "Do you really think you have the right to parent me? One, I'm over forty. Two, you left the family of your own accord and abdicated all parental rights. Three, you're an evil demon and therefore hardly a voice to which I would listen."

Abigor stared at her in shock. Apparently people didn't talk back to him. Surely he hadn't forgotten family life so soon.

"Mom, Harry. Come on. Let's get out of here." Julie motioned them towards her.

"No. She's a demon trying to trick you. Come with me." Julie Deluxe spoke from behind her shoulder.

Julie swung around and stared at her in disbelief. The demon even had the same clothes on as she did. Julie folded her arms, disgusted with her father. "This is so lame, Dad. Like Harry and Mom won't know who I really am."

Her father smiled. "Then we'll need to confuse them, Princess."

The room began spinning, slowly at first and then faster and faster, like one of those amusement park rides where you're backed against the sides of a big cylinder, holding onto metal poles and once the ride is twirling fast enough, the floor drops out, centrifugal force holding you against the walls.

She had no nearby wall or poles to hang onto today. She lost her balance and dropped, yelping as her hip landed hard against the white floor. She rolled, knocking into Julie Deluxe, who'd fallen beside her. The demon reached out and hung on to her. Julie found herself face to face with her mirror image. She hadn't realized her eyes were quite that rich a shade of brown, or that her nose had that little scar on it. And she really did need to moisturize more often.

The room picked up speed and the two of them rolled together, bumping into Jean, who was flat on the floor but hanging on to Abigor's leg to keep in one spot. Smart woman. Julie rolled toward Harry's leg and stretched an arm toward the neat cuff of his pant. The room tilted again and she and Deluxe rolled in the opposite direction.

Finally, the frantic motion of the room slowed, coming to a halt. Julie lay still, gulping in air, waiting for her head to stop spinning, too. When she was reasonably sure that her legs would hold her, she stood. Julie Deluxe shadowed her actions. Across the room, Julie saw her mother hold onto the wall as she got to her feet.

Abigor and Harry had both stayed standing. Different center of gravity, apparently.

Abigor smiled. "Sorry about that, but I wanted to mix up the Julies. This seemed the easiest way."

"Like that's going to work," Deluxe said, her tone holding the exact amount of dry sarcasm that Julie's would have. "Mom will always know her own daughter. Won't you, Mom?"

Jean held a hand to her head as if still disoriented, but she took a step toward Deluxe.

"Mom!" Julie couldn't believe it. "*I'm* your daughter. You gave birth to me, for Pete's sake."

Jean paused and looked between the two, obviously confused. "That was the olden days. I was sedated, totally under during the birth."

Julie turned to Harry, disgusted. "Harry, don't tell me you're fooled, too."

"Remember the blackout?" Deluxe interjected.

"Hey," Julie stared at her, appalled and embarrassed. "How do you know about that?"

"Because I was there, demon." Deluxe stared right back at

her. "Harry's not going to fall for your little game."

Julie looked at Harry in frustration. He stood, legs slightly apart, arms crossed over his chest. He didn't look in the least perturbed.

"No one is going anywhere for a while," Abigor interjected, obviously satisfied with the results of his manipulation.

Harry slowly unfolded his arms and walked to Julie. He took Jean's elbow as he passed and brought her along with him. He stopped at Julie's side and briefly put his palm against her cheek. The touch was fleeting, but it marked her, soothed her. "You know me," she whispered.

"Of course," he responded.

Julie shot a triumphant look at her father and placed a hand on the shoulder of her mother and Harry. Julie Deluxe blinked out of the room.

"You're making a mistake, Julie," her father warned. "You're part demon. Gehenna calls to you. You will return."

"No. I'm not like you. I don't belong here." Her voice wobbled. Harry put an arm around her waist. Harry, so strong and honest. "I don't belong here," she repeated, more firmly.

"Jean. Stay." Abigor looked at her mother.

Jean took the papers that Harry was still holding. "I found these in your office. Do you want them back?"

His face hardened. "No."

Jean watched him as she tossed the papers in the air. They floated slowly to the ground. Julie could make out a faded pink crayon heart on one of the sheets. She knew it had the words "I love you, Grandpa" scrawled across it. The other sheet was a letter that she could recite by heart. Her love and sorrow were poured onto that page, along with the tears she'd been shedding when she'd tucked both of the folded pieces of paper into the inside pocket of her father's suit coat as he lay in the casket.

"I'm going with my daughter."

Abigor's face didn't change. "She's come into her powers, Jean. She belongs to me."

"You can't have her, Abe. I won't let you have her."

Abigor didn't say anything. Instead, his eyes, dark with promise and intent, swung to Julie. Bone-deep fear chilled her. This wasn't the father she remembered.

"Take us home," Julie yelled, the words tumbling out in panic. They had to leave. Now. This second.

A wild rush of power whipped through her. A mad exultation of unlimited strength and possibility.

"You are above good and evil, Princess. You will return." The words echoed in her head.

Her gaze locked with her father's as she vanished from the room.

"I can't believe you're here." Julie looked up from her computer in disbelief as Joe walked into her office.

"I'm kind of surprised you're here, too," Joe grumbled and dropped in the chair in front of her desk. He set his latte carefully on the armrest.

Despite everything, Julie still liked Joe. Call her crazy. She leaned forward, taking in the dark circles under his eyes. "So, what happened in Gehenna after I left?"

"Let's just say all hell broke loose."

She smiled. "Stop it. It's hard to hate you when you make me smile."

"Believe me, I'm not feeling very funny today, so hate away." He sipped at his coffee.

"Are you in trouble?"

"Not really. I got you to Gehenna."

Julie leaned back in her chair. She picked up the pencil in front of her and tapped the eraser on the desk. "Why are you here, Joe?"

"I'm just shooting the breeze while I take a coffee break."

"No. Why are you *here*? As in not in Gehenna."

"I told you," he said slowly, meeting her gaze. "I don't give up easily. I'm going to convince you the slow burn is better than fireworks."

Her eyes narrowed. "That was the line you used when you wanted to seduce me so I'd go to Gehenna with you. Did Dad give you the job to get me back?"

"Nope. You are no longer a duty."

"Then what gives?"

"You are a pleasure," he said simply. "I don't have many of those."

"Joe," she exhaled his name softly.

He sipped his coffee, not meeting her gaze.

"Stop talking like this. You're a demon. You can't care about people."

"You're a half-demon, and you care about people. Abigor cares about your mother."

"Obviously my non-demon gene is dominant in this case. Caring about a person means putting them first. Dad, and you, too, Joe, don't know how to do that."

"And Harrison does?" Joe stood up and tossed his empty paper cup in the waste can. "Maybe we do put ourselves first, but Harrison puts the law first. You won't come any higher on the totem pole with him."

"Charming. Is that supposed to make me jump in your arms?"

"No. Not today. But I'm putting you on notice. Someday you will."

"Go away, Joe."

He walked to the door and paused. "Go home and get some rest, Julie. Yesterday you were in Gehenna. Hell can suck the life out of you."

"Goodbye." She didn't want his concern. But the minute he left the office, she laid her head on the desk, exhausted. She'd come in to work to take a break from thinking about the craziness her life had become. She'd forgotten the craziness had filled every little nook and cranny of her existence.

After returning from Gehenna yesterday, Harry had left

immediately for London with Bas. They planned to consult with the Council on a way to get rid of Marguerite's curse. If Marguerite found the key to Lobolo in Harry's mind, and released Ashakarin and the rest of the Lost Souls, the havoc caused by the recent demon activity would seem minor by comparison.

Luc had gone in search of Marguerite, who'd disappeared. Harry said she was managing to hide her whereabouts from him, too. And Tasha had left for her dorm in a huff, still angry Julie hadn't taken her to Gehenna.

That left Julie alone with her mother.

They needed to have a serious conversation. Instead, they had sat in the living room, staring at each other for about a half hour, both too tired to talk about what had just happened. Mom finally went into the guest bedroom. She'd left for Chicago this morning, saying she had business with the Gigis.

They were going to become a dysfunctional family if they didn't start talking about all this stuff pretty soon.

Julie straightened from her desk and laughed out loud. What was she thinking? They might become a dysfunctional family? They were the poster family for dysfunction. Her life would send daytime talk show hosts into a feeding frenzy—Next Up: What to do when your Demon Dad returns from the grave.

Could her quiet middle years get any less quiet?

A knock brought her attention to her open door. Several people stood just outside her office. She didn't recognize any of them, but one or two of the women wore pink Gigi T-shirts. Worried that something may have happened to her mom, Julie stood and rounded her desk.

"Hello. Can I help you?"

A man stepped out of the group and into her office. Large, muscled forearms were bared by his rolled-up sleeves. He wore faded jeans and work boots. Black hair lay flat on his head, like he'd just taken off a hat of some sort. He looked about her age, his face weathered by the outdoors.

She met his gaze and took an involuntary step backwards.

Contempt blazed from his pale green eyes.

"Are you Julie Dancer?" His voice held a midwestern twang.

Since her door had a nameplate beside it, it probably wouldn't do much good to deny it. "No," she tried anyway.

He ignored her. "By the power invested in me through Triad Law, I place you under arrest."

Eighteen

BAS WALKED into Harry's office and closed the solid oak door. "There are three Dancers sitting in the lobby with Heidi. Each one of them has offered to sleep with you to break the curse. Go pick one."

Harrison could barely hear Bas through the barrage of images pelting his brain. Marguerite was no longer a worm in his head. She'd become a raging elephant. He lifted his head from the obscenely large desk he worked on. What had Bas said? Three Dancers? Did that mean that Julie, Tasha and Jean were here? He frowned, not sure he'd understood correctly. "Go pick a woman?"

"Sex, Harrison. Combine power with a Dancer in the old-fashioned way and possibly break the curse."

"Is one of the women Julie?" He despised himself for asking.

"No. There isn't any danger you'll bond with one of these. Unfortunately, they don't begin to have Julie's power, either." Bas frowned. "Maybe if you have sex with more than one at time, the power will be cumulative."

Disappointment. And adding to that, disinterest. "I don't think I can."

"I don't think you have a choice. Even though Marguerite knows the truth about Belle, she hasn't the capacity to break the curse. Ashakarin has too great a hold on her. She is his puppet."

Harrison slumped in his chair, not hearing the rest of whatever Bas said. Every ounce of his will focused on keeping the key to Lobolo hidden. He heard a rumble that he assumed must be Bas's voice, but he didn't really care.

Bugger Marguerite. She sifted through his memories, bringing them to the surface, forcing him to relive every one as she worked through them. Time became non-existent. He was a young boy again, holding tightly to his father's hand as they approached the massive double doors of South Haven Academy. Now he was a young man, reading a historical text, learning his father's role in ending the Great War. He flashed again to childhood, in the library, studying. He couldn't track the flow of minutes or hours. Bas's voice echoed. Pain rocketed through his head, pounding, pounding.

Insidious, dark tendrils, so small and innocuous that he almost didn't notice them, began to snake through his brain. Wisps of smoke, seeking to grab hold, take root. He staggered to his feet and knocked against something. His desk. Fear and adrenaline coursed through his system.

This wasn't Marguerite. This was the evil that fueled her making an attack.

Black clouded his vision, pressed against him. He couldn't breathe. He grabbed at power, shaped it into a strong beam and directed it toward this foe that had no end. He couldn't possibly win. Already he felt tired, weakened. But he couldn't lose.

He fought for his soul.

Luc appeared in the office beside Bas just as Harrison slid, boneless, to the floor. Bas ignored him and dropped to his knees beside Harrison.

"I've found Marguerite." Luc sounded strange, hollow.

Bas placed a hand on Harrison's forehead. "Where is she?"

Luc waved his hand and Marguerite sprawled on the floor beside Harrison. She wore the white linen pants she favored, with a loose, blue cotton shirt. Both were smudged and wrinkled as if sweaty hands had pulled at the cloth. Marguerite's usually perfect nails were cracked and broken, indications that her own hands had made the marks.

Her long, silver hair, usually immaculate, tangled around her head. Her eyelids, closed tightly, twitched as if even the light of the office pained her.

"Help her, Bascule." Luc clenched his hands into fists. "Nothing I've tried has worked. Help her," he repeated, the words a terse order.

Bas laid a gentle hand against the woman's forehead. She jumped, as if his touch hurt. He didn't leave his hand there long. "Ashakarin uses the connection she forged to try to take control of Harrison. Marguerite is a conduit for the demon."

"What can we do?" Luc asked.

"Hope that she doesn't burn out, that she can handle the bile flowing through her. She will be tainted for life if she does survive."

Luc watched his sister, face expressionless. "And what of the Balance?"

"The Balance fights." Bas closed his eyes for a moment, the muscles in his jaw tightening. "Harrison is mortal. He can't win against an immortal. The power Ashakarin brings against him is immense. That Harrison has resisted so far is a miracle. He does the impossible."

"The angels must help." Luc looked around as if one would materialize any moment. "This can't be allowed."

"The angels wait and watch."

"What for?" Frustration edged Luc's voice.

"I don't know." Bas glanced at the heavens, his lips twisting slightly. "I've never been one to wait and watch." He looked once more at Harrison and then seemed to come to a decision. "Don't let anyone enter this room until I return. Your sister, Ashakarin and the Balance are tied in a delicate triangle and must not be disturbed." He walked to one of the large windows in the office and opened it. "I go for one who can help."

Julie's prison cell looked like a Valentine's Day card gone wild. The two predominant colors were red and white, and for some strange reason an enormous number of heart-shaped items littered the room. The color scheme was the exact opposite of the sterile white of Gehenna, but still, being held captive was growing old fast. She glanced at her watch. She'd been in this comfortable, window-less room for seven long hours already and hadn't seen anyone. Thank goodness there was a small, attached, also window-less, bathroom.

She could, of course, leave at any time. At least, she thought she could. She still didn't totally trust her ability to wield energy. But if she could get out of Gehenna, she sure as heck shouldn't have any trouble getting out of London.

Harry kept her here. Flouting the laws that Harrison upheld didn't seem like a good idea. Besides, she desperately wanted to see him again. Sitting in the Seat of Judgment might be the fastest way.

She'd explain her side of things, the Council would understand and everything would be fine. Hopefully. She kept remembering the look on Harry's face when he'd ordered her not to go to Gehenna, and she'd gone anyway. And now there was the additional issue of her being a potential wild power.

She walked to the white dresser and picked up a brush that sat on top of a heart-shaped doily. Looking in the heart-shaped mirror, she sighed and began brushing her hair. Not that it did any good. How had Deluxe managed that soft, silky wave?

She set down the brush and paced the room. She flopped back on the red, silk duvet that covered the bed and stretched out. Hadn't Linda Hamilton kept in shape doing chin-ups while she was in a mental hospital during the first *Terminator* movie? She kicked off her sensible shoes and began flexing her toes. She didn't have enough energy for chin-ups. She'd start small with toe flexes, and maybe she'd work her way up.

Here she was with plenty of time and no work that had to be done. She could think great thoughts or figure out answers to pressing world problems…or check out the closets.

She stopped the toe flexes (who wanted bulging toes anyway?)

and hopped off the bed. Inside a pair of wide doors was a closet full of clothes. She frowned and checked several tags. They were all new and all her size. Exactly how long was she going to be here and did all prisoners get a new wardrobe?

Pushing aside hangers, she wondered who had picked out the clothes. They weren't her usual style, which leaned toward casual comfort. These clothes looked more like something Julie Deluxe would wear.

Maybe she should try one of the outfits on. Someone had gone to a lot of trouble to pick them out. She quickly shed the brown slacks and cream-colored shirt she'd worn to work that morning and slipped into a deceptively simple black dress. It was sleeveless with a round neck and a zipper up the side. It hit her legs mid-thigh.

She stepped over to the full-length mirror. How could something so simple look not so simple once it was on her body? The material of the dress was soft and clingy, and hugged her in a good way.

She padded back to the closet and studied the rows of shelves that held shoes. A pair of low-heeled black sandals reminded her of a pair she had at home. Her eyes kept straying, however, to a pair of shiny red, sex-on-a-heel shoes with ankle straps. She pulled them out and buckled them on. Whoa. She sauntered to the mirror, one hand on her hip, and grinned. Not bad, Dancer. Not bad at all.

A knock sounded on the door. Julie started in surprise and turned toward it. Her stomach knotted as the door handle turned.

Linda marched into the room. Dressed in her purple outfit, the massive woman shut the door behind her. She paused, silent, and took in the white rag carpet, the bed with a red, silk comforter and the white dresser and chair. Then her eyes settled on Julie. "Before he chased after you to Gehenna, the Balance told Heidi to get a room ready for you in case you were arrested." She shook her head as if to clear it. "The Council is not into torture, though. I'll get you another room. And some shoes that won't stretch your gastrocnemius like a rubber band."

Julie had no idea what that was, and she didn't care. She ran to Linda and gave her a big hug. She even got teary at the scent of dead cow. "I'm so glad to see you!"

Linda lifted Julie off her feet to set her an arm's length away. "Going a bit squirrely, I see."

Julie grinned, happy to see a familiar face or any face for that matter. She sat on the edge of the bed because her ankles were a little wobbly. "Tell me what's going on. Where's Harry? How is he doing? Is he okay?"

"Don't know. Haven't seen the Balance."

"How do I post bail?" She'd hunt him down herself.

Linda regarded her with pity. "There's no bail, mate. You're here until the next Judgment Day. Of course, they're not really days. Judgment Day can last a long as a month, depending on the quarterly caseload. Don't know for sure when you'll be seen."

"What!" Julie jumped up. "I can't stay here for weeks!"

Linda shrugged. "Should have thought about that before you made a deal with a demon in front of half the Walkers and Dancers in America."

Julie sighed. "Go away, Linda, and bring me Harry."

"The Balance won't meet with a sand bag."

"Excuse me?" Why on earth couldn't Linda speak plain English?

"A sand bag. You're extra weight, throwing off the balance of the Triad."

"Am not." Julie automatically sucked in her stomach.

"You're a sand bag until proven ballast."

"Where's Bas?" No point in discussing this.

"He's off getting women for Harrison to sleep with so the curse can be broken."

"He's what?" Sharp prickles danced along her skin and settled in her chest. She closed her eyes and counted to ten. Then she took a deep, cleansing breath and opened her eyes. Julie still wanted to shake Harrison, Bas and any woman in their vicinity.

"Why did you come here, Linda? Are you trying to cheer me up?"

"I'm your Guardian. I'm checking to see if everything is all right."

"No. Everything is not all right." Harry might be having sex with another woman while she languished in prison. Okay, it was a nice room, with killer clothes, but she was still languishing.

She tried to pull her thoughts together and think clearly. How could she be selfish enough to be angry with Harry when she knew he needed to break the curse? Would she rather he suffer with Marguerite in his head or have sex with another woman? Afraid to think about it too closely, she spoke. "Can you get word to my mother, Dorie and Tasha about where I am?"

"That's not in my job description." Linda folded her arms and tapped a foot, encased in what looked like purple alligator skin.

"Linda, please."

She shrugged. "Already have. All three of them are on a plane on their way here."

The news cheered her and worried her at the same time.

Linda nodded at her. "That was some feat, you pulling all those folks out of Gehenna. Twice. Absolutely brilliant work. Made all Triad members proud."

Yeah. But not proud enough to ignore a little thing like making a deal with a demon. Besides, Julie wasn't sure that she could even be considered a Triad member, with her mixed heritage. A thought occurred to her. "If I'm not a Triad member, can I be held to Triad laws?"

"Don't go there, Dancer. You better be a Triad member."

"Why?"

"If they decide you're wild, you'll get banished. If they decide you're a demon, nobody's gonna want anything to do with you."

"I don't have cooties, you know. Just a demon father. It's not contagious." She tried not to be hurt. "You all have a real thing against demons, don't you?"

Linda just stared at her.

"Okay. Sorry. Root of all evil. I know." She sighed.

"There's no easy way out for you. The Council will put you through the wringer, and then Harrison will pronounce judgment. He's known for his strict interpretation of the law."

"Doesn't Harry have to recuse himself on account of possible bias?" He knew her. He'd kissed her. He'd been to Hell and back with her. Surely that counted for something.

"Balances aren't biased."

"Ever?"

"Ever."

Linda sounded very sure of herself. Which made Julie slightly less sure of the outcome of her trial. She'd counted on Harry to have a bias toward finding her innocent. But what had Joe said? The law would always come first with Harrison. Adventure had come first with Jack. War and evil came first with her father. Maybe her demon blood led her into her own personal little hell of bad relationships.

She began pacing the room. "What are the chances I'll get a not guilty verdict?"

"Did you make a deal with a demon?"

"There were extenuating circumstances," she hedged.

"Did you make a deal with a demon?" Linda repeated.

Julie sighed. "Technically, yes."

"You're guilty, Dancer."

She stopped pacing. "What will happen to me?"

"The Balance likes you, so you may just be sent to Lobolo for a couple hundred years."

"I'm so glad he cares." With friends like that…it was time to plan a prison break.

Bas suddenly appeared in the room.

Julie jerked and fell back on the bed. "Bas! You scared me." She pushed up on her elbows.

"Sorry." He spoke tersely as he took her arm and pulled her to her feet. He wore jeans and a white T-shirt today. His lips were set in a tense line.

Julie felt a flicker of concern before she remembered what Linda said he'd been doing. Pimping for Harry. But why would that make Bas worried? Women were no doubt lining up to sleep with the man.

"Come." Bas tugged on her arm. Julie stepped toward him, her heart racing. She'd never seen Bas like this before. His face was hard and his eyes glittered, filled with a vast and ancient power. Gone were any signs of his usual humor and charm. Something was seriously wrong.

Quick as a whip, Linda broke his grip with a wicked swipe of her hand and inserted her body between them. "The Dancer's not going anywhere. She's under Triad arrest and can only be released by Council edict."

Bas gritted his teeth but spoke calmly. "Peace, Guardian."

Linda stiffened and stepped aside, quickly and silently. Bas gripped Julie by the waist and pulled her against him. She locked her hands on his arms, driven by a sudden, desperate worry for Harry.

Then she stood in what appeared to be a lush office. Her gaze swept the room quickly, logging details. A large, mahogany desk took up most of one side of the room. Two laptops and a neat stack of paper looked lost on the massive surface. Beige walls and gleaming hardwood floors gave the space its only hint of warmth. Several black and white pictures broke the monotony of the walls. Ansel Adams? Oddly enough, the room held no furniture other than the desk and chair, giving it an empty feel. Except for the fact that Luc stood in front of the desk, frowning at the floor beside it.

Not at the floor. At someone on the floor. Julie was already moving when she saw two shining wingtips poking out from behind the side of the desk.

Harry.

She brushed past Luc. She barely noted that Marguerite lay on the floor beside Harry. She dropped to her knees. Harry didn't move. His face scrunched, as if he were locked in the act of lifting a heavy object. Her hand went immediately to his heart. It beat quickly under the soft, white silk of his shirt.

"What's wrong with him, Bascule?" She gently smoothed the hair away from his forehead. He felt cold, stiff. "What has she done?" She couldn't even look at Marguerite.

"Your father's enemy, Ashakarin, uses the link he helped Marguerite forge to access the Balance's mind. Ashakarin is attempting to invade and take over the Balance."

"Why?"

Bas squatted down beside her, his eyes trained on Harry's face. "Ashakarin lives for two things—to escape Lobolo and to get back at your father for putting him there. Very few people have access to the lost dimension. Only a few of the Immortals. And Harrison. The Balance is given the knowledge by the previous Balance, when he assumes the position. For the Triad, it is the place of ultimate punishment."

"So Ashakarin can gain his freedom if he controls Harry," Julie said slowly.

"Yes."

"He must be very powerful to be able to attack Harry like this from another dimension."

"He is."

"How did my father defeat him?" Her hand traced Harry's jaw as her mind worked furiously. She had to touch him, connect with him. She had to save him.

"Ashakarin is powerful but your father is brilliant. Abigor tricked him."

Julie took in a deep breath and leaned toward Bas. "If I have sex with Harry right now, will this all end?"

"If you can have sex with Harry right now, you're even more powerful than I think you are." Bas nodded toward the still man on the floor. "It's not going to happen. His energy is focused on the battle he wages against Ashakarin. He's fighting for his soul."

Julie's hand went again to Harrison's chest and she rubbed gently, as if she could give him her heat. He was so cold.

With frightening clarity, the perfect solution popped into

her head. She ignored it. "I'm a social worker," she said loudly, just to remind herself. "I *help* people." But while she subscribed to the Social Work Code of Ethics, she hadn't actually sworn to a Hippocratic Oath. Okay, where did that last bit come from? Her heart started beating faster. "Shut up, brain."

Bas frowned. "Julie?"

She spoke quickly. "What if Marguerite dies? Will that break the link?" She was gathering information, nothing more. Luc made an odd noise, but she didn't look at him.

Bas watched her with interest. "You're going to kill Marguerite?"

Julie finally turned to the woman beside Harry. Marguerite seemed to be in agony. She fidgeted restlessly, her hand thrashing out toward Harry. "She's in a lot of pain. I bet she would ask me to do it if she could. It would be a mercy, a good thing." She looked up and met Bas's steady gaze. Her voice fell to a whisper. "Isn't Harry's life worth more than hers?"

Harry had given his whole life to the Triad from the time he was a child. No one had ever loved him. Except maybe Bas, and Bas was hardly a warm fuzzy. This brave and good man deserved so much more than to have his soul destroyed because of this woman's stupidity.

"Marguerite is nothing." The words rasped out of Julie's throat, surprising her.

"You judge her harshly," Bas commented quietly.

"I could kill her, couldn't I?" Julie rubbed both hands against her thighs and contemplated the idea. She felt the power in the room, pushing against her skin, hers to shape.

"Think it, and it would be done," Bas agreed. "No fuss, no muss."

"Then Harry could get up and walk away from all this, free and whole."

"Yes," Bas said quietly.

Julie tried to think it through clearly, but emotion swamped her, confusing her. The only thing she knew for sure was that

Harry could not die. She could not let that happen.

Bas said nothing.

Luc's voice came from above her head. "You can't judge my sister. You can't kill her. You don't have the right."

She looked up, anger emerging, bright and clean. "She gave up her rights when she allowed Ashakarin into her head, when she allowed herself to become a conduit of evil. What right does she have to kill Harry?"

"If you kill Marguerite, you are no better than she." Luc met her gaze, unflinching.

"Ha! Is that supposed to make me feel bad? I'm far worse than she." Julie stood slowly. "I'm the evil she only channels."

"No. You're not." Luc shook his head vehemently but took a step backward.

Julie turned to Bas, who had one hand on Harry's arm, one on Marguerite's. His eyes were narrowed and his face intent, as if he could monitor the flow of energy between the two people on the floor. "What should I do, Bas?"

Bas opened his eyes fully, his gaze unfathomable. Very slowly he removed his hands from both Harrison and Marguerite. "Kill her, Julie."

Nineteen

"WHAT DID you say?" Julie couldn't believe her ears.

"Kill her," Bas repeated. "Harrison is weakening. He can't hold out much longer."

Julie stared at Bas for a moment, fear for Harry paralyzing her ability to think. She slowly knelt beside Marguerite and placed a hand against her forehead. Marguerite felt warm, damp and very alive.

Julie closed her eyes and thought back to one of her lessons with Bas. She visualized herself as sponge. She gasped when the lights in the room actually dimmed as energy soaked through her pores. She'd never even made a light flicker during her lessons. Heat and energy filled her, tingling up her arms. She opened her eyes, and her gaze flew to Bas.

He smiled. "I told you once you started to use and shape power, it would flow to you more easily."

Marguerite twisted under her hand. With a slight tug, Julie knew she could reach in and pull the life force from the woman. She turned toward Luc. "I'm so sorry."

"Julie, you can't do this." Luc said the words with certainty.

Of course she could. Demons kill. She was half demon. So why was she hesitating? Years of contact with Ashakarin had probably damaged Marguerite past repair. "It would be a kindness to kill her." She repeated her first argument.

"A kindness to kill. A merciful act." Luc choked out a bitter laugh.

"That's me, a regular Mother Teresa." Murderer to saint in one neat twist of logic. Maybe she could get a job as a political spin doctor after this was all over.

Her gaze slid to Harry, so still on the floor. *Harry, I can do this. I won't let you die.* Her hand started shaking, and she closed her eyes again, not wanting to look at Marguerite while she killed her. She took a deep breath then sniffed more deeply. The faint bite of cinnamon scented the air and calmed some of the fear and anxiety swirling in her brain.

You always have a choice.

Her eyes flashed open, searched for Bas. He still bent over Harrison. He hadn't spoken, had he?

"Bas."

His head swung toward her.

"I'm sorry. I can't do it, I can't kill her."

"Good."

"Good?" She stared at him for the space of two heartbeats. "What do you mean? We don't have time for games, Bas."

"I don't play games. Make no mistake Julie. Your choice in this is deadly serious."

"Well, now that I'm not going to take Marguerite out, we need to come up with a Plan B." Harry looked paler, as if all the blood had headed somewhere far away from the organs that needed it. Every passing second, tension wound tighter inside her. She had to act quickly.

"I think you can bind with Harrison and join power without having sex," Bascule said.

Well, why hadn't he said so sooner? Wait a minute. "Bind together. Is that the blood-mate thing Harrison mentioned?"

"Yes. I can perform the ceremony that will bind you."

Whoa. Harrison definitely didn't want to bind with her. He'd been crystal clear on that point. Even in the grip of very strong passion, he'd backed away so that it wouldn't accidentally happen.

Luc spoke from behind her. "You may give him back his

soul, but you'll take away his reason for existence."

Julie shot him a questioning look.

"The Council won't allow a demon-bound Balance."

Giving him his life would take away his reason for life.

Great choice. But, then again, no choice. She wouldn't let Ashakarin have him. Besides, he couldn't really be mad at her for not letting a demon take over his soul, even if meant he was tied to a half-demon, and he lost his beloved job, right?

Of course he could.

"Do it, Bas. Bond us together."

Bas took her left hand and before she had time to wince, he sliced a deep cut across her palm by moving his finger above it. He did the same to Harry's hand. Then he joined them, palm to palm. Julie swallowed hard and curved her fingers through Harry's, holding him tightly, mixing their blood. She tried to will her life force into him. Please, please, she prayed. Help him. Help me help him.

Bas cupped his hands around their clasped ones and began chanting in a language she didn't understand. Latin, maybe. But since the words "veni, vidi, vici" comprised the sum total of her Latin—and they weren't mentioned in the binding ceremony, thank you, God—she couldn't be sure.

"It's done." Bas released their hands.

Julie kept her fingers entwined with Harry's. "I don't think it worked. I don't feel any different. Shouldn't I feel warm and tingly and connected to Harrison?"

Bas gently tugged at her hand until she released Harry. He ran a finger over her cut and then Harry's, closing the skin.

"Bas," Julie said urgently. "You need to do it again. The blood bonding didn't take. I don't feel Harry. I'm not joined with him. I can't help him fight."

"Julie. Be still. He shields himself against Ashakarin. To break through those defenses will weaken him. You have to ask him to let you in."

"He's unconscious." She pointed out the obvious.

"Ask him," Bas repeated quietly.

Right. She turned to Harry and put a hand on either side of his face, feeling the rough scrape of whiskers against the palms of her hands. She shut out the sound of Marguerite, still moaning. She shut out Bas and Luc, whose worry sat like a brick on her shoulders.

"Harry." She spoke the words in a whisper. "Let me in, love." She paused, felt nothing. "I know you're used to fighting alone, but you don't have to anymore. I'm here."

Still nothing. She needed to get closer. She gently straddled his waist, one leg on either side of his ribs, and sat on his stomach. "Harry, we're bonded now. We're family. Let me help you."

A mental door slowly creaked open, and she caught a glimpse of him, felt the edges of the terrible battle raging inside him. How had Harry survived this long?

A thread of energy Harry couldn't spare focused on her for a moment. "Go! Ashakarin will have you."

"If you let me in, we can stop him together." She willed him to trust her, to open to her.

The door began closing much too quickly. She searched desperately for a way to convince him to let her help. "Harry, if we defeat Ashakarin, we can have sex."

Maybe he was going to do it anyway. Maybe he didn't have enough energy left to close his mind to her. Maybe he was a typical guy.

Whatever the reason, Harry's mind opened to her in a rush that pushed her flat against his chest. She screamed as energy cascaded through her, overwhelmed her, drowned her.

She couldn't breathe. She couldn't think. Then abruptly, the whirlwind stopped and everything stilled. She cautiously opened her eyes.

Julie thought for a moment that she'd landed in that movie with Robin Williams, the one where he follows his wife through the afterlife to pull her out of Hell. The scenery seemed to shift and blur, and everything was just a shade too intense to be real.

A grassy field stretched as far as the eye could see. Peaceful, in a bizarre sort of way that totally freaked her out. She slowly turned a circle, trying to get her bearings, trying to find Harry,

Suddenly, the pastoral landscape dissolved into a huge Coliseum. Tiers of crowded seats sprouted and rose around her on all sides. The grass beneath her feet flattened and turned into packed sand. The roar of screaming voices filled the air, along with a sense of rising excitement and anticipation. The hair on her bare arms prickled, and she turned, as if tugged by a string, toward her right.

Harry stood twenty feet from her, bare legs spread in a firm stance, body tense and coiled. She'd never seen him like this— elemental, dangerous, fierce. Stripped of his polish and elegance. Stripped, period. He wore a skimpy loincloth secured only by a few clever tucks of cloth.

When she dragged her eyes away from that interesting bit of clothing, she noticed the very big sword gripped in his hands. He looked sort of like Russell Crowe in *Gladiator*, only more naked. His hair captured the sun and his golden eyes were narrowed, intent. Facing him stood a giant of a man dressed in a plain black tunic, holding an even bigger sword. Ashakarin.

The demon had red hair. She squinted her eyes. And freckles across his nose. He looked more like an overgrown leprechaun than the heart of darkness. If anything, this whole experience had taught her the fallacy of stereotypes. Evil didn't have a particular face. In fact, it could be looking back at you in the mirror.

Ashakarin shifted his feet. He was going to skewer Harry.

"No fair!" She yelled out her first thought. "The swords should be equal size."

Harry didn't spare her a glance, his attention focused on the demon in front of him.

A familiar female voice answered from behind her. "You know size doesn't matter. It's all about how you wield the weapon."

"Mom." Julie twisted around. "How did you get here?"

Her mother looked so normal, dressed in a pink T-shirt and

a pair of worn jeans, pink toenails peeking out from her favorite Birkenstocks. "I'm not here. Not really. Except that I'm your mom, so I'm always a part of you in some way or another. You just decided to separate me out for this little scenario that's playing out in your head."

"You mean this whole fight in the Coliseum isn't really happening?" Her attention focused again on the two opponents warily circling each other.

"Oh, the battle is very real, but you're interpreting it in a way you can handle. Someone less addicted to movies and more into sports might view this as a boxing match, or someone more into strategy might see it as a chess competition or something."

"A chess competition?" She should have come up with that one.

Swords clashed. Julie gripped her mother's arm as Ashakarin brought down his massive sword, forcing Harry to parry his attack. Harry absorbed the shock of the hit then danced backward out of reach. But not quite far enough. Ashakarin lunged and nicked his bicep, drawing blood.

"Ashakarin." Julie spit the word and tried to run to Harry's side. Her mother held on to the back of her dress, stopping her.

Ashakarin stepped back out of Harry's reach and lowered his head in a courtly gesture, seeming to notice her for the first time. "Spawn of Satan," he greeted Julie solemnly.

"My father is not Satan!" She turned to her mom and lowered her voice. "Is he?"

"I have no idea," Jean whispered back.

Harry darted in and backward again, scoring Ashakarin across his massive thigh.

"Go, Harry!" Julie jumped up and down, not easy in the red shoes, and made a megaphone out of her hands. "Slice him, dice him, don't be nice ta him!"

"Thank God you didn't make the cheerleading squad in high school," her mother commented.

Julie frowned as Ashakarin pushed Harry back with a series

of feints. The crowd cheered wildly, obviously not rooting for the underdog. "He's never going to win. Ashakarin has a longer reach and doesn't look tired at all. What can I do?"

"Besides distracting Ashakarin with your cheers? Nothing. Ashakarin is too big and too strong."

"Mom!" Julie glared at her. "What if Erin Brockovich had believed that California power company was too big and too strong to go after?"

"Julia Roberts wouldn't have gotten an Oscar?"

Julie didn't bother responding to that. Everyone knew Julia Roberts would have eventually gotten an Oscar for something. Instead she began patting her dress, wishing for pockets. "I should have brought a weapon."

"Only things of power exist on this plane. Even if you had a gun on you in Harrison's office, it wouldn't be with you here. You're not really here. Just your essence, your soul, is."

A gasp from the crowd focused her attention back on Harrison. "Ashakarin got Harry's other arm. He's bleeding pretty profusely. Enough of this. I bonded with Harry so we could join power and defeat Ashakarin together and here I am, standing on the sidelines. I need a sword."

"You're going to fight for Harry?"

"Hellooo—I did the whole blood thing. Of course I'm going to fight for him."

"You never fought for Jack," Her mother pointed out.

"Jack wasn't fighting a demon."

"Wasn't he?"

"No. He wasn't fighting anything. Except me." She paused. "Oh. That means he was fighting a demon. This is getting way too complicated. Leave Jack out of this. He's not important."

"He never was. That was always the problem."

There was a kernel of truth there. Maybe part of the reason Jack left was because she hadn't cared enough to fight for him. He'd been fun and exciting, sort of like a Cosmo on girl's night out—not the sustaining milk of everyday life. But, however startling this sudden insight was, she didn't have time to mull it over right now.

Because she did care enough to fight for Harry.

"Julie. Leave!" Harrison bellowed the words as he retreated yet again. His bloody arm moved with lightning swiftness, blocking the immortal's ceaseless attack.

"I can't. I love you."

Ashakarin laughed, which gave Harry an opening. He punched a shallow thrust into Ashakarin's chest, pulling back quickly to avoid the giant's roaring counter-attack.

Harry glanced at her as his sword flashed. "And you're telling me this now because?"

She didn't want to say she felt the need to tell him her true feelings before he died. Somehow that didn't sound supportive and positive. "I thought it might motivate you to fight harder."

Ashakarin's sword narrowly missed his left ear. He leaned back with amazing dexterity. "Ah. I was lacking motivation. Thank you."

This time Harrison managed to cut a thin line across Ashakarin's cheek. Ashakarin didn't even blink. Which reminded Julie of one undeniable fact. Harrison was not going to win this battle by killing Ashakarin. Immortals don't die. Ashakarin was merely waiting for Harry to tire.

And Harry would tire. Already sweat glistened on his muscles, and his lungs heaved, trying to take in more oxygen.

"You can't stop a storm, but you can sure shut a window so it doesn't get into the house." Jean murmured the words she'd said during each thunderstorm that Julie could remember as a child.

Huh? The fake sky was a bright, cerulean blue. Julie frowned at her mother, wondering what she was talking about. Her mother looked pointedly at Ashakarin and comprehension dawned. This storm was Ashakarin, the window, Marguerite. Marguerite was the conduit Ashakarin needed to reach out to Harrison from Lobolo. If Julie could close that conduit, remove Marguerite from Harrison's mind, Harrison would be safe.

"Where is she?" Julie scanned the packed stands. Finding Marguerite in this crowd would be impossible.

"I taught you to use your mind better than this," Jean said, exasperated.

"No, you didn't. You put me in front of the television set whenever you wanted to read a book or talk on the phone with friends." Julie's eyes moved restlessly over the sea of faces, though part of her attention was riveted on the sword fight happening beside her.

"You get that smart-mouth from your father. And I made sure it was public television."

Ashakarin was using Marguerite to access Harrison. It made sense that she'd be close to him. Julie stopped looking in the stands and instead focused on the arena floor. She'd thought it deserted except for the four of them. Now she saw that there were several areas of deep shadow along the edges of the stands. "Mom, yell if Harrison needs me. I'm going to hunt for Marguerite."

"Julie, I can't do that. I'm not really a separate person. Where you go, I go."

Julie stared at her, frustrated. "This is so blasted bizarre. Okay, I'm going to find Marguerite as quickly as I can." She looked at Harry who appeared to be holding his own for the moment. "I'll be right back!"

Harry and Ashakarin didn't pause in their grim assault on each other. She watched for a moment, then gave a little hop and put one hand on her waist. The other she fisted and pumped into the air above her head. "Fight, fight, fight! With all your might, might, might. Harry! Go, fight, win!"

Harry ignored her, but Ashakarin stumbled, his eyes widening at her antics. Harry took advantage of the fact his opponent was off-balance and disarmed him with a mighty upswing of his sword. Ashakarin's sword went flying in the air and landed at Julie's feet.

She grabbed it, amazed she couldn't lift it. She needed to work out more. Tugging at the hilt with both hands, she dragged it across the sand, trying to get it out of Ashakarin's reach. Ashakarin laughed at her and pulled another sword out of thin air.

She could really hate this whole magic, energy-wielding, immortal thing.

Not letting go of the sword, she reached the side of the arena and began scanning the shadows. There, curled in a small huddle, sat Marguerite.

Julie pulled the sword over to her and collapsed on the ground beside her, breathing hard. "Marguerite. You can't let Ashakarin destroy Harry."

Marguerite raised her head from her knees. Julie gasped. She looked ravaged and hollowed out, twenty years older than the last time Julie had seen her. "This wasn't supposed to happen. I just wanted to free my grand-mère."

"Stop Ashakarin, Marguerite."

"I can't!" Both hands pulled at her hair as if it hurt her and she wanted it off her head.

"What do you mean, you can't? You got in here. Get out the same way. Reverse the curse or use a counter-curse or something"

"This is the first curse I've ever attempted. I don't know how to reverse it," Marguerite admitted.

"Of all the stupid—" Julie stopped. Name calling wouldn't help. "You're an idiot." Okay, it helped a little. Julie had absolutely no sympathy for this woman, even though channeling a demon looked like it did pretty nasty things to a person.

Julie took a deep breath and stood. With a huge effort, she lifted the sword over her head. "You're not really here, so if I put this sword in you, maybe it will force your spirit to seek your body and you'll leave."

"And maybe you will sever her soul from her body forever and leave her in some sort of limbo," her mother piped up from behind her.

"Are you my conscience, Mom?"

"Yes," Jean said simply. "Ask Freud. I was very instrumental in the development of your super-ego."

Julie lowered the sword. "Great. Is Freud somewhere around

here, too? Harry's going to have a major headache when this is all over."

"I meant that rhetorically."

"I don't have time for rhetorical. If I can't do the sword thing, how do I get Marguerite out of Harrison's head?"

"Push her out."

"Excuse me?"

"You can gather energy from light and earth, probably from wherever immortals get power too. Gather power and push her out."

A loud cheer broke out from the crowd. Julie swung around to see Harrison on his knees, parrying Ashakarin's powerful blows with straining muscles. Determination flowed through every line of his body. Sweat glistened on his chest, and she could see his thigh muscles bunch as he fought unsuccessfully to rise to his feet.

Without thought, without a plan, Julie tightened her grip on Ashakarin's sword and ran toward Harry. She lifted the sword as if she'd morphed into Wonder Woman and met Ashakarin's downward swing with the block of her own blade. The impact of the hit bruised every muscle of her body, down to her toes. Harry surged to his feet and stood at her shoulder, sword raised, ready.

"Get behind me," he ordered.

"I just saved you," Julie protested, not sure she could move to get behind him.

His eyes never left Ashakarin. "Thank you. Get behind me. Now."

Ashakarin roared. He didn't look happy at all. As if in slow motion, he swung his sword to the side and began a low arc that would probably lop both of their torsos from their waists. Harry pushed her flat down against the sand with one strong arm and stepped toward Ashakarin, his sword extended in his other hand.

Julie panicked and mentally reached out. She grabbed every energy source she could find—earth energy, light energy and energy she didn't even recognize. She directed it all toward Marguerite in a mighty effort to push her out of Harry's head and break the curse.

A howl echoed around the arena as Ashakarin recognized her purpose.

"Please, Marguerite. Help me break the curse. Release Harrison."

Unbelievably, she felt the window allowing Ashakarin access to Harrison begin to close. Marguerite added her will to Julie's.

Too late. A triumphant laugh filled her ears as Ashakarin's sword finished its mighty swing and bit into the skin covering Harry's rib cage.

"No!" With a last panicked push, Julie felt the bonds of the curse shatter. Marguerite flew from Harrison's mind, sucking Ashakarin with her like a vacuum.

Unexpectedly, Julie followed. Her last look at Harry was of him lying on the dirt of the arena floor, blood spilling into the sand.

Twenty

JULIE'S PHYSICAL senses came back slowly. First were the smells—warm cotton, sweat and Harry. Then came the pain, as if every muscle and ligament in her body had been pulled, twisted and hung out to dry. Finally, she became aware of her torso and limbs, splayed like a limp jellyfish across Harrison's chest. She bumped up slightly as he breathed and started to roll to the side. Hard arms came around her and held her fast against him.

He was alive. Thank you, thank you, *thank you*, God.

"Are you okay?" Her voice sounded funny, distant.

"I don't know," he spoke slowly.

She struggled to sit up, but his arms wouldn't let her go. "Are you bleeding? Ashakarin, the sword…."

"No. That wasn't our physical bodies. They were here in this room. If Ashakarin had succeeded, he wouldn't have killed me, he would have had my soul." Serious, golden eyes met hers. "Thank you."

"You're welcome." When his gaze didn't waver, she licked suddenly dry lips. "Do you remember everything?"

His brow furrowed. "If I forgot something I wouldn't know it."

She almost smiled at his response—pure Harry—but her stomach was too upset. She buried her head against his chest. "We did the blood thing." She said it quickly, before she lost her nerve.

"I know."

He didn't sound angry. He didn't sound happy. He didn't sound anything she could identify. He had a poker voice.

She lifted her head again to look at his face. No help there.

"Pretty funny, huh?" She tried for a jocular tone.

He didn't smile. "Which part, bonding with me or banishing an evil demon and saving my soul?"

She cleared her throat. "I meant funny in a sort of ironic big picture way. First you wanted to have sex, then you didn't because you didn't want to bond with me, then we bonded while you were unconscious and now we can have sex."

"Ah, irony." He paused. "The humor is still escaping me."

She pushed at his chest, needing some distance. He didn't let her go.

"This is only ironic if now that I can have my heart's desire, I don't want it," he said calmly.

For a moment, she couldn't breathe. His gaze held her more securely than his arms.

"You both survive an attack by an immortal, and you're talking about irony?" Bas crouched down beside them. "Glad to see everyone is feeling okay."

Julie jerked and turned her head, meeting Bascule's amused gaze. How did Harrison make her forget that they weren't the only people in the room? Marguerite lay only inches away from them, strangely silent after all her moaning. Luc knelt beside his sister, holding her hand.

"Go away, Bas," Harrison ordered.

"Not yet, friend. You've both been through a major ordeal. I want to check you out."

Harry's arms dropped reluctantly from her, and Julie rolled off his chest. She took the hand Bas held out, pulling on it more than she would have expected as she stood. She smoothed her dress neatly over her thighs and reached down to adjust an ankle strap. Harry rose slowly, grimacing as if his joints pained him.

"What of the Moonflower?" He turned to Marguerite.

Bas shook his head. "She lives. I don't know what her fate

will be. She'll need time to regain her energy and heal."

"I'm taking her back to Le Quatre Horizons." Luc stood and lifted Marguerite in his arms as if she weighed nothing. "I'll find a way to rid her of Ashakarin's taint.

Bas nodded. "I'll visit when I can."

Luc looked at Harrison. "I apologize for my sister."

Harrison put a hand on Luc's shoulder. "She's a strong woman who fell prey to evil. I'll help in her recovery any way I can." His jaw firmed. "However, she's broken Triad law and will be held accountable when she has healed."

Luc held his sister closer. "I know."

Harry briefly touched Marguerite's hair. "Ashakarin has been working on her for many years. Her road back won't be easy." He didn't add it might not be possible, but the words hung in the room. "Luc, she saved me twice. Once in Gehenna she kept me from falling into Abigor's trap. Today she added her power to Julie's to help break the curse."

Luc took a deep breath. "Thank you for telling me that." He turned to Julie. "I have a message for your daughter. Tell Tasha that time is too slow for those who wait. For me, time is eternity."

Julie nodded, confused.

Luc's lips curved in a small smile. "She'll recognize the quotation. I'll contact her when I can."

Julie nodded again, relieved this dazzling man was going back to France. She'd had enough of Walkers for a while. She didn't want her daughter dating one.

When Luc and Marguerite left, only Bas, Harry and Julie remained in the room.

"Where is Ashakarin, Bas?" Julie rubbed her hands up and down her arms.

"In Lobolo, raising hell, no doubt."

At Julie's steady glare, he grinned. "You demons are excellent targets for bad jokes. I can't help it."

"You owls are just a hoot," she shot back.

Bas stared at her blankly and then started laughing. Julie had a feeling that he laughed more than the joke called for. He'd been under tension, too.

Harry didn't laugh. "Bas, leave."

Bas controlled himself. "Okay. But this isn't over yet, Harrison. There are still issues to settle."

"Later." The word left no room for negotiation.

Bas didn't say another word. He walked to the office door, opened it and walked through. When he closed the door, the lock snicked into place.

Harry turned to her with a look that made her nervous and excited. His eyes travelled from the top of her head down the length of her body to her shiny, red shoes. "Let's discuss irony."

"I'm sorry that I bonded with you against your will. Bas said it was the only way and…." The flow of words dribbled to a stop when Harry moved closer to her.

"You risked your soul for me." He watched her closely. "Why?"

"I had to." The words whispered past her closed throat.

"Why? Because I'm important to the Triad? Because you wouldn't have let anyone lose their soul to Ashakarin?"

The vulnerability behind the words pierced her. She reached out and touched his cheek. "Those sound like noble reasons and are probably true."

"But?"

"If Ashakarin took your soul, I would have spent my life finding a way to get it back." She didn't need blood to bond her to this man. He'd already seeped into her system and become a part of her.

"Say it straight out, Julie."

"I thought I did. I love you, Harrison Chevalier. You're mine, to cherish and to protect."

He grabbed her upper arms, pulling her tight against him. His head buried in her neck. "Julie," he whispered, his breath warm against her skin. Then his lips moved, finding the curve between her neck and shoulder. She stretched her neck, shivers of fire igniting her blood stream.

He lifted his head and stared at her, his possessive gaze roaming her face like a touch. He reached out and threaded the strands of her hair through his fingers. "I love your hair."

She smiled, feeling a little wobbly. "You're crazy."

"Yes." His lips took hers, thrilling her with their intensity. Her head arched back, only to be cradled in his large palm. Their clothes were gone, and she had no idea who had gotten rid of them. She didn't care. She felt his strength, his firm muscles, flexing beneath her touch.

Then she was on the floor, the smooth wood cool against her back. Before she had time to shiver, a soft, furry rug cushioned her.

"You're getting good at that," Harry murmured against her lips.

"Practice makes perfect," she gasped as his hand slid up her side and framed her breast.

"You're perfect without practice."

The words were so awfully corny, and he said them with such sincerity that her heart melted. "Harry."

She spread her legs and pulled him more firmly against her. Every inch of him touched her, skin to skin. His penis, a hot, hard length, slid against her lower belly. She closed her eyes, lost in pleasure and sensation.

He groaned. "Open your mind to me."

She slowly raised her eyelids. "It is."

With the next breath, she felt his familiar presence in her head. Then, his eyes steady on hers, he brushed his palm firmly over her nipple. She drew in her breath, feeling the pleasure of his touch. Feeling his pleasure in the touch.

"Harry." He moved against her, a slow, rhythmic rock. His mouth replaced his hand, and his teeth played with her, tugging gently. Her fingers curled into the soft rug. On the surface of her skin, running beneath her skin, warm bubbles of sensation tumbled and caressed her.

He lifted his head. "Your breast is amazing." He bent to her other breast, his tongue circling her nipple while his hand began exploring the curve of her bottom. "I dream about touching you, tasting you."

She laughed, really more of a moan, then arched her pelvis and sucked in her breath at the burst of pleasure as he rubbed against her. Her hands slid down his back, cupping his firm behind. "I was so scared I'd lost you."

"Shhh," he commanded, then took her nipple firmly into his mouth. She moaned and moved her hand around to grasp him. As she touched him, she felt the biting edge of his passion, the aftertaste of the fear he'd felt for her, the savage need to drive himself into her, to take her, own her.

"Condom." He ground the word out.

Condom? She tried to concentrate. Suddenly the thin sheath formed beneath her hand. Okay, that was seriously cool. No pausing, no fumbling. Safe sex with minimal hassles. Then she didn't think any more. He raised himself, arms firmly planted on either side of her shoulders, and with one smooth thrust of his hips, slid inside her.

She felt filled, utterly possessed. Hot bolts of lightning ripped through her, and she thought sparks might be coming from her fingertips. She caught the faint scent of burning fur but ignored it. She couldn't separate what she felt from what he felt. Pulsing, pounding, she spiraled, twirling into a circle tighter and tighter, until she thought she'd explode.

"You're mine." The thought roared through her head, a triumphant shout. Then she screamed as she splintered into a thousand shards of intense pleasure.

She couldn't open her eyes. Her lids were too heavy to lift. "How come it's raining inside your office?"

"Don't know," Harry mumbled. He rolled off her onto his back. "Oh, bloody hell. It's the sprinkler system. We set the carpet on fire."

270 @ HOLLI BERTRAM

"That would explain the irritating beeping noise." She pushed herself up on one elbow, finally opening her eyes. "The fire alarm."

Harry waved a hand, and the fire alarm and water stopped. Which allowed them to hear the loud banging on his office door.

"Mom! Are you okay? Mom! Let me in." Tasha's voice.

Julie's muscles suddenly sprang into action, and she jumped to her feet. "Tell me I didn't just scream at the top of my lungs during love-making while my daughter was in the next room."

"Julie, calm down."

"Tell me I'm not standing naked in the middle of your office!"

"I rather like it," Harry offered.

"Tell me there's not a body outline singed into the white carpet." She took a closer look. "I'm not really that fat, am I?"

Harry actually laughed, his hair hanging in wet strands around his face, his chest glistening with water. She'd never seen him look so carefree and happy.

She grinned, until the banging on the door started again. Clothes, clothes, clothes. Julie turned her back on Harrison, which really wasn't a better position because she'd never gotten around to doing those glute-tightening exercises Dorie had told her about. She thought jeans and a sweatshirt and relaxed slightly as she felt the cloth slide over her body.

"Mom!" Tash's voice held a note of panic.

Julie glanced backward only long enough to see that Harry wore black pants and a white shirt and then ran toward the door. She unlocked it and swung it open. Tash halted with her fist in the air.

"Mom. What's wrong? You were screaming. Is there a fire? We heard the alarm but couldn't get in." She shot Bas an accusing look. "Bas wouldn't help."

Julie felt her cheeks redden. "No, no. I'm fine. I just got—frustrated—with Harry and…screamed. What are you doing here?"

Harry stepped behind her and wrapped a hand around the back of her neck. Julie shivered at his touch, every nerve still attuned to him.

"We hopped on the first plane we could when Linda told Grandma you were under arrest in London. We called Linda when we arrived at Heathrow, and she told us to take a taxi here." Tasha paused. "Why was the fire alarm going off?"

"A small fire started in Harry's office. The reason I got so frustrated with him—you know, when I screamed—was that he wouldn't help put it out," Julie improvised. Okay. She lied.

"The fire was not small, and I did a lot to help put it out." There was definitely laughter in Harry's voice.

Dorie and her mother stood slightly behind Tash, both giving her a curious look. They each held long sticks with cardboard attached to the ends. The cardboard rested against the floor.

Linda leaned against one wall, shocked amazement on her face. Obviously she had a good idea of what had been happening in Harry's office. Heidi sat at her desk oblivious to everyone but Bas, who lounged on top of it, idly swinging one leg. He winked at Julie. "Fire department's on their way up."

Julie glared at him. "Stop them."

Bas got slowly to his feet, a resigned look on his face. The elevator doors opened at that moment, and five firefighters in full regalia with hatchets and helmets rushed out.

Bas held up a hand and the group halted. "There is no fire," he said.

"There is no fire," repeated the lead fire fighter.

"Go back and reset the alarm. It was set off by accident." Bas waved his hand, in the exact way Obi Wan Kenobi did when he was redirecting Empire soldiers in the first—which was really the fourth—*Star Wars* movie.

Everyone watched in silence as the firefighters crowded back into the elevator and headed down to the lobby. Julie made a mental note to ask Bas if he knew George Lucas.

Jean broke the silence. "So what exactly has been going on here?"

"We've broken the curse." Julie didn't feel the need to talk about what had happened after that. "Harry is free of Marguerite."

Some of the confusion left Tash's face to be replaced with relief. "That's great! Does that mean this jail thing is all cleared up, too?"

The jail thing. She'd forgotten all about that, what with fighting Ashakarin and having wild sex. Harry's sudden stillness told her that it wasn't all cleared up.

Linda straightened from the wall and walked over to the small group. "That's why I'm here. I've come to take you back to your holding room until the Balance is ready to judge you."

"This is ridiculous!" Jean turned to her. "I won't stand for having my daughter brought to judgment because she wanted to rescue her daughter."

Linda shrugged. "Sorry, Jean. I don't make the rules. I don't even enforce them. I'm a guard, and I'm guarding the Dancer until I'm told not to."

The room grew silent again, and all eyes turned to Harry. He was the only one who could tell Linda not to. Harry dropped his hand from Julie's neck and stepped away from her.

"Guard her well, Linda." He sounded cool and professional.

Julie must have misunderstood. She turned toward him. "You want Linda to take me back to the holding room? You're going to pass judgment on me?"

"I'm the Balance." His face looked remote, but she felt his mind touch. *Julie.* The aching tenderness and regret in the word caused a knot in her chest.

And being Balance is more important than us? She touched his arm, trying to understand.

"I'm the Balance," Harrison repeated.

"You may be the Balance, but you're also a jerk." Jean stuck her chin out, ignoring the gasps from Linda and Heidi. "Julie didn't do anything that any good mother wouldn't do. We won't let you convict her." She tugged Julie away from Harrison and stepped between them. The sign in her hand flew up, almost hitting Harrison in the nose.

Written in bold letters were the words FREE JULIE. "I'll camp outside the Council door with my sign until my daughter is released. Won't that bring some unwanted attention to your sham company, whatever it's called?"

"Bright Promise Energy," Heidi piped in, pointing to a sign on the wall. "It's quite legit. We have a thriving research and development group."

Everyone ignored her. Dorie raised her sign, identical to Jean's. "I'll be camping out, too. Though I can just stay a week, because Jim can only get off work for that long and someone has to watch the kids."

"Me three." Tash stood shoulder to shoulder with Jean and Dorie.

Julie tapped Dorie on the shoulder. All three women did an about-face. Suddenly she didn't feel so empty and alone anymore. "Dorie, thank you, but go home. You need that vacation time for your family trip out West this summer."

Dorie shook her head. "Like I want to spend my vacation keeping the twins from falling into the Grand Canyon anyway. You're my best friend. I'm not going anywhere."

Julie tried to frown at her daughter, though her lips trembled. "Tasha. School."

"Mom." Tasha smiled slightly. "Forget it. I love you. I'm fighting for you. I'm in your corner all the way."

Julie turned to Jean and just looked at her.

"I know, baby. We'll straighten this out. It will be okay."

With those words, the three of them surrounded her and hugged her, their arms wrapped firmly around her like a warm cocoon. Her eyes met Harry's, standing stiff and aloof outside the circle.

Linda sniffed and swiped at her cheek. "We're all going to be bawling if you don't cut this out now. Let's go off to the torture chamber, and we'll be back before the Council in no time."

"Torture chamber?" Tash tightened her hold on Julie.

"It's a bedroom," Julie assured her. "Very comfortable."

"Oh, I'm so glad you like it!" Heidi clapped her hands.

Before she could say thank you and goodbye to everyone in the room, and most of all before she could yell at Harry or get on her knees and beg him to love her, Linda reached into the circle and grabbed her arm. A quick swirl of stomach and she was laying flat on her back on the red bedspread in her prison room.

Linda loomed over her, a serious expression on her face. "You hurt the Balance and I'll have something to say about it," she warned. With that, she turned on her heel, walked out the door and slammed it shut.

Julie didn't even bother to sit up. She just stared up at the ceiling, pain permeating every cell of her body. Hours might have passed before she shifted and a sharp edge nudged her ribs. She lifted herself on one elbow and saw the leather-bound book Bas had given her to read. *Words of Wisdom*. She curled her fingers around the binding and lifted it. Propping herself up on two white bolster pillows, she began to read.

"You're quiet," Bas commented as Harrison adjusted the black ceremonial robe worn on Judgment days. They stood in Harrison's office, adjacent to the Council chamber.

"I'm always quiet. You're the one who comments on everything."

"Part of my duties as ancient wise man." Bas wore a black T-shirt and jeans today, in total disregard of the formality of the Council proceedings.

"Any words of wisdom on how to handle my current situation?" Harrison glanced at his watch, then at the wall clock, to check its accuracy. The hands on the dial hardly seemed to move.

"My wisdom doesn't extend to matters of the heart. Nobody's does."

"You performed the blood-bond ceremony on Julie and me," Harrison pointed out.

"I wasn't concerned with your heart when I did that. I was

concerned with your soul. Are you sorry I did?"

"No. However, the bond will make my decision on Julie's judgment more closely scrutinized than most. The Council is meeting after this case to decide if I will remain Balance." Harry gave a small smile. "The only reason they're still letting me hear this case is because no one else wants to touch it. It's political suicide almost any way you look at it. Put Julie in Lobolo, and you piss off a powerful demon, not to mention Jean, which is almost as bad. We don't even know if Lobolo will hold Julie. She can skip in and out of Gehenna like she's going next door. On the other hand, let Julie go free, and you've set a very poor precedent for future wild powers. Julie can't fully control her energy and there's the real possibility that she'll expose us to humans."

"You're balancing between a rock and a hard place."

Harrison walked to his desk and stared down at the empty surface. "The law is very clear on wild powers."

"The letter of the law or the spirit of the law?" Bas perched on the edge of Harrison's desk. His face held none of the amusement with which he usually regarded the foibles of the rest of the world. "You have trained to be Balance your entire life. What will you do if they remove you?"

"I don't know." He had never imagined a future that didn't include his work, his service, as Balance. "This is a particularly bad time for a change in leadership. We're just starting to build trust, appoint regional Lions and get the Threes back into action." He shut his eyes, seeing nothing but black until an image of a woman with brown hair and brown eyes formed behind his lids. He opened his eyes and met Bas's gaze with a small smile. "But no one is irreplaceable. As you know, we've been carefully monitoring the boarding school assessments since I took office. No clear candidate has emerged as the next Balance, which is unprecedented. No one since Lia has been marked as a future Balance."

Lia Chevalier, a distant cousin of his, had tested through the roof on all of the measures of intelligence, leadership and power used to choose a new Balance. She was ten years younger than him, but had unfortunately died in an accident when she was nineteen. Each year, several children who reached puberty were chosen to go through a modified form of the Balance training. As they grew to adulthood, they formed a pool from which an interim Balance could be chosen if no chosen Balance was available to lead. Because they were seldom required in that role, those who were thus trained usually became the Lions of their respective regions. "The Council will choose someone from the interim pool, and I will likely be chasing after my mate, making sure that she doesn't blast open the Gates of Gehenna or something similar."

"The Council is handling the news of your bonding quite well. Especially since there is no chosen Balance in the wings, they may be open-minded about it. After all, there are no written rules against a Balance blood bonding. The fact that none has before you is beside the point. And there are certainly no rules against blood bonding with a demon hybrid."

Harrison shot him a wry look. "Only because no one envisioned the possibility. I don't consider a week of intensive research into archaic laws and histories on bonding and mixed heritage, hours of non-stop questioning and endless debate as 'handling the news well.'" He glanced at the wall clock again. Had the hands moved at all?

"Obviously they haven't read *Words of Wisdom* lately." Bas didn't look pleased at the idea.

"There is no place in that whole damn book that talks about a Balance bonding with a demon hybrid. I wouldn't have forgotten that part."

"Interpretation. Prophets aren't allowed to say things straight out. Most prophecies are only realized after they happen."

"How very convenient for you prophecy writers."

"Not always." Bas tapped his fingers against a side table, looking unusually morose. "Imagine watching people you care about heading towards a train wreck because they refuse to use the map you gave them."

"*Words of Wisdom* isn't a map, Bas. It's a word maze. You can't blame two trains for crashing if you're not clear what track they should be on."

Annoyance flickered in Bas's eyes. "Having a book of prophecy doesn't mean you don't take responsibility for your life, your decisions and what track your train rides on. You have free will. I can't interfere with that, no matter how much I might want to."

The pain in Bas's voice stopped Harrison's flip answer. He studied his enigmatic friend. "When have you wanted to interfere with someone's free will?"

Bas ignored him. "I saw Julie a few days ago."

The words distracted Harrison, as Bascule had no doubt intended. "How is she doing?" He hadn't seen her since the day they'd made love in his office, over a week ago.

"Getting antsy, like you. She wants to go home."

Harry bristled at the idea that he was getting 'antsy' and glanced at the clock again. "Has she asked to see me?"

"No."

She hadn't made a single attempt to join minds with him, either. "Does she understand why I haven't been in contact with her?"

"I explained how inappropriate that would be. She said that she'd hate for you to ever be inappropriate."

Bollocks. "What is she doing? How is she spending her time? Is she enjoying the clothes?" The full wardrobe of designer clothes had been Heidi's idea.

"She's been engrossed in reading *Words of Wisdom*."

Harrison hadn't meant for her to get that bored. "Wasn't she provided with any movie she requested?" He'd envisioned her blissfully watching Jane Austen movies, crying at each happy ending.

"Apparently she preferred my book," Bas spoke smugly. "You should have mind touched with her, Harrison."

"Contact by the Council or the Balance with those coming for judgment is forbidden once they've been arrested." He recited

Section VII of the Council's Policy and Procedure Manual.

Bas looked less than impressed. "You already had contact with her after she was arrested. You blood-bonded with her, fought a demon with her and made her scream in your office."

Harrison ran a hand through his hair. "If I went to her, Bas, I wouldn't be able to leave her."

Bas gave him a pitying look. "You should have told her that. You have a lot to learn about being part of a family."

A family. The words conjured feelings he didn't know what to do with.

"Family means sacrifice," Bas said. "Sometimes it means ignoring rules, forgetting about work and spending way too much time worrying."

"How do you know? Have you got family?" Bas always traveled alone.

"I consider you my family, Harrison. And believe me, I've got the breaking rules and worrying part down to an art."

"Bas." He looked at the strong, enigmatic man who had been responsible for every good moment of his childhood. This man had brought him out of his black and white world and introduced him to a life full of color, a life shaded with gray. This man had sent him to Julie. He couldn't find words to fit the emotion that weighted his chest.

A deep bell tone vibrated through the air. Bas's lips curved. "Showtime, my boy."

Harrison nodded. He turned to his desk and gathered the opinion papers of each of the Council members. "Julie will understand. She knows about duty."

Bas shook his head. He opened the door that led into the Council chambers and stood to the side to let Harrison enter the room first. Harrison paused before stepping through the doorway and put a hand on Bas's shoulder. Bas was always present when he most needed him.

When Harry didn't move through the door, Bas gave him a questioning look. "Thank you." Harry squeezed the other man's shoulder, cleared his throat and walked toward Julie.

Julie decided that whoever had designed the open, sunny Council chambers could re-do her living room when she won the lottery. Large floor to ceiling windows filled one wall, a brilliant gateway to the morning light. The sun warmed her cheeks and she smiled for the first time since she'd been confined to the Red Room. She reached out with what she'd begun thinking of as her mental hand and touched the light, comforted by its presence, comforted by her ability to access its power.

A large, oval oak table sat in the middle of a deep red carpet. Linda, her constant companion, ushered her to the one white chair at the table. The Seat of Judgment. She gingerly sat in it, finding it quite comfortable. She and Linda were the first in the room. Her lawyers had been meeting with the Council for days. This morning, she would face them alone. This morning, she would finally see Harry again.

She brushed the lapel of her black, silk blazer, wondering if she had over-dressed. No one had given her a dress code but she felt good in this outfit. The black pantsuit and white blouse were simple, elegant and powerful. While Julie would never hire her as a room decorator, Heidi had an amazing eye for clothes. Maybe when this was all over, she'd agree to a shopping trip with Julie.

Julie turned to Linda, who had taken a seat to the right of her chair. "If the Council sees criminals in here, aren't they afraid that the bad guys will use their power against them?"

"The room is shielded. You can't wield energy in here." Linda fiddled with her brown leather vest, a conservative choice for her.

Julie frowned and nudged a chair with her power, causing it to move an inch. Linda shot her a sharp glance but didn't say anything. Obviously the shield didn't work on her. Guess the Council never envisioned a demon hybrid in their midst.

A door on the far wall opened, and her gut clenched as she turned toward it. Twelve people, six women and six men, none of them Harry, marched into the room. Each was dressed in a long white robe. Either a church choir had taken a wrong turn or these sober-faced individuals were the infamous Council.

Unfortunately, nobody broke into song. The group silently approached the table and each chose a chair, leaving the one directly across from Julie empty. Linda had explained that council member wore a small symbol on the left shoulder of their robe—a triangle that was colored either yellow if a Dancer, blue if a Walker or green if a Penumbra.

"Hello." Julie smiled in an attempt to lighten the grim atmosphere. Linda groaned and nudged her sharply with an elbow.

"Speak only when asked a question." An older woman, a Penumbra, finally broke the outraged silence, her voice carrying a heavy German accent.

"I'm sorry. My Guardian explained the rules to me, but I thought they didn't start until the Council officially went into session."

The woman crossed her arms across a tiny bosom. "The Council is in the room."

But Harry isn't. Julie kept a polite smile on her face and just nodded. No need to antagonize the people you need on your side.

Her cell phone rang.

"Didn't you switch that off? Frau Scheller is going to freak," Linda hissed anxiously in her ear.

"I forgot." Julie fumbled in her purse for her phone, saw the call was from Tasha and looked apologetically at the woman she assumed was Frau Scheller. "My daughter," she whispered, hoping that whispering didn't technically count as speaking. "She'll worry if I don't pick up."

Julie flicked open her phone, her eyes on the older woman, whose shoulders now looked as if she might have a case of premature rigor-mortis. "Bad time, Tash. Can't talk."

"Mom, I just want you to know, when they find you guilty, we're going to fight. We'll get Grandpa to help if we have to—"

"No!" She forgot to whisper. "Don't. Do. Anything. Don't

let Grandma do anything. I'm going to be fine. I'll call as soon as this is over."

A sharp movement beside her brought her gaze to Linda, who had buried her head in her hands. How unusual. Linda didn't have headaches. Slowly, she swiveled to look at the Council members. Every person in the room stared at her, with the same stony expression. A shiver prickled up her spine. She swallowed. "Gotta go, Tash. I love you." She quickly disconnected and turned the phone off. "So sorry." She belatedly lowered her voice to a whisper again. "Kids—what are you going to do with them?"

"Guardian, it is your duty to silence your charge."

Silence her charge? That didn't sound good. Julie turned to Linda, who looked like she wanted to be sick.

"Frau Scheller, I'd rather not. I don't think it's necessary."

Frau Scheller lifted an eyebrow. "That's not your decision to make." She nodded toward a younger member of the Council, a Walker, who sat beside her. "Mr. Kodak, you do it."

Mr. Kodak, short and husky with slick, dark hair, pushed back his chair, went to a desk in the corner of the room and then came to stand behind Julie. Before she could twist her head to see what he was up to, he slapped a piece of wide tape over her mouth. She couldn't budge her lips. With a quick movement, he grabbed her wrists, pulled them behind her chair and clasped cold metal around them, probably so she wouldn't tear the sticky stuff off her mouth. It all happened so quickly she didn't have time to protest. In just a few seconds, Mr. Kodak sat back in his seat.

Julie blinked, horrified. This was barbaric. She breathed deeply through her nose, and unexpected tears burned her eyes. Frau Scheller's lips flattened in a satisfied smirk. Good Lord, who were these people? Were they all raised in rigid, cruel boarding schools? She needed to talk to Harry about changing the system. Harry. Julie didn't want Harry to see her like this. She looked at Linda, silently asking for help.

Linda bent her head toward her. "Shit. Scheller has a stick up her butt," she muttered. "No energy wielding can occur in this room, which is how they get off using the tape and cuffs. Sit tight. The Balance will be here soon."

Which was precisely the problem.

Every minute of every long hour spent locked in that room, she'd wanted to see Harry. At first, she'd truly expected him to contact her, reassure her. Then Bas had explained any contact would violate the Council rules.

Ha! Surely a man who really cared about a woman, who made love to her with such exquisite tenderness and passion, would scoff at those rules. But no cake with a nail file appeared. No note slid under her door. Harry didn't attempt even one, single, furtive mind touch.

She forced herself to face reality.

She'd given her heart to an insensitive, non-romantic, rule-bound man. The paranormal version of Darcy in *Pride and Prejudice*. More than that, she'd forced him into a commitment he hadn't been ready to make. That was not something a proud man would take lightly.

After her lightning bolt of insight, she'd then spent every moment wanting to see Harry so she could apologize. That phase, thankfully, didn't last long.

As time passed slowly in the Red Room, she'd fantasized about telling him to his face that he was a no-good bastard. She'd imagined explaining very clearly that her feelings were transient, induced by a mixture of post-traumatic stress and a midlife crisis. He was her shiny Porsche convertible.

Now, finally, she was going to see him, and she was trussed up like a turkey. Life could be a bitch sometimes.

Any normal demon hybrid would dissolve her bonds, free herself and hang Frau Scheller naked out the window by her toes. For a moment, she contemplated doing just that, the gleam in her eye bringing a panicked look to Linda's face.

But, no. To do so would be a clear indication that she didn't hold herself accountable to the Council. Harry would be in even bigger trouble—bonded not only to a demon hybrid, but to a rogue demon hybrid who didn't recognize the authority of the Triad.

One of the men pushed a button embedded in the table, and a deep bell sounded in the room. Instinctively, Julie knew the bell called Harry. She straightened her shoulders, not even able to brush away the tears she felt sliding down her cheeks. With her stomach twisted into a tight ball, she watched a door on a side wall of the room slowly swing open. For a breathless moment, no one walked through. Then Harry, dressed in a long, black robe, stepped briskly into the room.

Twenty-One

HARRY'S GAZE immediately found her. He stopped in mid-stride as if someone had pressed a pause button and freeze-framed him. Julie could read nothing in his expression. After one brief flare, the golden eyes blanked. Bas quickly sidestepped from behind him to avoid slamming into his back.

Bas frowned and looked confused by Harry's sudden halt. He glanced around the room and stiffened when he saw her. His hand immediately reached for Harry's arm, as if to restrain him. Harry didn't need restraining. If anything, he needed a push.

Every bit of her wanted to wield energy, to open up the floor and drop through, to disappear from this mortifying situation.

Instead, she raised her head and lifted her chin. She couldn't look directly at Harry again. She wasn't that brave. She looked at Bas instead.

She thought she read a brief flick of compassion in his expression and that almost caused her tears to start flowing. Then he grinned and winked and she felt like he'd handed her some much-needed courage. Harry began moving again and walked to the table, taking the empty seat across from her. Bas stood behind him.

"Why is Ms. Dancer gagged and cuffed?" Harry spoke calmly, not looking at her but at the Council members.

"She broke the Council rules, Balance," Frau Scheller responded.

"Ha!" Linda spoke up. "She got a phone call from Tash, Balance. Her only crime is forgetting to turn off her cell phone."

Julie felt a rush of warmth and gratitude toward Linda. She couldn't imagine that the Council looked very kindly on Guardians speaking up, either.

"Ms. Dancer is not familiar with our ways," Harry said quietly. "Release her. I'm sure she'll show proper respect to the Council." He still didn't look at her.

"Balance—" Frau Scheller began.

"Release her." The words snapped from him. The sharp edge of his tightly controlled anger caused Julie's muscles to contract.

Tension drummed in the room. Bas smiled easily and walked around the table until he stood behind her. "No need for anyone to get up. I'll do it."

Bas gently lifted her wrists, and she felt the shackles loosen. He didn't need a key to open the handcuffs. Apparently the shields on the room didn't affect his ability to wield energy, either.

Julie immediately brought her hands to her mouth and tugged at the itchy tape. She managed to get one corner free. The evil Frau Scheller must have bought special superglue-backed tape. This was going to hurt, big time. Okay, suck it up, Dancer. When you take off a sticky bandage, it's better to pull it quickly, all at once.

Closing her eyes, Julie gripped the loose corner in her fingers and gave a mighty yank.

The scream must have been hers. She didn't want to open her eyes and look at the tape she'd dropped on the table, knowing her lips and a good portion of her cheeks were stuck to it. Was it possible to do lip transplants these days? Was she going to bleed to death?

Bas's hand covered the lower portion of her face, and she felt immediate relief from the stinging pain. "I would have removed the tape for you," he murmured in her ear.

The pain diminished and she could breathe again. Bas's hand worked better than a morphine drip. Julie slowly opened her eyes and met Harry's gaze across the table. The man looked like a slab of granite. Hard, no emotion, no concern.

Why did she fall in love with men who didn't give a flying fig about her? Okay, maybe she was wallowing in self-pity, but she couldn't help it. Harry's disinterest ripped at her soul. Even Bas couldn't help her with this pain.

Julie reached up to touch Bas's hand. Harry's eyes followed the movement. Her anger, built up over the days he'd ignored her, dissolved away in sorrow. They might be bound together by a blood ceremony, but Harry wasn't hers and never had been. Harry belonged to the Triad. And the Triad needed him more than ever, with demons and Skaven popping up all over the place.

She would not keep a man tied to her who didn't want her. Besides, she had things to do, her own destiny to figure out. She didn't need a man distracting her.

She carefully removed Bas's hand from her face, but kept hold of it for courage. Her lips felt almost normal. She looked around the table at the unsympathetic faces, bracing herself for what she needed to do. She cleared her throat. "I'm sorry for the scream. I don't do well with pain."

"No apology required, Ms. Dancer."

Harry's formal voice felt like a slap. Bas squeezed her hand. She looked up, directly at Harry. "May I address the court?"

"This is a Council. We have been in extensive talks with your lawyers and representatives, Ms. Dancer. They have presented your side of the events that led you to bargain with a demon and enter into Gehenna. Your mother and daughter have phoned and emailed us daily, as well as started a popular blog on the secure Triad server. We have enough information to render a decision in this case."

"I would still like permission to speak." Her gaze challenged him.

He nodded. "Granted."

Julie gave Bas a brief smile and released his hand. The young man who had put on her handcuffs and tape pulled out a small flat disk and pressed a button. Apparently a junior member served as secretary, and he was responsible for recording the events of the Council.

Julie cleared her throat again. "I know there has been concern about the ability of the Balance to remain impartial while rendering a judgment on his blood-bonded mate."

"That is not the issue before the Council," Harry broke in.

"I think it is one of the issues before the Council today." Julie pushed herself to her feet, aware that the Council members were listening to her carefully. She saw the truth of her words in their eyes. "Harrison Chevalier was bonded to me against his will while he battled the demon Ashakarin. I forced the bond on him so that I could join him in the fight. Ashakarin was vanquished mostly due to the Balance's courage and stamina. The bond is no longer needed and I intend to dissolve it."

Total silence met her announcement. After a moment, Frau Scheller spoke. "You can't. A blood bond can't be broken."

"I've spent much of the time since my arrest reading *Words of Wisdom*." Julie turned and looked at Bas. "There is a way, isn't there?"

Bas watched her as if fascinated. He slowly nodded. Voices broke out around the table as the Council protested, asked questions and generally made a lot of noise. All except Harrison. He sat still, his gaze never wavering from her face.

"You didn't think to mention this, Bas?" Harrison's voice sounded strange to Julie's ears. Tight.

She felt Bas shrug. "I told you to read the book, Harrison. Several times. I can point out the path, but you must walk down it yourself."

"The Book of Wisdom has been studied by master scholars." He folded his hands loosely on the table before him. Julie's eyes were drawn to that casual grip. "No one has ever spoken of the possibility of breaking a blood-bond."

Julie answered. "The passage is rather obscure." She glanced over her shoulder to frown at Bas. "You need a modern translation of the book. This reads like the King James edition of the Bible."

"Because I used some of the same translators. The King James Bible came out in 1611. This edition of *Words of Wisdom* was completed in 1618."

"Can we have the history lesson later?" Harrison's voice remained calm, almost pleasant.

"Sorry, but it's rough reading. More people would have a go at it if he updated the language. Anyway, the passage I'm referring to is in the first section of the book, part of the ancient stories that outline the beginning of the Triad. It says something like "'And again Yesmi opened her palm. The blood flowed fresh and free, winding a river between them.'"

"I know that verse," Harrison broke in. "That's from the story of Patre and Yesmi, father and mother of all energy wielders. That verse follows the recitation of twelve year separation and represents a renewal of their blood-vows."

"I'm impressed." Bas sounded pleased. "You're right. The verse has usually been interpreted that way. Scholars teach that Yesmi blood-bonded again with Patre, strengthening and reaffirming the connection between them."

Harry didn't even glance at Bas. "How do you interpret it, Julie?" He didn't seem to notice he hadn't called her Ms. Dancer. She glanced at his hands. His knuckles were white.

"That verse ends the story of Yesmi and Patre. We never hear of them again. I believe when Yesmi opened her palm again, she shared blood with another man. The new blood-bond opened wide a river between Yesmi and Patre, breaking their original bond. If I blood-bond with another, our tie to each other will be broken."

She couldn't look away from Harry. The intensity of his gaze physically tied her to him. "Bas?" Harry rapped out the word.

"Julie correctly discerned the meaning of that passage," Bas answered.

"This is what you want, Julie?" Harrison asked, as if only she could hear him.

No, you idiot. I want to live with you forever, maybe even have our babies and love you for the rest of my life.

But she didn't say the words out loud or in his head. She broke free of his gaze and looked instead at the Council members. This was Harry's life, where he belonged.

"Yes, Harry. This is what I want."

He regarded her silently for a moment, and then jerked his head, once, in a sharp nod of assent.

"Shit." Linda cursed loudly, causing several in the room to gasp. "I don't care if you can do it. You shouldn't. This is wrong."

"We will discuss the details later," Harry said, as if the matter were now of little importance. He straightened his shoulders and seemed to grow larger, to effortlessly command the attention of everyone in the room. "Sit and hear the judgment of the Council."

Julie sat down hard.

"Julie Dancer, though the blood of demons runs in your veins, so, too, does the blood of Dancers and Walkers. You were born into the Triad through your mother's line, and are thus bound by Triad laws. The Council has duly taken into consideration the fact that you were raised without knowledge of your heritage and the customs and conventions that bind you. Testimony has been received from your mother, Jean Dancer, your daughter, Natasha Morgen, and from your neighbor Doreen Lessing corroborating this. The Council accepts that you broke our laws out of a mother's desire to save her child, not with any thought of malice or personal gain."

Did that mean she was considered innocent and free to go? She tried to feel excited and happy.

Harrison continued. "The Council has received additional testimony from the demons known in Gehenna as Abigor and Josephius."

Julie sat up straighter, a twinge of anxiety piercing her numbness.

"This testimony has been disregarded. While demons may be retained as legal council, they are not reliable or truthful witnesses.

Therefore, Julie Dancer, I have determined that in this specific instance you will not be held accountable for breaking Triad law. However, you are required to take classes in Triad government and must submit a certificate of completion of said classes to the Council secretary within six months of this date." Harry met her eyes and she saw a well of dark emotion, quickly shuttered behind his usual enigmatic stare. "An additional concern has been raised regarding your potential as a wild power. The one known as Bascule has pledged responsibility for your training. He vouches for your ability to control yourself in such a manner as to not place the Triad in danger. You are free to go, Ms. Dancer."

Julie knew the words signified more than just her freedom from the Council. She stood, silently commanding her shaking legs to hold her, and nodded respectfully to everyone in the room, including Frau Scheller. Then, with the surprised gasps of the Council ringing in her ears, she gathered energy around her and popped out of the room.

"Julie, you are going to Sexy Cindy's Halloween party whether you want to or not," Dorie nagged at her through her closed bedroom door. "It's not healthy to stay in your room, eating chocolate. No man is worth hardening your arteries and gaining weight over."

"How do you know I'm not doing sit-ups or practicing yoga positions in here?" Julie asked around a bite of chocolate, not bothering to lift her head off her pillow.

"Because a trail of empty Hershey Kisses wrappers leads to your room."

Was there no privacy in this world? "I'm over forty. I can eat what I want."

"Yes, you can eat anything you want if you don't care if you die early." Dorie was trying to push her lock open with something. Probably a bent paper clip. When it came to opening anything locked, Dorie could give Charlize Theron in the *Italian Job* a run for her money.

Julie sighed and sat up, stuffing several silver wrappers under her pillow. "I won't die early. I think I might be immortal. Or half-immortal, at any rate." Jeez, what did that mean? She'd only live half of eternity? You couldn't really get halfway through something that had no end, so technically, if you were any fraction immortal, you were immortal, period. She frowned. Was that right?

Dorie succeeded in opening the door and stepped triumphantly through. "All the more reason to be healthy. Can you imagine living that long if you feel like crap?"

Good point.

Dorie walked over, pushed aside her rumpled comforter and sat down beside her. "Tasha's worried about you. To distract her, I sent her out to the backyard to rake leaves. She's been trying to convince us to do an intervention on you."

"You don't do interventions on depressed people. You give them therapy."

Dorie's hand was gentle as she smoothed tangled hair away from Julie's face. "Well, chocolate therapy doesn't seem to be working. You look horrible."

"You also don't tell depressed people they look horrible. That's too…depressing." Besides, who cared if her hair was a mess? She hadn't brushed it since returning from London two days ago.

"The good news is that you don't need a costume to go to Cindy's party as a haggard, old witch."

"That is so funny I forgot to laugh." Julie fell backward against the bed and covered her face with a pillow. "If you weren't my best friend, I'd zap you. I want to be alone." The words were muffled.

"Too bad, Garbo. You're going to get into the shower, eat a healthy dinner and then you're going to the Halloween party with me. Jim's volunteered to watch the kids while we go."

Julie peeked from behind the pillow. "Wow. Sole custody of sugar-saturated kids. He must be really worried about me."

"We all are, sweetie. You've been through a lot these last weeks."

Julie pushed herself to a sitting position and hugged the

pillow to her stomach. "He just let me pop out of the courtroom and come back home. He didn't try to stop me."

"Did you want him to?" Dorie asked. "I thought you told him you wanted a divorce or whatever you Triad guys call it."

"I did."

"So you're angry because…?"

"He didn't care enough to fight for me." The words hurt as they bubbled out her throat.

Dorie didn't seem to appreciate the fact that Julie had just revealed the genesis of her depression.

"You are a grown woman." Dorie stood, facing Julie with her hands on her hips. "You know better than to play these kind of I'm leaving you, but I want you to chase me games. If you want the man, tell him. Otherwise, get on with it."

"He's better off without me," Julie mumbled, resolving to find more empathetic friends.

"What are you? Miss Low Self-Esteem of Michigan? The man is crazy about you. You're a unique, powerful, attractive woman who is normally fun to be around. Why is he better off without you?"

Julie jumped off the bed. "Are you being deliberately obtuse? I'm part demon." She shouted the words.

Dorie looked unimpressed. "I'm part German, part Italian. Your point is?"

"Demons are pure evil."

"So are some Germans and Italians. Hitler. Mussolini." She jutted her chin at a stubborn angle. "Your point is?"

"I'm older than he is. Maybe he has some kind of mother complex about me."

Dorie just shook her head. "Maybe you have some kind of son complex about him."

"Oh yuck." Julie took a step back. "That's just…yuck."

"Precisely."

"Dorie." Julie met her met her friend's eyes, took a deep breath and tried to explain. "Balances don't blood bond. I forced this on him. He will lose his job, which is everything to him. He doesn't want me. "

"Yeah. Just like you don't want him." Dorie didn't look convinced. "Have you tried contacting him with that mind touch thing bonded people can do?"

"No. He just got Marguerite of his head. He's an intensely private person. It didn't seem polite, since we've decided to separate."

"Coward."

Julie opened her mouth to argue the point, and then decided Dorie was right. "I might resort to begging if I spent any time talking with him."

"In order to really separate, you have to find someone else to bond with, right?" Dorie started making her bed while she talked, probably hoping to keep Julie from jumping back in. "Got any candidates?"

"Mom knows some Dancer families in Chicago. She's going to introduce me to a couple of men. I'm not looking for passion. Just someone who will leave me alone."

"So, let me get this straight. You want to bond with a guy— let him into your head—but keep him out of your pants? Good luck with that one."

Tash knocked on the doorjamb and walked into the room. "Mom! You're up."

"Hi, honey." The relief on Tash's face increased Julie's mountain of guilt. She smiled an extra-large, I'm-not-depressed smile at her daughter.

"You okay?" Tash gave her an odd look.

"Fine. I'm feeling much more rested."

"You should come outside with me for a while and get some fresh air. Maybe if we sit quietly on the deck we'll see the giant squirrels."

Julie and Dorie looked at each other. "Giant squirrels?" Julie asked.

"Or whatever. The leaves in that old oak tree in Harrison's

yard are shaking like some really big squirrels are up there."

Julie dropped her pillow and vaulted over the bed to the bedroom window. "Did you see any shoes? Wingtips?"

Tash looked at Dorie for help. Dorie just shrugged. "Mom. Squirrels don't wear wingtips. Nobody wears wingtips any more."

Julie sank back against the windowsill. "I don't see anything."

"Mom! Get a grip. Come on downstairs and I'll get you a cup of tea. Or some anti-psychotic medication. Maybe both."

Tash was right. She needed to go downstairs. Julie gave her a quick hug and ran down the steps, past her mother sitting in the living room and out the front door. She didn't stop until she stood beneath the huge oak, looking up into the canopy of bright yellow leaves. "Harry?" she called breathlessly.

Silence.

"Bas?"

Nothing but the sound of rustling leaves. She squinted, and saw two squirrels, normal sized and shoeless, running along one of the upper branches.

Julie pivoted and ran for Harry's side door. She knocked so hard her knuckles hurt. When no one answered, she peered through the glass window in the door, but the house looked dark and deserted. Her chest felt hollow, her whole body felt hollow as she turned and slowly walked home.

"Where were you off to in such a hurry?" Jean asked as she entered the living room.

"Mom's looking for squirrels in wingtips," Tash said as she and Dorie came down the stairs.

Jean gave Julie an interested look. "Really? I prefer my squirrels in running shoes."

Julie sat down across from her mother. "I want to talk to Harry."

Jean smiled. "It's about time. If you want to talk to him, mind touch with him."

"You're right. That's the easiest way. I will."

Three pairs of eyes looked at her expectantly.

"When I'm alone." For some reason, she felt nervous about communicating in such an intimate way with Harry while everyone watched.

"Do it soon, Julie. James and Robert are popping in from Chicago tonight to meet you. I don't want you distracted."

"Robert and James?"

"Two brothers from a very nice Dancer family. Their mom is in the Gay Grays with me. I told them to come in costume because I knew you'd be over at Cindy Lui's party."

Julie looked at Dorie.

"You'll have fun." Dorie grinned, unrepentant.

"Just remember," Jean cautioned, "tonight is a blue moon. The very air seethes with power. Very strange things have been known to happen when a blue moon is in the sky."

Julie stood under a maple tree in Cindy Lui's backyard. Knights, monsters, aliens and ex-presidents bobbed in and out of the shadows caused by the full moon and a string of pumpkin lights attached to Cindy's deck. Julie tried one more time to reach Harry via mind touch and sighed when she met with a blank wall. So much for the blood-bond giving her special access to Harry. Where the heck was he?

"You're so gorgeous I could go ape over you." The growled compliment came from behind her.

Julie swung around to see King Kong step from behind the tree.

"How many times have you used that line tonight?" Julie asked dryly. Impossible to tell if she knew the person under all that hair and plastic.

The man laughed and reached up to take off his ape head. Twinkling, brown eyes and damp, dark hair were revealed. "I've been reserving it for a true beauty. You must be Julie Dancer."

Julie gave him a polite half-smile. "Do I know you?"

"No, but you will. Your mother showed me your picture. I'm James Morris."

James, one of the Dancers her mother wanted to set her up with. She looked at the attractive man and stepped backward, almost tripping over her long, white skirt. This felt wrong, like cheating on Harry.

James's friendly smile faltered, and she gave herself a mental shake. She and Harry had agreed to separate. She wasn't doing anything wrong.

It took an effort of will to stretch her hand out to the man. "Hello. It's nice to meet you."

He reached for her hand and grimaced when he noticed his furry paw. He took off the ape mittens, dropped them to the ground and warmly grasped her hand. "And I'm very, very pleased to meet you." His voice deepened. "Has anyone ever told you that you look like an angel?"

She wiggled one of her white-feathered wings at him, discreetly trying to pull her hand out of his. "As a matter of fact, yes."

"I bet you could take me to Heaven." His lips curved in a boyish grin.

The man had more lines than a Tolstoy novel. "I don't know about that, but I can definitely take you to Hell."

James frowned. Then his good-natured face beamed a smile, as if she were joking. He stepped closer, still holding her hand firmly. He jerked when a crack of thunder shook the air directly above them.

Julie quickly reclaimed her hand and looked up at the star-studded sky.

"That's odd." James shrugged and reached for her elbow. "Maybe we should head inside and find a drink."

The moment he touched her, a bolt of lightning arced through the sky and struck the ground at his feet. Several people screamed. James jumped backwards and fell in a hairy heap. The back of Julie's neck tingled at the electric power charging the air.

Cindy Lui, sleek in her Catwoman costume, appeared in front of them. She helped James to his paws. "Are you okay?"

He rubbed his head. "I think so. That was too close."

"We all better go inside until this lightning storm passes." Cindy raised her voice and began to direct the crowd toward her patio doors. She looked pale, shaken by James's near miss.

James turned to Julie, and she waved him toward the house. "I'll follow in a minute."

"You shouldn't stay out here," he argued.

"Go," she ordered. He walked toward the house without another word.

When she was alone in the yard, she turned back toward the tree. Harry leaned against the trunk, ankles crossed, his white shirt gleaming in the shadows, blond hair messed as if he'd been running his hand through it.

"He's an ass," Harry observed in a mild tone of voice.

"Actually, he's supposed to be King Kong." Her heart beat too quickly. "You could have hurt him."

"Yes. I could have. I have excellent aim with lightning." His lip curved in a decidedly unsettling way. "If he had touched you one more time, he would have been Queen Kong."

"Ha-ha." Her throat closed on her attempt to lighten the atmosphere. He regarded her silently. She took a step toward him, trying to see his face. He obliged her by turning his head slightly so the faint glow from a pumpkin light caught his cheek and brow. Deadly anger glittered from his eyes.

"Are you upset with me?" Her voice went an octave higher in surprise.

"No. Definitely not. Upset is too bland a term."

She paused, waiting for him to elaborate. He didn't seem in a big hurry to speak. She cleared her throat, more intimidated than she would have admitted. Power seemed to crackle around him. "I know this is an awkward situation, Harry, but how am I supposed to find someone else to bond with if you emasculate the possible candidates?"

He folded his arms across his chest. His eyelids lowered, partially shielding his expression. "That's an excellent question."

"Thank you. And the answer is?"

"Obvious. You don't."

"Harry." Suddenly his behavior made sense. "You're worried I might be the One from the prophecies, aren't you? You're determined to stay bonded with me to ensure I don't cause chaos and tear the Triad apart." He would do anything to preserve the balance, to preserve the Triad.

Harry's arms dropped to his side, and he straightened. "You think I want to remain bonded with you because I'm a bloody hero?" He laughed, a short, bitter sound. "I'm not a hero. I'm a selfish bastard. I know you're not the one in the prophecy."

"How do you know I'm not?"

"Because I know who is," he said, impatient. "Why did you leave the Council room so suddenly?"

"There was nothing to stay for." And she didn't want him to see her cry.

He stiffened. "My mistake then."

She searched his face. "Why are you so upset? You want to break the bond. I forced it on you. I'm a liability."

"You're fucking blind." He rubbed a hand across his eyes. "I told the Council I won't break the bond. They removed me from my position as Balance."

Her brain took several seconds to process his words. "You did what? No! The Triad needs you. You need the Triad."

"I need you." He took a step forward. "What I don't know is if you want me." He studied her, face impassive. "You called me family. You told me I was yours to cherish and protect. Then you left me."

"I thought the best way to cherish and protect you was to leave." She whispered the words, her throat tight.

He moved, framing her face with his hands. "Understand this. Marguerite's curse was my blessing. It brought me to you. Before I met you, I was damned near empty. Aside from my friendship with Bas, being Balance was all I had, all I knew. Now I have you—and with you comes Tasha, your mother, Dorie, a whole host of demons and who knows what else. You fill me, Julie. You take away the empty spaces." His jaw firmed. "Tell me what I need to do to make you stay with me."

Her legs started shaking. "I don't want to screw up your life."

"Then don't. Stay with me."

She tried to say something but her tongue wouldn't work. The flash of vulnerability in Harry's eyes released her voice.

"Shhh." She put a finger against his lips when he started to speak. "You had me at 'you're fucking blind.'" She didn't just say that, did she?

He gripped her hand and held it against his chest. "I probably should have just said hello."

Wait a minute. "You've seen *Jerry Maguire*?"

"Tom Cruise, Renee Zellweger. I liked her better in *Bridget Jones's Diary*."

"You saw *Bridget Jones's Diary*?" She couldn't quite picture Harry at a chick flick.

"Tasha let me borrow your DVD collection while you were in custody awaiting the Council judgment." He didn't meet her eyes. "Watching your favorite movies made me feel connected to you, closer to you."

He'd watched chick flicks to feel closer to her. Oh. My. God. "You love me."

"Of course. That is not the issue under discussion." He spoke calmly, but beneath her hand, his heart pounded.

"There *is* one thing that you need to do if you want me to stay with you." She met his gaze, her face serious.

An eyebrow arched. He watched her intently.

She went up on tiptoe and spoke against his ear. "Just breathe."

As she said the last word and brushed her mouth against his ear, his hand cupped the back of her head, positioning her with gentle force so that her lips covered his. His kiss effectively kept them both from breathing. Okay, so maybe he didn't need to do anything to make her stay with him. Heat exploded inside her—

tiny, internal fireworks. The taste of him loosened her muscles and pleasure spilled into every cell. Harry. Finally, the world felt right.

The next moment she was in her house. In her bedroom. On her bed. Flat on her back. Naked.

Harry, also naked, crouched over her, knees on either side of her hips. His hands began a slow, firm journey from her waist up her ribcage. She groaned as his fingers moved to cover her breasts. His palms brushed her nipples in an intoxicating rhythm. Her body arched into him.

A brief knock sounded on the door. "I'm coming in!"

"Mom!" Julie yelped, pulling Harry down on top of her. "Go away!"

"Dorie thought you'd be in here! Honey, the comforter on that bed wasn't cheap." The door cracked open and an arm appeared. Jean tossed a large, shiny silver blanket across the room to them. Harry managed to snag it and drape it over his back in one smooth motion, covering them both.

"Use that to sleep on," Jean said, her head briefly appearing. "It's made of a special fire-retardant material. Should keep the smoke detectors from going off all night." She winked and ducked back out. "The Balance is almost as hot as Paul Newman," she commented to someone, hopefully not Tasha, as she shut the door.

Julie groaned. "Welcome to the family."

Harry lowered his forehead against hers. Laughter rumbled in his chest. "I'll have to remember to lock the doors."

She smiled, and then cupped his cheek. "Harry, about the Council, what will happen, who will take over?"

The laughter stilled and then he gave a small shrug and lowered his head to rest his cheek against her breasts. "There are several people who could serve as interim Balance. That will be decided by the Council in the next months. Regardless of who leads, the Triad needs to rebuild and remember its mission. I intend to be a part of the process, though I don't know yet what my role will be."

She threaded her fingers through his hair. "One more question. You said you know who the person foretold in the prophecies is."

"So do you if you think about it." He nuzzled her nipple, making it hard for her to think at all. "'A daughter shall be born in light and shadow, a guardian who rises out of evil. Wild power circles her and chaos will follow her footsteps.'"

Julie grabbed his chin and tugged, so she could see his eyes. "That sounds like me except...."

"You're not a guardian. The Penumbrae are the guardians and you have no Penumbrae blood."

"So who has both Dancer and Walker blood—light and shadow—plus has Penumbrae blood and rises from evil, which I assume is demon blood? Do you know anyone like that?"

Harrison lifted himself over her, and his mouth brushed hers. "No, but I hope to know that child quite well, eventually."

Julie's eyes widened. Warm joy bloomed inside her. "I have a feeling I should be more nervous about this than I am. Wild power, chaos? God help us."

Harry's lips found her collarbone. "He will."

Fireworks danced along her nerve endings, and cheers and clapping rose from Cindy's party as the colored lights lit the night sky. Julie pulled Harry even closer. "So much for my quiet middle years."

⁓*⁓

Acknowledgements

This book would never have been published without a lot of powerful magic. I don't personally know any Walkers, Dancers or Penumbra, but in my life the Brown-Eyed Girls wield some wicked energy. Colleen Gleason, Mara Jacobs and Liz Kelly—I wouldn't be here without you. Seriously. And life would be nowhere near as fun. Thank you for your friendship, support and wisdom.

Editing a book requires focus, attention to detail and the ability to turn off the brain's auto-correct mechanism to see the errors that are on the page. In other words, editing is crazy hard. Erin Wolfe made my part of the process fun. Her sidebar comments kept me laughing. Thanks also to Ann Mooney for reading through the manuscript and for being so enthusiastic about it, even though she doesn't usually read romance. And thanks again to Liz and Mara for their final eagle-eyed read through. Any errors that remain are totally on me.

Lyndsey Lewellen has true magic. She took a few tidbits of information, focused her amazing creative energy and designed the perfect cover. Working with her was a joy.

And finally, this book would not have been the same without the men in my life, Scott, Ben, Sam and Jacob. They're intelligent, honorable, opinionated males who know how to love with their whole hearts. Is it any wonder I write romance?

Holli Bertram grew up in Detroit, Michigan. She most often had her nose in a book, lost in the magic of a good story. She solved crimes with Nancy Drew, rode the Black Stallion to victory, and cried for three days when Rhett frankly didn't give a damn. Holli eventually discovered that real life holds its own magic. She attended the University of Michigan, found her own true love and has three wonderful sons.

Holli's second novel in the Magic Destiny series, Lost Magic, will be available in January, 2014. For more information, visit her website at Holli Bertram.com or find her on Facebook at Holli Bertram Author.